"I put off reading Mack's new book because his first book kept me up all night. Once again, the same thing happened with *You Just Never Know*. Once I got sucked into the plot, I couldn't put it down. I spent a very groggy next day recovering. So be forewarned. For thrills and action, I'll take a Mack Cameron book any day over a John Grisham book."

Wyatt Emmerich

The Northside Sun, Jackson, Miss.

"Mack Cameron's second book, *You Just Never Know*, is a fascinating sequel to his excellent first book. I could not put either of them down once I got started."

Bert Case

WLBT-TV, Jackson, Miss.

You Just Never Know
Mack Cameron

Mack Cameron
Post Office Box 321244
Flowood, MS 39232

Visit our Web site at http://www.msbluffs.com

First Edition: January 2013

Cameron, Mack.
    You Just Never Know / Mack Cameron. – 1st ed.
        p.cm.

        ISBN-13: 978-0-9801434-3-0
        ISBN-10: 0980143438

Dedicated to all of my family and friends,
without whose support I could have not completed this novel.

Chapter One

The wind felt good on Tony's face as he traveled up the bayou. The clear, blue sky contrasted nicely with the golden hue of the marsh grass. This April day of 1976 was like so many days he had experienced growing up in Sicily. It was warm but not hot, and there were few clouds in the sky. The bright sunshine of spring time almost illuminated the grass and trees.

Handsome, twenty-eight year old Tony Gable had arrived in Bay St. Louis, Mississippi by rental car late the night before and had checked into the Beachfront Hotel, the only hotel in the downtown area. He had wanted to make sure he got down to the city dock area before seven in the morning. It had not been hard to find his ride there for his trip into the swamp. An overweight man named Bert, he had been told, would be waiting for him with a boat. He would be wearing a New York Yankees baseball hat. It took Tony, dressed in casual slacks and a golf shirt, every bit of ten seconds to find him.

"Are you Bert?" Tony asked as he walked on one of the docks up to a man wearing the distinctive hat.

"Yep. I guess that means you're Tony," the overweight man said with a slight smile on his face.

Tony walked over closer to the boat and said, "That's me."

"Then step on board and we'll boogie up the bayou."

Tony put one hand on a piling to help steady himself as he thrust a leg forward towards the boat. His six foot tall, one hundred ninety-five pound, solid frame landed gently on the floor of the small boat. Tony could see from the size of the engine on the back of the boat that this little trip would probably be taken at a fast clip.

After removing the bow line from its anchor to the dock, Bert moved his large frame toward the back of the boat, causing a dramatic shift in the tilt of the small ship's position on the water. Tony moved to immediately grab the side of the boat and eased himself onto a padded bench in front of the low pilot house. The motor suddenly came to life, initially jarring the boat and Tony, who was surprised by its power, and deep sound. Whoever was going fishing in this boat, if indeed that was what it was being used for, was going to get to their fishing area in a minimum amount of time. Guided by its heavy captain, the twelve foot vessel eased away from the dock and out into the large body of water known to locals as the Bay of St. Louis. As soon as the boat was far enough away from the docks, Bert opened the throttle and the bow of the boat rose up out of the water as the vessel began its trip.

Tony was immediately taken by the beauty of the trees and

marsh grass of the area. It was so completely different from the barren waterfront area near his home in Sicily. Tony felt alive and it was a wonderful feeling. But he had to remember why he was making the trip and he had to remember, as he had been told, to be extremely careful about anything he said once they reached their destination.

Not a word was said between the two travelers as the boat made its journey upstream. After having traveled on open water for the first few moments of the trip, the boat turned into a more defined body of water that, while still relatively wide, easily showed in the distance both shores of the water way. It wasn't too long and the body of water began to meander first to one side and then curve in an opposite direction, all the while showing its beauty in the full sunlight.

After a while - a period longer than Tony had expected - as the vessel came around one of the bends in what now was a more narrow, but still wide, body of water, in the distance could be seen some type of structure. As they got closer, Tony could finally see what it was - not one but two huge, connected concrete docks. Behind the docks was something completely out of place, a high, concrete wall up against what appeared to have been at one time the facing of a bluff. Tony could see figures standing on the two docks. Other boats similar to theirs, tied up to the docks, were now riding on the waves created by the entry of their means of transportation into the area.

Bert guided the boat towards the dock to their left and eased it into contact with, what Tony could now see, was solid concrete flooring resting on wooden pilings. With their boat making that contact, one of the men on the dock reached forward as Bert threw him a rope attached to the boat. Tony waited until the line was secured before he made the attempt to stand up and move over to the concrete structure. He wanted to make sure Bert put the boat at least in one position that might stay the same during the time Tony tried to leave the boat. He had witnessed the results of boats carrying someone as heavy as Bert, which were that one or more people who had not taken enough care usually fell either inside the boat or, on a few occasions, even overboard.

As he finally stepped on the dock, he looked around and saw something that immediately caught his eye. He noticed that a man standing about halfway up the stairs, which appeared to run from the floor of the dock up the side of the cement wall to its top, had an AK47 automatic weapon hanging from a strap running over his shoulder. Tony looked toward the other side of the wall and saw another person standing there also with another one of those extremely reliable weapons hanging from a similar shoulder strap. His examination of the two men was interrupted by a voice.

"Ahhhhh Tony!" The voice, coming from a very large, grey-headed man, was deep and at the same time controlled.

Tony turned around and was greeted by a full bear hug, followed by a handshake and a pat on his upper right forearm.

"Welcome! Welcome! Come with me." Tony didn't say anything, remembering his previous directions to that effect.

His six foot four inch, almost three hundred pound greeter began working his way, with a lot of effort, up the cement stairs. Tony noted that everyone, the six or so men on the dock, were quiet, and they were all watching the two of them. As he reached the top of the stairs, Tony could not help but notice that right in front of him were the remnants of a swimming pool, which location overlooked the bayou from the top of the bluff. As both of the stair climbers paused to catch their breaths from their effort, Tony surveyed what was in front of him. There were seven massive, beautiful trees located around the immediate area, with something hanging from each of them that swayed in the breeze. Even though it was a pretty day, the material gave the place a sort of eerie appearance. He decided he could at least ask his host that question.

"What is that stuff dangling from the trees?"

"It's called Spanish moss. It's unique to some areas down here."

Pointing to the left, the grey-headed man then said, "Over there was where the men's bath house was." Then motioning to the opposite side of the dilapidated, empty pool, he said, "Over there was the women's bath house. Behind it, you see there is the guest house, where we will have our meeting." Then motioning directly in front of them, about seventy-five yards away, towards six white columns, he said, "Those columns are all that is left of the old mansion."

Tony could almost feel his jaw dropping open as he began trying to imagine how it might have looked back when. The columns were huge, just simply huge. He looked back at the guest house, which was nice enough itself that it could have served as an upper class home back in Sicily, if it were there. And then there was the swimming pool, built way back when on this bluff overlooking the bayou.

His thoughts were interrupted as they began to make their way toward the guest house. It was then that the man said while gesturing to his left, "Back there, behind the old mansion, was a race track." Tony actually stumbled, losing his step as he quickly shifted his eyes to look for what he had just been told. Regaining his balance, he could just make out the oval of the track. Out here in the middle of nowhere!

They soon were at the steps leading up to the small porch of the guest house. Tony noticed another man standing near the corner of the guest house, also with an AK47 hanging from a shoulder strap. After they climbed the five stairs to the porch area, his greeter turned and pointed toward a group of men standing on the opposite side of the pool where the location of the men's bath house had been.

"Those are our friends from Phoenix, Las Vegas, New Orleans and Kansas City." Then motioning towards another group standing not too far from the columns of the old mansion, he said, "Those are our friends from Chicago, New Jersey, Miami and Detroit." He then turned and entered the small house.

When Tony entered, he was facing a round wooden table surrounded by heavily padded chairs. He noticed several men standing around who all looked at him as they entered the room.

"Come around and sit next to me," the man said, and Tony followed closely behind him, glancing at the men he passed but not really making permanent eye contact with any of them. He could feel all of their eyes following him as he worked his way around the table.

Stepping back, the man motioned for Tony to walk in front of him, saying, "Have a seat right there," as he pointed to a chair to his left. At that point, four other men who had been standing around the room walked over and took their positions behind various chairs. Tony could tell this part had been all planned out because he noticed that there was not an empty chair left after those four men, and he and the grey-headed man, had taken their positions. Then, as the grey-headed man pulled his chair back and moved to sit down, the other four did likewise, as did Tony. After everyone was settled into their chairs, the grey-headed man began.

"Thank you all for being here. We are gathered today to

6

discuss Madeline Benedetti's will. At stake are eighteen gas wells and approximately one hundred and ninety-one million dollars. Madeline saw fit to not spend hardly any of the money that was deposited into her accounts from the gas wells."

As the older man was speaking, Tony casually looked around the table. He noticed that each man sitting there was looking intently at the speaker. He also noticed that standing against the wall behind each man at the table was one other man, except he saw that two were now standing just behind the speaker and him, and two others were standing at the doorway they had just walked through.

"I propose that the rights to the gas wells and the one hundred ninety-one million dollars be divided six ways."

One of the men seated almost directly across from the speaker leaned forward and said, "Godfather, there are only five families in our organization. Why is everything being divided into six parts?"

"Because one of the parts is going to the young man seated to my left."

The same man, leaning forward even more, immediately said, "Why does he get a portion?"

The Godfather answered, looking directly at the questioner, "Because, right now, he owns all of it."

There was an audible sound from some of those seated around the table. The questioner eased back into his chair. After a slight pause, the Godfather continued.

"Years ago, Al Capone sent Nick Gable down here to purchase all of this land so that he could set up an operation shipping booze in from Cuba during prohibition and then sending it all over the southeastern United States. I knew Nick in New York when we both had just arrived there. He was a few years older than me. Well, it wasn't too long and he went to Chicago where he hooked up with Al, who had also been in New York."

Taking a deep breath and leaning to one side of his chair, he continued.

"After a while, as a result of things that happened in Chicago and Detroit, Nick was one of the few people that Al trusted, and he trusted him completely. That is why he sent Nick to establish the operation down here. To provide a cover for Al, everything was put in Nick's name. It was extremely successful, extremely. Unfortunately though, Nick was eventually arrested and convicted. Before he was sent away, Al had Nick transfer title to all of this down here to Nick's sister, Madeline, who had worked with Nick in the operation. Then Al had all of his problems. Each of you knows about all of that."

Looking around the table, he continued. "Well, Nick was picked by the United States military to help with the invasion of Sicily. He was taken out of prison, along with two others with a similar Sicilian background, trained and actually landed there before the invasion so that they could help guide the American forces that landed there. After that successful invasion, his friends in the military appreciated all that he had done for them. At the end of the war, so they would not have to send him back to jail in the U. S., they arranged for his apparent death. It worked, and he lived quietly in Sicily after the war. Eventually he got married, but his wife died after a serious illness. A few years ago, Nick passed away. Now Madeline Gable Benedetti has passed away. Tony here, whose full name is Anthony Gable, was Nick's only child. Being Nick's only child and Madeline being a widow without any children, Tony is Madeline's only heir."

Looking around the table, he then said, "Tony was thoughtful in that he contacted us when he was notified of his inheritance. His dad had mentioned a few things to him through the years and told him that, even though most of Al's organization has long since been forgotten, he should get in contact with us should this happen. I am proud to say that he has done what his dad wanted and has agreed to the split I mentioned, so that there are no problems about it all."

Looking around the room, he then said, "Are there any other questions?" After a short glance around the table, he continued.

"Hearing none, there will be a meeting tomorrow morning at 10 a.m. at the Monteleon Hotel in New Orleans in suite 301, at the end of the hallway. There each one of you may pick up your share of the money. We will work out with you how the payments will be made. It is up to each of you how that will be done, but it will be done tomorrow. Any other details will be worked out with your representatives as to how everything will be taken care of."

Now looking around the table, he then said, "Okay, this meeting is adjourned until 10 a.m. tomorrow."

As he stood up, the others stood up. The four men shook hands with each other and then each one, with few comments, took their turn shaking Tony's hand. Within just seconds, the last person had left the room and only the Godfather and Tony were left standing there. Tony turned to the man standing next to him, shook his hand and said, "Thanks, Uncle Marty."

Chapter Two

Tony had flown into New Orleans from New York four days before the meeting out at the bluffs in Devil's Swamp. Uncle Marty, otherwise known as Martin Gable, was a first cousin of Tony's dad, Nick Gable. They had been raised in the same area of Sicily and knew each other well even though Nick had been eleven years older than Marty. Marty's family, Tony had long ago been told by his dad, had been successful in getting Marty over to New York City a little more than a year before Nick had come over. They had tried to help Nick once he had arrived but had been unable to get him a steady job. It wasn't too long and Nick knew he would have to try his luck in this fabulous country at some other location. It was then that word came back from Chicago that a young Italian named Al Capone, who had also come to New York City when he had first arrived in the country but had eventually gone on to Chicago, might need some manpower to help him in his efforts in that midwestern city. Nick decided that he would go by train to Chicago in hopes of hooking up with Capone's operation there. It had been a wise decision.

Capone's organizational skills had resulted in the establishment during prohibition of a business that, had it been legal, would have ranked among the top enterprises in the United States. Tony's dad, Nick, had been assigned the task by Capone of buying literally thousands of acres of land in Mississippi, most of it in an area of Hancock County called Devil's Swamp, as the receiving point for illegal booze being brought in by Capone from Cuba to be delivered throughout the mid-south region. Title to all of the property had been put in Nick Gable's name. The operation had been enormously successful and, even though Nick had been arrested and convicted of smuggling booze, the operation had never been shut down. Nick had signed the property over to his sister, Madeline Benedetti, after he had been arrested and sentenced. Capone had allowed Madeline to keep the operation running, letting her believe that she was in control of it when in fact he had assigned one of his close male associates to watch every move she made and report back to him. A hurricane had hit the Devil's Swamp location, leaving Madeline without the full use of her mind. There was no need for Capone to change anything with his men already being at the location. The docks were quickly repaired but the huge mansion at the site was not rebuilt.

With Madeline's state of mind being at a level that she didn't really know where she was, and didn't care, she was not in any position to interfere with the continuation of the operation. Capone decided that she would be provided with a fairly significant stipend that kept her in place as a front for the operation. That stipend continued to be paid from a nice percentage of the profits made from the operation that had been kept in an account at a local bank. Capone had his man there assign one of their associates to check on her and take care of whatever financial business needed to be dealt with. Because the owner of the bank knew Capone well and spent time with him on almost every trip Capone made to the coast over the years, he knew that it was best, even after Capone's demise, if everything were left as it was, which meant that a large amount of money had begun to accumulate even before the finding of the Bayou Gas Field under a lot of the swamp land that had been bought. The bank officer did not want mobsters coming after him concerning the money set aside to take care of Madeline. Even after the repeal of the Prohibition amendment to the U. S. constitution and eventually Capone's arrest and conviction for income tax evasion, nothing had really changed for her since she was barely able to function anyway.

Over the years on rare trips to the business area of downtown Bay St. Louis, Madeline occasionally would pass out candy to some of the kids playing in the city park there. Other than that, even though she was still a nice looking woman, she often could not even respond to a statement because of her lack of understanding of what had been said to her. So she just didn't say anything. Sometimes, she would focus what attention she had on a yard boy that had been hired to cut the grass around the house where she lived. Usually though, after a brief sexual encounter with her, the yard boys had actually refused to return to perform their duties, once the rumor made its rounds about how she may have had one of the yard boys killed for a derogatory comment the boy had said about her to her face. It was said that the young man had been buried right behind where the mansion had been. That way, she could sit in her rocking chair on one side of the

13

front porch and look over at where he was buried. Apparently she felt good knowing that the person who had said such nasty things about her was no longer walking the face of this earth. It was said that when she looked in that direction, a strange smile would come over her face, one that said, "Gotcha."

Nick had contacted Marty several years after he had been declared dead in Sicily by the United States Army and asked him to discretely check on Madeline's situation and health. Marty was by then in the upper levels of the mob and well-connected in what had become a nation-wide crime syndicate. He was easily able to make a call to Juan Bartolli, the head of the organized crime family in the mid-south area, so that an inquiry could be made about Madeline's status and health. Marty got Nick to agree to a division of any funds that existed as a result of Capone's operation, as long as Nick's son, Tony, got an equal share. This agreement was able to keep Bartolli happy and satisfied to the extent that he felt no need to try to do something that might cause problems with his New York business associates. So when Madeline had died, being unmarried and leaving no children, her only existing heir was her brother, Nick, who was by then deceased also, leaving Tony as the sole known heir to the property and any funds. Nick, having already put Marty on notice to let him know when Madeline died, had predeceased her by several years.

There was simply no way that Marty was about to not follow through on his word to his relative and longtime friend to make sure his son was taken care of in any settlement. When Marty had been informed about her death, he had called Tony and told him to come to New York immediately. Tony already knew what to do, having been told more than once before his death to do whatever "Uncle Marty," or his designee if he were dead, said do. After he had gotten the call, Tony flew to New York the next day. He had been warmly greeted at the airport by "Uncle Marty" and taken to a room at the Waldof Astoria. They had dinner at a quiet restaurant, spending most of the meal discussing how matters in Mississippi should be handled. Uncle Marty had already notified the potential attendees and arranged for the group to meet in Mississippi at the Bluffs the following Tuesday. Now had come the time, the next morning at 10 a.m. at the Monteleon Hotel in New Orleans, to settle up with everyone.

Tony had stayed at the Monteleon and was up at 7:30 to have breakfast. He ate by himself, having been told by Marty to not be seen in public with anyone. Even when he saw faces that looked familiar from the meeting the day before out at the Bluffs, he made no effort to recognize them, nor did they with him. At 10 o'clock, he went to the large suite at the end of the hallway on the third floor. He knocked in the sequence he had been told and the door opened. After stepping inside, he was almost overwhelmed by the activity in the room. He noted that the curtains for each of the windows of the room had been pulled so that there was no natural light in the area. Inside were at least six guys dealing with large briefcases and huge stacks of cash. Also in the room were five tables at which men in shirtsleeves were writing on sheets of paper at an almost continuous pace. Moving his eyes around the room, he saw two men with automatic weapons on both sides of the front door, along with two other men also with the same type weapons standing next to both side walls of the room. Sitting on four bar stools at the bar located to the back of the main room were four heavy-set figures, one of whom Tony quickly recognized was Marty. After working his way over to the four men, he was warmly greeted by his "Uncle Marty."

"Ahhhhhhhhhh, Tony! Welcome, welcome." Then pointing to

the three men with him, Marty said, "You remember these three gentlemen from yesterday?"

"Yes. Certainly," he said, nodding towards the other three men. He remembered their faces and that each one was head of a crime family in another city, but the only name he could remember was the one from New Orleans, Juan Bartolli. He also noted that the one missing man from the group that had been around the table out at the Bluffs the day before was the man from Detroit.

"We were just talking about how much we appreciate your father making sure that all of this took place," Marty said as he gestured to the other men while talking.

Tony felt obligated to say something, even though Marty had told him to say as little as possible.

"Well, thank you for saying that. He thought the world of you, as you know, and I am just glad it has all worked out."

As he talked, he looked at each man, one after the other, and was glad to notice that they were nodding their heads in agreement to what he was saying. It was about that time that there was another special knock on the front door to the suite. The door was opened and in walked the man from Detroit along with three men, two of them carrying black leather suitcases. A man at the door shook the leader's hand and pointed in the direction of the bar stools. As the man from Detroit began to make his way over to that area, his associates were directed by the greeter to one of the tables where they began setting up for business, pulling legal pads and pens out of the briefcases.

"Hello, Harry," Marty said as the man arrived at the bar stools.

"Gentlemen," he answered as he looked at the group with a

smile on his face. Not wasting a second, he then said, "So where are we? How is everything going?"

Marty answered, "Everything is on schedule. You each should be able to leave here within the next hour. Our host, Mr. Bartolli here, has arranged for our business to be taken care of by two separate banks here in New Orleans. One is a major bank well-known to everyone that he has a close relationship with and the other is a mid- level bank with which he also has a special relationship. The mid-level bank, which doesn't necessarily have the oversight the larger one does, may be helpful concerning any matters that some of you may have that may be, shall we say, difficult to deal with. Hopefully we will not have any problems that cannot be handled and we can bring all of this quickly to a close."

Harry answered, "Good. I was hoping there would be no problems. I need to get back as soon as possible."

Tony stood to the side as the men talked while at the same time keeping an eye on the activities in the room. At one point, some fifteen minutes after Tony had arrived, Bartolli was summonsed by his men over to his table. After a short visit with his associates, he walked back over to rejoin the group at the bar. Marty motioned for him to come stand closer to him and turned to Tony.

"Tony, come here for a moment." Tony responded by moving so that he was next to Marty with Bartolli now standing in front of him.

"Juan, I would like to ask a favor of you. Tony here would like to stay in this country for a while, see if he likes it here and if he does, maybe stay here." Bartolli watched Marty intently as Marty continued.

17

"Would it be alright with you if he stayed in this area? He has been here a few days and seems to really enjoy it here, like almost everybody else that visits here." With that, Marty let out a hearty laugh, as did Bartolli. Tony smiled, nodding his head in agreement.

"Sure," Bartolli answered. "Godfather, you ask me for a favor, I do that favor if at all possible. That would be fine with me."

"Good. Maybe you could even show him around, let him see a few things. Maybe he might even be able to help you with something, you never know," Marty said, looking intently at Bartolli. Tony knew that it would take a really good reason for Bartolli to not agree to show him around given the way the request was put by the Boss of Bosses.

"Yeah. We'll show him a few things, see how it goes," Bartolli answered, looking over at Tony.

"Thank you, sir," Tony said with a smile on his face. "I would really appreciate that."

Bartolli answered, "Good. We'll see what we can come up with."

Marty then said, "Thanks, Juan. I owe you one." Marty then gave one of his big smiles as he offered his hand. Bartolli put his hand out and shook Marty's.

"Good," Marty said. "Now Tony, I know you will do the right things while you are down here. Juan has a huge operation and can really be helpful to you. You be as helpful to him as you can, while you are in this area."

"Yes, sir," Tony answered.

About an hour later, the group had thinned out. The only men left were Marty's men and a few of Bartolli's. Everyone else had left. Bartolli himself had departed a few minutes earlier with two of his men.

Marty said, as he slapped Tony on his shoulders, "It's time for you to go, Tony. I'll be leaving in just a little bit. It's been so good to see you. Thanks for doing everything your Dad told you to do. He would be so proud of you. You are not even my son and I'm proud of you," he said followed by one of his laughs.

Walking Tony to the door of the room, Marty continued, "Let me know how it goes with Bartolli." Then he opened the door and walked out into the hallway with Tony. Looking both ways as he now shut the door, Marty grabbed Tony's arm and walked with him down the deserted hallway towards the elevators.

Marty lowered his voice and said, "Tony, the rest of us are not in the drug running business." Then he stopped in the hallway and began looking straight into Tony's eyes.

"We don't like what it does to people, to their families. We have all had several talks about that business and we all agree that none of us, none of us, should be involved in that."

Tony nodded his head in agreement. He had always prided himself on staying in shape, training so hard while he was in that school in France, and continuing to train hard when he had returned to Sicily.

"Uncle Marty, I have never even tried that stuff. While I was boxing and all, I always wanted to be the best I could be and do the best I could do. I wanted my dad to be proud of me."

"I am glad to hear that, son, I really am. Your father was so proud of you. I mention this because we have had reports that Juan is starting to get into the shipment of those types of things. I hope not, because it would really cause a problem for us, as a group. Some of the guys, like Harry, just hate that stuff. He had a son who ended up committing suicide because of getting involved with that. So we are against that. Now, there is only so much we can do. But I mention it to you because you might get exposed to some of what he is, like I said, probably doing. Just make sure you stay like you are. They may even try to get you to use some of the things they may be shipping. I am just telling you, do your old Uncle a favor, and don't experiment with that stuff."

"I won't, Uncle Marty. I have never understood why somebody would do that, but I promise you I will not get involved in doing that kind of thing. And if you want, I will let you know what I see."

"That would be good. Now, please understand, I am not asking you to do that. But I am asking you, if they are into it and they ask you to try it, stay away from it, please."

"I will, Uncle Marty. I promise."

"Good," Marty said as he began to give Tony a big hug, putting his head on first one side of Tony's head and then the other. "And Tony, find a church and go to it, ok? Your father would like that."

"I will, Uncle Marty. Have a safe trip back."

With that, the two parted, Marty standing there watching Tony as he walked down the hallway, and into the rest of his life.

Chapter Three

Deputy Sheriff Mark Patterson had the look of a law enforcement officer. He stood 6 feet tall and weighed a trim but strong two hundred twenty-five pounds. His clean cut features and dark hair, along with his build, gave him an appearance of strength. He was the grandson of a legendary couple in Hancock County, former Sheriff Wild Bill Patterson and his wife, Helen. Their son, Bart Patterson, had graduated from St. Richard's high school in Bay St. Louis and had fought in Europe in World War II as a tank commander in U. S. General George Patton's famous Third Army. Bart had received a Purple Heart when he was wounded in a tank battle not too far from Bastogne during Patton's effort to rescue the American forces holding out there. He was not seriously wounded and returned to the front lines within a matter of a few days since, at that time, every soldier capable of carrying a weapon was needed.

After the war, Bart had come home and attended Louisiana State University on a full scholarship, which was funded by an anonymous donor. Bart had tried on several occasions to find out the identity of the donor because he had wanted to thank whoever had done such a kind thing. He had been told by the financial aide officials at LSU that the agreement that had made the funds available to the school specifically said that the identity of the source would never be made available to anyone. They had also assured him that such an arrangement was not unusual because individuals, and corporations, that provided such assistance sometimes simply did not want their identity known. The implication was left by those officials that there was great appreciation throughout the country for what the veterans had done for their country and making scholarships available to returning soldiers was the least that some of them had felt they could do, but they did want to remain anonymous. Bart could understand such a feeling and decided to leave the matter alone. While appreciative, he did not have to know exactly who had done what he ultimately benefited from. Not too long after he had entered college, the United States Congress passed the provisions of the GI bill which provided government financial assistance to classmates of his that had served in the country's armed forces.

Bart married his college sweetheart, Amy Lovelace, upon his graduation from Louisiana State University and went back to Hancock County where he took a job in his father's sheriff's department. A few years later, when his father had passed away, Bart was elected to the open position and took his father's place as sheriff of Hancock County. His mother, Helen, was proudly seated on the first row during the swearing in ceremony on the front steps of the County Courthouse in Bay St. Louis. Not too long after he took over the sheriff's office, Bart and Amy were the proud parents of a bouncing baby boy, Mark Tyler Patterson. Grandmother Helen, when she was not playing the organ and piano at St. Richard's Catholic Church services, spent as much time as Bart and Amy would allow her with her new grandson. She welcomed the time she spent with Mark since he was always a pleasure to be around.

It was during the years that Bart was a teenager that events took control of so many lives of the young men in the United States. The Vietnam War raised its ugly head and became the deciding factor in many of the decisions made by those becoming 18 years of age, such as Mark. The United States still had a military draft which mandated that every male in the country, without a valid reason, could be forced to join the United States military in order to provide manpower for the country's war effort. That draft was something that every able-bodied young man over the age of 18 had to face. Those who were politically connected or whose families had influence were able to sign up for the National Guard or an Army Reserve unit and stood a good chance of not having to "go over" to what had become a dirty, seemingly no end war.

Mark's family, while well-connected, would never stand for the slightest mention of him not doing his duty for his country. Though his father was sheriff of Hancock County and his grandmother was well-known throughout the county for her playing such wonderful music on the church organ for so many years, there was never any discussion of the family trying to protect Mark by having him avoid the draft because they were able to get him into a unit that would, in all likelihood, remain in the states and not be sent over. He would do his duty as a responsible citizen should. Others may run away as "draft dodgers" to Canada or some other place, but under the law such an individual would face being banned for life from ever returning to the United States. Mark was never close to even thinking about not doing his duty for his country.

After two years in a local junior college, Mark graduated but had no interest in going any further for a higher education. Not being in school meant it was only a matter of time before he would be drafted by his country and probably become a private in the United States Army. Having been an avid woodsman during all of his young life, especially his years in junior high and high school, Mark was familiar with the outdoors and with guns, hunting rifles in particular. He had thought about being on active duty for a long time. He made the decision that, if he was going to be sent over to Vietnam, he wanted to be as prepared as he could possibly be.

For Mark, that meant he wanted to try to be part of the Green Berets, a very specialized, elite Army unit he had found out about that was highly trained and extremely particular about who was allowed to be a member. Through contacts made by his father, he learned that it would be best for him to volunteer for military service in the army and, once basic training was completed, if he finished high enough in his class he could then apply for further training as a Green Beret. If everything went well, he could indeed be selected to be part of that well-respected and admired group of soldiers.

Mark volunteered for the army two weeks after graduation from junior college and was sent almost immediately to Fort Benning, Georgia for infantry training. There he finished number seven in his class of 342 draftees and enlisted personnel. The appropriate contacts were made with both his instructors at the infantry school and, by his father, with political friends concerning his interest in the Green Berets. The United States

Army did not take long to decide that if this son of the sheriff of Hancock County, Mississippi wanted to be a Green Beret, then he was most welcome to try to see if, during training for that force, he could pass its stringent requirements. During the initial qualification period, only one in one hundred was allowed to move on for further training. Eventually, only about one in ten was awarded the honor of being finally selected to serve as a Green Beret.

It was just before his training began that Mark got a call from his mom. She tearfully told him that his father had been killed while on duty. Apparently, late at night he had gone to meet an undercover informant by himself. When he had not returned after several hours, a search had begun which resulted in the discovery of his body in his unmarked patrol car, which had been located in a deserted field overlooking a bayou. Mark was devastated, but even more so was his mother. He was granted emergency leave and flew to New Orleans, rented a car and drove to the family house in Bay St. Louis. Several relatives were there and hurried him in to see his mom, who was in his parent's bedroom in their bed. When she saw him, she started crying, so much that he began to worry about her. She kept hugging him, and simply could not stop crying. It was something he would never forget.

The turnout for the funeral was enormous for Bay St. Louis. His father was respected and admired and his tragic death seemed to have an effect on almost everyone. Time and time again during the trip, he was told how universally loved his father had been and how much of a positive influence he had been on so many lives. The burial service was attended by so many people that the church was full and the overflow crowd ended up just standing outside. With his continually sobbing mother on one arm and his tearful grandmother, Helen, on the other, the three exited the church behind the casket. Mark stood at the top of the stairs and briefly glanced around the church grounds at the hundreds of people standing on the front lawn of the church and also across the street.

He helped the two ladies down the stairs and to the waiting car for their ride to the cemetery. After they were all seated inside the vehicle, Mark thought about his father, not even noticing the crowd as they pulled away from the church. He literally could not believe that his father was dead. Such a thought had never crossed his mind, that his father, or his mother for that matter, would ever die - and certainly not this soon.

After the brief ceremony at the burial site, everyone, including his mother and grandmother, eventually left. The only people remaining in the area were those individuals working for the funeral home. Mark had told his mother and grandmother to go back to the house. He said that he would like a few moments alone at the grave site. After they had left, Mark had just sat there, by himself next to the open grave, thinking about how there were no answers as to why this had happened, and at this time in his life. Here he was getting ready to go into very serious training, hopefully training that would help keep him alive and at the same time do some good for the country's war effort, and this happened. All at once, everything seemed in doubt. Everything. That day, August 26, 1969, was not a day he was going to fondly remember. After losing a father he really had loved, Mark now felt most uncomfortable with the future. Raymond Burdette, his father's chief deputy, had been appointed to his father's position of county sheriff until an election could be held. Mark had training classes that were about to begin, very important classes that might help him stay alive in Vietnam. Life had to go on.

*   *   *   *   *

Mark managed to survive the Vietnam war. Oh, he had several close calls, and things had happened that he did not necessarily want to remember. Things such as the death of fellow soldiers that he had gotten to be close friends with. Soldiers such as Clark Bishop, a country boy from east Tennessee who had gone through Green Beret training with him. Because they were both from the south and from the country so to speak, they had become close friends. Clark was a medic and Mark never had understood the thinking of those serving as medics. They just seemed hell-bent on getting killed, constantly risking their own lives to try to help fellow soldiers who were wounded, or sick. Time and time again, he had seen Clark run across ground while the air all around was filled with bullets that were trying to kill him. If there was one goal of the Viet Cong soldiers, or VC as they were called, it was that they would try to kill every United States soldier serving as a medic that they saw. In particular, the VC would try to kill Green Beret soldiers serving as medics because of the good things they did to try to help everyday Vietnamese people just trying to survive. The VC wanted to make an example out of every soldier that was known for trying to help any Vietnamese. They wanted to kill that soldier, especially those serving as medics, and do so as gruesomely as possible.

Four months before he was to come home, Clark Bishop was killed just after helping several wounded Green Berets. It had happened during a successful ambush the unit had set up and

27

performed that resulted in the almost complete elimination of an entire Viet Cong company. The ambush had taken place in the Mekong delta south of Saigon and had lasted for the better part of an afternoon. As the battle had progressed, Clark helped his wounded comrades while under almost constant fire. After he had helped them all he could, he also tried to help a wounded VC soldier who had fallen close to the Green Beret positions. As Clark was tending to the soldier's wounds, the soldier pulled the pin on a grenade and both of them were instantly killed by the explosion.

That same battle resulted in their unit commander, Captain Andy Jones, being severely wounded. The battle was finally over when, due to the setting of the sun, both sides had managed to slip away as best they could. Mark's side ended up with three of his fellow Green Berets, including Clark, having been killed and four, including the Captain, having been wounded. Only Mark, Jim McDaniel, Bobby Ryan and Tom Simpson had survived the battle unscathed.

Finally, Mark's tour of duty was complete and he was given orders to return to the United States and go on leave to visit with his family. Flying over, wearing his uniform had been no problem because he had been placed on a chartered plane that flew fully loaded with soldiers going to the war. Coming back, his commercial flight leaving Japan for Spokane, Washington required him to wear his uniform in order to fly for free. When he arrived at the airport in Spokane, he and a few other uniformed soldiers had to walk through the gate at which the plane had landed, down a concourse and then into the main baggage claim area of the airport. There was only one problem. On the second floor surrounding the baggage claim area was a balcony. As Mark walked out into the open area under that balcony, he felt moisture hit him in his face and saw moisture spots appear all over his uniform. Looking up, he saw what had caused that moisture: it was from the spittle of over two hundred anti- war protesters, both men and women! Those protesters were spitting on the soldiers as they walked out into the open area. Mark, and others in uniform, began to jog to get out from under the barrage of spit, followed by chants of derision. Once they had made it to the next hallway, Mark leaned up against the wall, and almost threw up, looking at what was causing the disturbance. Raggedly dressed, mostly young people were screaming at the soldiers, yelling out words such as "baby killers," "murderers," "rapist," and other horrifying words.

Mark, now leaning against the wall of the concourse and breathing so hard that he had to support himself, could barely keep his feelings under control. It had been a good thing that the soldiers were not allowed to carry their weapons with them as they departed the planes. He knew that he would have felt no remorse firing up into that crowd. After taking a few moments to collect himself, he immediately went to the nearest men's clothing store in the concourse, picked out a suit of clothes, shirt, tie and shoes, and changed, throwing his military uniform into a trash can as he left the store. Buying an airplane ticket at the cost of $1245.00, he flew to New Orleans and caught a ride to Bay St. Louis, not stopping until he had reached his house. There, he slept almost continuously for over two weeks, except to eat small meals prepared by his mom. Finally going back to Fort Benning, he spent the next two years helping train other Green Beret units, particularly those individuals designated to be snipers.

After getting his discharge papers from the Army, he had returned to Bay St. Louis where the mayor, a long time friend of his father's, suggested that Mark go visit the new sheriff, who was none other than Raymond Burdette, his father's former chief deputy. Mark eventually did so, and with the support of the many political friends of his father's, Burdette decided that his office could indeed use a person like the former sheriff's son. He had worked in that office for a little under two years.

Now, Mark was on his semi-annual trip to Washington, D. C. Flying into the city's downtown National airport, he was greeted by one of the former members of his Green Beret unit, Jim McDaniel. After giving him a big bear hug and going with him to collect his suitcase, Jim took Mark to his house in nearby Alexandria, Virginia. There he got a nice greeting from Sarah, Jim's wife, and both of them helped him to his room.

Not too long after dropping off his bag there, Jim said, "Well, are you ready to make the visit?"

Looking at his friend, Mark said, "I am never ready to make this visit." Jim nodded his head in agreement.

"I know we say that almost every trip, but I will say it again. We both know if we were there, he would be doing what we have done, and are doing, and probably more,"

"There is no doubt in my mind that he would. No question at all. So let's go try to put a smile on his face."

Jim replied, "Let's do it."

With that, the two of them left in Jim's car for Walter Reed Army Hospital in Bethesda, Maryland. They needed to get there before three in the afternoon. At 5 p.m. visitation was limited to family members.

Walking into the huge facility, they approached the desk and Mark asked of the pleasant older woman sitting at the desk, "Captain Andy Jones' room, please."

Checking her register, she soon replied, "Room 212. Do you know how to get there?"

"Yes, ma'am. He was in that same room our last visit," Mark said.

"Okay. I think I remember you two. From about 5 or 6 months ago. You came to visit him then."

"Yes, I remember you too," Jim said.

"Thanks for always being so kind to us," Mark said.

"Gentlemen, with people like you two, it is always easy to be nice. I hope you have a pleasant visit."

"Thanks," Jim said as the two began to walk towards the elevators.

Room 212 was something they both remembered, without saying a word. It was a shared room. The problem had been that two of the last four roommates had passed away shortly after having been moved there. The result was significant depression on the room's remaining occupant, their friend and former commander, Captain Andy Jones.

The door to the room was partially open as they walked in. There, in the bed to their right, was Jones. They were both happy to see him, but they had to make sure they hid their sadness. That was because no part of his body existed below the lower waist of Captain Andy Jones. It had all been blown away. Yes, he was lucky to be alive, but that depended on how a person evaluated it. Captain Jones spent most of every day, almost all of each and every day, in bed because he had no legs. There were also other lower body parts that were missing from Captain Jones. Here, trying to sit up in his bed, were the living remains of a former excellent athlete, a leader of men among men. Now he was trying to continue to exist even though his roommates kept dying on him.

"Hi, Captain," Mark said with a genuine smile on his face.

Almost at the same time, Jim said, "Hi, Captain. We came to check on you."

The captain managed half of a smile and replied, "Hi, boys. Good to see you."

"Good to see you too, Captain," Mark said, now standing to the Captain's left, away from the curtain partition in the room.

"So are they taking good care of you, Captain?" Jim asked with as much of a smile as he could muster.

"Oh, I guess you could say they try, but, and you two of all people know this, there is not much they can do to put a smile on anybody's face."

A moment of heavy silence came over the three former comrades. It was then that Mark knew he had to try saying something that was on his mind from time to time.

"Captain, you know how awful I feel about ...." He could not finish.

"Mark, just stop it. We have been over all of that. I don't hold you responsible for what happened to me. It was the damn VC that did this to me, not you or anything you didn't do. So like I have told you before, please, just forget that. Things happen, especially in war. I will be alright eventually, at least I hope so. They have been telling those of us with problems like I have for three years now that they are working on new artificial limbs for us. The doctor told me just the other day that businesses working on all of that are finally beginning to make some progress. Now, I don't know if he is just telling me that or if it is actually true. He has been saying something almost like that ever since I can remember. But the tone of his voice seems to be more positive lately so, you never know. They may finally be close to coming up with something. So Mark, thanks for the thought, but again, there was nothing you could have done that would have prevented what happened. In fact, you saved my life, and that of Jim here, and Bobby and Tom. Hell, if you hadn't done what you did, none of us, you hear me, none of us would be on this earth, much less talking with each other here now."

It did make Mark feel better hearing that from a man he thought so much of. If Captain Jones had not insisted on their level of training being so high, none of them probably would have survived. They were only alive because, when trouble came to visit them in the swamps of Vietnam, they had been prepared.

After about a twenty minute visit, the two visitors began to bring the get-together to a close. As they were turning to leave the room, a heavy but perky nurse walked in. "Amanda" was written on her name tag.

"Well Captain, you didn't tell me what hunks you had coming to visit you," she said with a wide smile.

The Captain replied with a smile on his face, "Now boys, you see what I have to put up with around here."

The two visitors manufactured chuckles but Amanda continued.

"Captain, you do have to do a better job of letting me know when these two are coming to see you next time. I want to rearrange my schedule so I can get to know them a whole lot better."

"Sugar, I can assure you that these two can't handle you. You are going to have to save yourself for me," Captain Jones said.

Amanda quickly responded, "Now honey, I don't mind if you tell these two that I hopped up on that bed and tried every way possible to get you to take care of me. Did you tell them that? I don't want them thinking I didn't try to do everything I could to put a smile on your face."

Mark and Jim were already laughing by this time, as was the Captain.

Jim said, "Captain, I do believe you have a little more than you can handle."

Amanda continued, "Honey, I am just waiting, waiting I am telling you, for them to get him a prosthesis for his penis, one of those pump up things. That's why I am checking on him every day now, every day, because that is what I heard! If he gets one of those things, he could get hard any time we wanted! He just might be able to stay hard for a really long time with one of those things. I would just be totally in love then!"

Mark laughed as he smiled, then said, "Captain! You didn't tell us about all of that!"

Again Amanda chimed in, "Honey, he doesn't want you to know. Then all of you guys would be up here trying to get one of those things so you could get to me too. Now you know why I keep checking on him, every day, to see if his has come in yet!"

Captain Jones, Mark and Jim all responded by howling with laughter. Amanda then said, "It's time for you two to get out of here. I have a few things I have to check on the Captain, unless you two want to stand there laughing while I do it."

"No, no," Mark and Jim said at almost the same time.

"It's definitely time for us to go," Mark said laughing.

"I am with you, partner," Jim said with a big smile.

Both walked over and shook the Captain's hand. As they then moved towards the doorway of the room, Amanda said, "You two hunks come back soon now, you hear?"

Both men turned towards her and smiled.

"We'll be back, girl. You can count on it," Jim said.

Amanda turned towards the Captain and said, "Oh I just love it when a man wants to be with me."

The men left the room chuckling as they each said, "Bye, Captain."

They were both so glad that Amanda was the nurse for that station at the hospital. They could tell that she really lifted the Captain's spirits. There was no telling what other types of banter went on between those two. All of that was so much better than the atmosphere that had been there when the Captain had first arrived. Of course, his spirits had not been helped by the fact that the Captain's beautiful, redheaded wife, who had come to see him every other day for about two months after he had been put there, had walked in one night and put her wedding ring on the night stand next to his bed while he slept. They were divorced six months later.

Jim and Mark walked out to Jim's car not saying a word. Even after they got in the car and Jim began driving them down into the Georgetown area of Washington, not a word was said. Finally Mark spoke.

"He looked better this time than he has in a while."

Jim agreed, saying, "He seems a little better. He does." Then after a brief pause, he added, "It is all probably due to that nurse."

Mark chuckled a little and said, "Man, is she a breath of fresh air! Whatever it is she gets paid, that one should get more."

Jim spotted a parking place on the street, almost an impossible happening to Mark's recollection, especially at that time of the day. Getting out of the car, the two men walked down the streets of Georgetown to the "Brewmaster's Restaurant and Pub." Walking in the front door, they immediately spotted Bobby Ryan and Tom Simpson, two of the surviving members of their Green Beret unit, who both stood up as they approached their table.

"Hello guys," Jim said with a big smile as they all proceeded to exchange handshakes and hugs.

Tom gently pushed at Mark's stomach and said with a big smile on his face, "So they must feed deputy sheriff's regularly down in the deep south."

Mark smiled as they all settled into their chairs and said, "I try every way possible to not miss a meal. I learned that from that little trip we all took over to the Far East."

A young, male waiter appeared at their table and began passing out menus as he said, "Welcome to Brewmaster's, gentlemen. Anyone need a cocktail before you order?"

Jim looked around the table. As usual, since he had been the highest ranking member of the present group when they were in the army and he also had a pretty good idea what the group wanted to do as soon as the drinks could be delivered, he said, "If you would be so kind, I believe each of us would appreciate your bringing us a beer."

Seeing unanimous agreement, the waiter asked, "Any brand in particular?"

Jim answered following a quick glance around the table, "I think, for starters, a Bud for each of us would be fine."

"A Bud each it is," the waiter said and he quickly left the table.

Settling into their chairs, Bobby said looking at Mark, "So how is the State of Mississippi's crime element holding up under the efforts of the sheriff's office down there? Which county are you in, I forget."

Mark answered, "It's Hancock County, down in the southwest corner not too far from New Orleans, you may recall."

"He doesn't remember too much from his last trip down there," Tom commented as the others smiled.

"Is everything going Okay? You haven't had any close calls or anything, have you?" Bobby asked.

"Everything is fine, except for all the drugs being brought into the New Orleans area. With us being so close, we get a lot of overflow, I guess you could say, from everything happening over there."

Looking around the table, Mark just had to ask. "How are you guys doing? Has anybody had any feedback from that last time we were together?"

Jim quickly answered, "Everything is fine. No problems at all of any kind. I take it that each one of you are available if needed in the future." As he looked around the table, each of the other three men nodded his head.

"Good. Everybody was very happy with what the final result was and now it is as if it never happened. I will let you know if any other opportunities come up."

Everyone at the table could tell by Jim's tone of voice that he now did not want to talk any further about that last time. Bobby helped the situation out by asking, "So how was your visit with Captain Andy?"

Jim answered, after glancing at Mark, "Well, he seems to

be doing a little better. He's got this new nurse and his morale seems to be much better. You guys, of all people, will love this. She told us, in front of him, that she was looking forward to his receipt of an artificial penis!" The various members of the group let out chuckles upon that being said. Jim continued.

"Yep, it seems that the new ones being shipped in, which should arrive any day now, are of the pump up variety and she is looking forward to seeing how those things work!" With that, the whole group let go with a round of healthy laughter. Filled beer mugs were then placed in front of each one by the waiter.

Jim raised his in a toast, as did each of the others.

"To our missing comrades in arms. God bless them. May they rest in peace," he said.

The group then clinked their mugs and each man took a drink. At least two of them had tears in their eyes.

Chapter Four

Tony now had the kind of problem that every person on the planet earth wished they had at some point in their lives. What was he going to do with his over thirty-two million dollar share from Madeline's estate? His first thought was to go get drunk. His thought immediately after that was he had better take care of making sure that his share was protected. The more he thought about it, the more he knew he had to get his money into safe places so that it would be there for him, not only now but in the future.

He went down to the Huntington National Bank in New Orleans and met with Thomas Hester, a bank Vice President that Uncle Marty had specifically mentioned he should see, and arranged for ten million dollars to be wired back to his bank in Sicily. Since his father had made sure that an account had long been set up and used by Tony as he grew up, and since his father had also insisted through the years that he get to know the management people at that bank, Tony already had the appropriate wiring information for sending what he wanted to send, where he wanted to send it back in Sicily. He had made sure to take care of getting that vital piece of information before he had left Sicily.

Tony left the remainder of his money in the Huntington Bank, receiving assurances from Hester that he could start spending from his account at any time by using any of the small stack of checks Hester gave him. Tony asked where the nearest used car dealership was located and was told about a location in the downtown area several blocks away from the bank. He let Hester know that he was going to buy a used car that afternoon, if he was able to find one he really liked at the dealership, and that the dealership may need to call him to verify funds in the account. Hester told him he would be more than happy to let the dealership know any check Tony issued to them was good. He also had Hester give him a cashier's check for one hundred thousand dollars to take with him.

That afternoon, after eating a meal at a small restaurant on Canal Street, Tony hailed a cab and had it take him to the dealership Hester had mentioned. He saw the car he wanted right when he got out of the cab. It was a 1956 light blue and white, four-door Ford. He walked over to it from the street and soon was met by a salesman. The transaction took every bit of twenty minutes, after the phone call to Thomas Hester. Tony now had transportation and it was in the style of car that he had long admired.

Tony was going to stay in the United States, at least for a while, and what better place to be in than Bay St. Louis, where his father and Madeline had lived. So he asked for directions over to the coastal Mississippi town after buying his car. He felt his license to drive in Europe would keep him covered until he could get a place to live. Then he would get his United States license in that area. Tony had told Uncle Marty that he might do that and had asked Uncle Marty if there was a bank in Bay St. Louis that he should deal with. After telling Bartolli that Tony was thinking about going over to Mississippi to live and asking him for a banking contact there, Bartolli had told Marty that Tony should go see George Kovac at the Templeton State Bank in Bay St. Louis.

Tony enjoyed his drive over to Mississippi. Most of all, he enjoyed the pickup and power of the four barrel carburetor and the 406 cubic inch engine in his '56 Ford. Another thing he enjoyed was the beauty of the area as he drove over. The occasional glimpses of water from the highway took his thoughts back to his home area. He would miss it there, but he was also glad to get away. It was time for a change. He hated to say it, but he was glad Madeline's death had taken place when it did. It was the perfect time for him to leave, at least for a while.

He took the first exit off of Interstate Highway 10 onto Highway 90 and worked his way towards the town. He stopped along the way at a gas station and got directions to the bank's downtown location. Finally getting to the bridge over the Bay of St. Louis, he turned right and went down Beach Front Road which ran along the western edge of the large, beautiful body of water. Immediately he began to notice the nice homes along the road, some of which appeared to have been there for years. He was impressed by the neatness of the area and by its cozy character. He was soon at a stoplight and made the appropriate turns to arrive at the large building with the name Templeton State Bank on its front. He parked his car out front and walked into the building.

Going over to the first teller's window, he smiled as he asked, "Could you tell me if George Kovac is here?"

"He is. May I tell him who is asking for him? " the short, cute teller answered.

"Yes, tell him Tony Gable is here to see him."

The teller walked around from behind her window and went over to a closed door at the back side of the open entrance area. She knocked very lightly on the door and after a couple of seconds opened it. Tony could hear her say, "A Mr. Tony Gable is here to see you."

"Tell him I will be with him in a moment," Tony could hear a voice say.

The teller closed the door and walked over to him.

"He said he will be with you in a moment. Please have a seat in one of those chairs and he will be right with you," she very pleasantly said as she pointed to a group of six chairs around a coffee table in front of Kovac's office.

"Sure," Tony said and made his way over to the chair area. He took a seat there, making sure he could watch Kovac's door but also see what was going on at the teller windows. His first thought was that if all the girls down here were as cute as this teller and her two teller friends at the other windows, he was going to enjoy being here.

Once seated, he noticed the magazines on the small table which all seemed to deal with boating or fishing. He felt that he was going to like this place even more because of his interest in both of those since he had been big enough to walk. His Dad had made sure of that.

After about ten minutes, the office door opened and out walked a man about 5 feet 10 inches tall carrying a pot belly and wearing a white suit with a red bow tie. His hair was almost totally white and needed to be cut, Tony thought, for a man who was so high in a bank. Tony had certainly never seen a banker in Sicily that had his hair so unkempt. Another thing Tony noticed was that, as the man stuck his hand out to shake hands, he was not smiling.

"Hi, Tony. I was told you would be coming by to see me."

Tony stood up, shook hands with Kovac and said, "Nice to meet you."

"Come on into my office."

Kovac guided him through the doorway to his office and entered the room behind Tony, closing the door. There were two chairs in front of his desk and a small sitting area off to the left side of the room.

"Would you like something to drink?" Kovac asked, still without the hint of a smile, as Tony sat down in one of the chairs.

"Nothing for me, thank you."

"I hope you don't mind if I have a toddy. It's after noon and around here those of us who enjoy that sort of thing usually start having ours about this time."

"No. Not at all."

Kovac walked over to a cabinet along the wall and opened one of the doors, revealing a portion of a bar setup with numerous glasses and mirrors and bottles.

"So how was your trip over from New Orleans?" Kovac asked as he mixed his drink.

"It was very nice. I really enjoyed the drive. It is so beautiful here."

"Yes, we usually have nice weather this time of year, until some hurricane shows up."

Tony remembered hearing about hurricanes being down there, but they were not on his mind. At least they had not been until now.

With his drink now mixed, Kovac walked over and sat in the chair behind his desk and then asked, "So what can I do for you?"

"I am going to be living around here and need to put this in your bank and start a checking account." With that, he pulled out the folded cashier's check from his pants pocket and handed it to Kovac.

Opening the check and looking at it, Kovac said, "Ohhh nice check. We can take care of that for you."

Tony said, "There will probably be another one for a larger amount soon."

Kovac gave him a hard look, one that Tony actually took as jealousy. He had seen enough of those already in his life to know that look.

Kovac then stood up and walked to his door, opened it and almost yelled out, "Tina!" Then he walked back to stand next to Tony as the teller who had helped him before came to the door.

"The boy here wants to set up a checking account," Kovac said as he held out his hand with Tony's check toward her. "Take care of it for him." Then Kovac said in a much louder voice, "And don't screw this one up like you did the last one! You got that?" The girl cowered in front of him as she took the check, totally embarrassed with being talked to like that in front of Tony.

Kovac then said, looking at Tony, "You just can't find good help around here anymore." Then looking back at her, he said, again in a much louder voice, "You mess this one up and you will be looking for another job. Got that?"

The girl meekly replied, "Yes, sir."

Tony stood up and said, "I'm sure everything will be okay."

Kovac replied, "Well, don't count on it unless she does a better job with this than the last thing I assigned her to take care of."

Tina now had her head down and was cringing against the door at the entrance to the office.

"Let's go get it taken care of right now, Tina is it?" Tony said, trying to ease the situation as he stood up from his chair.

"Yes, sir," she replied as she barely kept from crying.

Tony turned towards Kovac as he got to the door and, as he stuck his hand out, said, "Thanks for helping me get this taken care of."

"Sure. Well, glad to have you here. Come back any time. I'll see you around."

Tony looked at him, thinking briefly how he would have loved to have just slugged this asshole, right now, for embarrassing that girl like that. But there were things to do and he did not need any problems right now at the beginning of his stay in the Bay St. Louis area.

After walking over to Tina's window, it didn't take her ten minutes to set his account up. He smiled at her as she finished, thanked her for taking care of it for him, and took his new checkbook and checks out to his new, old car.

Next he had to find a place to live. He drove around town, getting himself somewhat familiar with the streets and the area as he looked for a place to live. He found a place on the southwestern edge of town that looked like the right size. It was a small, simple house near the end of one of the neighborhood roads. He got the telephone number off of the sign in the front yard, went to a pay phone and called about it. He got the agent to come meet him at the house around dusk and give him a tour. Tony found that it was furnished, not nicely, but furnished. He rented it on the spot, writing a check for the deposit and first month's rent.

The next morning, after breakfast at one of the restaurants overlooking the beautiful Bay of St. Louis, he called the Hancock County sheriff's office, as Bartolli had told him to do once he got settled, and asked to speak to Sheriff Raymond Burdette.

"Hello," the sheriff answered when connected to Tony by his clerk.

"This is Tony. You may remember our mutual friend suggested I call you once I got settled here."

"Ahh yes. Tony. Welcome to town. Did you get set up alright?"

"Yes. I am now an inhabitant of the town of Bay St. Louis."

"Good. So things went well?"

"Yes, no problems at all."

"Good."

"Do I need to plan to be available today or on into the next few days for anything?"

"Well, actually today would be fine, if it is alright with you. We need to run over to the New Orleans area about eleven or so, make our way down there south of the city a little ways for a visit."

Tony was somewhat surprised. So they were going on over there today. That was good. He might as well get started finding out about what all they wanted him to know. He certainly didn't have anything else to do.

"Today is fine with me."

"Okay. Did you come in on highway 90?"

"Yes, I did."

"Okay. Let's meet at that motel at the intersection of highway 90 and highway 603, the Bay St. Louis Inn. Its there on your right as you are going west out of town."

"Yes, I remember seeing it on the way in."

"See you there out front at about 11:00."

"Eleven it is."

The sheriff was right on time, driving up in his black, unmarked patrol car with the long antenna hooked to his back bumper. Tony got in.

"Hello there, traveler," the sheriff said as he offered his hand.

"Hello, sheriff. I am glad today worked out being good for you."

"I am, too," he responded as he shook Tony's hand. "The Boss wants you to get familiar with things as quickly as you can. You may be able to help us out once you know more about what's going on."

"That's fine with me."

The sheriff pulled onto the highway and increased his speed, quickly reaching seventy miles an hour, Tony noticed with a glance at the speedometer.

"Tell me about where we're going," Tony asked, hoping that conversation might slow the sheriff down a little.

"Boss said to show you some of the operation around here. So to start with, we are going to the Boss's farm. It's over there south of New Orleans. Down past where the War of 1812 New Orleans battlefield is. A couple a hundred acres. He has a nice big house on it. Has lots of pigs back behind the house a ways, in a big corral area. The Boss has some of his, shall we say, more serious problems taken back there to be dealt with."

"To a pig corral?" Tony asked, a little surprised.

"Yes. You know what is left of "things," shall we say, that are fed to pigs, don't you?" the sheriff asked with a smile on his face.

Tony did not answer immediately so the sheriff continued.

"Nothing." He looked over at Tony to measure the affect of what he had just said on Tony. "Nothing is left. The pigs eat everything. Fingers, toes, everything." Now smiling a big smile, the sheriff said, "Then we have no more problem. It's a nice, easy solution. He's got some good butchers that come out there. They can get a body ready for the pigs in just no time. They work in some of the best places in town. Some of them work in factories and places and some of them even work at famous restaurants." Then he let out a big laugh.

"People going to those restaurants have no idea that the same guy preparing their fine, upper class meals has occasionally spent time cutting up some of the Boss's problems so the pigs can, shall we say, dispose of them." He then let out another hearty laugh.

Tony decided to get him off of that subject. The sheriff was getting too much enjoyment talking about the cutting and the pigs.

"Tell me about the Boss."

Taking a moment to gather his thoughts about what he was going to say, the sheriff said, "Well, he's the most powerful man from Dallas to Atlanta. He can get almost anything done anywhere in this part of the country that he wants to get done."

"What is the biggest problem your Boss and your group face?"

Tony was intrigued now and wondered what the answer was going to be.

"Well, it was the judges down here. Boss one time a few years ago heard about how a federal judge that had presided over a trial had helped the defendant, a major sugar cane company, win a case even though the evidence was very much against the company. When the Boss heard what had happened, he said, 'I've got to get me one of those.' Well, I asked him, 'One of what? A sugar cane company?' I mean, I didn't know why he would want a sugar cane company. But Boss said, 'Hell, no, not a sugar cane company. A federal judge!' After laughing a bit, he said, 'You just never know when you might need one of them."

Finishing with that statement, the sheriff let out a big laugh. Tony had to smile, not only from hearing the story but from seeing the sheriff enjoying telling it so much. After taking a moment to catch his breath, the sheriff continued.

"Boss has always said that it's nice to have some dirt on somebody who has more power than you do. Sure enough, not too long after he said that, Boss was able to befriend a federal judge through fishing trips, a few prostitutes, and eventually some money. The time came when one of Boss's operations had a lawsuit over the payment of substantial funds for services that had been rendered by one of his companies and the boss won the case, with a little help from his new friend." The sheriff continued driving at what was a speed well above the posted limits.

"Now, he has a retired judge that was on the Fifth Circuit Court of Appeals on his payroll. Judges on the Fifth Circuit rule on cases from all over the south. They have the final say on most cases unless one is accepted on appeal to the United States Supreme Court and that court rarely takes cases from the Fifth Circuit unless some really big legal issue is at stake. So these guys down here on the Fifth Circuit who retire, those retired judges, still have access to the offices and corridors of the place where they used to work. They can go see and talk with people that ordinary folks like me and you don't have access to. Those retired judges can go where the judges' offices are and just walk in, close the doors and talk to them about anything. His Fifth Circuit friend has already done that on a few special cases. He doesn't do it on many but just particular ones, where a lot may be at stake for Boss, or his friends. That retired judge has already passed around over $100,000 to two judges on a three judge panel that ruled on a case involving another of Boss's companies. Boss wanted to make sure that the result would be to his liking. And it was."

Tony mentally went over what he had just been told. It definitely was a surprise to him, mainly because he had never had any idea that a judge in the United States would be involved in something like what he had just been told. That surprised him.

He was even more surprised, though, by the six columned mansion he now saw in the distance that was located on what appeared to be almost flat farm land. There was a fence all around the front of the property along the highway that led to the farm. The huge white house, down the access road after they passed by a small guardhouse and through the front gate, seemed to Tony so out of place here on what was now level ground. They did not go into the house because the Boss was not there. They did, though, go around back next to the pig pen area. Not too far from the pens were two large barns in which were several horses that, Tony was told, were race horses. Behind the barns were pastures bordered by various trees and, the sheriff said, swampland that eventually backed up near the levees of the Mississippi River.

Tony was impressed, but the one thing he kept thinking about as they later drove back to Bay St. Louis was what he had been told happens in those pig pens. He would catch himself thinking about that at various times for the next several days.

Chapter Five

Every town seems to have its own, for lack of a better term, "regulator." That individual is usually someone who is definitely well-known and somewhat respected. They consider themselves to be the one person who can make the individuals in office pay attention to them because of the respect the community has for the "regulator." Often times, the targets of such attention cater to those who pay attention due to the fact that it is usually much easier for the target to let the "regulator" have their day in the spotlight so that other things can go forward without being either brought to light or tampered with.

In Bay St. Louis, there was no question that the individual almost everyone in the small town would identify as that location's "regulator" was Ms. Bertha Sue Peabody. Bertha Sue was a retired school teacher who had never met the appropriate man to marry. Many in town said it was because of her high standards and that none of her former suitors in that town, who had shown an interest in her when she was younger, were up to those standards. So Bertha Sue was what the town wags called "an old maid."

Granted, she had taught many a student in her years of teaching how to negotiate difficult mathematical subjects such as Algebra. In addition, she had guided her students in the every day art of how proper citizens should conduct themselves in the small town. Having gained a reputation as a very demanding teacher and one who also put up with no foolishness out of those under her guidance and care during their time in class with her, it was often said that at times it was possible to hear a pin drop in her class room. It bothered her not at all to send even the most respected citizen's son or daughter to the principal's office for even the slightest of violations of her infamous classroom "code of conduct."

Developed by her over the many years she was in the teaching profession, her "code of conduct" consisted of stringent requirements of behavior which eventually became the subject of no small amount of conversation throughout the town. She also demanded excellence, and in a town where sometimes others did not come close to even approaching the success her students had in class, she was the subject of constant conversations, at least while she had been working.

Now she was retired, having earned that status by enduring for thirty-five years the burden of preparing local students for the future. Any student in her class considered just passing whatever subject they had taken from her a monumental achievement. Indeed, numerous now grown individuals who occupied positions of importance and power in the city almost fell over each other trying to get to the front of the crowd anytime the "regulator" let them know that some course of action should be followed that would lead to the betterment of the town and its people. For example, the small park in the center of town had long been a place where young children could gather and play. The park was close to a railroad track though and, with the "regulator's" efforts and leadership, attention was paid by the railroad to ensure that crossing guards and warning lights were more than adequate around the park area.

Then there was that time when Miss Bertha Sue, as she was fondly called by many, led the charge to get a very nice water fountain in the park for the children. Now this was no ordinary water fountain. Bertha Sue's fountain, or B. S. 's as it was called, was particularly special because she had made sure, after much research, that the fountain finally selected by the city fathers was in the shape of an elaborate swan whose water was released through the swan's beak with the mere turn of a handle. Bertha Sue considered it one of her biggest contributions to the area's beauty. Others had more basic comments about the expensive fountain, and the swan on top of it. Bertha Sue merely considered it to be just one of her many accomplishments.

Now, as she stood there looking out the back picture window of her extremely clean, well-kept house, she constantly stroked and petted her well-fed black cat, Tricksy, while thinking about her next challenge. Looking at the clothesline in her back yard that ran from one stout metal pole to another one about ten feet from her picture window, she pondered how she was going to get the attention of Mayor Steve Finley and Sheriff Raymond Burdette concerning what she was now continually hearing was simply an epidemic of drug availability in the area. The more she thought about students, similar to the ones she used to teach, getting more and more into experimentation with marijuana, the more determined she was to do something about it. The Vietnam War had caused such a loss of respect for authority and one of the results was the proliferation of drug use. "That demon weed," as she often called it, was becoming the downfall of many a decent kid and it was only because, in her mind, the grownups in the area were too weak to take a stand against its use. It was simply time, she concluded as she bent over and put her cat on the floor, for her to go into action.

The first thing she was going to do was mention it to her weekly bridge club. The eight ladies in the club were known by everyone and could get access to anybody in the county. So her first effort was to mention it to her bridge club friends and to have them join her when she met with the mayor and with the sheriff. Since she had brought it up, almost all of them agreed to be present to support her if she was able to arrange meetings with the two officials. Many in the group sympathized with her feelings about drug trafficking, but two of them in particular were hesitant about being too obvious in their opposition. They had good reasons to be careful due to what had become a real problem in each of their households. Both of them knew that one of their children was experimenting with smoking marijuana. They had tried to have discussions with the offenders about such use and one child had been somewhat responsive. In the case of the other child though, there had been outright rebellion. So when the "regulator" began setting up the meetings, those two bridge club members found that it just happened to be in a conflict with something they had already scheduled for that time. The "regulator" would have to do with just the support of the five other members of her club.

The meeting with the mayor went very well. Held at his office in the small city hall across from the massive Hancock County

Courthouse, the group came away with the feeling that the mayor would do everything in his power to keep this somewhat new social problem away from the town. He made sure that they understood that he could not do anything about those areas outside of the city limits and that the group would have to pursue other officials for those purposes.

Feeling good about the meeting the group had with the mayor, Bertha Sue contacted the sheriff's office to follow up on the mayor's guidance. Not too long after the meeting with the mayor, a subsequent group met with the sheriff, except this time there were only four members of the bridge club present, Bertha Sue and three others. Sheriff Burdette cordially received them and patiently listened to Bertha Sue's presentation. However, recognizing that the former teacher was, he felt, setting him up to take all the criticism for the explosion in drug trafficking in Hancock County, he told the ladies that, of course, he would do what he could and was supportive of their idea. In fact, he said that he had already increased patrols and would be asking for a larger budget for his office, which would increase salaries and allow him to hire more people so that he could have adequate manpower to bring the drug dealers and shippers to justice. The group walked away feeling like they had been successful in bringing their concerns to the attention of the two office holders and that they had been well-received. Only Bertha Sue felt that they had been conned by their own sheriff.

At the Baked Tomato most every Thursday after work, four girls got together for drinks. The small group of girlfriends had consistently met at the establishment on that day of the week for about three years. The group consisted of Molly Cooper, who was a hairdresser; Sarah Johnson, who worked in a department store; Sue Stephens, who worked in the office of a small independent oil company; and Karen Thompson, who taught the third grade in the local public elementary school. Molly and Sue were married, Molly since high school and Sue since her time at a junior college where she had met her husband. Sarah had never been married because the boy she was going to marry when he returned from Vietnam was killed there. Karen, the most beautiful of the group, had been married right out of high school but problems had started when her ex was caught robbing a local liquor store while he was drunk. He had a drinking problem that had only gotten worse the longer time went on. He eventually got to the point where he would come home from his job running his father's gas station and, after drinking a few beers, start verbally abusing and even sometimes hitting his beautiful wife. After he had put her in the hospital the third time, she decided to get divorced or her parents one day were going to be coming to get her body to bury her because of him.

The girls really enjoyed each other's company during their get-togethers. There was a lot of laughter every time; a lot of flirting some of the time; a lot of drinking most of the time, the more so the later it got in the evening; and there was usually a lot of discussion and comments made about every person that walked through the doorway of the bar. Tonight was no exception. This particular night, however, a subject was brought up that would have consequences that none would have ever expected.

"Girls, have to tell you about something that happened at the store today," said Sarah.

The other three girls leaned forward so that they could hear over the background music being played early in the evening.

"Come on. Don't tease us," said Molly, the heavier set one of the group.

"Today, not too long before I came down here, in walked

58

that sorry excuse for a human being, Kovac," Sarah said, almost whispering at the end of her sentence as she looked around to see if anyone could hear her except for her little audience.

"Don't tell us that he did it again!" Karen said, with an agitated voice.

"He did! He did," Sarah said more softly now, again looking around. There was an audible sigh from the group. They each knew that what Sarah had said meant that he had bought lingerie for his rather large wife, and also for his much smaller, younger girlfriend.

"That bastard," Sue said with a sneer.

"Well, he did it. Didn't seem to bother him one bit either," she said as she gritted her teeth.

There was a moment of silence, and then very softly Sue said, "I told you last time, at Valentine's Day, when he did that what you should do. Next time, you ought to do it. Swap what you put in those boxes." The three girls looked at Sue, not saying a word as each one thought about what had just been said.

Chapter Six

Several years earlier, Tony had seen his dad, Nick, in Sicily sitting on his favorite chair-backed wooden bench on a promontory overlooking the Strait of Messina in the distance and the nearby town of the same name. A light breeze was always in the air near the waters of the Ionian Sea and the Mediterranean Sea, especially on days like today when there was not a cloud in the sky. The sole tree on the uppermost portion of the elevated area provided the only shade, though that always depended on the location of the sun during the day. His dad spent hours up there, usually by himself, and Tony tried to leave him alone, not wanting to risk interrupting his dad's thoughts. He had a good relationship with his dad. His dad had stayed in Sicily after World War II, something Tony had never understood since his dad had often talked about how wonderful living in the United States had been. His dad's comments had instilled in him a hope that one day he could go to America and see what was so great about living there. As for right then, being fourteen years old, Tony intended to explore more of his present world. To further that end, he turned and began working his way, as he had many times before, down to the base of the promontory so that he could go see if his cousin, Vinnie, was at his nearby home. There were endless possibilities the two of them could come up with to occupy their time once they got together.

Nick saw his son out of the side of his sunglass covered eyes. He yelled out to him before Tony got out of eyesight.

"Tony! Tony!" He could see his son had heard him because he turned to look at his dad, shielding his eyes from the bright sun. He motioned for Tony to come join him, which was the ultimate compliment Tony could get from his dad. He loved his dad, thought the world of him, and welcomed any opportunity to spend even just a little bit of time with him. It wasn't often that he got an invitation like this one. He responded by jogging up the hill to where his dad was sitting.

"Have a seat with me for a little bit, son," he said as he patted part of the bench next to him. Tony quickly sat down next to his dad.

"Where are you going, big guy?" his dad asked as he put his arm on the back support of the bench behind his son.

"I was going over to Vinnie's if that is alright," he answered looking at his dad.

"That's fine. Let me just talk with you for a little bit before you go about something you might be involved with when you are older. It is better for me to mention it to you now so that you are aware of it because one day I may not be around and you may have to deal with it."

Tony could tell by his dad's tone of voice that, whatever it was he wanted to mention to him, it was important because his dad's voice was in a low, serious tone. He knew that voice was only used when there was something those who heard it needed to listen to.

"What is it, dad? Are we going to America? Are you taking us to Switzerland? You're not going to send me away to school in France, are you?" Tony remembered a discussion he had overheard between his parents about the advantages of Tony possibly spending time in an all boy's school in France.

Looking at his son, Nick again appreciated how smart his son was, how much common sense he had. Hopefully, it would help keep him out of trouble in life and also help him get ahead.

"Well son, your mom and I have talked about that. We want you to get the best education possible to prepare you for the rest of your life. We both want you to have every opportunity to make a good life for yourself and, if you have an education, you will have so much better of a chance to eventually have a good future."

"But I don't want to leave here, dad. It's so nice having so many friends like I do and having all my cousins around to play with and spend time with and all."

Nick looked at his son. He could well understand how he felt, he really could, but he also knew that there was not really any future for Tony if he stayed in Sicily. In fact the opposite was probably true, that he would never improve himself and would be very limited as to what he would be able to do to support himself when he grew up, and a wife and family if he should be so lucky to have one or both.

"I know, son. But you are going to need extensive training to handle things that you might have to face in the future years of your life."

"What things in the future are you talking about, dad?"

Nick turned more to sit so he was almost facing his son. It was going to be very important that his son understood what he was about to tell him.

"Tony, there may come a time when you will have to go to the United States to deal with a matter over there. If that ever were to happen, and it might, you will need to know how to speak excellent English. You will need to know a lot about financing, how to handle money, how to make sure that the money you have is safe and all."

Tony was now looking directly at his father and could tell he was as serious as he could be about what he was saying.

Seeing that he had his young son's attention, Nick decided that it was time to tell the boy as much as he felt comfortable with telling him. Hopefully, telling him now would start getting him prepared to deal with what all might happen in the future. He continued.

"There may come a time that you will have to go over there to deal with my sister, Madeline's, estate. The property she owns is located over in Mississippi, not too far from New Orleans. That property, and any money associated with it, will become yours if I am not alive. With your mom being as sick as she is, if she does not overcome her illness and passes away, then once I pass away you will be my only heir." Tony knew that his mom had recently been diagnosed with an aggressive, incurable form of cancer and probably would not live much longer.

His dad continued, "In other words, if your mom is not alive when I pass away, you will get everything we own, both here and anything over there I might be entitled to if I were still alive when Madeline passes away. With you being the only child I have, unless she does something to try to disinherit me, you may have to deal with it all. From what I am told, she will not try to do that. In fact she is very worried about what might happen if certain other people or I were to ever find out that she was trying to do something else with everything there."

"What other people do you mean, dad?"

"Well, in particular I mean your Uncle Marty in New York for sure and there may be others. You remember Uncle Marty. He has been over here a couple of times and you have met him. Remember?"

"You mean that really big old fellow that's so hard to understand with that accent? Wasn't he from New York?"

"Yes, son, that's the guy. He is a very close friend of ours. You can trust him and when what I am talking about happens, when Madeline has passed away and the notification arrives here, if I am not alive you should get in touch with him immediately. Let him know, if he doesn't already know, that I have passed on and that you would then be the one receiving whatever might be due to me because of Madeline passing away. If he is not still alive at that time, then talk to his oldest son, Jerry, who will also know about everything."

Nick watched his son's reaction, being very interested to see if he was able to understand what had just been told to him. He was pleased that his son seemed to grasp what had just been said. He was even more pleased by what his son said next.

"I understand, dad. I am to call Uncle Marty when you die if mom is not alive, and talk to him or, if he is dead, his oldest son.

I promise I will do that but, dad, if I am going to do that, you need to give me his phone number."

Nick could not help but laugh out loud, which he did as his son smiled.

"I will, son. When we get back to the house today, we will take care of that, okay? I'll write it down and we'll put it someplace safe. You just don't forget where we put it, okay?" Nick said with a big smile.

"Daddddddddd, you know I won't. Now, what about this sending me off to school and all? Are you serious about that? Is that something that's going to happen soon? I mean, I don't want to leave."

"I know, son. I know, but please believe me; it will be in your best interests that you do that. Especially if your mom does not survive her illness, it would be better for you to be where you can be properly looked after. We need to get you away from here so you will have a chance of learning things so that you can take good care of yourself in the future. Believe me, I love you so much, son, and if it weren't in your best interest, I wouldn't think twice about it, but it is. And I hope you know I only want what's best for you. You know that, don't you?"

With a big smile, Tony said, "Awwwwww dad, I know that."

Patting him on his back, Nick smiled and said, "Thanks, son. I have always been so proud of you, I really have been. I could not have asked for a better son. And I promise that if you do end up going off to school, either I will come see you or arrange for you to come visit with me about every two or three months or so. I would want to keep up with how you are doing. We will talk more about this soon. We will see how your mom does. Be sure and give her a big hug tonight before you go to bed, okay? For now, run on, tell our cousins 'hi' for me and be careful."

Tony got up from the bench and, now standing, turned to his dad and said, "Do you think mom will make it?"

"It doesn't look good, son. That's why it is important for you to give her as many hugs as you can right now."

Thinking about it a moment, Tony then said, "I will, and thanks, Dad, for all you have done for me."

"Thanks for saying that, son. Now go have fun, and take care of yourself. Don't worry; it will all work out, as long as you do your best. Now, go! But behave yourself! Don't let Vennie get you into any trouble, you hear me?"

"I won't, Dad."

"Good, son, See you in a couple of hours for dinner."

"Okay. See you later." With that, Tony was off at full speed running on the narrow path down the small hill towards his cousin's house. He needed to make sure he paid special attention to his mom tonight because, from the way his dad had just talked, she might not recover and that thought made him sad. He also had known that it wouldn't do any good to try to argue with his dad about going off to school. Besides, he thought the world of his dad and, if his dad thought what he had just told him would be the best thing for him, then he would do what his dad wanted. He just might end up having a lot of fun in France.

Nick had not wanted to tell his son about his mom being in bad health but he felt Tony needed to know. That time had been as good as any to tell him. Nick truly loved his son but, right now, it was time for his son to go be a boy. He was glad his son had his cousin to go spend time with because Nick was ready to be left alone. Alone in his thoughts, in his recollections.

Yes, he had been fortunate that the United States Army had agreed to let him stay very quietly in Sicily at the end of the war, where he had grown up and had so many good memories, instead of shipping him back to that awful prison in Louisiana where they had first met with him. He was grateful to Colonel Brock, the man to whom he had reported during those years he helped prepare Allied forces for the invasion of Sicily and then the invasion of Italy. Colonel Brock had arranged, in appreciation for what he had done for the Allied cause, for Nick to be reported as killed in a car accident so that his file was closed just before the end of the war.

Oh, there were a few bad memories from Sicily, such as the times when he had been eighteen that he had to go, at his father's explicit direction, and have a talk with one of his sister's suitors to convince the boy that he would no longer be able to see his sister because of his telling his friends what all he had done with her. He still could not believe he actually used to do that, to try to protect her, as his dad had said. Nick later realized that the real reason was to protect the family name because unfortunately his sister, Madeline Benedetti, had gotten a reputation for being very accommodating to the boys she spent time with by allowing them to do just about whatever they wanted with her.

Other memories about Madeline were not pleasant to recall, particularly those associated with how she had sold him out to the Internal Revenue Service in Louisiana in order to take over his position as the head of Al Capone's operations there. He had been arrested, tried, convicted, and sentenced to 25 years in prison for his activities involving the shipment of massive amounts of illegal liquor from Cuba into the Bay St. Louis, Mississippi area. It was all due to her finding out that he had been the one that, at Capone's specific direction, had killed her second husband who had been providing information to IRS agents about the operation. Capone had been livid when he had found out from his then-new Detroit allies, the Purple Gang, that Madeline's husband had been the one providing the information that had led to the eventual loss of what amounted to millions of dollars of booze. Capone had made sure that Nick understood that either he was going to kill Madeline's husband because he was the one that had introduced him to Capone and the gang, or Capone was going to not only kill Madeline's husband himself, he was also going to kill Nick. Nick had had no choice because he knew about all of the people Capone had personally killed.

Nick's thoughts then turned, as they sometimes did, to that day in early 1943 that he was notified in his Louisiana jail cell that he had a visitor. He had not had many visitors so anyone coming there to see him was a special event. It was as if he had almost disappeared off of the face of the earth, as far as any of his associates and so-called friends had been concerned, after his conviction.

"Follow me," the jailor had said after unlocking his cell door. Together they had walked down the jail hallway, then over to another part of the large facility where mostly administrative staff for the prison worked. They walked down a hallway and stopped in front of a closed door. The jailor had knocked on the door and announced, "Officer Johnson here with the requested prisoner."

The door had soon opened and the officer had motioned Nick to enter the room. As he had entered the room, he had seen two men, one in a military uniform and the other in a civilian suit.

"Do you want me to remain with the prisoner?" Officer Johnson had asked.

The man in the suit replied, "No, officer. You can leave us

alone but please do remain in the hallway in case we need your assistance." The officer had nodded his head in the affirmative and exited the room, shutting the door behind him.

"Have a seat, Nick," the man in the uniform had said as he motioned towards an empty chair there next to the table in the center of the room.

The man then continued. "For the purposes of this meeting, my name is Roger and this is Brad," he said as he motioned to the man in the suit. "We are familiar with your record and why you are in here. I guess you know that you are to spend another eight years here before your sentence will be completed."

Nick looked at both men and then replied, "I don't know who you are or why you are here, but I can assure you that I know the exact amount of time I have remaining to spend here."

"What would you have to say if we told you that there is a way for you to leave this place and go do something to help with this country's efforts in the war we are in?"

Nick had been completely shocked by Roger's statement. He would have given almost anything to get out of that hell-hole.

"I would be most interested in hearing what you have in mind," Nick had evenly replied.

The man identified as Brad spoke up, saying, "First of all, Nick, we need to know something." Looking straight at Nick, he then asked, "Do you consider the United States your country, Nick?"

"What do you mean by that?" Nick answered, looking back at the man.

"Where is your loyalty, Nick? I mean, this country has put you in prison and you have been here for a long time. Do you hate this country for doing that?" Brad had asked, now standing just a few feet away from where Nick was seated at the table.

Surprised by the question, it took a moment for Nick to answer but, when he did, it had been in a firm, even voice.

"Look. I got caught doing something I was not supposed to have been doing. What I was doing was illegal, and I knew that. But when I came over to this country, to try to do something better than just stay in the poor section of Sicily, I could not get a job in New York. I tried and tried but nobody would hire a person from Sicily. Finally I was told I might have a better chance of getting a job in Chicago. I didn't know anything about Chicago, but I knew I could not seem to get a job in New York. So I went to Chicago, and the only way I was able to get there was because a few friends of mine from Sicily put together a little money to pay my way there by train."

Both men had been intently watching Nick as he told his story.

"I got to Chicago and I couldn't get a job there. Not even there. The only person who offered me a job of any type was Al Capone, and I took it. You two know that, and I have to tell you that for the most part, he was good to me. He took care of me, but of course I took care of him too."

Nick looked at the two men to see what reaction they might have to what he had just said. They actually seemed relieved.

Roger then said, "Nick, this country is going to invade Sicily."

Nick's mouth almost opened when he heard that.

Roger continued, "We are looking for a few people we can trust to go into Sicily before the invasion, help put together information about where the German troops are, especially the German tanks." Now looking directly at Nick, Roger asked, "Nick, is that something we can trust you to do for us?"

71

Nick, for a moment, had been at a loss for words. As he pondered Roger's statement, Brad said, "We want you, and a few others, to go in and help us there."

After thinking about the matter for a moment, he asked, "If I do this, what you want, what happens to me?"

Roger said, "Well, first of all, you will be let out of this stinking prison. We can't guarantee anything after that except that you will be out of here and going home. The only thing we can tell you is that if we are successful, we both will do everything we can to see that your sentence here is shortened."

"You mean that if I go over there and help you Americans, put my life at risk and probably that of my family over there if I contact them, you are not willing to tell me you can set me free?"

Both men turned their heads away from Nick for a moment, not comfortable at all with what they were having to tell him. Brad faced him again and said, "No, I cannot tell you, at this time, that we can guarantee that you will be freed when it is all over. I mean, we don't know what you are going to do, how well you are going to do it, and how successful we will be as a result of what you do. We don't know all of that right now. All we can tell you is that we will train you, which means time away from here, we will feed you, which means more time away from here, and we will house you in a special place, which will also be away from here. Then at some point, if everything works out, and we are comfortable with you and with putting you over there, and we are successful with it all, then we shall see what happens. That is all we can assure you of at this time."

Roger then said, "Think about it for now, Nick. And we will too. We have our necks on the line for even thinking about this operation, much less putting it into action. But I can tell you that, so far, we have one guy, also from Sicily, in another prison in this country that has already agreed to do it. In fact, he wants to go over there right now. He can't stand the Germans and what all they are doing to his people there. We hope you will feel the same way."

They left and he was taken back to his jail cell. It hadn't taken him long to come to the conclusion that he would do it if offered the opportunity. Why sit in that horrible place, wasting away, when at the very least he would be on the outside, doing something that might help his fellow Sicilians.

Nick's mind came back to the present for a moment. He looked around for Tony and did not see him. He knew that Tony had probably now worked his way over to his cousin's house. He would have to make sure he checked on him there if he did not show back up at their house in a little while. His mind drifted off again, this time to what had happened next.

They had come back and offered him the opportunity to take part in the operation and he had agreed. They spent the next six months training him in various things, especially radio operation, weapons training and some medical procedures, just in case he should ever need that knowledge over there.

Then almost all of a sudden, they told him that he was being shipped out to Africa to a place called Tripoli. After his trip by boat to get there, which had taken what seemed to be forever, he had finally been put on a submarine and taken to Sicily. The sub surfaced in the middle of the night near a cove on the western side of the island that he had become familiar with during summer camping trips as a kid with his relatives. Reconnaissance airplanes had determined that, hopefully, he could land nearby and not be caught. Once ashore, he destroyed his inflatable raft and buried it back off of the beach. Two days later he made contact with the resistance at a pre-arranged location.

The resistance fighters were very brave because, if any of them were ever caught by the Germans, they would have been tortured until they disclosed who their families and their contacts were and all of them would have been executed. Just before he had gotten to his area near his home, three resistance fighters had been captured trying to blow up a communications facility. After a week of interrogation, the three fighters and fifteen local citizens had all been hung from trees and poles placed in the local park area in the center of town. They had been left there for a week. No one had been allowed to cut them down and bury them until that week had passed. The local German commander, Captain Herman Bronfman, made it his intention to stop any resistance efforts in his area of control. His ruthlessness had almost worked.

Nick had finally been able, through the efforts of his relatives, to get a job cleaning at the headquarters where Captain Bronfman had his command center. The Germans, he remembered, had run investigation after investigation on him, but nothing ever showed up because he had been gone for so long from the area. It helped him when he was able to give the German Captain bits of information that helped them capture five resistance fighters from the northern part of Sicily. Nick had not cared because those fighters were communists who had turned in, to the Germans, resistance fighters associated with the British in an attempt to get an edge on taking over if the Germans were ever forced out. They had even turned in an Australian nurse who had been landed to help with casualties resulting from the resistance efforts. The German captain had done awful things to her in order to get her to give up the names of her contacts, including the removal of most of her skin. Nick remembered one thing about that Australian nurse; she had never said a word to the Germans about any of her contacts, much to the chagrin of Captain Bronfman who prided himself on his ability to make people talk.

Finally, the day came that the Allied invasion took place, at locations that had been pinpointed by Nick and the other two spies sent from the United States at about the same time he was. The three of them had never been allowed to see each other, in case any of them were ever captured and tortured. Their efforts led to such success that General Patton's army had been ashore for almost two whole days before there was any contact with German forces. His landing had been unopposed and all of his armor had been put ashore before any fighting began. The operation had been a huge success.

There had been just this one problem. Nick had been working at Captain Bronfman's headquarters and the Captain had gotten worried. Patton's forces were approaching. Bronfman told Nick that all German forces were being withdrawn to Italy so they would not be captured in Sicily. Bronfman even told Nick that he was welcome to come with them as they made their escape. The offer was made because of Nick's assistance with identifying the communist partisans.

"Come go with us, Nick. It will be bad for you here if you stay, having worked with us like you have."

Nick knew that Patton's army was nearby and would be in the area of the headquarters in just a matter of minutes. Nick's partisans had already been sniping at the remaining German soldiers. Captain Bronfman, being the arrogant leader he was, wanted to make sure he was among the last to leave his post area. Nick had seen the Captain's Lugar pistol in the holster on his belt. Nick had pulled a gun out of its concealed location next to his desk and walked into the captain's office. The German looked up to see Nick standing there holding his gun.

"Where did you get that weapon, Nick?" the German had asked with a demanding attitude.

"I got it from the resistance, captain."

The German then reached for his Lugar, sliding it out of its holster.

"And I thought you were on our side, Nick."

"I know you did, captain. But I am on the side of my people."

Gunfire outside the building began to sound closer and closer.

The German said, "I am disappointed in you, Nick."

Nick replied, "I am disappointed in you and what all you have done, captain. So I am going to see to it that the same thing happens to you that you did to those that you hung from those poles out front."

Captain Bronfman quickly answered, "That's not going to happen, Nick." Then he brought his Lugar up, pointed it at Nick and pulled the trigger.

Click!

Shock registered on his face as Bronfman immediately realized that the gun did not fire. He pulled the trigger again, and then again, and nothing was heard but clicks.

As he looked at Nick with a quizzical expression on his face, Nick said, "I changed the bullets out last night, captain." Raising his own gun so that it pointed at the captain, Nick said, "I thought you might try to do that." Nick then squeezed off his own round, purposely guiding it at the German officer's right shoulder.

WHAMMMMMMM!

Nick's round knocked the German to the floor, a mere eight feet away from him. The impact knocked the gun out of the German's right hand. The stunned look on the Captain's face, as he now lay on the floor with his back against the back wall, also showed the pain the bullet had brought to him.

The gunfire nearby outside had become much louder.

Looking up at Nick, the captain had said, "Go ahead, finish me off."

Nick had coolly replied, "Not a chance. Remember, you have to spend some time hanging from one of those poles outside, but not until I'm finished with you." He then pointed his gun at the German's left shoulder.

WHAMMMMMMM!

Nick watched as a bullet hole appeared in Bronfman's chest. He turned around and there was Johnny Cantonni standing in the doorway, holding a .45 pistol.

"Get out of here, Nick. Now, before it's too late."

Nick turned back around and saw that Captain Bronfman was not going to hurt any more people. He and Johnny then ran from the building, barely in time to avoid the last of the German infantrymen who came to get the Captain.

Nick remembered it all as if it had been yesterday. His next thought was back to today. With it now being 1962 and Tony being fourteen years of age, Nick watched as his son had become infatuated with United States President John F. Kennedy, reading everything he could about the man and his family.

It wasn't too long afterward that Nick's wife had passed away and that Tony, indeed, had been sent to school in the south of France that had an outstanding reputation for its education. Yes, there had been a really good English department at the school, there had been a really good program for athletics there which had included soccer, and there also had been extensive training classes there in personal physical protection. The school had specifically been known for producing students who excelled in the physical arts of self-defense, such as boxing, karate and other similar types of courses.

Over the years following the assassination of President Kennedy in 1963, Tony had continued to read everything he could get his hands on about the handsome former President Kennedy. That continued up until and past Tony's father's death in 1974. Now, a couple of weeks ago, almost two years after his father's death, had come the call from Uncle Marty telling Tony to come to New York City as soon as possible. Madeline Benedetti had finally passed away.

Chapter Seven

Tony received word from Burdette that Bartolli wanted to see him out at his farm. Having already been shown how to get there by the sheriff, Tony was told to be there the next morning at precisely 10 a.m. Burdette was adamant that Bartolli did not like it when people coming to meet him were late. He thought of it as a waste of his time, inconsiderate, and felt people who were late could not be counted on when it mattered. Tony clearly understood that feeling since he felt the same way. So Tony made sure he was up and traveling over to south of New Orleans early enough so that, if he got lost, he would still be able to find Bartolli's farm in plenty of time so as to not be late.

Driving down the highway, Tony felt good when he passed the New Orleans War of 1812 battlefield marker since he knew the farm was past that landmark. Finally, he saw the small guard house at the gate to the white fenced-in field. In the distance was the mansion, sitting back among trees that, by their orderly location, seemed to indicate they had been carefully planted in years past. Seeing that the guard house was not occupied, he drove on up to the mansion, pulling off to the side onto what appeared to be a small parking area. It was then that he noticed a man standing over by the side of the house where the driveway went by on its way to those areas behind that large structure, such as the infamous pig pen.

Getting out of his car, Tony waved to the man and said, "Hey."

"Hi," the figure replied as he gradually began to walk towards him. It was then that Tony noticed the firearm in its holster on the man's hip.

"I was told to come out to see Mr. Bartolli. Is he here?"

"Yes, he's in the house. Just knock on the front door and they'll let you in."

"Okay. Thanks," Tony said as he turned and began walking towards the front door. Looking to his right he admired the open land between the trees near the house and the trees bordering on the highway. The lush green grass of the house's front yard covered what Tony estimated to be at least ten acres of land.

Knocking on the front door, Tony could hear footsteps coming toward the door's direction in response. As the door opened, Tony saw a rather large man in slacks and a casual shirt. The man's ruddy complexion showed the results of hours spent in the sun. The grey hair around his ears set off the jet black color of the rest of his hair.

"I'm Tony. I was told to be here at 10. I'm a little early but I didn't want to be late."

A hint of a smile crossed his greeter's face. "Yes. We were

expecting you. I'm Hank," the big man said as he extended his hand for a hand shake.

"No, you don't want to be late to meet with the Boss. He's in his office waiting for you. Come on back."

Tony was glad he had arrived early. He followed the massive shoulders in front of him over to the right corner of the huge entering room and then down a hallway to a doorway on the right side. The large shoulders in front of him managed to make their way through the room's entrance way and Tony followed.

"Tony's here, Boss," he announced.

Tony walked through the doorway and saw a little man in a white suit sitting behind a huge wooden desk. It was Bartolli, the man that Uncle Marty had asked to let Tony hang around for a while. He stood up as Tony approached the desk.

"Tony, Tony! Welcome to south Louisiana," he said as he stuck out his hand. Tony put his hand out, having to lean across the desk to shake hands because of Bartolli's short 5 foot 5 inch stature.

"Thank you, sir. And thank you so much for letting me hang around for a while."

"Oh, glad to have you here. And thank you for the way you handled that estate situation. Letting us all share in that was a smart move, Tony. Such a smart move. Took a potentially bad situation and turned it into nothing at all. Good job."

"Well, thanks for saying that. I wanted to be as cooperative as I could be. I mean, after all, I am a guest here and just wanted to do things in a way so everybody could be happy, if that was possible."

Pointing toward the two high backed chairs facing the desk, Bartolli said, "Have a seat. Make yourself comfortable."

Tony took his seat in the chair to Bartolli's right, sitting so he could still observe, to some extent, the doorway he had just walked through. He noticed Hank quietly leaving the room and closing the door behind him. Bartolli eased himself back into his very large, black leather chair behind the desk.

"I understand Sheriff Burdette brought you over and showed you around a little bit."

"Yes, sir, he did. We came over a couple of days ago."

"So how has it been for you here so far?" Bartolli asked as he leaned back in his chair.

"Good. Everything has been good. I really enjoy this weather you have here. It is so nice. Reminds me a little of home."

"Yes, yes. I was over your way one time years ago and, yes, it was like this over there. I was down around the toe of the boot; I think it was named Reggie something."

"Maybe Reggie di Calabria?"

"Yes, yes. That was it. Pretty little town."

"My Dad used to tell me about crossing the straits there to the town of Vila San Giovanni, a smaller town right there on the coast. As a kid, he used to make that trip every day to work in a winery in that area."

"It was a nice area. Very pleasant there," Bartolli said as he shifted in his chair. Then he continued.

"Look, I have been thinking since Marty asked me about your staying down here what we could have you do that might help us out. You know it's always good to have another face around in an area, keeping eyes on things, sometimes hearing things, sometimes doing things. You know what I mean."

"Yes, sir. Sure. If there is any way I can help you, just let me know what you want me to do," Tony said, interested now in what Bartolli might have in mind.

"Well, the first thing is I think you need to see some of our operation and all. Seeing a few things might help you understand why we might need certain things, or access to certain people who might be able to help us. With you being unknown in this area, you may be able to do things that our other associates might not be able to do."

Tony understood what Bartolli was saying and agreed with him.

After taking a breath, Bartolli continued.

"For an example, there is this deputy sheriff, Mark Patterson, over in Hancock County, Mississippi. He is the son of the former sheriff and well-thought of over there. Fought over in that stupid Vietnam war and came back to work there in the sheriff's office. Well, Sheriff Burdette has had a hard time sort of guiding him in our direction."

"What did you have in mind?" Tony asked, not having any idea what to expect next.

Taking a moment, Bartolli looked out of the windows on the right side of the room and then said, "I think what we should do is have you try to make friends with him. Meet him, get to know him. Find out his likes and dislikes. What kind of a person is he really? What his weaknesses might be. Almost every person has those. You do. Even I do. Find out what his are and let's see if we can't persuade him to give us some slack. Hell, he has cost me over a million dollars in seized shipments. A million dollars! I need that to stop."

Bartolli slowly shook his head from side to side. Then he looked back at Tony.

"Get to know him. Don't take too much time, but also don't move too fast either. You know what I mean?"

"Yes, sir. I do."

Already, Tony was wondering what the product was that the deputy had been seizing. He remembered that Uncle Marty had told him that the families had all agreed that they would not get into drug shipments, but then Marty had mentioned to him that he thought Bartolli's family had become involved in it.

"Good. It's just got to stop. You see what you can do. Burdette told me you are living in a place over there. Go to a nightclub over there called the Baked Tomato. Patterson is usually assigned to the club on Thursday, Friday and Saturday nights in case there are any problems with those rednecks that show up there. See if you can meet the deputy; tell him you just moved to town. He usually sits at the end of the bar, with his back to the wall and his side to the bar, wearing cowboy boots and sometimes a big ole cowboy hat. Start some conversation with him. See how it goes. In the meantime, I'll get some of the boys to show you around a little of our operation, just so you can know about our efforts and how he is messing us up with what he is doing."

"Okay."

"We got this retired judge from the federal appeals court here. Finally got him and he has really been worth the money we pay him because he has gotten results. He got a three judge panel there at the Fifth Circuit Court of Appeals to rule in my favor in a case, even though the law was completely, completely against me!"

He then let out a big laugh as he rocked back in his oversized chair.

"So let's see if we can't do something like that with this deputy. Get him to look the other way at certain times, maybe even help us some times. That kind of thing."

Bartolli then yelled out, "Hey, Hank!"

"Yeah, Boss," came a quick reply from outside the room. The door opened and Hank walked in.

"Make sure our new friend here is shown around a little bit, just so he gets a feel for what's going on."

"Sure, Boss. Anything in particular you might want him to see?"

"Yeah, get him out to the rig, let him meet Jim and see all that out there. Get him over to the Rigolets and the barge. Let him see a few of the things happening around there. It also might be interesting for him to see the pasture thing." With that, Bartolli let out a laugh.

"What he will show you on that pasture is something I bet you won't see over in your part of the world." With that, he let out another big laugh. Tony could not imagine what they were talking about and now he really wanted to see what it was. At least he thought he did, but he wasn't going to ask about it now.

"Hey, Boss. While we are at it, you want me to get him over to the rooster fights?" Hank asked.

Bartolli looked over at Tony and said, "What do you think?"

Tony looked at the two men incredulously, and then said, "Rooster fights?"

Hank said, "Man, yeah. Every Sunday morning, starting about 10 over in northern Harrison County. Out in the middle of nowhere, they have this little place there and they have these cock fights. Hold them in this little stadium place. An actual little stadium, built out of cinder blocks."

"For chicken fights?" Tony asked, almost wondering if they were pulling his leg.

Bartolli answered, "Yes, of all things, chicken fights. And the crowd there loves it. There will be about 200 people there. On a Sunday morning, of all things. And the fights will last until the late afternoon. So much money is bet there, you would not believe it. Lots of money. At a farm, out in the middle of nowhere, on a Sunday."

Tony just sat there. He didn't know what to say. His mind was still trying to picture what he had just been told. First they had mentioned pastures and then chicken fights, on Sundays. He was having a hard time imagining it all.

"Those chicken fights may be a little too much for our new friend right now," Bartolli said, followed by another of his laughs. "Maybe that's something we can show him after he sees a few other things first."

Hank smiled, then said, "Whatever you say, Boss."

"Okay. Any more questions, Tony?"

"No, not now. I am still thinking about those chickens," he said followed by his own chuckle. "In a stadium, at that!"

The Boss started laughing. Then he said, "Yep. Lot of strange things go on over there. But keep a low profile and see what you can do for us."

"Okay. Sure will."

With that, Bartolli stood up, followed by Tony, and they shook hands.

"Get back in touch with me once you have made contact and let me know how it's going," Bartolli said.

"Okay. Will do."

"And Hank, take Tony here with you on Wednesday night and let him see that part happen," Bartolli said with a grin.

"Okay, Boss."

With that, Tony turned and followed Hank out of the office. As they walked out of the front door of the house, Hank said, "Meet me in the side parking lot of the Bay Inn there in Bay St. Louis at 11: 30 Wednesday night. Wear some blue jeans and a dark, long sleeved shirt and boots, if you have them."

Tony thought to himself that the next few days were probably going to be very interesting.

On Wednesday night, Tony got to the Bay Inn parking lot fifteen minutes early. He parked his car and sat there, waiting for Hank. A few minutes before 11:30 Hank pulled up in a brown Ford pick-up truck with dents in its side.

"Do you want me to follow you?" Tony asked.

"Nah. Leave yours here and come go with me," Hank answered.

Tony got out of his car, locked it, and climbed into the passenger's side of the truck cab. They were soon headed north on what Hank said was state highway 603.

"We've got a pick up to make tonight. Boss thought you might want to see that part of our little business," Hank said as they rode down the two lane highway.

"Is there anything I am supposed to do?" Tony asked, wondering what he might be getting himself into.

"Nah. Just stay close to me. You'll get to see how we do some things down here. We're going up not too far from where those chicken fights happen."

"We're gonna see chicken fights tonight?" Tony blurted out.

Hank let forth a big belly laugh.

"Nah! They don't do that at night. Where we are going is just not too far from where all that happens, over in the northern part of Harrison County. It's the county next to this one. Nah, no chicken fights tonight." With that, he let out another belly laugh.

About forty-five minutes later, after using Interstate 10 to go east and then going north off of that four lane highway, they turned back to the west on a paved two lane road. Several minutes later, they pulled off onto a dirt road that weaved its way back into the moonlit countryside. Tony could see open fields of what looked to be gently rolling pasture land.

Eventually seeing what appeared in the distance to be a large barn, they made their way over to that building. As they got closer, Tony saw that there were two pickup trucks and a van parked not too far from the side of the structure. After they had pulled up close to it, Hank turned the motor off. A figure appeared from the barn's shadows and walked up to the driver's side of their truck.

"I was wondering when you were gonna make it," the figure said as he leaned on the open window area of Hank's door.

"Had to go pick up my passenger here. The Boss wanted him to see this tonight." Turning to Tony, he said, "Let's get out and we can stand over there next to that corner of the barn and watch it all." Hank opened his door as did Tony and they both exited the truck and began walking over towards the far corner of the barn.

"What time are we looking at things happening?" Hank asked of the man now walking with them.

"Something should happen a little before one or so. The boys have already spaced the lights out on both sides of the area that's going to be used."

"Well, these guys are always on time. I mean, they are better than the airlines about being on time so 1:15 it will probably be."

After reaching the corner of the darkened barn, the man who had met them said in a somewhat hushed voice, "I need to go check a few things. Y'all be sure and stay around here. There's a lot of firepower out there and they're already on edge, as you can imagine. So don't do anything to make them wanna start using it."

"We won't. We'll be right here," Hank answered.

The man then disappeared into the trees along the edge of the field in front of them. There was now total, absolute silence.

After what seemed like a long time but really was only about twenty-five minutes, there was a noise that gradually became louder. Tony didn't recognize it at first because it was such a soft sound. A string of lights suddenly came on, running along both sides of an open area of the pasture. Then, in a matter of just a few moments, it appeared. It was an airplane, flying about 150 feet above the ground, coming in over the tall pine trees at a really slow speed. After it cleared the trees, it dropped down quickly to land on the somewhat level field of the pasture. The single engine plane with what seemed to be oversized wings came to a stop within sixty yards. It then turned around and made its way over towards the barn, guided by a light that appeared at the end of the field some twenty yards from the building. The lights on both sides of the pasture runway were then turned off.

When the plane came to a halt near the barn, six men ran out to the side door of the plane as the motor of the van parked near the barn was started. The van quickly pulled up to the plane and stopped next to the aircraft's door. After the sliding side door was opened, bale upon bale of some product already wrapped in plastic was then unloaded directly into the van. From his viewpoint, Tony was not able to count how many bales were delivered, but there were many. He guessed it was probably marijuana. Upon completion of the transfer, the side door of the van was slid shut. It then pulled away and traveled down the same dirt road that they had driven in on.

While the van was going down the dirt road, one of the pickup trucks pulled up next to the plane and the same thing happened. After its bed was full, a tarpaulin was pulled over the product and tied down to the sides of the truck. Then that truck pulled off down the same dirt road as had the van.

The very second that the pickup truck had pulled away, another pickup truck pulled up and was loaded. A tarp was also tied over its cargo and it pulled away. The very instant that the second truck had pulled away, the side door was closed and the plane began moving. The lights along the runway area again came on like clockwork, guiding the plane as it immediately lined up and then began to gather speed. Within approximately forty yards, the plane was airborne. Within seconds, it had disappeared over the trees.

Hank said, "Let's get out of here." They both ran to the truck and jumped in. Within just a few minutes, they were riding down the state highway on their way back to Bay St. Louis.

Tony couldn't help but ask, "Was that marijuana?"

His driver turned to look at him and, with a slight smile on his face, nodded his head in the affirmative before turning back to watch where he was driving.

Tony then asked, "How often does this happen?"

Hank answered, "More often than you could ever imagine. There's a lot of demand out there for our shipments. We just make sure it's taken care of because it's growing more and more every day."

Tony could not help but be impressed.

The next night, Thursday night, at about nine o'clock, Tony drove his '56 Ford to the downtown area. He had already scouted out the location of the Baked Tomato, so he had some idea where he wanted to park. The area was packed, with cars circling the bar for blocks trying to find parking spaces. Tony decided he would just park in the first open space as close as he could get to the bar, and that was five blocks away and two blocks off of the water front. After taking a lot of time to parallel park his car, Tony ambled his way towards the Baked Tomato with the bar's music and noise getting louder the closer he got to its location.

Reaching the front door area, he noticed the large grouping of young people standing out front trying to get in. The two guys and a girl at the front door were making sure that only those who were old enough to be in the bar were allowed in. At least that was what they were supposed to be doing. The fact of the matter was that if someone wanted in bad enough, even if they were a year or in a few special instances more than a year below the proper age, they could get in if they knew the greeters or looked interesting enough to be allowed in.

Tony had to admit that the musical sound coming from inside

was fabulous and the crowd outside was intent on getting in to hear it, and dance to it. To look at the girls lined up to go inside, Tony knew that the competition in the bar must be strong because the girls he was looking at were trying their best to stand out. They were decked out in tight jeans, tight tops of all sorts, strong perfume and even stronger hair spray. It was show time and the show was on, generally for everyone. Tony thought that it would take an extremely confident woman to enter that place without looking her best, and this was Thursday night. He could only imagine what Friday or Saturday nights would be like. He made a mental note to definitely find out, as soon as possible.

Tony finally got in the doorway, after spending a lot of time watching others in front of him get checked for age determination. He entered the relatively small lobby area and noted the locations of the restrooms on each side of the entrance. Walking on through the lobby, he entered the dance area only to have his ears be even more challenged by the loud sound of the vibrating music. His first thought was how different this was from the many places he had been in all over Europe. Those places served the same functions that this one did, the mingling of men and women looking to meet one another along with the enjoyment of good music in the background. The more he stood in the doorway looking out over the dance floor and bar, the more excited he got. There was as much, if not more, energy in this room than almost any comparable room in similar locations he had visited in Italy, France and Switzerland, much less Germany and England. Yes, he liked it here. A lot.

Tony took a few steps over to his right just after he had entered the huge dancing area and moved slowly through the crowd to position himself up against the room's back wall. Standing there, he gradually ran his eyes around the room, going from one side to the other and then back again. As he came back and looked more slowly over the bar area, he saw a man sitting at the end of the bar that fit Deputy Sheriff Mark Patterson's description. Appearing to be about 6 feet tall, the figure had broad shoulders and was wearing blue jeans. Tony noticed that a jacket was over the back of the chair. Since it was rather warm outside, Tony guessed that the jacket concealed the deputy's weapon because one was not readily visible. The figure was also wearing a western style hat as were several others in the room.

Standing next to the chair was a woman who, Tony guessed, was in her late twenties and looked to be about 5 foot 7 in height. She was wearing a long, full blue jean skirt, a tight white blouse that absolutely showed off her ample breasts, and brown boots. Her brown hair was long and obviously had received a lot of attention. Tony could not clearly see her face just yet so he ran his eyes once again over the crowd. Most of the women were wearing jeans or jean skirts and either boots or heels. Any change by those present from wearing jeans was obviously done at a risk to the wearer. The men were almost unanimously wearing jeans and cowboy shirts, but the difference was that the men were also almost unanimously wearing cowboy boots. The other consistent condition for the men was that they all looked rather unkempt. Unlike the bars in Europe that Tony had been in, the show in this bar was the female side of things. The men, for the most part, almost all looked like they had just come in from off of the farm.

As he surveyed the room, Tony noticed the groupings of those who were already in the room. Two couples consisting of two men and two women occupied most of the tables. However, there were several tables of nothing but females, usually in groups of four and almost all deeply in conversation with one another as they observed the goings on in the large room. Most of the men not seated at the tables were either sitting at the bar or standing along the walls.

The more Tony looked around, it began to sink in on him. This room was built with an absolute minimum of items that were movable and breakable. The wooden tables were heavy as were the wooden chairs next to those tables. The posts located inside the building were thick and solid, not the kind that would be damaged in a normal bar room brawl, which Tony guessed happened with some regularity in this building. Yes, the more he looked around, it became apparent to him that somebody had designed this establishment to withstand the various assaults its designer and builder had probably witnessed on various occasions in other locations. This building was built to withstand the probably constant, physical battles in which those in attendance there engaged.

Looking around the vast room, Tony noticed what appeared to be two tall, muscle-bound men who seemed to be there to keep the peace. He watched them as they constantly looked around the large room at those enjoying their Thursday night away from their daily lives. He also noticed how the two men slowly walked the room, one going one way and the other going the opposite way. While they did that, the man appearing to be Deputy Sheriff Mark Patterson continued to talk with the sexy lady standing next to him, occasionally shifting his eyes to check around the room. Yes, that had to be him, but Tony was content to stay put at his observation post for the time being.

After the live music stopped for what the band's singer said was a short break, Tony observed another girl joining the two at the bar. She was a redhead, who appeared to be out of place in her white, one piece dress that was belted at the waist and rather short. Her dress emphasized her figure which, Tony knew from past discussions with other girls, was the exact reason she was wearing it. While a little above average looking, Tony could only give her a grade of B, and that was for trying because she was carrying some extra weight on her frame. She was now standing on one side of the chair while the much better looking girl was leaning against the bar in front of the man, talking with him as she scanned the crowd.

Again looking around the room, Tony was able to find the table he thought he had seen the redhead get up from when she had walked over to the bar. At that table were three girls whose eyes constantly scanned the room. All three did not stand out as far as looks were concerned but they had done, in Tony's opinion, the best they could with what they had to offer. Tony had a thing about evaluating females, and he estimated that at least two of the three had long time problems trying to attract male attention. One of the three, a sandy blonde girl with short hair and full lips, was attractive in her own special way. Her eyes acted like radar antennae. As her head gradually moved back and forth across the room, this girl's eyes took in everything. As she had been scanning the room, her eyes had briefly rested on him, evaluating him like they had probably done before to hundreds, no, thousands of men, and probably even several female competitors. Tony avoided looking into her eyes, lest she think he was interested in her. He had to admit it was hard not to look back at the table because of her mannerisms.

After about ten minutes of watching the crowd without the music, Tony decided it was time to meet the man that he was pretty sure was his target. He gradually ambled over until he was eventually standing at the bar right next to the dark-haired beauty.

He nodded and smiled to all three of them as he now leaned against the bar. The two girls nodded back as did the man in the chair.

"Bud," was his statement when the young bartender immediately came over to him It was at that point that he realized what he should have thought of before he ever walked in the place. He was a new face and nobody knew who he was. After the bartender put his beer in front of him, he paid him and then raised the beer can in his left hand and took a sip. It tasted good, was cold and just what he needed at that time. He then turned just enough so he could look at the three standing next to him. Two of the three were looking at him, the man and the redhead. The beautiful one continued to look out over the dance floor. None of the three were saying anything. Tony decided it was time to move into action.

Looking at the male, he smiled and said, "Hi, my name is Tony." Keeping his eyes on the male, Tony continued, "I am new to this area and came here to meet some people."

The man sitting in the bar chair looked at him for a moment and then stuck his hand out.

"Hi. I'm Mark Patterson. Welcome to Bay St. Louis."

"Thank you," Tony smiled and said as he shook Patterson's hand.

Nodding his head towards the beautiful girl leaning against the bar, Patterson said. "This is Karen." Then nodding towards the redhead he continued, "and this is Carol."

"Nice to meet you, ladies."

Karen said, "You have an accent. Where are you from?"

"I was born and raised in Europe," Tony responded, still smiling. "Came over here for business and decided to stay for a little while. This is beautiful country. First time I've been here. What about you? Are you guys from here?"

"Oh yes. All three of us," answered Karen as Carol nodded her head in agreement. Patterson leaned back in his chair, now listening to the conversation.

"What do you do here? Do you each work?" Tony asked, genuinely interested in what their answers might be.

"Well, I am a school teacher," Karen said. "Carol has her own little business running land titles all over the county." Tony slightly nodded his head at that piece of information. "And big boy here is a deputy sheriff, but don't tell anyone," she said with a really cute smile.

"I really am undercover, but Karen is constantly telling people, like she just did with you, what I do for a living so it's not working too well," Mark said with the hint of a smile on his face.

Carol piped in, saying, "Well, we are constantly trying to find out whose cover he's under, but she seems to be the only one that knows where he is."

Tony immediately recognized the voice of jealousy. With that one statement, she had let him know that Karen and the deputy were an item in bed. By the same statement, she was also letting their new friend know that Karen was basically taken, which by Carol saying what she did, meant that she was probably available.

"Carol!" Karen immediately said, giving her a look of disapproval. "We try to find out what cover Carol is under, but there are too many possibilities," she answered back along with a "gotcha" look. Carol did not respond.

Tony's first thought was that these two girls were cats, just pure cats. With this taking place right after they had just met him, he could imagine what might be said after they got to know him or, even more so, after he was out of hearing distance.

To change the subject, Tony asked, "Is this the best club here, in this area?"

Mark answered, "Depends on what you are looking for. The best music? None better. The best looking girls? Absolutely. Now if you want the best food? Not here. The cleanest kitchen? It's at the bottom of the list. If you want really good food, go across the road out front to The Overlook Café. During the day, the view out on the back deck over there is beautiful and the food is really good."

"I'll have to try that out," Tony said, glad that the two girls were back to watching the male traffic walking nearby. Turning to the two girls, he said, "I need you two girls to introduce me to some of your friends. I am single and would like to meet some girls here."

Karen said, "Well, if that is what you want, come go with me. There is a table of my girlfriends that will just love meeting you."

Tony answered with a big smile, "Sounds great to me. Lead on."

With that, the two of them left the end of the bar area and Tony followed Karen over to the table with the three girls he had briefly watched earlier. All three of them were sitting there though one of the girls, the one he had dodged making eye contact with earlier, was talking with a man holding a drink standing next to their table.

Arriving at the table, Karen said, "Girls. I would like for you to meet Tony, a single guy who is new to the area and wants to meet some of my friends."

Now motioning towards the nearest girl, a nondescript sandy blonde, she said, "This is Molly." Pointing to the girl sitting to Molly's left, she said, "That's Sue." Then pointing to the girl involved in the conversation, who was now turned to face them, "And that is Sarah."

With a big smile, Tony said, "Nice to meet you ladies."

About that time, the band started playing again. Karen grabbed Tony's hand and literally pulled him out on the dance floor. He immediately said to her, "Look, are you trying to get me in trouble with your boyfriend back there?"

She leaned over next to his left ear and said, "Oh, don't worry about him. He doesn't dance." With that, she pulled back and turned around to take a look at the band as she moved to the music without missing a beat.

After about two hours, Tony had danced with every girl at the table, some two and three times. He also danced with Carol, the redhead who just kept looking at him with this smile on her face that sort of said, "You are my next target, big guy." There was just something, though, about that look. He eventually slipped away after visiting the men's room in the front of the building. Enough contact had taken place for the first evening.

Chapter Eight

Tony liked his little two bedroom house. It was on the edge of town, but it had a screened-in back porch and a side garage with a door that pulled down. The front door opened into a living room that also had a small kitchen and breakfast area to the rear. To the left of the living room was a hall that led to the two bedrooms with connecting bathroom. A door in the rear of the living room led to the back porch area. Occupying a center location along the wall on the right side of the living room was a nice fireplace with book shelves on each side of the mantel.

The one thing Tony liked about the house from the moment he first saw it was that the place was completely furnished. The family that owned it had moved to Texas and had tried to sell it but, not having found a buyer for the place, agreed to lease it for the time being in order to get some income from the house. Granted, the furniture was not the best, but everything he would need was already there. There were double beds in both bedrooms and an easy chair and couch in the living room along with end tables and lamps. A small table with four chairs was snugly fitted into the kitchen area and a swing hung from the ceiling of the screened-in back porch. It was all he needed, at least for the time being.

The one thing that had been in the corner of the living room that he did not completely understand was that there had been a stand made of circular iron in which stood three umbrellas along with an old hickory cane about three feet long. As much as he thought about the umbrellas and that old cane, he could not figure out why they had not been taken by the family. He had asked the real estate agent when he was first shown the house, but the only thing that portly gentleman could offer was that the family that had lived there just had not wanted to take those items with them to Houston. After a while, he quit thinking about it.

Several nights since he had started renting the place, Tony had come back to the little house, put his car in the garage, pulled down the garage door and gone inside to fix himself a sandwich. Sometimes he would just sit there and think. He made sure all of the curtains were pulled, even the ones hanging over the glass area of his front door. There was one TV that had been left in the living room, but it did not give a clear picture most of the time, so often he would not even bother to try to turn it on. He was convinced, by everything he had heard and been told during his short time in Bay St. Louis, that it was best for him to keep a low profile, at least until he got familiar with the area and sort of got his feet on the ground, so to speak. He remembered how people in his home town back in Sicily felt about somebody new moving to the area. For one thing, everyone was aware of a newcomer arriving to live there, especially since it didn't happen very often. At first, everybody was suspicious of the person, and certainly not comfortable in their presence, at least until there was more to be found out about them and what their purpose in being there really was.

He felt the same was probably true in Bay St. Louis, especially with it being such a small town, relatively speaking. Besides, it wasn't as if he wanted a lot of people asking him questions about what his purpose was in being there. So for the time being, until he was a lot more familiar with the area, he would just keep to himself. Maybe in the near future he could begin going to New Orleans on a more regular basis. He had liked what he had seen of that city during his trips there to take care of his banking requirements, but he had not wanted to have too high of a profile until he was more comfortable knowing more about those with whom he was now dealing.

In the living room as he sat in almost complete darkness in the easy chair, which was very comfortable, he thought about so many things. He had already spent several evenings going over what all had happened since he had arrived, remembering things about his family back in Sicily, even wondering what in the world he was doing here. He was a nice looking guy with a good personality, he thought, who now had lots of money. But he constantly went over in his mind what he was being shown down here in this part of this wonderful country. The question he had to answer for himself was whether he wanted to be part of any of it.

He was thinking this particular night about his beautiful, kind girlfriend back in Sicily, Amanda Votano, who he had absolutely loved. They had dated for almost three years and everybody thought they would be getting married. But she had been killed in an accident not too long before he got the message that he had to come to the United States. The bus she rode every day to her job at a jewelry store in the nearby seaside town had been hit by a drunk driver as she was coming home from work. The bus had been thrown over a cliff and all but two of the fourteen people riding in it were killed. She had been one of the twelve.

Tony had been devastated. In fact, he was still devastated. They had not gotten married sooner because she had wanted him to get away from the illegal activities that his father had gotten involved in upon his return to the area after World War II and had continued to be involved with. Tony felt that he could not do so, especially while his Dad was alive. His Dad had seen to it that Tony had gradually been made a part of the activities. But his Dad had died and Tony had thought that the time might have been right for him to begin to extricate himself from the mob. Then his girlfriend had died in that tragic accident. That had been five months earlier and, now, he had come to America.

It was about 1:30 a.m. when Tyrone Hamilton normally made his efforts. This night, he decided to go ahead and do what he just felt he had to do, even though it was only a little after 10 p.m. Tyrone decided it was time to break into another deserted house. After all, nobody checked on those types of places and every now and then he would come across a place that had something of value in it that he could sell to his buddies in Louisiana. They didn't care where the merchandise came from and a lot of the time it didn't even matter what it was. His friends were capable of selling almost anything that had any value at all.

His last haul had been from an old warehouse just on the edge of town and had resulted in a nice sum of $382 being paid to him for several items he had taken, among them being a couple of lawn mowers and various yard tools such as clippers, saws, shovels and hoes. It hadn't taken him fifteen minutes to get inside the building and get the items he was able to carry to his truck. The sale of those stolen items had taken only the few moments it took for his friends to look at them and give him a price, which he quickly accepted and left the premises. With part of that money, Tyrone had loaded up with several bottles of Ripple and had enjoyed himself for the rest of that evening. Life was good.

Now it was time to find out what he might be able to take from this old deserted house near the end of the block on the outskirts of Bay St. Louis. He had cruised the neighborhood for several days and had now been watching this particular house, riding by at night to see if there was any activity around it, and a few of the other houses in the area that he thought might also be deserted. One day, as he passed by the house he had been happy to see that the man and woman, who had been living there, were putting suitcases and two chairs in the bed of a pickup truck. Checking it out several times since then, he had seen no activity when he had passed by. It was now time for him to see what he might be able to quickly take from the house so that he might have a little spending money for the upcoming weekend.

Parking his pickup truck next to the adjacent empty lot, he walked up to the front door, carrying in his right hand a six inch knife with a large handle. He didn't anticipate any problems but just in case, as he always did, he carried his knife with him. It would be better to have it already in his hand if something were to happen. The knife had been his since he was a kid, and having it with him made him feel, well, special. He had only threatened to use it one time, when he had broken into a house during the day and a white woman had pulled into the driveway. As she opened the garage door, he just stood there and showed her he was carrying that knife. He had laughed when, she was so scared, she dropped her bag of groceries that she had been carrying and started screaming. He decided to leave by her back door and eased himself into the very thick woods behind her house. As he made his way deeper into the woods, he could still hear her yelling as she stood in the street in front of her house. He laughed about that whole scene sometimes, when he thought about it.

CRASHHHHHHHHH!!!!!!!!!!!!!!!!!!!!!!!!

Tyrone's use of the butt of the knife to break the glass pane just above the door knob had been successful, after he had tested the knob and determined it was locked. He immediately thrust his hand through the opening, found the inside door knob and twisted it so that he could push the door open. He moved through the open doorway and quickly shut the door behind him. He was now inside the house. He put the knife in his belt and began trying to move around the room. It was totally black inside the house, the darkest he could remember. He finally found the wall to his right and began to feel around with his hands for drawers to pull out or shelves to pull things off of to see if there might be something he wanted to take. He could barely make out the small fireplace located a few steps away from the front door. It was then that it happened.

Click!

A lamp located on the opposite side of the room was turned on. Tyrone wheeled around, pulling his knife out of his belt as he turned. Startled, he stood there, knife in his hand, as a white man began to stand up out of the easy chair he had been sitting in.

"You picked the wrong house," the man said as he now was standing up.

"Whaaaaaaaaa????" Tyrone said. Realizing that another human being was standing there facing him, Tyrone said, "Man, you scared me! What'd you say?"

Tony answered, "I said, you picked the wrong house."

Looking at him, Tyrone's first thought was, this white boy doesn't have a gun. His second thought was, I'm about four inches taller than him. His third thought was, I'm also bigger than he is. He then thought, but I don't need any fight here, so he said, "Look, honkey, I'm gonna just leave now so you stay put while I do that."

Nick said, "What did you just call me? A honk? What is that word?"

"I said honkey, white boy. That's what it means." Now starting to twist and turn the knife he was holding in his right hand out towards Nick, Tyrone said, "Now I'm going to ease out of here so you just stay put, chu understand that?"

Standing with his legs slightly spread, his hands now clinched but hanging down next to his side, Nick said, "Can't do that, black boy."

"What chu mean? I'm gett'n ready to leave, just don't try to stop me. Understand?"

"Can't let you do that. You broke my window. You shouldn't have done that. You're not leaving."

"Oh, really? You think you gonna stop me? I got dis here knife," Tyrone said as he raised it up, twisting it slowly as he showed it to his opponent. Now having sized him up, Tyrone made his decision.

"I've cut other people with this knife. I guess I'm gonna have to cut you." Tyrone then thrust his knife towards Tony to stab him.

It was at that point that things happened, quickly. Tony brought his left hand up, fist clinched, and parried the thrust of the knife, pushing it off to Tyrone's right. Then, in the blink of an eye, Tony did a front forward snapping kick with his right foot, one that he had practiced so many times before on his way to his black belt in karate. That kick, performed much like that of a forward kicking field goal kicker in American football, caught Tyrone right between his legs. The kick was delivered with such force that it literally lifted the taller, heavier black man off of his feet. It also immediately crushed his left ball below his penis.

Tyrone yelled in pain as he fell to the floor, the knife falling out of his hand as he grabbed for his crotch with both hands. Tony quickly reached down and picked up the knife as Tyrone writhed on the floor, now screaming.

Walking around his prey, Tony said, "So you were going to cut me? Huh? You were going to cause me some pain, were you? Huh?"

Tyrone continued to have both hands between his legs, continuing to scream with every breath while now lying on his left side.

Tony walked over to the iron holder and took out the long hickory stick. Walking back over to Tyrone, he said, "You were going to hurt me? Huh? You were going to use your big, bad knife on me? I think you need a little something else to remember me by."

With that, Tony raised the hickory stick over his head and, using both hands, brought it down as hard as he could on Tyrone's upper right arm.

"AYYYYYYYYYYYYYEEEEEEEEEEEEE!" Tyrone cried out. Tony knew Tyrone's upper arm was probably broken. He had heard a snap when the hickory stick had hit it. Tony walked over to the stand and put the stick back in it. Turning, he walked over to the now constantly moaning Tyrone.

Watching Tyrone curl himself up almost in a fetal position, Tony began thinking about where he was. He was not in Sicily. He was in the United States, in Mississippi, and he was supposed to keep a low profile. Yet, here was this man on the floor of his house, probably with a busted testicle, but surely with at least a broken arm. The more he thought about it, the more convinced he became. He had to take this poor excuse for a human being to a hospital. He remembered where he had seen one while he had ridden around town after he had bought his car. He knew what he had to do.

He walked over to Tyrone, who was still moaning on the floor. Reaching for his left arm to help him up, Tony said, "Alright, mister bad ass. Come on. Stand up."

Every movement caused extreme pain between Tyrone's legs, yet Tony insisted.

"Get up. Come on. Get up. I've got to get you out of my house and to my car. I'm gonna take you to the hospital so come on. Get up."

With a lot of effort, accompanied by continuous moaning, Tony helped Tyrone out to Tony's car and finally eased him into the passenger side of the front seat. Tony then drove him to the hospital he had previously noticed.

Pulling up in front of the hospital, Tony went around and helped Tyrone out of the car. Putting Tyrone's left arm over his right shoulder, He helped ease Tyrone to the front door of the hospital. As they entered the lobby, the nurse behind the desk hit a button and then quickly came around to help hold Tyrone.

Tony transferred Tyrone's left arm so it was around the nurse's neck as he saw two other nurses running down the hallway towards them.

"He had a bad fall," Tony told the nurse. As he turned to leave, he said, "I have to go. Take care of him."

With that he left the building, got into his car, and drove away.

Later that week at the Baked Tomato, Tony walked in as the music was blaring, though the crowd was light since it was early in the evening. He walked over to the deputy, who was sitting at his normal perch at the end of the bar, with his back to the wall as always so he could see the whole room.

"Hello there, Mr. Deputy," Tony said with a wide grin on his face as he watched two girls dance by themselves on the dance floor.

"Am I safe in your town tonight?"

The deputy turned his head to look at Tony and replied, "Hello, Tony." Turning back to get the same view Tony was looking at, he answered by saying, "I don't know. I am beginning to wonder."

"Oh, really?" Tony answered as both of them now watched the two dancers.

"Well, it seems that a few nights ago a black man was brought into our local hospital here and checked in." The deputy turned his head away from the dancers and looked at Tony as he continued. "Seems he had a broken arm."

"Really?" Tony said as he continued to watch the dancers.

"Seems that he also had been kicked in the balls so hard that one of them was completely smashed," the deputy said as he continued to look at Tony. Tony kept watching the two girls.

"He's going to be there at the hospital for several days," he continued.

After a moment, the deputy then said, "Won't talk to anybody about who did that to him or why it might have happened. Without him being willing to press charges or talk about it, there is really nothing we can do."

After a few moments of just the music playing, the deputy said, "Seems that he was brought to the hospital by a man driving a '56 Ford." Pausing for a moment, he then said, "There are not many of those in this area." Tony, now beginning to move with the beat of the music, still kept watching the girls.

"Don't you drive one of those?" the deputy asked, now closely watching for Tony's reaction.

Tony turned to look at the deputy and said, "Those two girls really should not be dancing just by themselves." With that, he turned and walked, keeping some semblance of a beat, out and joined them dancing.

The following Monday, after he had spent some time thinking about the deputy's inquiry, Tony went down to the hospital to see Tyrone. When he pushed open the door to Tyrone's room, he saw the patient's right arm in a cast. After he shut the door, he also noticed that Tyrone's legs were spread wide open on the bed and there was a large wad of padding at the top of his thighs. When Tyrone realized who had just walked in, his eyes quickly got very wide open. As Tony took a few steps over towards the bed, Tyrone's eyes got as wide open as they could get and his mouth dropped open. He saw a glass vase holding a dozen red roses in Tony's right hand alright, but it was what was in his left hand that immediately grabbed his attention. What he saw was that cane!

"Hi, Tyrone," Tony said as he looked first at Tyrone's open mouth and then at his cast and bandages between his legs. Tyrone could not answer. All he could do was stare, and most of his stare was directed at that cane.

"Brought you some flowers," Tony said in a firm voice. Tyrone continued to look at the cane after briefly looking at Tony as he had spoken. Tony put the flower vase on a table that was not too far from the side of the bed. He then slowly walked around to the foot of the bed and stood there as he brought the cane up so that he was now holding it in both hands. Tyrone still did not say a word but looked at the cane and then up to Tony's face, then back down to the cane.

"Brought the cane too," Tony said with sort of a sneer to his voice.

"You remember this cane, don't you?" he asked as he stared directly into Tyrone's eyes. Tyrone was now pressing himself back into the head portion of the bed.

Lowering his voice, Tony said, "Tyrone, if I ever hear about you ever, ever breaking into somebody's home and trying to steal something from anybody, you hear me?" Then Tony slowly dragged out the next words, "Anybody at all." After a short pause, Tony finished his sentence, saying, "I am going to hit you with this thing on your other ball." As soon as he had said the last word, he quickly pulled the cane up above his head and, gripping it with both hands, brought it down with all the force he could muster right between Tyrone's spread legs.

"Whumppppppppp!"

Tyrone almost passed out. If he had not been so scared, he

probably would have. Instead, after checking his senses and realizing that Tony had not, in fact, hit him between his legs, he slowly opened his closed eyes. He saw Tony still standing there, but he was now lifting the cane up off of the bed where he had slammed it.

"Do I make myself clear, Tyrone?"

Shaking almost all over, Tyrone raised his eyes as he followed that cane being lifted up off of the bed. Then he shifted his look up to Tony's face and nodded his head in the affirmative, his eyes still wide open.

"Good," Tony said, now in a more jovial tone of voice.

"Now that we understand each other, hope you get well soon." With that, Tony eased his way back towards the door, holding the cane up in his right hand as he did. He then opened the door and walked out, closing it behind him.

Two weeks later, Tyrone was told he was going to be discharged from the hospital. Two orderlies at the hospital helped him carefully get dressed and then into a wheelchair. A nurse pushed him down the hallway to the front desk for him to check out. One of his five sisters was there to pick him up and take him to her house where she could help take care of him.

"Mr. Elliott, your bill is $24,783," said the woman behind the desk.

Tyrone looked at her with a blank look on his face. Then he said, slumping over even more in his wheelchair and looking down at the floor, "I can't pay that."

The clerk answered, "Oh, you don't have to. It's already been paid, by the man that brought you in that night."

Chapter Nine

Bartolli had long ago decided that he would be the one who determined what his operation would be involved in, not some old men living in other parts of the country. Since there was so much demand for drugs Bartolli was determined that he and his organization were going to supply that need, regardless of what other crime bosses might say.

Now that Tony had been made aware of Bartolli's involvement in that effort, in spite of the other crime families having taken the position that none of them should be involved, Bartolli was pleased that his new visitor had registered no objection to what he had seen. That being the case, Bartolli determined that he would arrange for Tony to go out to one of the drilling rigs also being utilized for the shipment of drugs into the area.

Tony realized it really was an attempt by Bartolli to show

him how smart he had been in utilizing the rig, unbeknownst to its owners, as one of the major trans-shipment points in the operation. Tony was interested in seeing how extensively Bartolli's outfit was involved in drug shipments and also how the operation was performing that portion of its activities. He was told by Hank to be down at the Scabelli Corporation docks in New Iberia, Louisiana at 7 a.m. Tuesday morning. He was also told to bring with him an easy to carry overnight canvas bag and to dress in jeans, lace-up boots and a work shirt. Hank said for him to look for a man with a beard named Jeff who was stocky, about 6 feet tall and about 35 years old.

Tony drove to the docks in his '56 Ford, getting there about thirty minutes early. After getting out of his car, he opened the trunk and took out his overnight canvas bag. He slammed the trunk closed and, carrying his bag, began walking towards the dock area. As he walked, he saw a man fitting Jeff's description break off from a group of men and approach him.

"I'm Jeff," the man said, without a smile.

"Hi, Jeff. I'm Tony."

"How do you like that Ford?" Jeff asked as he looked at the parked vehicle.

"Gets me where I want to go. At least it has so far," Tony answered, noticing the man had not offered to shake hands.

"I always wanted to get me one of those but never did. It's got that big engine in it, a 406 I think?"

"Yes, that sounds about right. I'll let you drive it one day if you would like," Tony said, trying to establish some common interest somehow.

"That would be nice," Jeff answered, now with the slightest of hints of a smile on his face. "Bring your bag with you and come with me. And Tony, stay close."

They walked towards what appeared to be some type of an oil service boat. Tony had never spent any time around offshore oil rigs but had seen pictures of boats that worked around them on television from time to time. This boat had a large, flat area which covered over two thirds of the boat's entire length. The front portion was similar to that of a tug in that it had an elevated cabin that provided a good view all around the boat. Tony presumed that was where the captain was and that the area underneath that elevated portion was a crew quarter. The appearance of the white superstructure and the black hull both evidenced having been involved in bad weather. The vessel obviously had not been painted for some time.

As Tony followed Jeff onto the back tail section, they wandered over to a corner just behind the pilot house. Six other men, four white and two black, soon followed them onto the back of the boat, taking their places by sitting on the floor of the open back area. There was a minimal amount of conversation between those in the group.

Promptly at 7, the boat cast off from the dock and eased down a short, wide canal, eventually making its way into open water. At that point the captain opened up and increased the boat's speed. Jeff leaned over and said, "We are supposed to have some bad weather out near where we are going so it might get a little rough." Tony nodded his head in acknowledgement of the warning.

The deep sound of the boat's engine made any conversation difficult to hear so there was no further discussion. Soon the ship encountered seas similar to what he had witnessed so many times in the Strait of Messina between Sicily and the Italian boot. He had never liked the boat rides he had taken in that area and this was no different. In fact, the further out they went, the rougher the seas got, and they had not yet even encountered any bad weather. Oh, there were clouds in the sky moving rather rapidly, but the sun was out and the breeze felt good.

There was just that one problem. The further they got away from shore, the deeper the swells got. While their boat seemed to handle the progressively bigger waves well, it wasn't too long and the entire vessel was almost disappearing between the waves. As the captain pointed the vessel into the now 20 foot high waves, the boat went up and down like it was a roller coaster thrill ride at some entertainment park. Tony began gripping the side of the boat he was seated against with all of his strength, resting only a little bit as the boat entered one of the many troughs between the high waves.

After what seemed like an extremely long time, Tony could see the outline of a drilling rig in the distance. At about that same time, the sky began to darken and the wind speed increased. He finally leaned over to Jeff and literally screamed out so he could be heard, "I sure am glad we are about to get there." Jeff smiled and yelled back, "This is not too bad. You should be out here on one of these things when it really gets bad."

"No, thanks," Tony quickly answered. Jeff laughed.

As they got closer to the rig, Tony was impressed at how massive the structure was. With his boat riding up and then down about 30 feet from the rig, Tony began to hold on tighter, if that were even possible. As they pulled within what Tony felt was dangerously close footage of so much steel, Tony saw the arm of the crane permanently located on the rig begin to swing out so that it was over the area of their boat's constant up and down movement. Tony began to have doubts. How in the world was he going to get up onto that oil rig? He estimated that the flat service basin, the area where he was sure most of the supplies and equipment were landed on the rig, stood about 60 to 65 feet above the water on which he was riding. As his ride continued its up and down motion, Tony wondered if he would keep his breakfast down. He was glad he had not eaten much because it definitely was too late to worry about that.

As he watched the structure supports rise and fall now almost adjacent to the vessel, he became even more fearful. It was then that Jeff screamed at him, "Okay, when that crane swings right over the boat, you will have to stand up and stick your arms through the harness at the end of the chain. Grab it and put your arms through it, then hold on, really tight."

Tony looked back at him in disbelief. He could hardly imagine himself standing up on this rocking boat deck, much less grabbing the material on the end of the chain now coming down towards him. And he was going first? Were they crazy? It was as if they were going to test it all out and see if it worked with him and, if it did, the others would then do it. Now was the time to admit it. He was scared. No, he was petrified, so scared he could not move. He watched one of the huge pilings of the rig as his little boat went up at least 25 feet with each wave and then down, right next to the piling.

The first time that Jeff told him to grab it, he did not move. He could not move. He was frozen. It was all simply too much. It was then that Jeff jumped up and pulled Tony over to the appropriate spot. When the next wave had the boat at its highest point, he quickly put the halter around Tony's back and under his armpits. It wasn't what seemed like a second later and the boom literally jerked him off of the back of the boat. Or at least that's what it felt like. In actual fact, the boat he was standing on started going down into the trough of the wave, leaving Tony suspended by the harness. Tony tried to utter a sound but couldn't get a noise out because he was so scared. He was now hanging from a chain about fifty feet long which was connected to the arm of the huge hoist on the rig. One glance down and Tony saw how far it now was down to the boat deck below him. As he saw the deck starting to come back up towards him, he realized that he was going to get slammed by the rising deck. It was precisely at that moment that the hoist operator pulled on the chain holding Tony so that he was lifted up out of harm's way from the boat. Now he was suspended, dangling from the chain connected to the hoist, over the boat and the water.

The crane operator began to swing the crane's chain around so that, in an instant, Tony was literally laid out almost parallel to the ocean as he was swung around the rig. He was definitely thinking that his time had come. He was not going to survive this event. He was going to die swinging from the arm of a crane on a Gulf of Mexico oil rig south of Louisiana. He knew he was now trying to scream but nothing was coming out. Not one sound. He then realized that screaming wasn't going to help him one little bit.

As the strong wind fought the crane operator's efforts to bring Tony to the landing deck of the rig, Tony could only imagine how horrible his impending death was going to be when he would soon be slammed into the hard metal of the rig's landing area. As he was being brought closer to what he knew was going to be a sure collision of his body with the landing platform, what he considered a real miracle happened. The crane operator set him down as lightly as a feather. Two men came out and grabbed him as he neared touching the hard platform. It was at that point that Tony felt the two men trying to forcefully pry his fingers away from their tight hold on the hoist that was around his back and under his armpits. They kept trying to pry his fingers loose but he continued to hold on to the hoist as tightly as he could. Then one of the workers said, "Man, if you don't let go, that crane operator is going to pull you up, swing you back out over the water and put you back down on that supply ship. There are others that have to be brought up here."

Vaguely realizing what the helper had just told him was getting ready to happen, Tony was able to relax his grip, at least to the point where his fingers could be pried loose. He was then helped to the edge of the landing area. For a brief moment, he didn't ever think his life would be the same.

Jeff was the next person to be lifted off of the supply boat and onto the rig. As soon as he was on the landing area and his harness was removed, he looked for Tony and, seeing him leaning over against a wall on the deck, ran over to him.

"You alright?" he asked.

Tony could barely speak. As hard as he tried, he could only say what amounted to brief sounds. Jeff started laughing.

"We need to get you inside," he said as he started guiding him to and then through a metal doorway. He took Tony to a mess hall area, sat him down and brought him a cup of hot coffee. Tony slowly drank from the cup as he braced himself against the metal table. Not a word was said, but Jeff continued to smile. After Tony had finished his cup of coffee, Jeff got him to stand and slowly walked him up some stairs to the sleeping area. There, Jeff showed him which bunk was his.

Over the next two days Tony observed the drilling operation and, more importantly, the smuggling operation. Anytime one of their operation's supply ships would come up on the south

121

side of the rig, it was met by Jeff and one of his associates, who had already decided where that particular shipment would be stored. Supply ships on the south side appeared to be going back and forth from other rigs south of the one Tony was on. In fact though, they were going south alright, but south to meet incoming shipments from so-called "mother" ships, which were old merchant ships and fishing vessels of various shapes and sizes that were being utilized in the trade. Tony was surprised at the number of times just during his short stay that a vessel would come up on the south side and be met by Jeff and his worker. It was at least two times a day and that was just at that one rig.

Tony was also introduced to the rig boss, a man of some sophistication in that he was wearing regular pants and a shirt whereas almost everyone else on the rig was in work clothes. Tony's meeting with him was brief, being cut short when Jeff interrupted the conversation by letting them both know that an "arrival," as he called it, was imminent. Jeff later told him that the rig boss could expect to make upwards of an additional $50,000 a year if operations ran smoothly.

Early into his visit, Tony had seen where door hatches on the huge legs of the rig were opened and spiral stairways utilized for access to storage areas inside the leg. The level of the waves determined how the work boats docked at the leg in order to either drop off or pick up shipments.

On the second day out at the rig, Jeff had told Tony to be ready to catch one of the service boats back to the dock. Tony immediately protested.

"Man, you have got to find me another way to get back to shore. I cannot, hear me, cannot ride on one of those boats again. Really. I just can't."

Jeff couldn't help but tease him about it.

"You mean you can't take a little ole boat ride back to the shore? You mean you are, let me get the right word, is it "afraid," of going back on one of the many boats that will be available to return on?"

"Let me answer that for you real quickly. Yes." They both laughed. Jeff understood. He had seen this reaction before, more than once. In fact, more than just a few times.

"Okay then. The other way to get back is to fly on one of the helicopters, if the weather is nice. You probably would have been brought out here by copter if the weather had not been so bad. More and more of our manpower is being brought out here that way. There will be a couple of them coming out here tomorrow, if you want to wait."

"Let's just count on that, okay?" Tony said smiling. Jeff just laughed.

"And I thought you were a brave person, a person of little fear, a person who would go through most anything in the pursuit of knowledge," Jeff said while again laughing.

"Let me put it to you this way, okay?" Tony responded. "There is no way I am going back on a boat, unless it is a very big boat and I don't think you can get any of those as close to this rig as I would need it to get."

"Okay. Okay. You convinced me. Then tomorrow at 7:30 a.m. be on the landing deck with your gear. You will have a short briefing before getting on the copter. Everybody who is a first timer has to do that. You and the others who will be flying at that time will meet with the pilot in the room just inside the doorway to the landing area."

The next morning at about 7:15, Tony was sitting in the room along with two other men. In walked a person who could best be described as "grizzled." His head was partially bald; what hair that was left on his head was grey along with his eyebrows and his goatee; his tee shirt was stained; his pants had obviously not been washed for what appeared to be weeks; and his demeanor was about as friendly as a cactus.

"Any of you ever flown in a helicopter before?" he asked the group.

Tony was the only one that had not. The pilot briefly glanced at him with a look that said, "Where have you been living your life?"

"Alright. First, and foremost, when you get in, put on your seatbelt. If you don't, you might fall out. Secondly, put on your shoulder harness. If you don't, you might fall out. Thirdly, hold on to something with both hands. If you don't, you might fall out. Any questions?"

After every bit of three seconds, the pilot said, "Okay, follow me."

With that, he left the room followed by his three passengers on his way to the deck where the copter was sitting. Tony threw his bag in a web harness area in the rear of the copter and sat down in the back facing those who sat in front of him behind the pilot. He made sure he followed the pilot's directions, locking his seatbelt and shoulder harness, as did the two sitting opposite him.

The pilot started the engines and, after a brief time, slowly lifted the copter up until it was about three feet off of the pad. He then gradually began to back the copter, moving it away from the built up area. There was a wind, but not nearly as bad as it had been when he had come out to the rig.

It was at that point that he noticed that the surface under the copter slowly eased away from being under his means of transportation. Tony remembered that third thing the pilot had mentioned, about holding on tightly, which he now did by grabbing the shoulder harness, with both hands. It was then that he looked over to the left side, and then guided his eyes down. It was now not three feet down to something to land on. It was 65 feet down, to the water! The pilot quickly rotated the copter, pointed its nose down towards the water so it was almost at a 45 degree angle and then applied the juice to move the copter forward.

Tony tried to scream, but again nothing came out, especially when the pilot made what Tony thought was a very sharp left turn to get away from the rig. The two guys sitting opposite him looked on in total dismay as he made strange sounds in his efforts to scream.

When he finally got back to his house, he still had a hard time walking. The thought of that copter, nose pointed down, then making that left turn so that it, in essence, was almost on its side, just kept coming back to his mind, over and over again. As he unlocked his side door next to his open garage, he noticed something standing at the edge of his house. He took a step over towards whatever it was and stopped. It was a baby, brown and white, cocker spaniel. He bent over as best he could and the puppy came over to him. He petted it on its little head, which set the cocker's short tail to wagging. He picked it up and carried it inside. That little puppy was a welcome addition to his household. It had arrived at just the right time.

Chapter Ten

Bourbon Street could be called the crossroads of the world. In every shop, bar, restaurant, or strip joint there are usually people from everywhere. A person wandering down that infamous street may just as easily run into somebody from Honduras as from Los Angeles or Vietnam or west Nebraska. It is one of those few places on earth where a person with a history that they might want to escape from can go and, depending on what they are willing to do, make a nice living and not have to worry about somebody asking them questions they might not want to answer.

That was exactly what Sung Lu wanted. She wanted to be somewhere where she did not have to worry about answering too many questions about her background, such as where did she go to high school or did she work while going to college. There were extremely good reasons for her feeling that way. She had grown up in a rice paddy in South Vietnam in a family of seven, whose members, all of them, were always looking for their next meal. At the very young age of 14, she was forced by her father to go to work in a bar in Saigon where, because of her good looks by comparison with the other girls working there, she quickly went from being just a bar maid to being a prostitute. Her life was hard enough, being in that profession, with the constant changing of the many American soldiers she had sex with to the few Vietnamese that wanted to be with her, but who also shunned her if they ever saw her in public. But she began to make enough money that she was able to help her family out, at the constant insistence of her father since she still lived at home.

Then there was that period of time in 1969 that one of the brash lieutenants in the South Vietnamese army that she had been seeing from time to time, Nuguan Dao, got promoted to First Lieutenant. He then got promoted again and then again, eventually rising very quickly to the rank of full Colonel. He had been promoted those several times because of his interrogation and subsequent accurate evaluation of intelligence information obtained from captured Viet Cong soldiers, but also because the officers above him were continually being killed by the Viet Cong, or VC, assassination teams. Colonel Dao was taught by his American CIA advisors the art of getting the real truth from captured Viet Cong soldiers, and a few from North Vietnam. His specialty was the interrogation of a captured VC soldier while taking the soldier for a ride in one of the American huey helicopters. He had tried time and again to question VC soldiers in barracks, then in barns, then in sheds, and finally on the edge of the jungle.

He eventually found out that none of those locations or the techniques utilized by the young Vietnamese officer and his

CIA associates were as effective as taking his targets for a short helicopter ride. Most of the time he would take three, and sometimes up to as many as five, captured VC for that ride. He was usually, but not always, accompanied by his CIA counterpart on those helicopter rides, along with four to six members of his South Vietnamese army intelligence unit. Even though he continually asked his targets questions that he either knew, or at least felt, that they could have easily answered, the targets would almost always adamantly refuse to respond. Such refusal took place even though they had been told it was in their best interests to respond. Once the aircraft had reached an altitude of approximately two thousand feet and arrived over a particular location, usually ground that was open but not being used as rice paddies, the South Vietnamese soldiers would stand a VC man up and hold him in front of the open doorway on the side of the huey. Then officer Dao would ask the VC soldier one more time if the soldier wanted to answer a question that was then presented to him that the officer wanted to know the answer to. The question may be about his unit, its officers, its home base area, its supply routes, its next target for attack, or some other piece of information the intelligence officer wanted to know.

The dedication of the VC soldiers was admired by the intelligence personnel because, almost without fail, the first soldier would not answer the question he was asked. At the nod of officer Dao, that soldier would then be pushed out of the open side doorway of the traveling aircraft. After watching the soldier fall the first several hundred feet through the air, officer Dao would turn and face the second VC soldier and repeat the same process. It almost never failed that by the time the third soldier was stood up and put in the doorway, he was telling his interrogators, as fast as he could, information that they wanted and could use. Sometimes they would bring that soldier back to base and question him further, but other times if they had what they felt was all he knew or all they could get out of that particular soldier, they would push him out of the doorway anyway.

At first, when Dao was directed by and encouraged by his CIA associates to use the helicopter technique, he was horrified. But as time went on and he found out what the VC were doing to captured South Vietnamese soldiers that were part of his unit, he began to feel that what he was doing was not enough. He began to think that these VC captives needed to suffer more because the tortures used by the VC were so immoral as to almost not be believed. At least what he was doing was quick and easy. They either answered the questions or were given the chance to see if any of them could fly. None of the going several days and nights using absolutely brutal torture like the VC did.

To escape from that life, if even for just a little while, he began to go to strip bars. Even doing that he had a hard time forgetting, for just a little while, what he was doing and had to go back to. At first the strippers could not get his mind off of things that he was part of. Then one day at the infamous Sho Bar, he saw the very pretty Sung Lu.

Sung Lu had long understood, to survive in her world, that befriending powerful people could possibly help her, since she was this poor child coming from the rice paddies. Seeing the uniform of Colonel Dao, she knew that he might be the way things could be made easier for her in her world. She was smart enough to have learned the insignia of a South Vietnamese Army Colonel. The problem was that so had all the other girls at the Sho Bar. But the Colonel liked her look, and he felt there was something special about her. The result was a relationship that lasted until just before the fall of Saigon. She had developed such feelings for him that she wanted them to get married, but he felt that if he did so, the society he had been raised in, which was an upper class Catholic social system, would cause his family to be shunned by their friends,

When the Americans had left Vietnam, Colonel Dao knew it would not be long until the country fell to the North Vietnamese. He also knew that he would probably be killed if he was captured, but only after days of grueling torture. He told Sung Lu that he would find her a way out of South Vietnam. True to his word, he was able to persuade a CIA contact to let Sung Lu get inside the gate at the American embassy compound. There, she might hopefully get on one of the helicopter flights taking Americans and a few select South Vietnamese out of the country to aircraft carriers offshore. He said he would try to find her once he got out if she would go to Los Angeles, where he said many Vietnamese had settled. She had finally gotten on a helicopter flight the last day before the fall of the American embassy, but he was nowhere around.

She had eventually landed by boat in Los Angeles. She heard there that Colonel Dao had been killed while trying to get out of Saigon. He had gotten her out just in time, but he had not made it out himself. After several months in a refugee camp there, she was able to make her way to the Vietnamese community in New Orleans. Having no skill, she began working as a waitress at a restaurant first. She gradually got better with her English, but she was hardly making ends meet. It was then that she met a girl, Doris, who came to work part time as a waitress at the restaurant. Doris also worked at a strip club on Bourbon Street where she made a lot more money. With her help and introduction, it wasn't too long before Sung Lu was stripping in the French Quarter. It seemed that a lot of soldiers and sailors who had been in Vietnam wanted to see a Vietnamese stripper, especially one who was as pretty as Sung Lu. There was only one problem; Sung Lu had tried drugs in Vietnam and liked them, all types. They helped her forget about what she was doing. She hadn't gotten completely hooked in Vietnam and, while spending all that time on a boat in the Pacific before she got to the United States, she had forced herself to be clean. But then she had found out that Colonel Dao had been killed.

Soon after finding out about Colonel Dao, it wasn't too long before she was doing drugs again, this time on Bourbon Street. And this time, she worked herself into harder drugs, specifically cocaine. Also, she and another Vietnamese girl, Chu Ling, had become close friends. Chu introduced her to a man that she said could change Sung Lu's life. That man's name was Juan Bartolli. Bartolli was recognizable because he was usually wearing a white, three piece, polyester suit. He was also recognizable because of his short stature and having a full head of long, jet black hair. But the one thing he enjoyed was sex with, as he called them, his "two slant-eyed" girls. At the same time. Not two weeks would go by before he either sent for them or showed up on the spur of the moment at their strip bar with one or two of the muscle men who always seemed to be with him. There, the two girls would usually take him into one of the back cubicles and make sure they put on a show for him, and sometimes with him. He usually managed to make sure that they were more than happy with the money he left with them for their efforts.

He enjoyed everything about being with them, mainly because they never let him feel bad about being so short. In fact, they were always doing things and saying things that made him feel like he was more than just a man. They made him feel like he was their "stud." Ling remembered how the American soldiers that came to her strip bar in Saigon had always loved it when she made them feel like they were the best sex partners she had ever been with. In fact, it worked so well, she made sure she told each one of them that. And they loved it. Of course they had too many other things on their minds, like staying alive, to worry about how true it may have been. She had heard that Bartolli was a crime boss, and a very rich one at that. She had also heard about his involvement with drugs. When he had found out about her renewed and now more intense habit, he did what he could to make sure his entertainment had all of the drugs she needed, as long as he was taken care of.

On this particular evening, a rough looking young man came into Sung Lu's strip bar. From her experience, both in Vietnam and in New Orleans, she felt he was a cop. She couldn't explain it except to say that being around him just didn't feel right. Part of it was the way he was dressed. What he wore just almost screamed that he was a plain-clothed cop. They never seemed to know that what they wore constantly gave them away. It was as if they had all gone to the same store and bought the same clothes. The other indicator was the way he acted. The previous times this young, almost ugly looking man had come in, he hadn't said a word to anybody. He just sat over in a corner and watched things, just like the Saigon police had done. In particular, he watched every move she made, both on stage and while working the room. But up until now he had never even said "hi" to her. Yet, she always felt as if there was some other reason he was there. It wasn't too long and she found out what that reason was.

This particular night he sent word over by a drink waitress that he wanted Sung to come sit with him. She did and it wasn't too long and he was in there almost every night, always asking her to sit with him. She didn't mind since he was buying her drinks and tipping her for her dances. During their conversations, she found out his name was Joe Thomas and that he worked on off shore oil rigs as a deck hand. Eventually, after about two weeks of that, he told her that he wanted to meet her after work. She agreed to do that, but for a price. After he had suggested he might increase his payment if she invited him over to her place, she told him that she had a roommate but for him to meet her after the bar closed at around 2 in the morning. He stayed until it closed and then spent a couple of hours at her place. The sex was not good at all but the money was alright and, for that, Sung would endure the other, at least until there was a reason not to.

Juan Bartolli was often underestimated. He thought that happened mainly because he was so short, which probably did have something to do with it. Some people would never think that a person of Bartolli's stature would ever be smart. Those people usually figured that a person of limited height probably had limited intelligence, though there was no reason to reach such a conclusion. However, not only had he made good grades in school, he was able to usually be a step ahead of other people in every business effort he had attempted. It all seemed to be that people thought they could take advantage of him because of his height. It was a mistake that was to be to many a person's detriment.

Bartolli enjoyed being with the two Vietnamese girls. First of all, they were nice looking and that meant a lot to him. But they were also always happy and nice around him, even though he knew it was because he treated them well monetarily and supplied them with drugs. What they didn't know was that he had his boys completely check out the two girls. They had been followed, their phones tapped, and their friends talked with, all done very discretely of course. In addition, Bartolli had developed many information sources through the years, including one in particular in the local Drug Enforcement Agency office. So when Joe Thomas started seeing Sung, Bartolli knew about the efforts of the man under contract to that agency before the second meeting ever took place.

*   *   *   *   *   *

Certain portions of the mighty Mississippi River can be very dark, even on normal nights. On nights when there is no moon and there are a lot of clouds, it can be extremely dark around the well-known river. This was one of those nights. It was hard to see much of anything on the water except for one thing - large ocean going freighters. Even on the darkest of nights, the few lights on the forecastles of those types of ships provide eerie appearances for anyone witnessing the passage of such a massive vessel on the river.

On this particular night, just north of the town of Venice where the river is over 70 feet deep just over 50 yards from the shore, as this ship reached that point large packages wrapped in plastic were shoved overboard under the cover of the darkness. Eventually, the packages were gathered up, under Tony's watchful eye, by four men waiting on the banks of the river using grappling hooks. The packages were then loaded, one by one, into two large, previously empty minivans parked near the water's edge. The packages, all 36 of them, contained marijuana which would be transported to locations from Dallas to Atlanta over the next two days for distribution.

Chapter Eleven

As Mark waited in the heavy humidity of the Mekong Delta ambush site in South Vietnam, he had time to think about how he had gotten there. He could do that as long as he kept an active eye on what was happening in front of him as a result of the earlier ambush his Green Beret unit had initiated and the following three hours of battle. He thought about his family, especially his wonderful mother who had always been there for him. He also thought about his father, the personally somewhat cold but well-respected sheriff of Hancock County. He wasn't thinking about them being proud of him at this point in time. He was just hopeful that he could get back alive to see them after doing his job in a way that they might be proud of him, especially his father. His father had never complimented him much, if at all, even though he had been a good student and a fair athlete. He had never given them any trouble, always being aware of how others were watching him because of who his parents were.

Waiting for the next penned down Viet Cong soldier to expose himself gave him time to think about how the Vietnam War had been the deciding factor in so many of the decisions made by the now 23 year old.

Instead of being drafted, Mark had joined the army and had become part of what was known as a Green Beret "A" team. That meant that each one of the ten to twelve members were cross trained in various things such as armaments, medicine, communication, engineering, and in some cases familiarity with certain languages. With his experience as a hunter combined with his knowledge of the outdoors, it was soon apparent to his trainers that Mark's capabilities with a rifle made him uniquely qualified to be a sniper. While he did become familiar with the operations of light and medium automatic weapons, it was when he was holding and using a sniper rifle that he stood out.

Following what amounted to almost a year of intense training, his Green Beret team was sent to Vietnam. Before leaving, Mark had the opportunity to talk with others who had performed there as snipers. After numerous trips to the firing range during which he fired several different sniper rifles, he settled on the one he was most comfortable with, and most accurate with, the Schnizer 501 which fired a 405 bullet. He was told that he also needed to carry a .45 automatic pistol for any close-in experiences he might have over there.

Upon arriving in Saigon, the team had been assigned in the Mekong River delta to an area that was almost totally swamp, having only limited tree coverage. The commanding officer in their field of operation had decided to fight a guerilla style war against the communist Viet Cong instead of using conventional tactics. That strategy had proven to be hugely successful so far and showed promise for future actions. Mark's unit had conducted two successful ambushes of Viet Cong forces as they moved through the swampy area but they had lost two of the original twelve members of their "A" team. Having been trained together and having learned to trust each other and how each one of them functioned and thought, they requested that no new members be assigned to their team. Their request was granted and they had been sent out again to set up another ambush.

Now there he was, next to a narrow tree line in the middle of nowhere, southwest of Saigon on the edge of a huge, water covered rice field that had dykes, a foot to two feet high, running all over the place. Penned down in that open field was an entire company, about 150 men, of Viet Cong, at least those who had survived the initial burst of automatic weapons fire from Mark and his fellow Green Berets, and their subsequent fire for the next three hours. Mark's group had been in place for most of the day and had not been noticed by the VC as they had made their way across the rice fields. Once the VC group had gotten within 75 yards of the ambushers, the firefight had started.

Mark had used his rifle with deadly accuracy. After the initial ambush, the VC had tried to charge the tree line, only to be cut to pieces by automatic weapons fire and Mark's rifle. That attack had resulted in two of his fellow Green Berets being killed and two more wounded. One of the wounded kept crying out in agony, each noise drawing gunfire from the VC which was directed to the area of the cries. No one could go help the man. He had been trained to mend his own wounds, but he was obviously in bad shape. The other wounded man kept firing from his position hidden in the tree line. Mark had seen him hit twice and wondered how he was able to still function because, Mark was sure, one shot had shattered his left arm. He also wondered where the VC soldiers in the group were that had been carrying the rocket propelled grenades. He had seen the tubes that would launch the grenades and had hit two of the men carrying them when they had tried to fire those deadly weapons. But there had been more than two, at least five or six. He kept searching for those identifying tubes.

"They are trying to get to our tree line!" their leader, Captain Andy Jones, yelled out. Mark could see that several of the VC, thinking that all of them would not be hit if a small group made the effort at the same time, were trying to run and crawl over the dykes toward the same tree line that Mark and his fellow soldiers were hiding in. Mark sited, fired, hit scored; sited, fired, hit scored; sited again, missed, fired again, hit scored.

"Sam, come with me! We've gotta stop them!" shouted the captain, who then attempted to crawl along the base of the tree line in an attempt to intercept the VC flanking effort. The captain's words drew fire, which Mark and his unwounded friends returned. Then there was quietness.

After a short lull, three VC got up at the same time and started running towards the tree line, which was now only about twenty yards from them.

The captain fired, hitting two but as he was firing at the third, up popped a VC gunner with a tube. Mark sited, fired, but not before the gunner had gotten off his round, which landed at the Captain's feet.

WHAMMMMMMMMMMMM!!!!!!!

Mark saw the explosion throw the Captain up in the air and back into the trees. He then looked back towards the gunner. He had hit him, but it had been a split second too late.

AHHHHHHHHHHHHHHHHHHHHHHHH!

Mark felt something pulling on his right arm as he screamed out. He jerked his arm away, taking his fist back to punch whoever was tugging his arm. It was then that he woke up. He saw it was Karen that had been pulling on his arm. She moved back, putting both of her hands up to protect her face. He had hit her before when this had happened. Mark realized that he was in her bed, having stayed there after spending time having sex with her and then going to sleep.

She stared at him, apprehensive about what might happen next. Seeing him hesitate, she knew she had better say something, very calmly but something.

"It's okay, honey," she said softly, watching as Mark's hard breathing began to lessen. "It's okay. It's me," she continued as she then gently moved forward to hold him. She slowly put her arms around him, and cuddled him as he began to cry.

"That's okay, honey. Just let it go, its okay." Mark began sobbing deeply as she held him. After a few moments, he turned his head towards her, tears running down his face.

"I'm so sorry," he barely was able to mumble before he turned his head away from her and began deeply sobbing.

*   *   *   *   *

Tony knew the minute he might be spending some time on the Mississippi gulf coast that he had to have something sent to him from Sicily. It was just that he felt that there wasn't going to be much to do around Bay St. Louis that would be a lot of fun and there was one thing he did know, from so many past experiences,

141

that would be fun for him to have with him. That was his Ducati 750, his motorcycle. Now the Ducati was not just any motorcycle. It was world famous. That was why he had one because, since he had been 16, he had ridden motorcycles. When he had gotten to where he could afford one for his very own, he already knew about the Ducati. Anybody who knew anything about motorcycles knew about the Ducati 750. It was just the coolest motorcycle on the planet. Not only that, it was considered by most people who knew anything about motorcycles to be the very best. And oh by the way, it just happened to be considered by those who knew those kinds of things as the fastest motorcycle on earth. With its sleek lines and absolute power, it had been a thrill to ride every time Tony had ever gotten on his and gone anywhere. So he did what only a motorcycle lover would do, and he could afford to do it. He sent back to Sicily and had his cousins have his motorcycle packaged and sent, by airplane, to New Orleans. From there he had it shipped over to Bay St. Louis to his little, somewhat dilapidated house at the end of the street.

The first thing he did when it was delivered was to unpack it, which took quite a while because of the excellent job that had been done in Sicily preparing the motorcycle for its trip. He next put some gas in it from a portable tank he had purchased at a local hardware store and filled up in anticipation of the arrival of his playtoy. His first ride around the outskirts of town was simply exhilarating and was soon followed by daily excursions, both to enjoy his toy being there but also to enjoy the beautiful local weather and scenery. The feel of the wind in his face and the deep, throaty sound of his machine gave him a feeling of total freedom and independence. Almost every time he was thinking about taking his ride out for a spin, he would at some point think of one of his favorite American made movies, "Born to Be Wild," in which two relative unknown actors in a low budget film had become famous, in part, because of riding a motorcycle. That movie had been criticized by many due to its somewhat rebellious tone but, to Tony, it had symbolized freedom. Though he and his father had a good relationship, it still felt like nothing else to get on his cycle and go feel the wind.

As Tony settled into his home, he began to enjoy the company of his little visitor, the baby cocker spaniel that he soon named Buddy. He named the puppy that because that was exactly what he was. He was Tony's buddy. Tony found a local veterinarian and had the puppy vaccinated. It wasn't long and he decided that he needed to have it so that Buddy could go along with him on his motorcycle rides. First, though, he had to have something made for his new little friend to ride in. So he went by the local hardware store where he described the type of saddlebag he wanted so that he could carry his puppy with him on his excursions around town and out into the countryside. A very kind salesman at the store was able to identify an individual at a blacksmith's shop that would probably be able to make that special saddlebag for him.

After a short ride out into the northern part of Hancock County to a stable area on a farm where the blacksmith worked, Tony was able to describe to the bulky, overweight worker what he wanted made. Being told to return in about a week, Tony had been able to finally get his saddlebags after a two week delay due to what the blacksmith called "unusually high demand" for his services. It seems there was a rodeo and horse show coming up soon and those from the local area who would be participating in that event in the state capitol of Jackson just demanded that their needs be met first.

Tony now had the immediate problem, if he wanted the little fella to ride with him on his motorcycle, of getting this brand new being, his puppy, used to the loud sound of a motorcycle engine.

The first time he started the engine of his motorcycle around his puppy, he had the small animal tied to one of the railings of the garage door. Tony just knew how massive the mechanical beast must seem to the puppy so he took the cycle out into his front yard all the way down to the street before he started it. Needless to say, the little animal was put into constant motion by the loud noise as Tony neared the house riding it. The puppy tried every way possible to get away and go somewhere safe from what, Tony could tell for sure the dog thought, was a scary noise.

Tony took his time trying to get his little friend used to the sound. First tying the puppy to the garage railing, he would then drive up the street and back down. He would pull into the driveway and then drive back out. Gradually, over a period of the next three days, Buddy became more and more accustomed to its sound, especially when Tony started holding the puppy as he walked over to the machine, got on it and started it. Eventually he was able to let the animal gradually be aware of the louder sounds of the motor by gunning the engine while the motorcycle was idling. The day finally arrived that he was able to put his small friend into the saddle bag behind him and take him down the driveway. Not too long afterwards, he drove him up the block. From then on, taking a ride was a piece of cake for the puppy, as long as he could be down inside the saddlebag, sometimes with just his nose sticking out and occasionally with his head completely showing. Tony gradually began driving around the area, sometimes even going down beachfront road and into the downtown Bay St. Louis area of stores and buildings, usually with his puppy in the right side saddlebag. To his even greater surprise, after a few short rides with the puppy in one of the saddle bags, if Tony got on the motorcycle and looked like he was going to leave Buddy at the house, the dog would literally bark his little head off. He did not like being left alone at the house by his master.

On this particular Saturday morning, Tony was taking his young friend for a ride downtown. When he turned off of Beachfront Road and headed towards the massive Hancock County office building, he noticed a beautiful girl walk out of one of the dress shops along the street. It was Karen. She looked stunning in the sunlight where he could evaluate every curve of her body. She had been impressive that first night he had met her but now, she almost caused him to run into a parked car. She had that air of confidence that some women have if they know they are good looking. But at the same time, she was not offensive about it, just, well, confident.

Tony slowed down and pulled over to the right side of the street as much as he could and then eventually stopped in front of the good looking female animal. He admired the view. She was in a light green tee top, fashionably tight, white pants, and beach flats. He couldn't resist saying the first thing that came to his mind.

"Want a ride?"

His big smile solicited from her a smile below the huge black sunglasses she was wearing under her stylish, white straw hat.

Looking at the puppy's little face as it protruded from the cover of the saddlebag, she said, "Thanks, but the puppy's in the way." She reached down and petted the small animal on his head, then continued, "Besides, I don't ride motorcycles. I ride horses."

Tony said, "Oh really? Well, I don't ride horses because they are so unpredictable." As she began to stand up, he continued, "I ride my motorcycle because I know it will do what I want it to do."

After a brief look over his cycle, she answered, "I ride my horses because they do, exactly, what I want them to do." Her grin was just too much for him. He couldn't help but chuckle.

"I bet they do. If I was one of your horses, I certainly would." With a horn now beginning to blow from the car behind him, he smiled and waived, saying, "It definitely is time for me to be leaving."

She smiled and said, "Don't get lost in this big town, ok? And take care of that little puppy. He's cute."

"I will. His name's Buddy. Good to see you. See you at the Baked whatever it is." With that, he pulled away.

That night, at Karen's house in her bedroom, she and Mark were resting from their latest sexual encounter. That had been going on for almost a year now. Usually once or twice a week, sometimes even three times, they would meet, usually at her place, for fun and games. At first, for her it was an attraction thing for sure. Mark was in excellent shape, the result of his years of training in the army but also his continued effort to maintain his strength in case he found it necessary to use it as a result of his job. He did not want to get caught short of having whatever strength he might need. If he ever did need physical strength, he knew that it was something that had to be planned for in advance because it surely was not going to just appear when he had to have it.

Karen was attracted by Mark's looks when she had first met him. She was happy that he had shown an interest in her because she had been told by her little gang of friends that Mark was very quiet and not what they called a "player", a guy who went from girl to girl. Not that there weren't girls who made themselves appear as if he was the most important person in the world to them because several had already tried that tactic. But Karen was

146

just herself, calm, cool and collected and the best part was that Mark seemed more willing to talk with her than almost anyone else.

So it hadn't been too long after they had started dating that they had also started having sex. That was the part that had surprised her. With his reputation as a quiet person, she was not sure what to expect in bed. Was she ever surprised and that, to some extent, had kept her coming back for more. What was great about it was he seemed to enjoy it as much as she did. Now, after all these months, she was ready to move their relationship to another level. She wanted to get married, but she also did not want to scare him off. At what she considered to be the old age of 28, she didn't know how many more men she would ever meet that she would actually get along with. She definitely wanted one that wanted to be with her because he genuinely loved her, not just because she was beautiful and, oh by the way she thought, good in bed.

Tonight was like other nights they had spent time together. After their first rather lengthy session, they usually talked, and tonight was no exception.

As they lounged in her bed, she turned over on her side to face him and said, "I saw your new friend, Tony, today."

"Oh, really. And where might that have been?"

"On the street, as I was coming out of Mrs. Myrtle's shop."

"Oh, was he going shopping at Mrs. Myrtle's? I was wondering about him, you know," he said with a slight grin on his face.

"Nooo! I don't think he is like that."

"Like what? Into things like Mrs. Myrtle's?"

"No. I don't think he was interested in Mrs. Myrtle's. He was driving by on that motorcycle of his and stopped for a moment."

"Oh, really? Put any moves on you?"

"Noooooo! He was nice. Had the cutest little puppy with him. Looked like a little cocker spaniel. Said his name was Buddy. Had him riding in a saddle bag he had over the seat behind him." She then sat up and crossed her legs on the bed facing her lover.

"What have you heard about him?" she asked, clearly interested in what her lover had to say.

Mark pushed with both hands so that now he could sit up with his back against the headboard.

"Why do you ask? Am I going to be traded off for this guy?" he playfully asked.

"Nooooo. Honey, you know you are not going to be traded off unless you want to be," she retorted in somewhat of a serious tone.

"The girls are all talking about him. He is a nice looking man and they have heard rumors that he was part of the estate of that woman who died recently. You know, the one who lived like a hermit by herself out in the swamp.

"Sounds like I should get the girls to help me get information on some of my cases. What else has the local intelligence group found out?"

"Wellllllllll, now that you asked, they say he is not married, that he came here just for the reading of her will, and that he may have gotten some of her estate money."

"Have they found out whether he is good in bed or not yet? I mean, for that group, that shouldn't take long to find out."

"You are so bad!" she said as she started laughing. "No, but I wouldn't put it past Carol to find out."

"Carol? Just Carol? I wouldn't put it past almost any of them to try to find out. If they all think he inherited a bunch of money from that estate, they will all be throwing themselves at the poor guy. Are you going to be doing that? Are you going to be getting in that line to see if you can get some of his money," he asked in a teasing voice.

"I've got what I want. I'm just having a hard time convincing him that I am what he needs," she said as she poked him in his ribs.

Reacting to her poke, he playfully said, "He's convinced! He's convinced. He just doesn't want to get married just yet."

"Just yet? How long are you going to wait? I don't have forever, you know. My clock is ticking. You know how I feel about that. I want kids, and I want them before I get too old to enjoy them. Don't you want kids too? You've told me that you do. Don't you?"

"Some day, you know I do. We have had this discussion a few times before, you know. I just don't want them now."

"Well, how long do I have to wait? Just tell me, how long?"

"I don't know. I really don't. I may never be ready. You know that."

"Look, I can't wait forever, you know. I really can't."

"I know. I know, Look, you know I have told you that if you want to date other people, go ahead. I don't want you to but I can't blame you. But I just can't commit to getting married right now, not with all the feelings I still have from Vietnam."

She looked at her handsome former soldier. He was nice looking, that was for sure, and he had a good heart, she felt. It was just that he was not going to budge, right now, about getting married. She would still just date him, for the time being, but the time was not far off that he was either going to have to make up his mind and marry her or she was going to find someone else to date. He knew that. She had told him that so many times already. So she might as well get back to the new guy in town.

"You are always priding yourself on your judge of character in a person. What's your feeling about him?"

Thinking for a moment, glad she had gotten away from the marriage issue, the deputy said, "He seems to be a nice enough guy. He doesn't seem to be like the average guy you would met in that place, but then he is not from here. There seems to be more to him, but now that doesn't mean I am recommending him to any of your ladies in that group of yours."

She paused for a brief second and then said, "He told me he wants to take me for a ride on that motorcycle of his." She watched for his reaction.

"What did you tell him?"

"I told him I didn't ride motorcycles, that I rode horses because I could control them. He said he could control his motorcycles," she said with a chuckle.

"Oh he did, did he? Pretty good answer, seems like to me."

After a brief second, he grabbed her and pulled her over on top of him. Before kissing her, he said, "We need to get some more practice on what we were doing before all this talk." After a long, deep kiss, she said, "You know how much I love practice." A long evening of it followed.

Chapter Twelve

Miss Peabody did not have a good feeling after her group's meeting with Sheriff Burdette. She had literally a lifetime of experience observing people, though granted it had been mostly that of young students. But she was more than comfortable with relying on her personal feelings and senses after experiencing the activities of males and females while serving in the noble profession of school teacher. So as she thought about the sheriff's reaction during their meeting, she continuously kept coming up with the same conclusion. The sheriff was very slick. His demeanor during that meeting, the cool way he observed them, the total lack of any response until almost the last moment of the meeting, just kept leading Bertha Sue to reach the same conclusion again and again. He was slick alright, and not only was he slick, he was hiding something.

When they had brought up the subject of drug shipments near

the beginning of the meeting, he had the same reaction to what was said to him as if they had been talking about dishwater, which was nothing. That reaction was the direct opposite of the mayor's. Certainly it could be said that the two men had completely different personalities, but there was just something about Raymond Burdette.

She had even felt a tinge of hostility from the sheriff towards the end of the meeting. That had happened at the point when the sheriff seemed to get tired of putting up with them and had decided it was time for them to leave. He had raised his voice, leaned forward and put his arms on his desk, and basically told them that he was asking for more money for his office and that should be enough of an effort by him so, now, go away and leave him alone.

After thinking about it for a few days, usually as she held Tricksy in her arms while looking out her picture window at her beautiful back yard, she came to a conclusion. She was going to have to come up with something that would get Sheriff Raymond Burdette's attention. He, being a public servant of the people, was going to have to show more "get up and go" about this issue. He was also going to have to show more appreciation for who he was dealing with. Whether it be by presenting classes at the public schools on the dangers of drugs or actively being at the forefront of seizures in the county, the sheriff was going to have to do something and she was going to see to it that he did. Maybe he was really just a wimp and all he needed was a push in the right direction. Well, Miss Bertha Sue Peabody was going to be just the person to provide this weak-kneed man with the push he needed.

At the next weekly bridge club get-together, Bertha Sue waited until just the right moment, about midway through their afternoon, before she stood up and said she had an announcement for them. With everyone's attention directed toward their courageous leader, she said, "All of you are aware of our efforts to get something done in our community about this horrible illegal drug situation. We had what I think we all thought was a good meeting with the mayor, who was very supportive of our effort. I, for one, really appreciated the mayor's acceptance of our presentation and his response, which I thought was most proper."

Taking a moment to walk away from the area where she had been seated to go to a position more between the tables, she then said, "And while we did get a pleasant reception from Sheriff Burdette during our visit with him, he really only listened and didn't do much else." Saying this, she saw two of the girls bend their heads down toward the table at which they were seated as if to say, "You are not going to bring this up again, are you?" But Bertha Sue insisted to herself that she was going to go forward with her new plan.

"Girls, I think we need to get a larger group together and go back to see Sheriff Burdette." Looking around the tables, she felt now was the right time to make her pitch. "I think we need to enlist our friends in the garden club, the various church clubs and every other public service club we have contacts with to support us in a follow-up meeting with the sheriff." She could see that each one was thinking about how it all might come together. She decided now was the time to press the matter further.

"I think that, if we could gather a nice sized little crowd at the sheriff's office, then he might appreciate more our sincerity concerning this very important issue. I think we need to identify others that might support us, have a little meeting to get a group together, set up an appointment to meet with him and then go see him, all together."

After a moment of silence, her longtime friend, Pippy Strickland, said, "I think that's a good idea. Maybe that would get his attention, if we just had more people there, to show him that we think that the drug issue thing is really important." Pippy saying that immediately took the pressure off of Bertha Sue and she breathed a sigh of relief to herself. She didn't want to be the only one in the room thinking it was a good idea. Why, if that had happened, she would lose a lot of her credibility.

"Okay, is everybody in general agreement with doing this?" she asked as she looked around the room.

Before she could say anything else, one of the girls who had been going through various problems with her oldest son spoke up.

"Bertha Sue, are you sure you want to get this far into all of this? I mean, we are talking about things that are illegal and isn't that something the authorities are responsible for taking care of? We have our daily lives to think about and, besides, they get paid for taking care of things like that. Is this something you really think we should get ourselves into?"

There was quietness in the room for a moment as everyone considered what had just been said. Then Bertha Sue again took center stage.

"Look, it's not like I would be asking any of you to go out on a patrol or make an arrest or go out interviewing people that might be involved in it all. All I am asking is for this club, and other clubs, to get together to impress upon the sheriff how important we think the illegal drug situation is in our community. You are right in that it's his job to do something about it. I just want to make sure he takes the drug problem in our county as seriously as we do and that he knows how we feel about it."

Pippy then said, "Okay, I am with you. I think if we don't do things like this, then he may not know exactly how strongly we feel about it. So I will get in touch with the girls in the garden club."

"Thanks, Pippy," Bertha Sue said, right before she asked, "Okay, who is going to contact the church clubs?" One of the other girls said she would undertake that effort and before too long, several other clubs were identified and girls designated as being responsible for contacting them.

It wasn't two weeks and a group had been put together representing seven different social clubs and church groups. It was decided that the sheriff's office would now be contacted to set up a meeting. When that contact was made, Bertha Sue told the secretary taking the call that she expected over thirty women to be present for the meeting. The secretary said that she would talk with the sheriff and get back to Bertha Sue to let her know when and where the meeting could take place. After a couple of days, the sheriff's office called to notify Bertha Sue that he would be happy to meet with the group in the circuit courtroom upstairs at the Hancock County Courthouse. It was big enough to handle such a crowd of citizens. The meeting was set for the following Tuesday morning at 10. Bertha Sue was convinced by some in her group that having the meeting in the morning would mean they would not have to miss performing their family duties at their respective homes, such as preparing dinner and helping younger family members with their homework, as they would if the meeting were held at 6 in the evening.

When the meeting took place, several county and city officials were in the room. Everybody wanted to know what the group was going to say and how they would say it. All of the officials wanted it to be well known that they agreed with the citizens' effort to support wiping out drug traffic in their community and the surrounding area. Bertha Sue was in her element. It was almost as if she was back teaching class as she guided the attendees through the bad effects drugs have on kids and communities in general. After her presentation, there was an extensive round of applause, not only from her club supporters but also from the attending officials and other members of the public. The mayor followed Bertha Sue and made a brief but very supportive statement which was followed by another loud round of applause. The sheriff then stood up to make his presentation.

"I want to thank Miss Bertha Sue Peabody for putting this all together. Let's give her another round of applause." Every pair of hands in the large room entered into a prolonged period of clapping, to which Bertha Sue smiled and nodded her head in appreciation. Then the sheriff continued.

"Certainly every elected official in the town of Bay St. Louis and every citizen in this county knows of her untiring efforts to better our lives. Now she has helped us all by focusing our attention on this epidemic of drugs that we are now enduring. Please rest assured, as I have previously mentioned to Miss Bertha Sue, that I will do everything possible, everything in my power, to see to it that the office of sheriff is fully equipped and fully manned in this fight against drugs. I will be asking the Hancock County Board of Supervisors for a substantial increase in funds to be made available to my office to help us so that we can combat this horrible assault on the lives of our families, our friends and our neighbors."

Now having the rapt attention of everyone in the large room, the sheriff said, "If any of you have any further ideas about how we might, together, fight this horrible problem, please contact my office and either let me or my top community specialist, Mr. Larry Brown here, know what you have in mind. Stand up, Larry, so if there is anyone here that doesn't know who you are, they will know you now." Larry stood up from his front row seat, smiled and politely waved to the crowd, then sat back down.

"We will be applying for more assistance from the State of Mississippi. A lot of that will depend on how much we get allocated to Hancock County from any additional funds appropriated by our state legislature."

Then after taking a short breath, he said, "Once again, thanks so much to each one of you for attending today's event. I'll look forward to seeing you around our beloved Bay St. Louis and Hancock County." As the crowd politely applauded, the sheriff moved back over to the rear area of the upper level where he had previously been standing. After a closing comment by the mayor, the meeting was adjourned just before 10:45.

Many of the attendees came over to Bertha Sue and complimented her on her presentation and her effort in putting the event together. As she and her cadre of associates began to leave the room, she looked over at the sheriff and noticed a hard facial expression that did not give her comfort as he looked back at her. She and her group left the building and Bertha Sue was back at her house by 11:30. As she picked up Tricksy and walked back to her picture window overlooking her pristine back yard, she thought about the event that had just taken place. It was then, the more she thought about it, that she realized that the sheriff had not once, not even once, said that he would do whatever he could to stop the drug activity. That realization caused her to have another slight feeling of discomfort.

Two nights later, the weekly gathering of the girls on Thursday

157

night at the Baked Tomato began with several comments about Tuesday's big event. But it wasn't long and Sarah just had to tell them.

"Girls, I have major news."

The chatter immediately stopped as each of the three other girls gave their full attention to the one who had spoken those words.

"It happened again yesterday," Sarah said as she looked around the table.

"Honey, you are going to have to be more specific," said Molly, the unofficial chairman of the meetings. "You know we do cover lots of topics in these little get-togethers. What are you talking about?"

Sarah leaned forward and almost in a whisper, said, "You know who came in yesterday and did it again. Bought both his wife and that girl more sexy lingerie."

"My goodness," Molly exclaimed. "That man has a problem."

"He did that again yesterday?" asked Sue, in an almost unbelieving tone.

"Yessssssss! Yesterday!" Sarah answered. "And I did it."

"You did what?" Molly asked.

"You didn't swap them, did you?" Karen all but exclaimed under her breath.

"You didn't!" Sue almost whispered.

"I did!" Sarah said with a big smile on her face.

"You actually did that?" asked Molly.

"You actually swapped their lingerie?" Karen asked in disbelief.

"I put things in the wrong boxes," she answered very quietly.

The three girls were quiet for a moment and then broke out in howls. The laughter grew louder as even Sarah joined them. After the initial outburst, it got quiet for a moment and Sarah continued.

"I have heard that both of them are just mad as they can be. The girlfriend wanted to know why he thought she was that fat. He had never thought that before with what he had bought her so it must be that it was intended for his wife. She was upset he had bought that lingerie for his wife. Then when he got home his wife screamed and yelled at him because she had this little thing that she obviously could not get into which meant it was for somebody else."

With that story being told, the group again broke out into loud laughter. In fact, their laughter was so loud that tables around them began to ask what was so funny. None of them confessed then, but by the end of the next day their little secret was all over town.

Kovac did not know how it happened, but he did know one thing for sure. It had happened. For the next few days, he caught it repeatedly from both women. By the end of the following week, he had moved out of his house. Not only that, now he had his so-called friends kidding him about it, having heard about it through the rumor mill. He was at the point that he did what he felt he had to do. Over drinks one afternoon, he told his friend, Sheriff Raymond Burdette, about his wife and lady friend getting packages, each meant for the other. He told the sheriff that the exchange had caused him to literally be thrown out of his house by his wife and that his girlfriend would no longer see him.

After taking another full sip from his bourbon and water, Kovac said, "I am sure that the clerk at the store did it. She swapped the items in the packages before she wrapped them."

Shaking his head almost violently, he turned to the sheriff and said, "Isn't there anything you can do about what that clerk did?"

Burdette looked at the banker and, after a moment, said, "You helped me with that last big deposit I made at your place. I'll see if there is something I can do for you." Kovac nodded his head as if to say "Okay" and then took another big swig from his glass.

Chapter Thirteen

Tony walked into the Baked Tomato and looked around. It was about 8:30 or so and the deputy was already in his normal place at the end of the bar with his back to the wall. Tony walked over to where the deputy was seated and said, "Hello, deputy. Mind if I join you?"

Looking at the new arrival, Mark said, "Not at all." Then he motioned to the adjacent chair and said, "Have a seat."

"Thanks," Tony said as he crawled up into the chair.

The bartender was over immediately and asked, "What can I get you?"

"A Bud would be just fine," he answered, to which the bartender immediately sprung into action by taking a couple of steps over to one of the large coolers behind him, sliding open the top and pulling out a Budweiser in a can. He then brought the can over and placed it on a napkin in front of Tony. Tony already had his wallet in his hand and pulled out a $20. The bartender went over to his register, taking a verbal order from someone at the bar on his way.

Mark then said, "Remember that guy I mentioned to you that was in the hospital here?"

Tony looked at the deputy and didn't say a word. After not hearing anything in response for a few seconds, Mark continued. "He said he was driven to the hospital in an old Ford four-door. He said the man who took him to the hospital also came to see him there a few days later."

Looking at Tony and not hearing anything in response to his statement, he specifically asked, "You don't know anything about any of that, now do you?"

After a moment of quietness, Tony said, "I don't know hardly anybody here yet, at least not to the extent that you might be interested. But I do know a few things about John F. Kennedy." That sentence definitely got the deputy's mind off of the hospital.

"President John F. Kennedy?" Mark asked.

"Yes, President John F. Kennedy, the one who didn't finish his first term as President here."

"Why do you know things about Kennedy?" Mark asked with a quizzical look on his face.

Tony took the change for his drink from the bartender and, now holding his drink in his hand, he turned his swivel bar chair towards the deputy.

"Because he is my longtime idol. I have read everything I can get my hands on about him, ever since I was a kid."

"You are a fan of his? Why is that?" Mark asked, really wondering what the answer was going to be.

Tony looked over at him, and then said, "Well, he was good looking, like me." He followed that with a chuckle and said, "Well, let me change that. Let me say instead that he looked like I always wanted to look. Handsome, well-dressed, great personality, good with everybody he met, especially the ladies, like I always have tried to be. I've read so much about him."

Mark leaned back in his chair and listened.

"I mean, he had all that money, that big family, did some good things while in the Navy during World War II, was a nice looking guy, had a beautiful wife, had those kids, and won that election for President that he really was not expected to win." Mark took a sip from his drink and continued to listen.

"I got really interested in the guy, everything he did, what all he tried to do, and then for that assassination to happen. It just doesn't add up. Never has, to me."

"Why not?" Mark asked as he took a quick glance around the room at the accumulating crowd.

"Well, for example was it really possible for Oswald to fire those shots that quickly with that rifle? And even if he did that, was he good enough to hit Kennedy with the shot that really seemed to be the one that killed him? That bolt action rifle he supposedly did that with, could he fire that thing three times and be that accurate with the car going away from him at the angle it did? Did you ever wonder about any of that?"

Mark kept quiet for a few seconds, with Tony staring at his face, studying it to determine if his question was going to be answered. Then Mark said, "What else have you wondered about with all of that?" Tony leaped at the chance to continue the conversation on the subject.

"Oh, I have thought about it so much. I mean, I admire the guy, how popular he was, how his family seemed to help him get elected, how his friends seemed to rally around him, how much money he seemed to be able to raise and how completely different people seemed to come together to support him and helped him get elected." He then took another sip of his beer before continuing.

"But the main thing is it all just doesn't seem to add up. I really thought that the Warren Commission investigation would have gotten into more things than it did. But you know how that came out, with it's report and all and what it said."

"What did you think of its conclusions?" Mark asked.

"Like I said, there are just too many things that don't add up, to me at least, the way that Commission thought they did. Those things, plus other things that seem to sort of dribble out every now and then just make me wonder even more. I mean, I really liked the guy, his charm, the way he was almost always surrounded by women who seemed to want to get his attention and yet, there he was, married to that beautiful, classy lady and they had those kids. I'll never forget that salute the little boy did at the funeral."

Mark looked at the man in the chair next to him. He was convinced that Tony was being truthful about his interest in Kennedy. The look on Tony's face and the tone of his voice as he talked set forth an aura of absolute sincerity.

"So do you think there is more to all of that about his assassination?" Mark asked.

"Absolutely. I do. Definitely. I mean, I think there is so much more to it than we all know and it already has been a lot of years since it happened."

"I think there are a bunch of questions about a lot of things that happened during his presidency," Mark said in a low, firm voice.

"Oh, really? Things such as what?" Tony asked with now all of his attention on the deputy.

Mark looked at him for a moment and then said, "Well, for one thing, why did he plan and start an invasion of Cuba, but then refused to provide it with air support at a critical point? Do you think some people might have gotten upset when that happened?"

At that time, Karen stood up from her table with her three friends, standing there speaking with them near the center of the room.

Tony quickly changed the subject, wanting to ask the deputy about her before she came over as it looked like she was getting ready to do.

"Hey, by the way, somebody told me that Karen there is your longtime girlfriend," he said quickly, hoping to find out a little bit about their relationship.

"Well, she sort of is, or at least has been. But she wants to get married and I am not quite ready for that. I am just not ready to move on into that yet. As a matter of fact, we just agreed the other day that we would start dating other people."

At that very moment, up walked beautiful Karen with a big smile on her face.

"Hi there, Tony. Where have you been? We were wondering where you had disappeared to?" she asked in a kidding manner.

"Hi, Karen. I am glad you guys missed me. I had to do a little traveling around and just got back. Had to go take care of a few things. How have you been?"

"Fine," she answered, and Tony could not have agreed more. She was definitely fine, to his thinking. It was just that he was thinking about a different kind of "fine" from what she was thinking.

Turning to Mark, Tony said, "I saw your girlfriend here on the street the other day and invited her to go riding on my motorcycle with me. I had my little puppy with me but she declined, saying that she would rather ride horses than ride on motorcycles."

Karen said, "Well, I can go riding with you now since he seems to not mind if I spend time with other men."

Not wanting to get in the middle of anything unsettled, Tony said, "Well, I just thought you might enjoy the ride, especially if you enjoy riding horses. I promise you that motorcycle riding is not as rough on a person."

"I'll tell you what, Mr. Easy Rider, I will ride on your motorcycle with you if you will ride horses with me. As I said, I can do that now that he doesn't mind me seeing other men," she said, obviously taking another dig at the deputy.

Looking at the deputy, Tony said, "If he doesn't mind, I'll do that. I'll agree to that challenge. As long as your boyfriend here doesn't mind. But I have to tell you that I have never ridden a horse. I guess it is about time."

"Well, he doesn't have anything to say about it anymore," she answered. "I have never ridden a motorcycle so we will both be having a first time experience."

166

Looking at Mark, Tony asked, "Are you sure you are alright with this? I don't want to cause a problem here."

The deputy somewhat reluctantly said, "It's her choice."

Looking back at Karen, Tony said, "Okay, I will pick you up in front of here this coming Saturday at 10 o'clock and we will go for a short ride, about a half hour or so. Then, if you will make the arrangements, we can go somewhere and I will try to ride a horse, for the first time in my life."

Karen looked back at Tony and said, "Getting a horse for you to ride is not a problem. We have some out at our farm. There is one in particular out there that you may really enjoy riding." As she finished saying that, she glanced at Mark with a slight smile on her face.

Tony knew if he was ever going to ride a horse, now would be as good of a time as any. Besides, he was looking forward to watching her ride a horse, which should include observing her and her magnificent breasts bounce around for a half-hour or so. Then he decided he had better do the nice thing to show the deputy he was going to be harmless with the deputy's somewhat "former" girlfriend by asking him if he wanted to be there.

Turning to Mark, he said, "You are most welcome to come watch her ride on my motorbike and to watch me ride her horse, if you would like."

Mark smiled at the suggestion, answering, "Oh, I think I will pass on watching her ride with you on your motorcycle but, if you actually do go out to her place to ride a horse, now that may be something I might want to see."

"Great!" Tony said. Turning to Karen, he said, "Okay, this Saturday here at 10 o'clock in the morning, out front. We'll meet and see how you do riding my metal animal, and then we will go to your farm. You'll have to let me follow you because I don't know where anything is around here. And I will ride one of your horses."

Looking first at Mark and then at Tony, now with a smile on her face, Karen said, "Okay. You've got a deal. Ten a.m. it is, this Saturday out front, then to our farm for your ride on a horse. And Mark can be at both of those, if you want to be there," she said, now looking back at him.

"We'll see how that works out, depending on what comes up with my job," Mark answered.

"Okay. Saturday morning it is," Tony said. He immediately began wondering if he had done the right thing or not. One thing was for sure, if Mark was there it might give him the opportunity to explore getting him to look the other way sometimes for shipments. He would have to be careful about how and when he presented that situation to the deputy sheriff. He also knew one other thing for sure. He wanted to spend more time with Mark discussing the assassination of his idol, John F. Kennedy.

Chapter Fourteen

Tony still was not comfortable being at Bartolli's ranch. There was just this feeling while he was out there that it was an evil place, a place where things happened that should only be happening in movies. The difference was that on the ranch it all was for real. Now he was back out there to find out what else the head man was going to allow him to see of his operation.

Tony greeted the man standing near the front door with a nod of his head. The man opened the door to the house as he said, "Go on down the hallway to his office. He has somebody with him but go on in."

Tony could hear voices, one of which he recognized as Bartolli's. As he got to the doorway to Bartolli's office, Bartolli saw him and motioned with his hand for him to come on into the room. He was talking to a man seated in one of the two high backed chairs in front of the massive desk with that cannon on it that he had noticed before. The short, stocky man sitting in front of the desk was wearing blue jeans and a short sleeved shirt that had the top two buttons unbuttoned. His dark complexion and black hair suggested that the man was either Vietnamese or maybe even Mexican. Sam was standing not too far from where the man was seated.

"So you want to work for me, huh?" Bartolli said.

"Yeah, I do a good job for you. Do whatever you tell me to do."

Bartolli eyed the man, not paying much attention to Sam or Tony. The sheriff and another man Tony had seen there before were in the room also. At that moment, a Vietnamese girl walked into the room and went over to stand right next to where Bartolli was seated.

"Well then, tell me, big man, how can you work for me and have me trust you when you are working as an undercover cop for the U. S. government?"

Tony saw the big guy was clearly shocked by what was said. The man's eyes immediately got really wide, like those of animals looked when they are scared or running for their lives.

"What chu mean saying that? Me, working for the government? Not a chance," he said as he shifted his eyes towards the Vietnamese woman.

Bartolli said, "You must really think I am a real dumbass." Sitting back in his chair, he continued, "Big guy, she found out about you." As he completed that sentence, Bartolli extended his left hand, which had a packet of cocaine in it, and the Vietnamese girl reached out with her right hand and took it. "She sold you out, my man. You see, she works for me and, in addition to that, she's my lover. She found out all about your being a supposed 'undercover' agent. She has a good friend that works in that little piss-ant agency you work for. She told me all about you last night while we were in bed together with her girlfriend."

In an instant, the big guy lunged up out of his chair towards Bartolli as if he was going to start hitting him. He probably had realized that his only chance was to somehow grab Bartolli and try to get out of there. It was then that he got a most rude awakening. With the forefinger of his right hand, Bartolli pushed a button on the back side of his desk and the cannon sitting on the desk fired! The cannon ball struck the agent in his left shoulder and knocked him to the floor. Sam, the sheriff and the other man immediately grabbed the now wounded agent and pulled him up off the floor. Bartolli said, "Take him down to the barn and work on him for a while. In about five or six hours, you know what to do with him."

"Okay, boss. We'll take care of him," Sam said. One of the boss's other men came in with his gun pulled. Motioning him toward where the agent had fallen, Sam said, "Clean up that mess over there that this asshole made." The man nodded his head and then left the room. Sam and the other enforcer then pulled the wounded man out of the room.

Bartolli looked over at Tony and, with a sinister sneer on his face, said in a monotone voice, "Go down there with them for a little bit and see what happens to those that try to get in my way."

Tony followed Burdette, Sam and the other man as they drug the wounded agent down to the nearest stable. What he saw there made him sick. The men took turns slugging the already wounded man first with their fists and then with a stick of lumber. Burdette in particular seemed to enjoy hitting the helpless man with the lumber. Tony quickly had seen enough of that and turned to leave the building to go back to see Bartolli. Sam left to go with him.

As they walked up the dirt roadway towards the house, Tony asked, "What will happen to him?"

Sam looked at him and said, "Boss likes to have guys like him really worked over before they die. Sends a message to the guys that work for us that the same sort of thing could happen to them if they don't do what he wants done. So he will probably spend, as the Boss said, the next five hours or so with guys working on him."

"What happens then?"

"Then, he'll be cut up and fed to the hogs," Sam answered in a very slow, serious tone of voice. After a moment of hesitation, Sam added, "They don't leave anything when they eat. They'll eat all of him, if given enough time. There won't be anything left for anybody to ever find." Tony remembered that the sheriff had told him the same thing.

As they now walked down the center hallway of the house, Tony was almost numb from what he had just been told. He realized he had to not think about that right now because they were getting ready to meet with Bartolli, who in front of his very eyes had just shot and ordered killed a man who apparently was an undercover agent of the United States government.

"Am sorry you had to see that but it had to be done. Anybody that stupid deserves to be dead," Bartolli said after Tony and Sam had entered the room.

Tony did not say anything, just stood there with Sam in front of that huge desk and the cannon that had fired.

"Have a seat. You too, Sam." Both men took their places in

the two chairs facing the desk, Tony noticing that he now was sitting in the chair at which the cannon had fired.

"How are you coming along with our deputy friend over there in Mississippi?" Bartolli asked as he leaned back in his huge chair.

"I have met him and we have talked. I intend to start going back to that bar where he works and talking with him some more until I feel comfortable sort of easing him into a discussion of what you want me to talk with him about. I don't want to be so obvious that he might wonder about things, if that's alright with you."

"Yes, that's fine. Just don't take too long. I think I mentioned to you that he has already cost us over a million dollars in seized shipments. That has got to stop. Like I said, I am willing to try this way for now, but at some point there has to be results or we will have to do something else. Eventually, we may have to kill him."

Tony was caught completely off-guard by that last sentence. After a brief moment of silence as what Bartolli had said sunk in, Tony said, "I think that, so far, it is going alright. Of course, he has no idea and I think that is the way it had to start off. I just wanted to ease into it for now. I'll let you know how it is going along."

"Okay. Good. Now in the meantime, I'll have some of the guys show you a little more of our operation around here, just so you know about some of the things that are going on that he has hurt with his seizures." Looking now at Sam, Bartolli said, "Go on and take him out to the blue boat. Let him see that and the race boats and maybe a landing out there. Also, take him to a cattle loading."

Sam nodded his head as he said, "Okay, boss. Will do."

At that moment, Burdette walked into the room.

"Too bad we couldn't let that old lady over in Bay St. Louis see what we are doing to this agent," Burdette said as he walked over to the side of Bartolli's desk. "You know, the one that's been asking all the questions and stirring up the people over there."

Bartolli firmly said, "Do I have to tell you again to take care of that situation? Do I?"

"No, no. I will. I just have to do it in a way so that she will get the message. I have something in mind. It has to be done the right way."

"It had better work," Bartolli quickly answered, "and it had better get the job done of getting her attention soon or we'll have to find a more drastic way."

Bartolli then turned toward Sam and Tony and said, "Okay. I'll see you, Tony, back over here in a couple of weeks or so. I'll let you know exactly when."

As Sam got up, Tony took that as his cue to also get up and the two men said their goodbyes and left the boss in the room with Sheriff Raymond Burdette.

Two days later, Tony got a call from Sam and was told to meet him at the gas station on the southwest corner of the Interstate 10 and Highway 603 intersection at 9 that night. Tony arrived ten minutes early to make sure he found a parking spot where he could leave his car for what Sam said would be about two hours.

Sam drove up just a few minutes early and Tony walked over to get into his old pickup truck.

"Where are we going tonight?" Tony asked as Sam pulled away from the station.

"Boss wants you to see something he is really proud of. He actually thought this one up himself, with a little help from a couple of the guys," Sam said as he increased his speed going north on highway 603. The truck weaved its way on the two lane road through the countryside, crossing a few creeks as it made its way into northern Hancock County. After traveling some distance, the truck turned to the right on a country road that went further into the middle of nowhere. After coming out of a sharp bend in the road that led them over a narrow bridge, they weaved their way through the area meeting only two cars as they traveled.

Finally, driving up on what appeared to be a ridge of open pastureland, Sam turned onto a dirt road that was blocked by a metal gate. Stopping in front of the gate, Sam got out, leaving the truck's motor running, and went up to the lock on the gate. Pulling a key chain from his pocket, Sam eventually opened the lock and pushed the gate open. Climbing back in the truck, he pulled the truck through the entrance, stopping far enough away that he was able to get out and go back and close the gate. Tony noticed that Sam made sure the lock was again secure on the gate before returning to the truck. With his lights on bright, Sam worked the truck down the dirt road for what Tony guessed was about a mile with rolling pastureland on both sides.

At that point Tony could barely make out a rather large barn in the distance next to a group of pine trees on the edge of one of the large pastures. It was then that they saw a man standing on the side of the dirt road as the road topped one of the rolling pieces of pastureland. Sam pulled up to the man and stopped the truck. The first thing Tony noticed was that the figure was carrying a shotgun.

"Where you been, Sam?" asked the skinny man who appeared

to not have shaved in at least a week, probably because he did not have to since he looked to be about 17 years of age, at the most.

"They got you out here tonight?" Sam said in mock surprise.

"Yeah, they needed somebody they could count on," the boy answered with a smile as he bent over to see who was with Sam.

"You just stay alert, you hear?" Sam said.

"I know. I know. You be careful up there," the young figure said with a chuckle.

"Take care of yourself," Sam said as he then pulled away going towards the barn. Tony looked around the pastured area and noted that it looked like it was completely lit up because of the reflection of the moon light on the landscape. He had seen that same look so many times back in his home country.

Sam guided the truck up towards the barn. As they got closer, Tony noticed three pickup trucks parked next to the barn. Sam pulled up, parking next to one nearest to the road. As they were getting out, up walked a young man who appeared to be in his late 20's, also carrying a shotgun.

"Hello, Barry. You checking us out?"

"Damn right," Barry said as he laughed.

"You'd better," Sam said jokingly. "How far along are you?"

"We've already loaded two up. Three to go," he answered as he turned to walk with them into the enclosed area.

"So it won't be long and you will be shipping out," Sam said as they approached five other guys standing near a large cow inside one of the corrals.

"They should be ready to roll in about thirty minutes or so."

"This group's going to Dallas?" Sam asked as he began watching the men work.

"Should be there by late morning."

Tony could not believe what he was seeing. On the floor of the barn were stacks of what looked like small bricks, each one wrapped individually with some sort of material. What he saw the men do was take one of those bricks and force the brick into the cow's rear. Tony was baffled at why the men would be doing such thing and looked over at Sam.

Seeing the quizzical look on Tony's face, Sam felt compelled to explain.

"Each of those blocks is a kilo of cocaine. A few of them are heroin, but mostly cocaine. We put them inside the cows for shipment. The only thing everybody sees is a bunch of cows going to market. There are huge places over there that don't do anything but buy and sell cows, thousands of cows," Sam said as he returned his attention to the work being performed by the men with the cow. Tony almost had to shift his eyes as one of the men shoved the next brick into the cow's rear and forced his arm inside to make sure the brick stayed there. The man's arm had eventually almost completely disappeared into the cow as he did that. After the first one stayed in the cow, the man took a second one and did the same thing again, forcing it into place.

"Two bricks are about the most that one cow can take. We've been doing this for a while now and it has really worked. We haven't lost a shipment yet. This is one thing nobody's looking for," Sam said with a grin on his face. "All they see is a shipment of cows going down the highway. Little do they know that each shipment of five cows, like this one will be, is worth almost half a million dollars.

177

Tony had to shake his head hearing that figure. That was huge, and the shipments were taking place right there in front of everybody. He had to ask, though, the one thing that popped up in his mind next.

"How in the world do you get the bricks out of the cow?" he asked in total wonder.

Sam answered, "Well, that's the worst part of it all, as you might imagine. When the shipment gets out there, usually the cows are bid off to, shall we say, certain people. The successful bidders get their cows and take them to their ranches and, at the appropriate time, take the bricks out of the cows."

Tony could not help himself. He asked it almost before he had thought about what the answer might be.

"And then the successfully bidding rancher does what? Does he kill the cow to get the bricks?"

Looking at Tony with as serious a face as he could muster, Sam said, "Oh, no. The cows are much too valuable to just kill them on every trip. No, each rancher has his men take the bricks out of the cow and we use most of those same cows again."

After thinking for a moment, Tony couldn't help but ask, "How does one take a brick out of a cow?"

Sam laughed, a deep hearty laugh, and said, "The same way they put it in, by having a man stick his hand up the cow's ass, grabbing it and pulling it out."

Tony was at a loss for words. He was totally unable to say anything as he thought about what Sam had just told him. Sam was still laughing at him as they drove away from the barn after the last deposits had been made in the cows.

Chapter Fifteen

Tony had heard Bartolli and Sam talk about a blue boat and make reference to it. Bartolli now seemed, after Tony's recent trip to north Hancock County, to want to try to impress his Sicilian friend by showing him even more of his operation so he decided that a trip out to the blue boat and other parts of the operation in that area was due. He had Sam call Tony and tell him to meet Sam at the same dock he had gone to for the trip out to the oil rig. Sam mentioned that Tony should bring an overnight bag with him and make plans accordingly because Sam was going to take Tony out to the blue boat.

Hearing that bit of news, Tony did not know what to expect. The mere mention of a "blue boat" did not bring up thoughts of any special place.

"Really now Sam, a blue boat?"

"Yeppers, a blue boat."

"What is located on this so-called 'blue boat'?"

"Boss wants me to take you to it so you can see for yourself. I don't want to spoil anything by saying a word. Just meet me there at 7:30 the day after tomorrow, bring an overnight bag and let's go have some fun. You may like it so much out there that you might want to stay two or three nights. Bring some shorts, a bathing suit, jeans, some deck shoes and a sweatshirt. And also, bring some extra spending money. You never know what you might get to spend it on while you are out there." Now Sam really had Tony wondering what all he was going to see out at the blue boat.

Using the next day, a Wednesday, to get ready for the trip, Tony went shopping for a bathing suit, shorts and deck shoes. He already had everything else he might need, he thought, including a canvas bag to put it all in. He had brought one of those with him from Sicily.

Promptly at 7:30 he arrived at the oil dock in south Louisiana where he parked his car as he had before. Again, the '56 Ford garnered a lot of looks and discussion amongst those who had an appreciation for it. That meant especially those who knew about its big engine. Sam was there waiting for him and, after greetings, said, "Let's go." Sam turned and walked, with Tony following him, to a small boat with an outboard motor sitting at the end of one of the long docks. In the boat was a bearded, mostly bald man who appeared to be about 60 years old. Tony was puzzled. He didn't see any blue boat anywhere and wondered what was going to happen next. In a rather short time, he found out.

The small boat ferried him out to a nearby seaplane, which was not too far offshore. Tony knew that the plane could have been brought closer for them to board and immediately thought that the plane was kept nearby offshore so that access to it was not easy. As they got closer to the plane, there was a man standing on one of its floats who helped pull the boat up close. Bags were transferred as well as Sam and Tony and it wasn't too long before the pilot had the plane in the air. Sam told him it was about a fifty mile trip to the boat's location.

As they took off, Tony was able to notice the massive operations at the port and also how vast the Louisiana marshes were to the north and east. They flew for miles with Sam providing an occasional description of locations of shallow open water and wetlands, along with the obvious sand islands bounded by the beautiful blue waters of the Gulf of Mexico. From time to time they would see what appeared to be rather large fishing boats moving either out towards the open sea or in a direction that Sam indicated was towards one of the launching ports for deep sea fishing.

After about thirty minutes, Sam pointed toward an image on the horizon. As they got closer, Tony could see that indeed it was a blue boat and it was large. Flying around it to make their landing approach on the water near to the boat, Tony could now tell that the boat was actually a very large, flat bottomed barge with a two story superstructure that had been constructed on top of it. The roof was flat and the boat remained stationary because of it being tied to two large groups of pilings near each end of the boat and on the same side.

Their landing indicated that the pilot had accomplished that feat many times before because there was hardly any impact on the two pontoons of the plane as they made contact with the water. A small skiff was sent over to take the two men and their bags off of the airplane, which immediately turned around and took off, leaving the area. Docking at the boat, they were greeted by a man Sam identified, as he walked up to them, as its captain.

"This is Captain Gardner Sims, the man in charge of this place. This is Tony, captain."

"Welcome to our little playground, Tony. Let me show you around." Motioning to the man that had picked them up in the small taxi boat, Sims said, "Throw their bags on the deck here, y'all grab them and I'll show you two to your rooms." Soon they were up on the second floor of the boat putting their bags in their adjacent rooms. Tony noted that the rooms were rather small but clean and in relatively good condition. The captain said, "Once y'all get freshened up and have some time, come to the bar downstairs."

Ten minutes later, both of the men were in the nice bar on the first floor. The bar had a dance floor area with tables around the edge that were attached to the flooring. At the far end away from the bar area was a small stage where three piece live bands sometimes played, the captain noted, "into the wee morning hours."

Walking the two of them down the outside of the bottom floor towards what appeared to be the back of the vessel, the captain mentioned, "Sometimes, we will have a few ladies come out here for these hard working fishermen. They stay in these rooms back here." Tony wondered about that part of the setup and was going to be interested in seeing how that worked out.

After their tour, they waited for about an hour in the bar before Sam told Tony to follow him, that they were going to get back into the boat that had picked them up from the plane. The two of them were going to be taking a boat ride. With Sam working the boat's motor and radio, the two men got in the boat and took off in a direction first to the east and then to the south of the blue boat's location. After about a fifteen minute ride, they pulled over to an exposed sandbar. Obviously, a lot of coordination was being taken care of by Sam because, after only two brief, three word conversations by radio, in the distance they could see a larger, much faster fishing boat heading towards the same sandbar, but probably still a mile away.

In what seemed to Tony as just a few minutes, a one engine airplane with massive, elongated wings appeared on the horizon, flying only about 75 feet off of the water. As the silver plane got close, Sam and someone on the other boat, which was now much closer, both held up a green flag so that the pilot in the plane could see them. It was the signal, Sam said, that meant that the pilot had approval to go ahead and land on the sandbar. He immediately did just that, landing the plane on a small area of the sand island close to the water. It had taken the plane only about 40 yards to come to a complete stop. Tony could not believe it. The plane immediately was met by three men from the other boat who opened the plane's side doorway and began to unload medium sized bales of marijuana. One of the men, who had jumped up into the plane, would hand one of the bales to a second man standing next to the plane. That man would then turn and pass the bale to the third man, who would then put the bale on the hard sand about four feet away from the plane. Tony could see that the bales were wrapped in plastic and were light enough so that one man could easily pick up and handle each bale by himself. He counted forty- two bales taken by the men from the plane.

After the last bale had left the plane, the side door closed. The plane revved up its powerful engine, turned around almost in one spot and took off, going only about thirty yards on the hard sand beach of the island before it was airborne. The plane had been on the ground only for about two minutes and forty-five seconds. As it left the area the plane only got as high in altitude as it had been when it had first come in. It disappeared into the horizon by the time the bales were all loaded onto the waiting boat. The fishing boat then left the area as quickly as it had arrived. The entire operation had not taken over six minutes. The hardest part had been getting the bales carried from where they had been unloaded from the plane through the shallow water and onto the waiting fishing vessel. The whole operation was accomplished without a hitch, in broad daylight.

That afternoon, they watched as boats came and went from the blue barge. Towards late afternoon, there were several boats that had arrived, tied up to the dolphins at each end of the boat, and the occupants had made their way to the barge's bar. One of the boats that had arrived was carrying five girls, who immediately went to rooms on the back end of the first floor. Soon the girls were in the bar dressed in tee shirts and shorts over their bathing suits. They began mingling and talking with some of the visiting fishermen. As the sun made its way towards the horizon, a boat carrying the band members and their instruments arrived. Not too long thereafter, lively music was coming from the bar and the dance floor began to be constantly occupied.

Sam and Tony sat listening to the music and watching the various fishermen, who now numbered about forty, attempt to dance with the five girls, who were now clad only in scanty bikinis. It was at this point that Sam said, "The Boss said for me to tell you that you could pick any one of them out you want and he would take care of it."

Tony looked at Sam, but waited for a moment before he answered. He wanted to make sure he didn't insult the boss by turning down his offer of hospitality but, at the same point in time, he had never been with a hooker and didn't want to be with one now. He was a handsome man and had always sort of been able to be with which ever girls he had wanted to be with without paying. He remembered his dad and the guidance he had provided to him. His father had always told him that he should "find a girl that you can get along with that likes you and that you like being around and stick with her because, just like men, there are not many of them that you can count on." Once he had found out about what Madeline, his father's sister of all women, had done to betray him, he understood his father's feelings. So he said to Sam, "You know that is really nice of Boss to offer that. It really is. But I think I am going to pass and just watch these guys and see who they end up with."

Then leaning over to get closer to Sam's ear while the loud music was playing, he added, "You know that doctors in Europe have just found out about a bunch of killer bugs that women are getting from some men now that the doctors just can't seem to get rid of."

Sam's eyes got real big as he heard, and his mind processed, that piece of information. Tony leaned back in his chair. There was no way he was going to be with one of these girls who were just being passed around. He noticed during the time that he was there that some of the others apparently felt the same way he did.

Later, as he got up to go to his room for the evening, a cute blonde sitting at the end of the bar near the doorway smiled at him and said, "Wanna get lucky?"

He looked at her and smiled back, saying, "No thanks, but you are a cute girl and if I was going to be with anyone, it would be you."

She made a fake sad face and said, "You just ruined my whole evening. Maybe you'll change your mind?"

"No," Tony answered, "but nice try. Happy hunting." Then he left and went to his room for the evening.

The next morning at the agreed upon time of 7:30, Tony met Sam for breakfast down in the bar. There were three other men there but none of the women. At 8:30 he and Sam were waiting next to the skiff that was going to transport the two of them to the seaplane that would take them back to shore.

The seaplane soon appeared and landed not too far from the barge. Tony and Sam were then taken by the skiff out to the aircraft and were soon on their way back to the mainland. When Tony got back to his house, he was greeted by Buddy. Tony could tell by the constant movement of Buddy's little tail that he was very happy to see him.

Chapter Sixteen

Karen had said she would ride Tony's motorcycle with him Saturday morning at ten. As he got ready to leave, Buddy was standing next to him. Seeing Tony pull his light leather gloves over his hands, Buddy was expecting to be taken for a ride, which he had now experienced several times before. When Tony showed him to the bedroom and began to shut the door behind him, Buddy looked at him as if to say he could not believe he was not being taken along.

"Not today, Buddy. I have a special rider today. Maybe after we get her used to riding, then you can come go with us. Okay?" The dog just stood there looking at him, no tail wag now, as if to say, "Boss man, I don't understand."

To Buddy's now continuous barking, Tony shut the bedroom door and made his way out to his bike. He was looking forward to this, he really was. He was also wondering if she would actually show up at the front of the Baked Tomato. He didn't want to be late. He took one last look at himself in the bathroom mirror. With his jeans and tee shirt on along with his boots, he was comfortable with how he looked though he continued to wonder if wearing the tee was a bit too much. Looking at himself one last time, and then again, he finally decided it was just time to go.

Tony opened the garage door, put on his sunglasses and walked up to his bike. He felt wonderful swinging his leg over its seat, putting the key in the ignition and starting up the loud, wonderful, and he thought, sexy, sounding motor. Its sound was one of pure, unadulterated power. He loved it. Pulling out of the garage, he eased down his driveway and onto the street. It was a beautiful day and now he was thinking, "Bay St. Louis, here I come!" With that thought, he gunned the engine and took off, thrilled by the surge of the mechanical beast beneath him.

After making his way the few blocks he had to travel to get there, he decided to ride a little bit down Beach Front Road, which ran on the high ground next to the open water of the Bay of St. Louis. He made his turn at the light and pulled up in front of the Baked Tomato. Not immediately seeing her, he began to wonder again if she actually would show up. He was at the location they had agreed upon, but he was a little early. He shut off the motor, put the kick stand down and sat there on his bike, watching the passing traffic. He was surprised at the number of cars traveling up and down the busy two lane road. He was also surprised by the number of people out walking the street front area, going into stores, looking at items on the sidewalk for sale in front of various stores, and how happy people seemed to be. He sat there thinking about how these people did not know about what all was happening in their little area of the world. He thought about what he had already been shown about the shipping operation. He also thought about how Uncle Marty had mentioned that Bartolli had specifically been told that he should not deal in drugs. Yet, that was a major source of his income. By showing Tony what he had already seen, Bartolli had put Tony in a tight spot. Tony felt that the more he saw, he was going to be in even more of a quandary about Bartolli's drug operation.

About that time, up drove a little two door, yellow Camaro. Its driver, Karen, pulled into the almost full parking lot of the Baked Tomato, circling around and eventually finding a place to park. She got out of her means of transportation and walked ever so slowly, looking ever so sexy, across the parking lot to his location. He enjoyed watching her tight jeans struggle to keep up with the swaying motion of her hips. He also enjoyed watching the bounce and sway of her breasts underneath her tight, white, tee shirt. Her hair was in a pony tail, her makeup was perfect, and her face showed a hint of a smile around the edges of her sunglasses.

"Hi, tiger. You ready for the experience of your life?" Tony asked.

She chuckled, then followed with, "If you think that riding a motorcycle would be the top experience of anyone's lifetime, you have led a sheltered life."

He had to laugh. Not only was she absolutely sexy and beautiful, she was smart. She was also quick with that mouth of hers.

He countered with, "Okay then. Let's just say that you are in for a special treat. Let me show you where your position is." Pointing to the leather seat behind where he was sitting, he continued, "After I get this thing started, step on that metal

189

piece sticking out down there and swing your right leg over so that you are riding like you would on your horse."

"Okay."

He then stood up, jumped on the starter lever on the lower right side of the motorcycle with his right booted foot, and the engine roared to life. He then turned the throttle on his right handlebar to rev the motor up a couple of times to a loud pitch. He then hit the kickstand with his left boot. Now he was balancing the cycle by standing on both legs. Satisfied that it was ready for her, he looked over at her and motioned with his head to climb aboard. She then got on behind him.

"Comfy?" he asked over his shoulder.

"So far," she yelled back.

"Okay. Now I have to tell you something. You have to put your arms around my waist," he said with a hint of a smile.

"Oh, really?"

"Well, we wouldn't want you falling off, now would we?"

"So there was a reason when you asked me to ride with you. You just wanted a hug you weren't going to get otherwise."

"It worked, didn't it? Now hold on tightly. Really tightly," he said as he turned the throttle so the powerful motor began to show off.

He then sat on the seat and began to ease the motorcycle forward. The two riders slowly began to be carried by the two wheeled vehicle. Karen did, indeed, begin to hold on tightly. He slowly drove down the street, finally making it to Beach Front Road. He turned right so that they were headed south, increasing the speed as they began riding next to the Bay of St.

Louis on a road that appeared to have no stoplights. It was now easy cruising.

The first thing Karen noticed was that the wind felt so good in her face as her hair was flowing behind her. The further they went, there was something else that she noticed. There was this constant vibration in the leather seat she was sitting on caused by the motorcycle's powerful motor. The longer they rode, the more she came to like the feel of that vibration. She had felt things like that before as she had ridden her horses, but that was more of a rhythmic thing caused by the movement of the horse. This was different, and constant, and after she was past her fears, it was pleasant and enjoyable.

After about thirty minutes of riding around the outskirts of Bay St. Louis and Waveland, the little town just to the south, Karen told Tony that it was time for him to take her back to the Baked Tomato. She had already had enough of this fun for a first time. What she didn't tell him was that she just had to get off of that vibrating seat before she embarrassed herself.

After she got off of the machine back at the Baked Tomato, she said, "Okay, now follow me out to our farm so you can ride one of my horses."

"Do I have to do that today?" he asked.

"A deal is a deal. Today it is. Follow me," she said as she turned to walk to her car. He enjoyed watching her body's movement as she made her way over to her means of transportation.

He followed her car on his motorcycle out to her family farm, which was some distance north of town. He noticed that the countryside was beautiful, with lots of large trees that, he thought, had to be very old. Following Karen as she turned to drive up a narrow dirt road, Tony dropped back to let the dust caused by her car, even though she had slowed down, settle somewhat before he drove through it.

Walking out of the barn as they pulled up was what appeared to be an elderly black man. Once she had parked and gotten out of her car, Tony pulled up not too far away and parked his cycle. He noticed the black man eying him as he walked over to her.

"Come over here and meet 'Snow.' He is our stable hand who has worked for us for, how long Snow? Over twenty years maybe?"

Snow, who was now slowly walking over, answered, "'bout that long, Missy."

Tony shook hands with the thin black man as he asked, with a big smile, "Has she been much of a problem all those years?"

Snow grinned and answered, "Naw, Missy never been nothin but nice."

"Thanks, Snow. That's sweet," she said.

"Well, Missy, it's true."

"So do you have Queen and the other one I asked for ready for us?"

"Yasssum, I'll go gettum for ya."

Not too long after disappearing into the barn Snow came out leading two already saddled and bridled horses. She took the reins of the brown horse and said, as she pointed to the other horse, "That one is for you." Looking at Snow, she said, "He has never ridden before so hold the reins for him until he is in the saddle and ready to go." Then looking back at Tony she said, "You have to always mount a horse from the left side so go stand there next to him, grab the saddle horn there with your left hand

192

while holding on to the back of the saddle with your right hand, raise your left leg and put it in the stirrup and pull yourself up."

Snow grabbed the reins closer to the horse's mouth as Tony moved so he was next to the left side of the big white horse. He then did as she had told him, grabbing the saddle horn, putting his boot into the stirrup and pulling himself up with the help of his right hand on the back of the saddle. Throwing his right leg over the saddle, he settled in so that he was now sitting on the back of the huge animal. Snow handed him the reins while still holding the part nearest the horse's mouth.

Karen said, "Okay, motorcycle man, are you ready?"

"Yeah, I'm ready. The question is, is the horse is ready for me,"

Karen chuckled and then said, "Take it easy on my horse now, okay? He is one of my favorites so be nice."

Tony answered, "I'll be nice, just because he is one of your favorites."

"Okay, Snow. Let go and let's see how much of a cowboy he really is." Snow let go and slowly backed away. Tony's horse immediately started moving forward, taking steps as Karen watched from atop her perfectly still horse.

After about five steps, Tony yelled over his shoulder to Karen, "See, there is nothing to this. It is just like I told you, this is not hard at ----------."

At exactly that moment, Tony's horse went straight up on its hind legs, its front hooves kicking in the air. The move by the horse caught Tony completely by surprise. As a result, he tumbled off of the back of the horse, doing a complete back flip by the time he hit the ground by landing on his rear, which just a second earlier had been sitting in the saddle on that horse.

Dust went up all around Tony as he landed. The horse's front two hooves came back down on the ground and the huge animal lunged forward, running a few steps as if it were charging out of a racing gate. Then it stopped and turned around to look at its former rider.

Karen quickly dismounted from her horse, threw its reins around a nearby fence post and ran over to her guest. Tony sat there, dazed and not sure what had happened, but finally realizing that he was sitting on the ground. Snow also came over to visually examine the former rider.

"Are you alright?" Karen asked as she squatted down next to Tony.

Tony was at a loss for words. He had to take a breath before he could even answer.

"I don't know. I think so, but I'm not sure." He then tried to move but immediately stopped his effort.

"Ohhhhhh my back. And my rear."

Karen had to control the urge to laugh. She had seen the whole thing: the perfect flip, the hard landing, the stunned look, all after such bravado. She knew, though, that she should not laugh, even though she really wanted to. She used her left hand to cover her mouth or else her wide grin would have showed.

Tony looked at her and asked, "What did you say that horse's name is?"

Looking at the former rider as she pulled her hand down, she said, "His name is Fireball." She could hardly keep herself from laughing out loud.

Tony could see she was having a hard time not laughing but said anyway, "Fireball?"

Karen nodded her head, with a big smile showing on her face.

"Now you tell me," he muttered as he glanced at the horse standing there looking at him.

After a moment taken to make sure she didn't start laughing, Karen was able to say, "Do you think you can stand up?"

"I think so," he said and then slowly moved himself to a position where he could try to stand up.

"Do you want me to take you to the hospital?" Karen asked.

Having finally, slowly stood up, he answered, "No, but I do think I need to go take care of this back."

"You can't ride that motorcycle home, can you?" she asked.

"I think so," he answered as he started to stumble his way towards his means of transportation.

Tony's ride to his house was not pleasant. His back was in extreme pain the whole way. He was just glad to pull up to his little house, park his cycle, and ease himself into his home, which did take some time. Buddy's barking was a welcome noise, but Tony limped straight to the bath tub and filled it with almost scorching hot water. He stayed in that tub for over three hours.

* * * * *

Miss Peabody stopped by the grocery store on her way home after a full afternoon of playing bridge. She had noticed that the conversation during her group's time together was not as lively as it used to be before her efforts with the public meetings had taken place. In fact, it was as if some of the ladies were not going to make many comments at all while they almost held their breaths as they waited to see what else she was going to bring up about the drug situation.

As she shopped at the grocery store for the few food items she needed to restock her freezer and food pantry, she felt a presence over her left shoulder as she reached with her right hand for a bottle of her favorite French dressing. Slowly turning, she saw lawyer Bradley Hamilton standing there next to her, appearing in his grey suit and red tie as if he had just walked out of the courtroom. Hamilton was a somewhat tall man, being about 6 foot 3 inches in height, and had kept himself in fairly good condition through the years. He had been in one of her classes way back when and, while he had usually behaved, she did always feel that she had to keep an eye on him. It had been somewhat of a surprise to her when he had finally become an attorney. He was in his late thirties now, she guessed, and while not one of the top attorneys in the area, he was one of the most well-connected politically in the whole county.

"Hi there, Miss Peabody," he said with a hint of a smile on his face.

She leaned back away from him a little since he had placed himself very close to her, in fact right next to her. Her first thought was he had a lot of nerve walking up behind her and standing so close. But then he had always been someone she had felt a little uncomfortable around.

"Hello, Bradley. I don't think I have ever seen you in here before."

"There are a few things my wife wanted me to pick up on the way home so I came on by," he said, still somewhat hovering over her. After quickly glancing around, Hamilton bent forward, lowered his voice and began.

"I was there at the courthouse the day you made your presentation about drug activity in the county." He then paused for a brief moment, as if to make sure she was listening to what he was going to say next.

"You had everybody's attention and you made your point. But I hope you will let those who have responsibility for those types of matters deal with them. There are very dangerous people involved in those activities and I would hope that you will not give them any reason to come do some horrible thing to you to stop your efforts." Hamilton was now talking in a low, firm tone of voice. After hesitating for a moment to let what he had just said sink in, he continued.

"I am suggesting that it's time for you to step back and let others deal with all of that, Miss Peabody. If you keep on doing what you have done, I am really fearful that something very bad might happen to you."

When he had completed his last sentence, she could feel her mouth drop open as she uttered a gasp. The look on Hamilton's face told her that he was as serious as he could be. She could not ever remember seeing him look like that.

"We don't want that to happen, now do we?" he continued with his face now only about a foot away from hers.

She caught herself beginning to tremble as she looked back up into a face that now looked completely evil.

Pausing a second to catch her breath, she muttered, "Why, no. Not at all."

Hamilton then pulled back and smiled, saying, "Good! Someone like you needs to peacefully enjoy the rest of her life. Have a nice day." With that, he turned and disappeared into the store as she stood there almost shaking.

While driving home, she couldn't even remember checking out. The more she thought about what had just happened, the more she knew what she was going to do. She was going to do exactly what he had suggested, spend her remaining days on this earth peacefully enjoying her life. She had done what she could. She would leave whatever else might need to be done up to others.

Later that week, Miss Peabody left for an extended stay with her sister in Atlanta.

Chapter Seventeen

Helen had been very pretty when she was a young girl. She could turn heads almost anywhere she went. But not many people could understand why she married Sheriff Wild Bill Patterson when she did. He was much older than she and not much to look at. She had been devastated when her first husband died in a tragic accident at a wood yard. She had thought she would be married to him for the rest of her life. He had been her companion, her reliable partner. Now he was gone forever. The biggest change for her, besides being so lonely, was that she was fearful for her economic well-being. Her husband had been a good provider in that his job at the local lumber yard had paid him well. However, his not having any life insurance to speak of had resulted in her security being basically gone.

Helen had thus eventually married Sheriff Patterson and he had tried to protect her somewhat. The biggest problem was that his being several years older than her had meant that a lot of times his interests were other places rather than at home. That eventually had led to her involvement with Nick Gable. She had basically fallen in love with Nick and had even gone so far, when she found out she was pregnant, as to let him know she would leave with him right then because she was convinced he was the father. Once she had told Nick she was pregnant though, he had backed completely away from her, leaving her alone, and not even trying in any way to see her. In short, he had just left her once she had told him she was pregnant. He had said it was for her own protection, but it had crushed her.

Something that had really gotten to her was when her husband had told her one night that he could not have been the one that got her pregnant. He said he had previously been injured to the extent that he could not possibly be the cause of someone becoming pregnant, something he had neglected to tell her while they were dating. After telling her that, he basically never mentioned it again. He had raised the child, Bart, as if it was his own, but he never showed the sincere love for the boy that he might have if Bart had been his own child. Bart had tried and tried over the years to impress his father. He had also never found out that the man he thought was his dad really was not. Helen had lived through raising Bart and seeing him become part of the sheriff's office. Bart had eventually become sheriff after Helen's husband, his supposed father, had passed away.

Bart had unfortunately been killed in the line of duty as sheriff during an investigation. His son, Mark, was in the Army when Bart had been killed and had come home on leave to Bay St. Louis for the funeral. Mark had then returned to active duty, eventually ending up in the swamps of the Mekong River in Vietnam with his Special Forces unit. Now he was a deputy in the office of the man who had taken over as sheriff after his father had been killed.

Helen had played the organ and piano at church and other events for almost fifty years now and she continued to love it. It gave her peace of mind and a chance to provide a hopefully good influence on the younger people she ran into through the church. She had been devastated when her son, Bart, had been killed. Her activities with the church had helped her keep her sanity. She was a little overweight now, but for her age she was just glad to be present to see what was going to happen next to the people close to her in her life and to those around her.

She regularly walked down the street from her small house to the downtown area of Bay St. Louis to do a little shopping and, at the same time, get her daily exercise. Her walks almost always took her by the small city park that was along the way. This day, as usual, she made a point to notice which kids were playing in the park and which parents were doing their duty of watching and protecting the future generation. That was necessary because the area was not as safe as it once had been. A person never knew if someone might appear in the area that may have bad thoughts in mind as they spent time around the park watching the kids playing there.

It was as she reached the far side of the park that she saw a younger man briskly walk around the street corner next to the park and head down the sidewalk in her direction. As he got closer, she almost fainted when she could clearly see his face. He looked exactly like a young version of Nick Gable, the man that she had fallen in love with oh so many years ago. She almost lost her balance as she stared at him as he approached. Then she really did stumble and barely managed to grab hold of a nearby lamp post.

"Are you okay?" the young man asked as he held her right arm that he had just grabbed so as to help keep her from falling to the ground.

She looked up at him and could not answer. He looked exactly like the man she had fallen so deeply in love with.

"Are you alright?" he asked again as he steadied her. She still could not answer as she literally kept staring at him. He slowly guided her over to a nearby park bench, easing her into a seated position there.

"Here. Just sit here until you feel a little better," he softly said to her.

She still just kept looking at him, not believing there was another person as handsome as her Nick Gable had been. This man looked exactly like him. Not just similar to him. Exactly like him. So handsome, so charming, so gentle he had been as he had helped her onto the park bench.

Finally she uttered, "Young man, would you mind staying with me for just a bit, until I get over the spell I just had?"

The handsome young man replied, "Of course. I would be happy to sit with you for a bit, until you feel better." With that he sat on the park bench next to his new acquaintance. After a few moments of silence, during which she continuously stole looks at the young man next to her, she finally was able to say more.

"May I ask what might be your name, young man?"

"I am Tony Gable," the man answered with the faint hint of a smile. "I am from overseas and staying here for a while."

She intently looked at him as he spoke. He talked just like her former lover of so many years ago. When he said his last name, she almost lost her breath. She felt that there had to be some way this man was related to him, but there was no way she felt comfortable asking that question, not right now. Maybe at least she could ask a couple of more questions before he would probably leave.

"Where are you from overseas?" she asked as she tilted her head to avoid the morning sun in her eyes.

"Well, let's just say I am from Europe, but I really am enjoying my stay here so far. Now how about you. Are you feeling any better?"

She looked at him and quickly judged his concern for her health to be sincere. It was then that she slowly answered.

"Yes, thank you so much for helping me. I almost passed out a few moments ago."

"Yes, you did. I'm glad you're feeling better. I was just visiting that motorcycle shop down the street over there and was going back to Beach Front Road to get my car."

"Well, I am so glad, young man, that you were here and I greatly appreciate your trying to help me. Thank you so much."

"You are quite welcome. Are you feeling okay now? Do I need to get someone to be with you?"

"No, no. I'll be fine. But thanks again so much for helping me."

"Okay. I am going to leave then, if that's alright with you. Now if you want me to, I'll stay with you a while longer, if you need me to."

She looked at him. He was such a nice person, just like her Nick had been way back when. Oh how she still missed him. Not a month went by that she still didn't think about him, but the last she had heard was that he had been killed at the end of World War ll in a car accident in Italy.

"No, you've been so kind. Thank you so much for helping me. Maybe some other time, when I am not so faint, we could talk a little bit more. You've been such a nice young man. Thank you again for helping me."

"It was my pleasure. Just please take your time before you try to walk again, and you take care of yourself. I too hope that one day soon we can sit here and spend a little time just talking."

"I would really enjoy that. I really would," she said with as much sincerity as she could muster at the moment.

With that, he slowly got up, patted her on her shoulder and said, "Now you just be sure and take your time before you start trying to walk again, okay? And if you want me to, I will get some medical person to come here and help you. If you would like, I'll help you get to where you live."

Showing him a faint smile, she answered, "You are so kind, thanks, but I don't think that will be necessary. I will just sit here for a moment and then try to work my way back to my house. It's just two blocks down the street from here."

"Okay. Please take your time. It was really nice meeting you, and I am glad that you are doing better."

"It was wonderful meeting you. You just be careful yourself, okay?"

"Okay. I will. Bye for now," he said as he turned to leave.

"Bye bye, and thanks again for being concerned about me," she said as he waved goodbye to her and left.

She sat there for several moments after he had left. So many thoughts came to her. So many remembrances from oh so many years ago. She knew she would be thinking for some time about how to find out exactly if he might be related to her former lover.

That was something that would be on her mind a lot for the next several days.

*   *   *   *   *

It rained for four days. Not just a drizzle, but a full fledged, pouring down rain, and for extended periods of time. Such was the way weather behaved in the Bay St. Louis area sometimes because of its nearness to the tropics. Every now and then a hurricane would blow through the area, but this time it was just day after day of nothing but rain. Finally, on the fifth day there was some slack off though occasional clouds were still in the area and the ground remained soaked.

Business had to go on. It had always been that way along the Gulf Coast after bad weather showed up. After a heavy rain like this one, the result was usually the same. Massive amounts of water had to make its way off of land and eventually into the various bayous and rivers along the coast.

There was only one problem. For activities such as the drug shipment business, there was simply no way that landings on pasture lands could take place. The possibility of the aircraft making the trip becoming damaged or mired in a saturated pasture was just too much of a potential risk. After days of heavy rains such as those that had just taken place, another location for the landing of the shipments had to temporarily be found, and indeed it had been.

Sam notified Tony that the Boss wanted him to observe another landing effort that particular Wednesday night. Sam mentioned that this particular type of landing had only been performed two times before so it should be something special that the visitor from Sicily would be interested in seeing. Tony had absolutely no idea what Sam was making reference to and was especially interested in what he might see.

That next Wednesday night, at about 2:30 in the morning, Tony left his car parked again behind the Bay St. Louis Inn not too far from the Highway 603 side of the motel. Within a matter of minutes, Sam pulled up in an old black pickup truck. Tony climbed in and they took off headed up 603 towards Interstate 10. When they reached the interstate, Sam took the entrance road that would take them onto the interstate highway headed west towards Slidell, Louisiana. They traveled in that direction for about fifteen minutes. Tony noted that there was almost no traffic, probably due to it being so late.

It was at that point that they saw a sheriff's department patrol car with lights on top that was pulled over on the right shoulder of the four lane highway. That car was parked about fifty yards before the portion of the highway heading west curved ever so slightly to its left. Sam pulled his pickup truck over on the highway's shoulder in front of the marked police car. He slowly moved down the highway's shoulder until he was around the curve in the highway and out of sight of the marked car. A thick forest of trees occupied the area between the two sets of highway lanes and was so thick that the east bound highway lanes to the south were not visible.

About ten minutes later, two unmarked black vans slowly pulled up behind their truck and stopped, both turning off their motors. Once the vans were parked on the highway's shoulder, Sam got out and then reached back under the front seat of the truck. Out he pulled a CB radio which he quickly hooked up with an antenna that he pulled out from under a tarpaulin in the bed of his truck. It didn't take long and Sam had connected the necessary parts and was ready to receive communications on a pre-selected CB channel. At precisely 3:17 a.m. a voice came over the CB and said, "Four minutes away." Sam quickly passed that message on to the patrol car they had earlier passed.

Sam then said, "One of Burdette's men in that patrol car we passed will begin blocking the highway with his car. When this highway was built, the federal government required that about every ten miles or so there had to be a one mile stretch that was straight as an arrow. They wanted that so that if airfields got knocked out because of some invasion or bombings, the air force could use portions of the interstate highways as landing strips. Tonight, we can't use our pasture landing areas because they are so wet. The stuff has to be moved so Boss decided that tonight, we will use this particular one mile interstate landing strip."

Tony looked at him and said, smiling, "You have got to be kidding!"

Sam let out a laugh and replied, "Naw, I'm not. Watch what happens in about three minutes."

"What about the lanes on the other side of the highway?" Tony asked.

"There's another sheriff's car over there now starting to do the same thing the one on this side is doing, which is stopping cars and checking licenses. There are also cars at the end of each one mile strip, just in case somebody shows up. But the landing itself is going to be over here."

After a few moments, a voice came over the CB again and said, "One minute." Sam clicked the microphone of the CB and said, "It's a go." He then started the motor of his truck and turned the headlights on bright, which illuminated the interstate highway. He then gave a signal to the drivers of the two parked vans by quickly clicking his headlights from dim to bright and back. They started up the motors of their vehicles, also turning on their lights.

About forty-five seconds later, Tony looked back to his left along with Sam, toward the east as he began to hear a relatively quiet hum of a motor approaching from up in the sky. Then it appeared out of nowhere, barely a hundred feet off of the ground. That same extra long-winged airplane that Tony had seen out on that sand beach was dropping down to land on Interstate Highway 10! After it touched the cement of the highway, the plane ran about 40 yards, eventually coming to almost a complete stop before rolling an additional fifty yards at which point it quickly turned itself around and stopped.

The two vans, with three men in each one, moved down the straight stretch of highway and pulled up next to the side door of the plane the instant it had completed its turn. Loading the first van with numerous, mid-sized bales of marijuana took about a minute and a half, after which that vehicle eased off down the highway headed west towards Louisiana. The second van was loaded with similar product in about a minute and it also left, headed west. As soon as the second van departed from the side of the plane, the aircraft's motors were revved up and it immediately began its take off effort. Within forty yards, the plane's wheels were off the highway's concrete. Within five minutes, both sides of the highway were opened up and the sparse traffic was moving once again.

Chapter Eighteen

Tony knew he had to go back to the Baked Tomato and continue his efforts to get closer to Deputy Mark Patterson. It would also give him his first chance to see sexy Karen since he had done his perfect flip off of the back of her horse. Walking into the busy place at around 9, he saw Mark in his usual perch at the end of the bar with his chair turned with his back against the wall so he could see everything going on in the room. He noticed Karen and her three friends out dancing on the dance floor. They were all loosely grouped together as they danced, but none of them had a male partner. The first thought Tony had was that they were all advertising, hoping some cowboy would like their looks, come up and start dancing with them. Tony walked over to Mark's end of the bar.

"Hi, deputy."

"Hello yourself there, cowboy," Mark answered, now with a broad smile on his face.

"Uh-oh. I guess that means you know about the results of my horse back riding effort out at your girlfriend's farm."

"Cowboy, your horseback riding effort is fast becoming well-known throughout the county," he answered, followed by a big laugh.

"Oh my," Tony said, shaking his head slowly from side to side. "Anybody sitting here?" he asked putting his hand on the back of the chair next to the deputy.

"It's all yours for the moment."

Tony climbed up onto the chair, resting his elbows on the bar. When the bartender came over, recognizing Tony he asked, "You want your regular?"

Tony nodded his head, thinking about how nice it was that already the bartender knew he wanted his regular Bud.

Mark then asked, "Don't feel too badly. There have been others that have found that horse difficult to ride."

"You mean she knew that horse might try to throw me off?"

"No, not really. But let's just say it was not the first time that's happened," Mark said as he gazed around the dance floor.

"I bet that never happened to Kennedy," Tony said with his head slumping somewhat.

"You talking about your idol again?"

Tony paid for his drink, took it in his hand and turned his swivel bar chair towards the deputy.

"Yes, and I have been thinking about what you said about him during our last conversation."

"I don't remember saying anything memorable during that conversation, especially about Kennedy."

"But you did. You just don't remember it, and it was more how you said it than what you said," Tony said with all sincerity. That sincerity caught the deputy's attention. Tony continued, "Your comment about the Cuban invasion. It sounded like you didn't approve of how he handled that."

Mark shifted his weight in his chair, made a cursory look around the room, then looked back at Tony.

"If he was going to invade Cuba, he should have been prepared to follow through with it. Do whatever it took to be successful."

"Well, he did let the CIA get involved. They were in on all the planning, all the recruiting of the Cubans, all the training. They ran the show," Tony said as he looked at the deputy.

"Yes, they did, but when it came down to it, when those Cubans needed his and the CIA's help the most, Kennedy would not permit the U. S. Navy to provide air support. When the invasion got in trouble, even though he had promised them his support, and U. S. air support from an aircraft carrier was already there, he would not give the order for those planes to go help them. But he had promised that air support would be provided."

"So what has that got to do with anything? He had already done so much for them."

Mark looked back at Tony and said, "Tony, how would you feel if you had been one of those Cuban invaders and had been promised by the CIA and President Kennedy's representatives, who put that whole thing together, that the air support would be provided, especially if it was needed, and then it wasn't? How would you feel if you were one of those Cuban invaders and that had happened to you? I know how I would feel. I would have felt betrayed, and I would have been really pissed."

"What does that mean, you would be going to the bathroom?"

"No, no!" Mark had to laugh at that. "Being pissed means that I would have been very upset. Angry. Mad. You know that some of those guys were executed and some of them were tortured."

"Yeah and later the United States got them all released to come back to this country."

"Well, do you think they just forgot about it all when they got back? Or do you think it is possible they talked about it. Do you think Castro and the Cubans in Cuba who supported him were happy about being invaded? You know Oswald, the guy that the Warren Report concluded fired those shots, hung out with the Fair Play for Cuba group in New Orleans, a group that supposedly supported Castro."

"How do you know so much about all of that?" Tony asked as he finished his beer.

"It was all in the newspapers down here. You know New Orleans is just down the road from here."

Tony then got out of his chair and said, "Let's continue this. Right now I have to go to the men's room." With that he turned and went in that direction.

Right after Tony had left his seat, up walked Carol who had just left the table where she had been sitting with the girls before their dancing effort, which was continuing on the floor.

"Hi sweetie," she said as she now leaned on the bar next to the deputy's chair. "I just want you to know that I think it is horrible that Karen is seeing that new guy in town, the one you were just talking with." Before the deputy could say a word, she continued, "I also just want you to know that I am available for anything, anytime, should you want me." Following a smile and a wink, she turned and went out on the dance floor and joined the girls already dancing there. An emergency call about a nearby accident caused Mark to have to leave and go outside to deal with that situation.

$$* \quad * \quad * \quad * \quad *$$

Two days later, an unexpected call was made to Bartolli's mansion while Tony was out at the ranch meeting with him. Tony was there to tell Bartolli about what the deputy had said the Thursday night before. Once Bartolli was on the phone, he was informed by Lenny, a local thug, that one of Bartolli's large shipments had just been hijacked by him and a few of his friends, who were trying to make a big hit. Lenny let Bartolli know that they also had Sam and were keeping him just to ensure that Bartolli didn't do anything stupid because they knew that Sam was one of the Boss's favorite men.

Bartolli remembered Lenny as a not too bright mid-level thug who was always looking to score a hit, regardless of who the target might be. This time he targeted Bartolli's operation as a place he might pick up some spending money for him and his boys. He was confident Bartolli would want his drugs back - and Sam. Lenny told him to be sure and bring one million dollars in cash that he, Lenny, had been told Bartolli kept at a secret location at his house. The boss readily said that he would meet them wherever they wanted so that he could get his shipment back, and Sam. It was agreed that they would meet at eleven p.m. that night at a deserted warehouse about 20 miles southwest of New Orleans. Lenny was happy because he didn't want to do the work necessary to go out and sell all of the marijuana he had seized.

Bartolli told Tony to come along with them that night so that he could see how Bartolli dealt with such matters. Tony agreed, but asked if he could borrow a little firepower from Bartolli for the trip. Bartolli took him to a hidden firearms room behind a false wall just off of the main dining area. Tony settled on a .32 caliber Colt automatic that had a 22 bullet clip and two additional clips to go along with it. Tony fired the gun in the yard behind the mansion until he felt comfortable with it.

The group arrived at the deserted wooden warehouse Lenny had designated as the meeting place. Bartolli knew that the old barn-like facility had ample locations where gunmen could be hidden. In addition to Tony, he had brought five men with him, three with mini machine guns and two with shotguns, which Bartolli knew would be very useful in close quarters if a gunfight broke out. The Boss was wearing his standard white suit with a matching white vest, white shoes and a light blue silk shirt. Tony was at a loss for words to explain why Bartolli would wear such an outfit to a possible gunfight.

Seeing a dim light in the large building, Bartolli called out for Lenny as he walked right into the building holding a large black briefcase. Tony stopped a few steps inside the entrance to the building, holding his weapon at the ready. Three of Bartolli's men spread out in the building behind Bartolli while two stood on each side not too far away from him.

Lenny walked out from behind two bales of hay. Standing on both sides of him a little distance away were two men, one with a gun in his belt and the other with a gun in his holster. The two groups stopped about fifteen feet apart from each other.

"Glad you used your head and followed directions, Bartolli,"

Lenny said in a cocky voice. "The marijuana is in the back along with Sam. You can have both of them when you give me the million dollars."

Bartolli put the briefcase down and pushed it towards Lenny. It came to rest about half the distance between them. Lenny looked around and finally stepped forward to check the contents of the black bag. He kneeled down and opened it. It was filled with newspaper. He looked up as he reached for his gun.

Bartolli said, "I'm really going to miss Sam" as he pulled his gun out and shot Lenny in his left shoulder. The two men standing on either side of Bartolli had already pulled their automatic weapons up and leveled the two thugs with Lenny.

Then a blast was heard in a back room. At the same time, a shot rang out from the balcony that ran around the inside of the warehouse. The bullet hit Bartolli on his vest and knocked him to the ground. One of the men carrying a shotgun shot the man in the balcony, causing him to fall from his perch to the ground.

As Lenny lay on the ground grasping his left shoulder in agony, Bartolli got up, walked over to him and yelled, while showing him the mark where the bullet had hit him on the front of his vest, "You stupid shit! This vest is bullet proof!"

Two of Bartolli's men made their way to the entrance to a back room, shooting one of Lenny's men in the process. In that room they found Sam lying dead on the floor. His head had been blown off. Seeing Sam that way, Bartolli told his men, "Take the ones not dead back to the farm. We're gonna take two, maybe three days killing them because of what they did to Sam. I'm really gonna miss him."

Tony felt bad about Sam. He had come to really like the man. He was going to miss him too.

Chapter Nineteen

Kenny Johnson had been one of Bartolli's muscle guys for a little over a year now. His large 6 foot 1 inch frame was carrying some extra weight, up to a total of about 310 pounds more or less depending on the day, but his appearance usually got people's attention. Bartolli liked that, getting people's attention when he wanted their attention. Bartolli's top enforcer and right hand man, Bruce "Bud" Merchant, considered Johnson to be a good man to have around, especially now that Sam was no longer there. Bruce knew he could tell Johnson anything to do and Johnson would try to get it done. It may take him a little while to get around to it, but he would eventually follow through with whatever Merchant, and particularly Bartolli, told him to get done, regardless of how unpleasant the task might be. Those unpleasant tasks may run from breaking somebody's fingers, one by one over about an hour, to helping clean up the barns behind Bartolli's house.

Johnson didn't enjoy the work around the barn, but he did like the fact that Bartolli and Merchant really seemed to appreciate that they could count on him to get things done, eventually. When he had first been told about Bartolli having all of his guys, and it would not be just Johnson, helping around his beloved farm, Johnson felt there were worse things he could be doing. Besides, he sort of enjoyed being thought of as one of the group's tough guys. There was something about seeing the fear in the eyes of those he had been instructed to deal with. He enjoyed that, probably more than he should, but he did. With Sam now gone, maybe Bartolli would begin to rely more on him than he had in the past. There was just that one thing that he had to be careful with. He liked to take a drink down there every now and then from a bottle he had hidden away next to the back wall of the barn. He would have to be real careful with that.

On this particular day, it was late in the afternoon and the shadows caused by the coming sunset seemed to make things appear so differently from how they had looked during a bright day. At least they did to this fifty-seven year old who had spent so many days during his lifetime out in the hot southern sun that his eyes were not what they used to be. Indeed, he was often kidded about not being able to see that well. His fellow work mates were always saying that, if a shootout took place, he should wait for one of them to identify the targets before he should shoot, just to prevent him from shooting one of their own guys.

As the darkness of night was completing its fall over the ranch in south Louisiana, Johnson was at work feeding the horses in the second barn, the one the farthest away from the big house.

This was something that he and another worker did and they usually alternated the days that they performed that task. As Johnson went about his business this evening, he noticed that the horse he was feeding was becoming skittish. It began to swing its head from side to side and then backed away from the hay being provided. Johnson had never seen that before and wondered what was wrong with the horse.

The more he looked at the animal, the more agitated the horse became, now even beginning to snort. It was then that Johnson had an idea, an idea that came to him in the form of Johnson now thinking something was wrong. Bad wrong. What could it possibly be? The horse was in its small corral inside the barn and the gate was closed. He didn't see anything inside the horse's area that should be causing such a stir. It must be something behind him, he decided, so he gradually turned to look over his left shoulder.

It was then Johnson saw that, standing at the entrance to the barn, was a large black bear! Johnson stumbled backward as the huge animal came into focus in Johnson's bad eyesight. He immediately tripped over a large bucket that was on the ground near the railing of the corral that was now behind him. Reaching his arm out to brace his fall, he knocked the bucket over on his way to the ground. Its remaining water contents went all over his clothing and on the dirt ground. Now lying on his back, gasping for air both from the fall and from the shock of seeing what he thought was at the very least a nine foot tall black bear, Johnson decided to began trying to crawl backwards through the now muddy ground, using his elbows and hands. At the same time, he was trying to convince his brain that he was not really looking at a black bear, especially one that big.

He must be having a heart attack, or a bad dream, or

something that he didn't even know about because he had never heard of a black bear being in south Louisiana and he had lived there all his life. His eyes had to be tricking him. That had to be what it was, and there it stood, in the doorway, on its hind legs, just looking at him. Johnson got even more scared as his next thought hit him. That bear looked at him like he was hungry! That bear looked like it wanted him for its next meal! It was then that he let out a piercing scream as he tried to turn over so he could stand up, and run! Get away from that place! Get away from that huge bear!

As he finally was able to stand up and turn around to see how close the animal was that might want to attack him and eat him, nothing was there. There was no bear. He steadied himself against the railing, blinked his eyes and then took off running through the open back entrance to the barn at a speed that was as fast as his big, overweight body could run. He was screaming at the top of his lungs all the way up the roadway to the big house. As he got to the back porch area, the door flew open and Merchant came out, holding a pistol.

"What's wrong?" Merchant asked, looking over Johnson's shoulders first to the left and then to the right.

Johnson braced himself on the railing of the porch at the steps, now breathing really hard from his run, and yelled as best he could, "There's a bear behind me!"

Merchant said, "A what?"

After taking another big breath, Johnson answered, "A bear! A big bear!" He then looked back over his shoulder fully expecting to see that huge animal lumbering up the roadway coming after him.

Merchant continued looking past Johnson and all over the area behind the house, gun held in hand.

"You saw a what?"

"A bear, I'm telling you. A huge bear, bigger than me." Johnson now turned to again scan the area down towards the barn, trying to find the large animal he was sure he had just seen.

"Man, there ain't been no bears around these parts for years."

"Well, I just saw one. I swear I did!"

They both stood there, scanning the area behind the house.

Merchant looked back at him. He noticed the dirt and mud all over Johnson's clothes, then said, "Man, you been drinking?"

Johnson looked again over the area where he had just run. Looking back at Merchant, Johnson said again, this time pointing towards the barn.

"I am telling you, Bud. I saw this big black bear. Right down there. At the barn."

Merchant looked down towards the area that Johnson had just pointed to.

"Alright. Show me." With that, Merchant started down the steps and began walking towards the barn. After taking a few steps, he looked over his shoulder and saw Johnson still just standing there, at the foot of the elevated back porch, leaning up against the handrail.

"Well, come on. Show me this bear."

Johnson pushed away from the railing and slowly began putting one foot in front of the other going back in the direction he had just run from. As he reached where Merchant was standing, Johnson said, "Look. I swear to you. I saw a damn huge ass bear down there."

"Okay. Come on. Let's go find him."

With that, the two men began their journey down the path leading to the barn the farthest away from the house. As they got closer, Merchant raised the gun in his right hand to a position where it could be pointed and fired immediately. Slowing their pace as they got closer, Merchant eased himself towards the side of the barn near where the entrance was, with Johnson nearby, but behind him. Johnson didn't have a gun, a fact of which he was now very aware.

After reaching the barn wall, Merchant leaned against it and eased his head around the wall's edge so he could see into it. He slowly ran his eyes from first right to left and then back left to right. No bear.

Now Johnson peered around Merchant to look inside the barn. He didn't see a bear either.

Merchant, now feeling safer, gradually eased through the entrance and into the barn, turning his head back and forth like it was on a swivel. The horse took a few steps in his corral but did not seem that agitated to Merchant.

Johnson stopped at the doorway, looked all around the inside of the barn from his position of what he felt was safety, and watched Merchant conduct his investigation.

Merchant pulled his gun down from its ready position and walked back to Johnson.

"There's no bear down here," he said in a mocking tone. Seeing the dirt and mud all over Johnson's clothing, Merchant said, "Come on. Let's go over to the bunk house and get you cleaned up." As they turned and began to walk away, both of the men looked back at the barn. They would both look back over their shoulders several times more before they got over to the bunk house.

* * * * *

Once again, it was Thursday night at the Baked Tomato. The group of four girls was at its regular observation table and they were already providing each other with their critical reviews of the newly arriving attendees. Deputy Sheriff Patterson was at his normal perch, that being at the end of the bar with his bar stool turned so he could view the entire inside area without much effort. Soon Tony Gable arrived and was the instant subject of a very complete evaluation of his handsome appearance by each of the four girls. He waived to the girls as he made his way over to the deputy, an act that had all four talking at the same time about him.

As before, during the course of the evening he danced with each one of the four. They all had the same opinion of his dancing ability. It did not come close to matching his drop dead handsome good looks. They all agreed with Molly that, while the fact remained that he was not that good of a dancer, each of them could forget that if they could just be on the dance floor next to him or just sit and look at and listen to this hunk of a man from overseas. It did begin to seem, to the other members of the group, that Tony was spending just a few more songs dancing with Karen than the other girls. That was somewhat annoying but not surprising to the others of their little group since that same thing had happened so many times before. The three of them had talked on several occasions, both with Karen sitting with them and without her being present, about how on the one hand they could disown her and make her feel uncomfortable being with them or they could let her sit with them and enjoy the attention they got because of her being with them. They decided to let her continue sitting with them, especially since they all really did like her as a person and a friend.

At about 10:30, with there being no new male showing her any particular interest, Sarah decided it was time for her to go home. She never did feel comfortable staying too late if she did not have a male companion to talk and dance with. She always felt it looked bad for girls like her and her single friends to be hanging around drinking late into the night, even if they were sitting together. Sometimes they would do that but tonight, Sarah felt, was a night she needed to go on home. So she got up to go to the ladies room, quietly letting her friends know she would be leaving for the evening after her visit to that area of the establishment.

After her restroom visit, she walked out of the building and got into her car, which was parked in the parking lot next to the entrance. She always tried to park in that lot and usually could because she and the others got there early enough so they could have their good viewing location starting early in the evening. As she pulled up to the street exit for the parking lot, a city police officer walked over to her car. He motioned for her to roll her window down, which she did.

"Ma'am, we are just checking to make sure that people coming out of the Baked Tomato are sober enough to drive home and not be a threat to other drivers."

"Okay."

"Have you been drinking tonight?" the officer asked as he slightly bent over next to her car.

"I've had a couple of drinks but that is what I normally have," she answered.

"Are you drunk or have you maybe even been smoking some of that weed tonight?" he asked with almost a sneer on his face.

She had seen the officer before but did not know him and was surprised that he had even asked her that question. She had only tried smoking marijuana once in her life and had not liked it though now a few of her friends were smoking it on a regular basis.

"No, officer. I am not drunk and I don't do that smoking type of thing. Now I am going to leave and go home."

"Not so fast, honey. Step out of your car, please ma'am."

"Why do you want me to do that?" she asked.

"Ma'am. Cut your motor off and step out of the car," the officer said, this time in a firm voice.

She did as the officer requested, getting ready to shut her door behind her after she had gotten out and was standing next to him.

"Can I search your car?" he asked while looking at her from about three feet away.

"Search my car?" she asked incredulously.

"Well, you say you are not drunk or smoking anything so you have nothing to hide or be worried about, now do you? Or do you?"

Thinking about it for a split second, she answered, "No, I don't. Go ahead. Make yourself happy."

She took a couple of steps to the side as he eased over and bent down so he could reach around under the dashboard of her car and under her front seat. She turned to look around to see if anyone was watching her go through this embarrassment. As she turned back to look at the officer, he now was on one knee on the driver's seat, reaching over under the passenger side seat. He then pulled back and stood up, holding a small plastic bag with something in it.

"Well, look what I found. Looks like a nice sized packet of marijuana."

Reaching for the handcuffs on his belt, he said, "You are under arrest for possession of marijuana."

She was in shock as he pulled her hands behind her and put handcuffs on her wrists.

"Officer, that is not mine."

"Yeah, sure honey. They all say that."

He began reading her rights to her as she stood there. After completing that legal requirement, he said, "Stand right here while I put your car back in the parking lot. You're not driving anywhere with that. You're going to jail."

He motioned to the place where he wanted her to stand. Then he got into her car, started it up, and drove it around so that he could park it back in the spot she had just left. After he got out of her car and turned to walk back to her, he gave a brief look over to the shadows of a nearby large live oak tree, where Burdette had stood hidden while he watched the whole thing.

Chapter Twenty

The Baked Tomato was definitely the favorite gathering spot for the local populace. Even Tony now looked forward to going to the hangout and seeing the new friends he had made there. He was especially beginning to look forward to how Karen would be dressed for the evening. Usually it was form fitting jeans and a tight blouse with boots but then that was what most of the girls there usually wore. Somehow though, she wore her clothing differently, or at least appeared to.

This particular evening, as he walked up to where the deputy was sitting, Tony was greeted in a completely different manner, for him. He was smiling.

"If it isn't the cowboy," Mark said with a wide grin on his face.

As Tony got up onto the adjacent bar stool, he couldn't help but smile back at him.

"You're never going to let me forget that, are you?"

"My cowboy friend, there are a lot of people that now know about your experience with that horse. I'm just the only one that feels he knows you well enough right now to kid you about it."

Tony could only shake his head and then said, "I can just imagine what all her group of girlfriends has had to say."

After a brief pause, Tony changed the subject and asked, "Tell me something. How long have you and Karen been dating?"

"Why do you ask," Mark answered.

"Well, I sort of consider you a friend now, and I just don't want to be with her, even as a friend, if it causes you any concern at all. I mean, she is so beautiful but she is also so nice and I don't want to cause any problems. I am just looking for some friends and I consider you both to be that." He knew he didn't want to cause a problem with the one person he had been asked to check out by his New Orleans associates and see if there might be some compromise way of doing things. He continued, "Look, I feel bad about even being out there with her because I really do consider you a friend. I actually feel bad about being with her just to ride motorcycles and my trying to ride her horse."

Feeling that Tony was being sincere about what he was saying, Mark answered, "I appreciate your feeling that way. I really do."

Taking a moment to shift around in his chair, Mark then continued.

"Look, we have been dating for about a couple of years. But she wants to get married and I am not comfortable with doing that the way I feel right now. I really am not. But she wants that to happen in the worst way. She thinks her clock is ticking for her to have kids, but I am just not ready for that yet and I really don't know when I will be. So the result is that she can date whoever she wants. I don't feel right restricting her and, at this point, she doesn't feel right about being limited to me if I don't want to get married. Don't get me wrong, I do care for her, but I think it's better, for me especially but also for her, to let me work out the problems I have. She really doesn't know what a load of mental baggage I am still carrying around from that Vietnam War. She has some idea, but not completely."

After thinking about what Mark had just said, Tony turned in his chair to face him and said, "Okay. I will just say this. I will still make sure that you know about any efforts we make to go try to ride both the motorcycles and her horses, so if you want to be there you can."

"Man, I appreciate your saying that. I really do. But that's alright. I don't have any say so over who she gets to ride her horses or who she rides with. But you really need to be careful about riding her horses, that one that threw you in particular. You were so fortunate to not have been badly hurt. I have known some people, especially while I was growing up here, that really got hurt from being thrown by a horse."

Tony thought for a moment and then said, "Well, I think I am going to try it again, at least if for no other reason, to prove to myself that I can ride a horse."

Mark kept his gaze on the busy room. After a brief pause in their conversation, Tony decided to bring the Kennedy subject back up. He had been thinking about what Mark had mentioned before and other things had come to his mind. He was looking forward to seeing what Mark's response might be to a few more observations and questions.

"I have been going over what you said the last time we talked about that Kennedy thing. Now tell me something, how do you know so much about that Cuban information?"

Looking back at his bar companion, Mark answered, "That all has been in the newspapers here. It just seems that nobody has thought that much about it and I wanted to mention a few things to you as we talked."

"What you said has really had me thinking about it."

"Well, add this to your thinking, Mr. Detective," Mark said as he leaned over towards him.

"What's that?" Tony asked, leaning forward to now give Mark his full attention because he definitely wanted to make sure he heard what was going to be said next.

Mark hesitated a moment, making the decision as to whether he wanted to explore the subject further, then asked, "What was Oswald doing in Mexico City at the Russian embassy?"

Tony fixed his eyes on the deputy. "What do you know about that? Not many people have talked about that. They have kind of left that alone."

"What's the answer to the question? Was that Lee Harvey Oswald at the front of the Russian embassy in Mexico City before the shooting? If so, what was he doing there? Why was he there? If it wasn't him, who was it that looked so much like him that was there and why were they there? And here is something else."

Pausing for a moment, Mark could see Tony's complete attention was focused on what he was going to say next.

Leaning really close towards Tony now, Mark said, "There are rumors that he went inside the embassy and spent some time there, inside. If it was Oswald, what was he doing going inside that embassy? If he did go inside, who did he meet with? And for how long? What was said, because as much as you have found out about it all, you know what the rumors are about who he met there."

Tony was almost on the edge of his seat by now, not saying a word, waiting to hear what Mark said next. After a quiet pause, Mark said, "The rumor is that whoever it was supposedly met inside with a Russian KGB agent known to the CIA for plotting and taking part in assassinations in this hemisphere and that they met for over an hour."

Tony tightened his grip on his chair as he sat there looking at Deputy Mark Gable. After a short pause, he said, "How in the world do you know about that? Not many people have ever talked about that. Some people have said it never happened. That it was not even Oswald that was there."

Tony now sat there looking at the deputy, taking into serious consideration what had just been said and Mark's lack of response to what Tony had just said. The conversation abruptly ended because up walked Karen, but Tony thought almost continuously for the rest of the evening about what the deputy had said.

Later, while dancing with Karen out on the dance floor, he invited her to go to the beach with him on his motorcycle the next day, which was Saturday. She agreed to go, saying she would meet him again at the parking lot of the Baked Tomato at eleven the next morning, but he would have to try to ride her horse again. He agreed. She then said she would bring sandwiches for both of them if he would bring the drinks. He agreed to that also.

The next morning they met at the parking lot. It was a beautiful day, a good day to be alive. This time she had a large knap sack that went over her neck and shoulders. Since he had Buddy with him, she agreed to put the paper bag holding her sandwiches in the right saddlebag so that the small puppy could be put in her knap sack, which he fit into without any problem. Tony already had beers and soft drinks in the left satchel behind where she would be straddling the motorcycle. Once she was in place, he started the motor, settled on his seat and off they went to a nearby beach down the road just south of town. Tony felt good and so did she.

When they got to a spot where he felt comfortable, Tony parked the motorcycle alongside the road. He took Buddy out of the knap sack and then they both put the drinks and the sandwich bag into the knap sack. Tony pulled out a light blanket from the left side of his saddlebags and they then made their way onto the sandy beach area overlooking the waters of the Bay of St. Louis. Once spread out, the blanket made a good place for them to sit down and start sharing a noon time lunch.

As they began to get their drinks opened, a beer for him and a coke for her, Tony asked, "So where do you stand with Mark?" he asked.

"Here I am with you and we are going to talk about my relationship with Mark?"

"He is the deputy sheriff, you know, and I don't want to run afoul of the law here," he answered with a big smile.

"You let me worry about him. But just so you get it again, from me, we are now dating other people. But you already knew that, or else I wouldn't be here."

Tony had to smile at her answer. One thing about Karen, she was direct in her answers. She was not playing games, at least not any that Tony had seen so far. And she was so beautiful. He could have just sat there on the blanket and looked at her. She would never have had to say a word, at least for a while. She was so cute petting Buddy, who was now lying down in her crossed legs as they talked.

"He likes you," Tony observed as Buddy seemed to not be able to get enough of her attention. If she stopped petting him, he immediately started looking for her hand to continue doing it again.

"It's time to eat. I do have plans for the afternoon and have to be back in a little bit," she said as she began to open the sandwich bag she had packed. They immediately began to enjoy the ham centered between two pieces of bread along with lettuce, tomatoes, and mustard.

"My friends have been telling me that you are somehow connected to that large house and all out in Devil's Swamp," she said as she watched closely for his response.

Tony looked at her and, after he chewed his sandwich so he could swallow and answer, he said, "What else do your friends say about me?" He wasn't going to confirm or deny anything, just yet.

Looking at him after she had sipped from her drink, she continued, "They say you may be involved in that huge estate out there, the house and those thousands of acres that go with it."

Studying her for a moment, he decided that she did not need to know too much right now. Maybe some day but not right now, not until he saw how things were going to unfold with his new friends in Louisiana and the sheriff of Hancock County.

"I only have a little part of that. You can go back and get them all straight about that. There are many others that had a lot more to be worried about in that situation than I did and they were in control." He was being truthful, but at the same time not necessarily forthcoming. There was still too much at stake. It was better left at what he had just said.

After further small talk, which included Tony agreeing to ride her horse the following Saturday morning, Karen told him it was time for her to get back. It was then that they began to pack up. As they got down to picking up the light blanket, Tony grabbed her as she was close and kissed her. Oh, did he ever kiss her, and she did not resist, enjoying every aspect of that romantic touch. When he finally ended the kiss, they both were somewhat stunned and just stood there. Finally she pulled away and said, "Uh look, I really do have to get back."

"Okay," he answered. They finished folding up the blanket, Karen ignoring Tony's almost constant stare at her, and then walked back to pack the motorcycle. After the packing had been done with hardly a word being spoken between them, he got on the cycle and she got behind him. Buddy was back in the large carrier slung over her shoulders. As she put her arms around his waist again, he looked over his left shoulder and said, "Just so you know, I really enjoyed that kiss."

"I'm glad you did. Now move it so I'm not late," she answered with a smile.

"No comment from you? I didn't know I was that bad of a kisser," he said, trying to lighten up the situation.

After a moment, she leaned forward and said in his left ear, "I did too, now go." He instantly noticed her hot breath.

He cranked up the machine's motor and they returned to town. After they pulled into the parking lot, Karen got off the motorcycle and stood next to the machine while handing Tony his puppy. She then stuck out her hand and, with a smile on her face, said, "Thanks for such a wonderful time."

He shook her hand and she turned and began making her way to her car. As he watched her magnificent rear end move as she walked away, he said, "You're very welcome."

Tony decided he may as well take a short ride around the Bay St. Louis downtown area and enjoy the beautiful day. After a tour of the area he happened by the small city park where he saw the older lady he had talked with there before, Miss Helen. Seeing her wave at him as she smiled, he pulled over and parked his means of transportation next to the corner of the park. Walking towards her, he was greeted like a long lost friend.

"Hi there," she said as he walked up to her. "I wondered if that was you on that thing."

"Hi, Miss Helen. Yes, it seems I enjoy riding them and feeling the wind in my face. May I join you?"

"Oh, sure! That would be so nice," she responded with a big smile.

Tony settled himself onto her park bench next to her and crossed his legs.

"I have been thinking about you since we met," she said as she looked over at him. "I really appreciated your help last time, when we met, and the more I thought about it, the more I had hoped I would see you again and we could talk. I would appreciate knowing more about you."

Tony looked at her and smiled, saying, "Well, I am not a very interesting person, but what would you like to know?"

"Oh, things like are you married, do you have any children, what about your parents, are they still alive; where over there are you from. Things like that."

"Ok. Well, I am not married. My girlfriend of several years

was recently killed in a bus accident. As for my parents, my father was over here for a while and came back to Sicily during the war to help the Allies. After the war he stayed and eventually married my mom and they had me. She passed away years ago because of cancer."

"I am so sorry, about your mother and your girlfriend," Helen said with all sincerity. "I would not wish that on anyone."

"Thanks, I appreciate that."

"Is your father still alive?" she asked, trying to hide her interest in his answer to that question.

"No, he passed away a while back. I miss him. We had a really good relationship." Tony dropped his head in obvious sadness.

"I am so sorry that he is also gone now. So what brings you here?" Helen asked as she tried to change the subject as she looked at his handsome face. She had just found out what she really had wanted to know.

Tony had to think before answering Helen's question. He decided it wouldn't hurt to let this person, who seemed genuinely interested in him, know a little bit. He knew from his discussion with Karen earlier that there was some information about him on the streets anyway.

"My father's sister was Madeline Benedetti. I had to come over and take care of a few things with her estate. Now, I want to ask you a question. Do you want to go for a ride with me on my motorcycle?" He could not help but grin as he observed her reaction to his offer.

"Oh, young man!" She immediately laughed and then said, "Fifty years ago, I may have taken you up on your offer."

"Really? Well, now is your chance."

"Oh, no. But that is sweet of you. So sweet."

"Okay. Well, I am off then. I enjoy riding my cycle. Feeling the power of my machine." Tony said as he stood up.

"Thanks so much for stopping and saying 'hi' to me, and for sitting with me," she said as he began to walk away.

"Oh, it was good to see you again. You be careful with your walking, ok?" Tony said as he stopped and looked back at her.

"You be careful on that thing you're riding," she retorted with a smile. "Bye, bye", she said as she waved to him.

He waved back as he turned and walked down to his ride. After getting on, he started up the powerful engine and then eased off down the street. She watched him drive away, thinking that she might have, indeed, enjoyed the excitement of riding, especially with such a handsome young man, if it had just been when she was younger. She also thought about her long lost love, his father, Nick Gable. She had thought about him so often through the years. She was just glad to find out he had survived the war and to also find out he was the father of this very nice young man.

Chapter Twenty-one

On the top floor of a large modern building in a major city, a trim man of medium build in a black blazer, grey slacks and white button down shirt opened the heavy wooden doors and walked over to the receptionist's desk.

"Hi, Marsha," the man said with a slight smile. "Is he available?"

"He's expecting you." As she stood up and began walking around her desk, she said, "Go right on in."

The man walked toward another thick wooden door, twisted the knob, and opened it with little effort. After he had gone through the doorway, Marsha immediately pulled the door closed behind him.

The visitor walked toward the massive desk centered in the

large office as the man behind the desk, dressed in a dark blue Armani business suit, stood up, offering his hand for a handshake.

"It's good to see you, Zack," said the man in the expensive suit.

"Good to see you too. Thanks for taking the time to let me visit with you."

Motioning to one of the two large, well-padded chairs facing the desk, the Armani suit said, "I always have time for you. Have a seat and tell me what's on your mind." The suit then sat back in his chair and clasped his hands in front of him, directing all of his attention towards his visitor.

As the visitor settled into his chair, he said, "You might remember that situation in the Gulf I discussed with you at our last meeting. Well, things are beginning to get out of hand. It may not be too long and that situation will have to be dealt with."

The man with the clasped hands slightly nodded his head in the affirmative, and then said, "What do you need from me?"

The visitor replied, "Whatever might happen, it will probably happen very quickly. If we don't get ready for it in advance so that we can do what is necessary to take care of the situation, it will be much more difficult to solve the problem. I need your approval for us to start thinking about how things might happen and what we might do to take care of it all."

The Armani sat back, his hands still clasped together, and he turned his head to his right and began looking out of the large window on that side of the office. After a brief, quiet moment, he turned back to face his visitor and began speaking in a low, firm voice.

"Things like this are why I hired you six years ago. You have done outstanding work for us, for me and this organization, ever since then. Not once have you made a bad decision. I have been impressed by your judgment. You have made decisions that I admire and that have resulted in us avoiding serious problems. So, with regard to this particular situation, you do whatever you have to do in order to deal with it. Do what you think is appropriate, when you think it is appropriate, but when the time comes to do something, take care of it, once and for all. I have complete confidence that you will make the right decisions. Now, at the same time, do keep me informed. I don't want to be surprised by anything. But start putting the pieces in place now and, when you think the timing is right, I am telling you to do whatever you think you have to do in order to take care of it. Completely, take care of it, sooner than later. We have put up with that situation for way too long."

Looking at the Armani, the visitor said, "You know that dealing with this has the potential to have ramifications that could go far beyond what we faced in our previous situations. It may end up affecting some of our friends much more so than in those other situations. At some point, you may have to even get the Governor of Texas involved."

The Armani knew exactly what the visitor was making reference to and knew that the visitor wanted to make sure that he was clearly aware of those possibilities.

After taking a moment, the Armani looked right at the visitor and said, again in a low, firm voice, "Noted." Then after taking a deep breath, the Armani said, "But start putting it together now and when the time is right, do it. Take care of it. Keep the others involved as much as you feel appropriate, but don't feel like they have to be familiar with all of the details. I trust your judgment as to what you tell them and what you don't.

The visitor slightly nodded his head in the affirmative, then said, "Okay. Just so you know, I think that, with this one, things may eventually come to a head so quickly that it might not be possible to get in touch with you before they actually happen."

The Armani looked directly at the visitor and said, "I understand. Try to do the best you can to let me know ahead of time but, make no mistake about it. You are authorized to do whatever you, in your professional judgment, feel you need to do. If anything, don't wait until it is too late and gets more complicated and more difficult to handle than it already is. The longer we wait to deal with that situation, the more likely it will be that things will get out of hand."

As the visitor then rose from his chair, he said, "I will see to it that things are taken care of as soon as we can get the pieces together and ready. And thanks for your comments."

The Armani stood up, walked around his desk and extended his hand to the visitor as he neared him. Shaking hands with him, the Armani said, "I meant every word of it. I have always been so glad that we have you working with us. We all owe you our sincerest heartfelt and deepest thanks for everything you have already done for us."

Opening the door for the visitor, the Armani said, "Good to see you. Have a safe trip back."

As he walked into the reception area, the visitor nodded towards the receptionist and said, "Nice to see you again, Marsha."

"Nice to see you, too."

With that, the visitor disappeared behind the huge hallway doors as the Armani went back into his office to deal with other matters.

Chapter Twenty-two

Tony received a call from the sheriff who told him to meet him out at the "farm," which meant Bartolli's ranch, the following morning at 10. Nothing else was said, and it should not have been, during that brief conversation. But for Burdette to call him and give him such short notice, something serious was going to be discussed. It wasn't like Tony was one of the key operatives of Bartolli's gang. No, something was on Bartolli's mind and he wanted to talk with Tony. Tony could only guess that it was something to do with the deputy.

Driving down to the ranch the next morning, Tony ran over in his mind what might possibly be brought up. He would have to be prepared for the ultimate question and that was if Mark was ready and willing to work with Bartolli's outfit. If he was willing to work with them, what was he willing to do at this time? Tony knew that as of right now, the answer to the question was a "no." The only thing he could do was to try to get more time so that he could find out if he could get some type of cooperation out of Mark.

Tony got out of his car after having parked it in front of the ranch house. Kenny Johnson walked up to him and said that they could see Bartolli in a few minutes, that he was in a meeting that had to be finished before Tony could see him. As they walked down towards the barns wasting some time while waiting, Johnson mentioned his recent sighting of a black bear when he had been down at one of the barns.

"He was huge, you hear me? Huge! Standing up he was almost like a third taller than me. And big. Just really big."

"Are you sure that's what you saw?"

"Aw man, not you too. Nobody believes me. I am telling you, I saw a huge black bear. Right down here. At sunset."

Tony began thinking that maybe Kenny had been into the spirits a little too much and had been seeing things. He could just imagine what the others there at the ranch were saying.

"How long has it been since anybody has seen one of those things around here?" Tony asked, trying to be pleasant and understanding.

"I don't know. Nobody has really said they knew anybody that has seen one. But I am telling you, I saw him standing about right there," Kenny said as they arrived at the spot.

"You saw him here?"

"Yeah, right here," Kenny said, as he pointed to the ground just as they had arrived at the entrance to the barn.

"Where did he go after you saw him standing here?" Tony

asked, really wondering at this point because Kenny was so sincere in his story telling.

"He just, uhhh, he was, uhhhhhhh, I don't know! I tripped over a bucket behind me and when I turned around to look for him while I was on the ground, he was gone."

"Just disappeared?"

"Yeah, just like that. He wasn't there. So I got up and went to get something to shoot it with and Merchant came back down here with me. But it was gone."

Turning around and beginning to walk back up the dirt road towards the big house, Tony said, "I bet you have caught a lot of grief about that, haven't you?"

Now walking beside Tony, Kenny said, "Yeah, but I know what I saw, and I saw a black bear."

"Well, maybe you'll see him again. Maybe soon."

"Yeah, but I'm carrying my gun with me now, everywhere I go around here. That bear could show up at anytime, but I'll be ready for him next time."

Kenny continued walking to the front parking area as Tony now opened the front door. Walking into the ranch house immediately told Tony all he needed to know. The man in the front hallway entrance was one of the guys Tony had seen before and now he was wearing a gun.

"He's in his office," the man said as he closed the front door behind Tony. "You can go on back now."

Tony walked down the short hallway and stuck his head into the doorway. Bartolli was by himself, at least for now. With Sam gone, Tony could understand why Bartolli might have a man at the door to the house. He could also understand why Bartolli

245

might start thinking that things needed to be moved along. The deputy was definitely a problem and Bartolli was not in the mood to suffer problems any longer.

"Come on in, Tony. Have a seat," Bartolli said as Tony walked into the room. Purposefully taking a seat in the chair with the desk top cannon pointing towards it, Tony was intently listening to find out what was going to be brought up.

"This thing that happened with Sam has made me rethink a lot of things. Makes me want to hurry things up, lots of things, many things you don't know anything about, but one you do. That deputy over there in Hancock County caused another seizure four nights ago. Wasn't a big one, just one of the smaller trucks hauling some stuff, but that deputy was there, at the seizure. I don't know where he is getting his info from, but it has to be somebody that knows what we are doing. With that happening, it doesn't look like you are making any progress with him. Where are you with that?"

"I am really just now getting to the point of talking with him about different subjects and all. He and his girlfriend have agreed to date other people. It seems he doesn't want to get married and she does because she wants to have kids."

"He doesn't want to get married? Sounds like we might have something in common after all," Bartolli quipped, followed by a forced laugh.

Then Sheriff Burdette could be heard as he was greeted by the man in the foyer, followed by the noise of his boots making their way down to the office.

"Sorry." Burdette said as he walked in and sat down in the other chair facing Bartolli's desk.

Bartolli pointed to Tony while glaring at Burdette and said,

"He didn't have any trouble getting here on time. What is your excuse for dragging in here late?"

Burdette was temporarily at a loss for words. After a moment, he said, "Traffic was horrible. There was an accident on the Interstate. Must have happened after he came through."

Bartolli looked at Tony and said, "He's telling me about the deputy's girlfriend. Do you know her?" he asked as he turned his attention back to Burdette.

"Yeah, I know her. Pretty little thing. School teacher. Hangs around with a bunch of little bitches. One of them was that girl that was arrested for marijuana possession in the parking lot outside that club over there. You know the one I am talking about."

Bartolli nodded his head in the affirmative and then said to Tony, "Go ahead with what you were saying before the sheriff here walked in late."

Tony said, "I was just saying that they have agreed to date other people and so I got her to go for a ride with me on my motorcycle. She only agreed to do it if I would ride one of her horses."

"Did the deputy know about her agreeing to this?" Bartolli asked.

"Yeah, he was sitting there when I asked her after she made a big point about how he wanted them to date other people. I even asked him if he wanted to be there when she rode my motorcycle. It's a Ducati, a pretty well-known motorcycle that I had flown over here from Sicily. Told him he could come along but he said he would pass on that, but that he might want to see me ride her horse." After a pause, Tony continued.

"So I took her to the beach and we had a nice conversation

247

there, a lot of it about the deputy. It gave me a few ideas about how I might try to approach him."

"Did you go out to her place and ride her horse?" Bartolli asked.

With a hint of a smile on his face, he answered, "Well, I went out to her place, but I don't think you could say that I rode her horse. When I got on him, he took about ten steps and then went straight up. I went straight off the back of that horse, did a complete flip."

Both Bartolli and Burdette let out howls of laughter.

"Put you on your ass, did he?" Bartolli asked, still laughing.

"I still don't know what happened, really. I mean, one second I am sitting up there and everything is fine. The next second, I am sitting on my rear on the ground! Don't remember anything in between." Both of the other men chuckled at that. Tony wasn't about to tell them about his latest motorcycle ride with her and the beach.

Bartolli said, "Well, you have got to move it on along. You really do. I just don't like having him out there messing up things. For him to think he can do that, and nothing will happen. I am going to have to show him he is wrong, unless you can get him to come around."

Shifting in his chair, Bartolli said, "I will give you a while longer, but not much longer. If we can't bring him around, we'll have to take him out and the sooner the better. So get after it. It would be better if he would just come on because those police guys get kind of strange about one of their own getting killed."

Looking at Burdette, Tony asked, "Did you ever say anything to him about sort of laying off or something?"

"Naw." Then Burdette explained, "We decided that it would be too dangerous to do that. He's smart, and he might start to thinking about that in his own mind and get to be even more of a problem. We decided to leave it alone from that angle,"

"Well, start getting into it with him. See what you can do", Bartolli said as he looked at Tony. "But I am telling both of you, if he doesn't come around, we are going to remove him. And if I have to, I'll do it in a way that will make it clear to everybody to stay out of my way." With that, he slammed his fist down on his table to emphasize his point.

"I'm not taking interference with my operation from anybody, least of all some two bit deputy sheriff in Mississippi," Bartolli almost screamed out. After getting his breath, he then said, "Kind of reminds me of Bobby Kennedy."

That comment instantly got Tony's attention.

"Did you know him?" Tony asked.

"I didn't but some people down here were picked up by him when his brother was President and taken to Central America."

"Taken to Central America? When was that?" Tony asked.

"Why are you asking," Bartolli said with a stare at Tony.

"President John Kennedy is somebody I have kept up with and studied my whole life. He had that beautiful wife, his handsome looks, and all of that money, and he was President. But, other than training some of those Cubans down there for the Bay of Pigs invasion, I've never known about any Central America connection. What was that all about?"

Bartolli settled back in his chair and after a moment of thought said, "Bobby, President Kennedy's brother, was Attorney General. At some point, even though his dad, ole man Joe Kennedy, had been in the bootlegging business, Bobby went after one of my good friends down here that was involved in a few things. Well, when he couldn't get my friend removed from the country by a court order, he just had the man picked up and taken to Central America and literally just dropped off on some road in the middle of nowhere. It took my friend about six months to get back into the United States."

"Bobby Kennedy just had him picked up and taken out of the country?" Tony asked.

"That's exactly what he did. Claimed he was in the states illegally."

"Boss, what would you have done if Bobby had done something like that to you?" asked Burdette.

"If that had happened to me, I damn sure would have done something about it. I probably would have taken him out. That's why I said this deputy sheriff sounds like Bobby Kennedy. He doesn't know who he is dealing with. Of course, a lot would have depended on the whole picture, you understand, just like it does with this guy." Tony was at a loss for words.

Not too long after that exchange, the meeting broke up. Tony now had something else he would stay up late thinking about.

* * * * *

The next day sales clerk Sarah Montgomery made her appearance before Judge Jonathan Banks in the Circuit Court of Hancock County. She still could not believe it was all happening because she had no idea how that marijuana got into her car. Her lawyer, Bradley Hamilton, was sympathetic, but she had been caught with the drugs. With the amount she had, unless she pled guilty, Hamilton told her there was a possibility that, if she was found guilty of possession, she could possibly be sent away to prison for up to twenty years. He told her that if she pleaded guilty, the judge might give her a five year sentence because they would not have tied up his court in a trial that could last for several days. Also, if she did decide to go to trial, she would have to pay Hamilton ten thousand dollars up front. She simply did not have that kind of money. It had been hard enough to get together the bail money she had come up with. With no family to count on for financial support or any other support for that matter, she felt she didn't have any option but to plead guilty and hope she got the reduced sentence that Hamilton had talked about.

The date of her hearing, her three friends from the Baked Tomato were sitting in the front row of the courtroom. A few other people were there who also had legal matters before the same court. The time came for Judge Banks to deal with her case. When asked to stand and tell the court what her plea was, she stood up and said that she was pleading guilty to the charges against her. It was then that things got out of hand.

"Hearing your plea of guilty, and giving consideration to the complaint against you in this matter, and giving further consideration to the recommendation of the sheriff relative to your sentence, I hereby sentence you to ten years in the state penitentiary at Parchman, Mississippi." Judge Banks then brought his gavel down, which resulted in a rather loud noise, and promptly declared, "This court is in recess." He then stood up and walked away from where he had been seated.

Immediately after the judge had finished reading out Sarah's sentence, Hamilton began assuring her that he would try to get her paroled after serving two years. But it was all too much for her to handle. Sarah collapsed. She fell on the floor and officers in the courtroom moved quickly to revive her. Cold, wet towels were brought in from the ladies room out in the entrance corridor.

After the attention she received from the courtroom officials, she was finally able to stand up. She was handcuffed and then began to stumble out from behind the table where she had collapsed. As two uniformed officers guided her towards the side entrance to the courtroom, she saw Kovac standing over next to the door leading to the judge's chambers with the sheriff, her lawyer, and the judge who had just sentenced her. As she was being led out through the doorway, Kovac raised his right hand and pointed his forefinger at her like it was a gun with his thumb acting as the hammer going down. She knew then that she had been set up for what she had done to him at her store.

Chapter Twenty-three

The more Tony thought about his effort to ride Karen's horse, the more his manly instincts told him he had to try to do that again on Saturday, as he had said he would. He had taken enough ribbing from Mark, Karen, and Karen's girlfriends that he knew he just had to try again. After all, it was only a horse, not some dragon or something unknown. It was just a horse, and watching her ride her steed during the first trip out to her barn and pastures had simply amazed him. A woman as beautiful as she was and as slight of build as she was gave no advance notice of how well she could control that huge beast. Making that big, approximately 1600 pound animal do what she wanted it to do was really something to behold.

So when he was kidded, once again, by the deputy about riding the same horse that had thrown him, he really didn't have any choice, at least not if he wanted to continue to try to protect the idea that he was a real man's man. In the presence of Mark and three girls, including Karen, who were standing at the bar, Tony confirmed on Friday night that he was going to ride the same horse again the next morning. Karen insisted that it be the same one that threw him because, she said, "You have to show that horse what type of person his rider is, and you are not going to be a scaredy cat, are you?"

"What is that? A what kind of cat?"

"A cat who is scared to try it again. Just afraid. Is that you?" she teased, right in front of what he felt like was everybody in that bar. So he said, "Not at all. I'll show you. Tomorrow morning at 10, I will be there."

He felt better after he said that with bravado. There was only one problem. As he thought about it, he remembered that the horse was so much bigger than him. Also, that particular horse had seemed to read his mind! He could almost swear the horse knew that he was just a little afraid of him. But he was going to try it again, especially with everybody there now picking on him. This was only going to be the second time he had ever tried this thing, this riding of a horse.

Mark was sitting at his normal perch listening to it all. Tony did not see any jealous feelings coming out of Mark concerning Tony going out to his girlfriend's farm and riding that horse, or at least trying to ride it. Tony even asked him, "Mark, you want to come watch history? I am going to ride that horse this time. I promise."

Mark actually smiled back at him and said, "Now don't go assuming that you are going to be successful with that. I am sure she has told you that particular horse has thrown more people than just little ole you."

Tony remembered hearing something similar from Mark before. Beautiful Karen had not told him that important piece of information. The fact that he was not the first one made him even more determined that he was going to ride that horse.

"I am going to do it this time. Come watch. You'll see. You can be my witness." Tony made sure he had determination in his voice.

With a grin on his face, Mark answered, "You keep on talking like that and I just might want to go out there and see what happens."

"Come on out, you'll see. This time, I am going to do it."

"I'll check and see if I've got anything going on with work for Saturday morning. If I don't, I just may come watch that."

Karen was all smiles when he said that. She was glad their budding friendship with this foreign guy was not being affected by some petty jealousy. She was glad that the two men seemed to get along so well. If anything, Tony actually loosened Mark up a bit. Mark was now getting to where he was kidding Tony. That was something new, at least for him. In the back of her mind, though, was that kiss on the beach the other day. As she looked at the handsome Tony, her thoughts went back to her feelings when he had kissed her. She had been surprised, which had made her uncomfortable, because she loved Mark, regardless of his resistance to marrying her. But then there had been that kiss.

Saturday morning at 10 a.m. Tony drove his Ford up to the barn area at Karen's family farm. He was not about to admit that he had been up most of the night worrying about how he was going to ride that huge animal. Karen was there as was Snow, the same stable hand that had been there the first time. Also there were Karen's two friends, Molly and Sue. The first thing that crossed Tony's mind was, here are two witnesses. These two girls will spread all over town whatever was getting ready to happen out at Karen's family farm. He had better ride that horse this time or he might not be able to even go back in the Baked Tomato again.

Snow already had two horses saddled, Queen, the same one Karen had ridden the first time, and Fireball, the one Tony had tried to ride. Tony looked at the animal and caught the massive horse looking back at him, almost staring at him. It was as if the horse was saying to himself, "This idiot is not going to try to ride me again, is he?" But Tony was determined. After Karen was in her saddle, the stable hand held the white horse by its bridle as everyone waited for Tony to mount the horse. Tony walked up to the left side raised his boot to put it in the stirrup, grabbed the saddle horn with both hands, and pulled himself up on top of the massive horse.

He immediately felt confidence flowing all over himself. He was handed the reins by Snow as the horse immediately began to turn almost in a circle.

"Pull back on the reins," Karen yelled.

Tony pulled back on the reins like Karen was telling him to do.

"You're pulling back too hard. Be easier doing that," she yelled out.

Tony loosened up a little and finally the horse seem to settle down somewhat. The two girls were clapping and cheering the hero. The stable hand was standing there, but Tony noticed he was not smiling or clapping so Tony remained on alert.

Karen said, "Follow me down this little path next to the fence." Tony noticed a wooden fence running on the left side of the path along the edge of what was an open pasture area. There were a few trees scattered along the fence line down the path. Karen had her horse headed in a direction away from the barn and Tony, now feeling more comfortable and in control, kicked the heels of his boots into his horse's ribs to encourage him to follow the leader. The horse moved its hooves quickly in response but, within a few feet, seemed to settle into a slow trot down the path, now being about twenty yards behind Karen and her horse. Tony was ready to celebrate. He was riding the horse and others were watching.

It was at this point that things changed quickly and dramatically. The horse all of a sudden took two faster steps forward, but moving over closer and now almost next to the wooden fence. It was at that point with the mass of weight moving forward, after gliding to its left so that it was now almost touching the fence, that the horse suddenly jumped back to its right. Tony and his weight did what every person who has not ridden much does in such a situation. He left contact with the saddle he had been sitting on and literally began an act of flight though the air over the fence. Eventually, after wisely letting go of the reins to the animal, he landed hard on the left side of his rear in what, just a split second before, had been an adjacent pasture. It had all happened in the blink of an eye.

At first there were exclamations of horror from the two girls back at the barn, which was still not that far away from where he had begun his flight. Karen had turned around to look at Tony riding but had instead seen him launched and flying through the air. She wheeled her horse around and immediately came back to check on him, at the same time trying her best to keep from laughing out loud. Finally, she could not resist anymore and let out the loudest belly laugh, followed by a wide grin.

Then, she started laughing again but tried to stop herself by saying, "Are------ ohhhhhh are you -------"? She just couldn't keep it inside. She now was laughing nonstop.

From his place on his rear on the ground, Tony looked up at Karen as she was laughing, then looked over at the horse. He could almost swear the horse was laughing also. The two girls came running up and Molly immediately asked, "Are you okay? My gosh, you completely flew through the air!"

"You did!" added Sue. Noticing that he was alright, they both started laughing. Uncontrollable laughter. He looked back at the stable hand who was now walking up to the group. Even he was at least smiling when he said, "Yassir mista, you was flyin through the air like an angel."

Hearing that, the three girls looked at each other and started laughing even harder.

Karen got off of her horse, wrapped its reins around a fence pole, then worked her way through the split rail fence and over to where Tony was lying on the grass. Molly and Sue began to crawl through the fence, all the while trying to muffle their laughter.

"Are you okay?" Karen was finally able to say without breaking out again in laughter.

Tony looked up at her. There was no way out of it. He was totally embarrassed. Totally.

"I think I'm okay," he was finally able to say. Then he moved to try to get up. Karen tried to help him with his effort. With her assistance and that of the other two girls, he was able to, slowly, stand up and then get through the fence and back out onto the path. He didn't think he had broken anything but one thing was for sure. He wasn't going to be running any races anytime soon. Almost every bone and muscle in his body hurt.

"I think I need to go get in a tub of hot water and spend some time there."

Assuring the girls that he would be okay as he slowly limped his way back to his car, he was finally able to get in and drive himself back to his house. There, he drug himself out of his car and made his way inside, now feeling like almost every joint in his spine was broken. He spent most of the afternoon and all of the early evening in his tub, refilling it with hot water about every fifteen minutes or so. Harley sat there next to the tub just looking at him for most of that time. At first, Tony could almost swear that the dog was laughing at him also.

*   *   *   *   *

The view from the top floor of the huge building was something Marsha enjoyed. The problem was she did not get to spend much time doing that. For one thing, her responsibility was to make sure that her boss, who besides being extremely wealthy was the head of one of the most recognizable business names in the world, functioned as efficiently as possible. The demands on his time were enormous with everyone from his company's business partners to literally heads of state insisting that he devote at least some of his attention to their interest of the moment. However, having worked for her boss for eight years, she knew exactly which of those striving to get his attention indeed needed it and in some cases absolutely had to have it.

Such was the person who was now on the special phone line on the credenza behind her desk. Not many people even knew that the number to that line existed and those who did know about it had such knowledge for a good reason.

Picking up the phone after its ring tone let her know one of those special people was calling, she merely said, "This is Marsha."

"Hello, Marsha. Is he around?"

She definitely recognized the voice because of its low, baritone pitch. No other person had a voice quite like it. She immediately noticed that he did not ask if her boss was "available." That meant this call needed a higher degree of response, like immediately.

"Yes, he is. If you will hold on for a moment, I will let him know you are on the line. He has some people with him so it may take a moment."

"Okay. It is rather important."

She knew immediately that, by the way the caller said what he had just said, it was not just "rather" important but was "very" important. She did not put the caller on hold. She just laid the phone down on the edge of her desk behind a rather large stack of papers and got up to go to the door to her boss's office. Reaching the door, she used a special combination of knocks that she and her boss had agreed upon just for situations like this. It was a knock that meant, "Boss, regardless of what you are doing, you need to get the visitors in there out of your office so that you can find out about what your 'loyal secretary' has waiting for you, either in person, on the telephone or by documentation."

After a couple of moments, she opened the door to see that her boss, today looking very stylish in a perfectly fitted light brown Armani suit, had already told his three visitors that something had come up that he had to deal with and so he would have to excuse himself from any further meetings with them at this time. The visitors said they understood and, after quickly shaking hands with their host, exited the room. Marsha showed them to the waiting elevator in the lobby and wished them pleasantries as she observed the elevator door closing. She then quickly returned to her boss's office and said in almost a whisper, "You have a call on the 'dedicated' line."

As he reached for one of the three phones on the credenza behind his desk, he said, "Thanks, Marsha."

After she had closed the door behind her exit from the room, he pulled the phone up to his ear and said, "Hello?"

"Yes, it's me."

Immediately the Armani recognized the caller by his deep voice. He could also hear the click of Marsha's phone being hung up.

"Okay," the Armani answered as he sat back in his chair.

"You wanted me to let you know, if possible, before something happened in that area we talked about."

"Yes."

"Things are coming together so we can move forward as soon as possible. Looks like the situation is at the point of getting completely out of hand. As we agreed, something will need to take place before that happens."

"Okay. Anything you need from me?" the Armani asked.

"No. I take it everything remains as we discussed before."

"Yes, it does. Good luck and be careful."

"We will be. I'll be back in touch once everything is concluded."

"How soon do you anticipate an event?"

"Pieces are on the move and almost in place. As soon as they can be brought to the table and the timing is right, it happens."

"Okay. I'll look forward to hearing from you."

"I'll be in touch."

"Okay. Thanks for the call," the Armani suit said with a finality in his voice which meant that the conversation was now over. The click on the phone indicated the voice had understood that and hung up. Things were getting ready to get real interesting.

Chapter Twenty-four

Kenny had barn duty at the Bartolli farm again this afternoon and he did not like it. None of the other guys did either, but the Boss had told them that it was good for them to be with the pigs in the corrals down the dirt road a little behind the house and with the horses as they were being fed in the barns just beyond the corrals. While they all felt like such chores were demeaning, the Boss assured them that, if they couldn't tend to the pigs and the horses, then he would have worries about them tending to the occasional body that had to be disposed of in that back area. Sometimes he would require them to put the bodies in huge vats filled with lye so that there were no finger prints or skin by which anybody might be able to identify the bodies. The problem with the lye was that it was difficult to turn a body over to the pigs for complete disposal after it had been in lye. Kenny preferred to just cut the bodies up and feed them to the pigs.

After he finished putting the hay in the troughs at the last barn, Kenny leaned his pitchfork against the wall and turned to walk towards the front entrance to the building. As he looked up, there it stood. It was that black bear and it was huge! The first thing Kenny thought of was that he was about 6 foot one inches tall and the bear was at least three or four feet taller than he was. It even looked bigger than he remembered! And he was not carrying his gun with him as he had promised himself he would do.

Kenny then did the same thing any ordinary person would do suddenly seeing a huge black bear standing in the doorway about ten feet away from him. He let out a yell. Not any ordinary yell, but an ear piercing, screaming yell. The bear, apparently annoyed by the yell, waved his huge paws in the air, as if he were clawing at something or soon would be, such as Kenny. Kenny turned in extreme haste to grab the pitch fork he had just leaned against the barn wall but, instead of grabbing it, he knocked it to the ground next to the wall. As he bent over to pick the implement up, he looked back and up at the bear, which now appeared to Kenny to be taking a step towards him. He panicked as he was reaching over to grab the pole of the pitchfork and fell down onto his knees. As he looked back up in his state of fright to see what the bear was now doing, that animal appeared to him to be enormous, so big that he seemed to be blocking out most of the light.

Kenny quickly turned his head to make sure he would get his hands on that pitchfork and he finally did. Now on his knees with pitchfork in hand, he turned back to face the bear, hoping he at least had time to raise it in his defense. There was no bear! He jabbed the pitchfork forward, blinked his eyes and looked again. The bear he thought he had seen was nowhere around. He cautiously stood up, looking around the inside of the barn but no bear. He carried the pitchfork with him as he worked his way over to the doorway where he thought he had seen that big black bear. Still no bear. Upon reaching the doorway, Kenny again did what any normal human being would have done - he began running, as quickly as a man as big and as overweight as he was could possibly run while carrying a pitchfork. After a few steps, being the smart man he considered himself to be, Kenny figured out that he could run a lot faster if he wasn't encumbered by carrying that pitchfork so he dropped it while in full flight.

As he got closer to the big house, he started calling out, "Hey! Hey! Hey guys!" As he got to the back porch area of the mansion, Merchant came through a doorway leading onto the porch area followed by Bartolli, who had an automatic pistol in his right hand.

"What's wrong?" Merchant immediately asked.

Gasping for air as he now stood in front of the two men, he said, "I saw that big ass black bear again. Remember the one I told you about before? I just saw it again. It's huge!" Not being able to really continue talking too coherently at the moment, he stopped to catch his breath.

Bartolli came down the back steps and went right by Kenny, saying as he passed, "Let's go get us a bear, boys."

Kenny looked up at Merchant after Bartolli had passed and Merchant said, "Let me get my gun, Boss."

Bartolli answered over his shoulder, "Don't worry about that. I've got mine. You two come on. Let's get down there before he gets away."

Kenny looked at Merchant again as if to look for guidance. Merchant shrugged his shoulders and said, "Let's go." The two of them joined the effort, walking a few steps behind the man with the gun.

When they got down to the barn, Bartolli walked into the barn with his gun extended and his eyes searching. Merchant and Kenny peered around the entrance, eventually walking into the barn, still a few steps behind Bartolli. They all saw the same thing- no bear.

After walking around the interior to make sure, Bartolli returned to the two men and, looking at Kenny, said, "You ain't been drinking, have you?"

"No, boss! I swear, I saw that bear here again. It's a big one."

"I'm starting to get worried about you, my man. This is the second time, and no bear."

With that, he stuck his pistol in the belt of his pants and began walking back up to the big house. The other two men began to follow Bartolli back towards the house, as Merchant again asked Kenny if he was sure he had indeed seen a bear. After all, no one else had.

*   *   *   *   *

As part of his continuing familiarization with at least part of Bartolli's operation, Tony had been told by Burdette to meet Chet Buchannan at the boat docks in Venice, Louisiana. Specifically, Tony had been told to go to the pier where the racing boats were docked. He was going to be able to identify Chet, he was told, because he would look and dress like a movie star and usually had two or three beautiful young girls riding with him on his sleek, white, 42 - foot Wellscraft Scarab racing boat. Buchannan had been racing for a few years now, which he thoroughly enjoyed during the times he wasn't making lots of money through what many people believed was a highly successful import/export business.

Chet's boat was the envy of most of his racing competitors. Its dual 750 horsepower engines, combined with Chet's risk-taking abilities as its captain, had made his vessel the one to beat in almost every local competition. Chet always seemed to be operating on the very edge of what would probably be a horrific crash if it ever happened. He loved having the reputation of a guy living on the edge but who so far had managed to successfully escape disaster time after time.

What Chet's friends and lovers did not know was that he had developed a strong need for artificial stimulation, now to such a point that it was something he just had to have on a daily basis. He readily provided his close gang of friends and the girls with them with a steady supply of not only marijuana but particularly cocaine and heroin. It had eventually gotten to the point where now he paid less and less attention to his business and more and more attention to the drug and female of the moment.

Tony recognized Chet the minute he saw him by the description Burdette had provided. Chet was dressed much as the upper class in Italy often dressed when they went boating. His white slacks and deck shoes were offset by the blue and white stripped shirt he wore which had the top two buttons unbuttoned so that the hair on his chest showed. His wavy blond hair and blue eyes along with his trim, medium build did give him, Tony agreed, a movie star appearance. Tony's blue jeans, tennis shirt, and deck shoes gave him the appearance of a person still attempting to make his first financially successful deal, an image that Tony didn't mind presenting since he was the newcomer in town.

He didn't want to appear to be a threat to anyone, especially someone like Chet who may have been concerned with a man that apparently had the attention of the Boss to such an extent that he was being allowed to make this special trip today.

Chet saw Tony as he was approaching the long racing vessel. Tony noticed that Chet seemed to have only one person with him, that being a rather burly looking individual who Tony assumed was a deck hand of sorts.

"You must be Tony," Chet said as he stuck his hand forward for a shake.

"I am," he answered while grasping Chet's offered hand.

"Good. Climb on board and we'll take you for a ride. That's Jeff over there," said the seemingly good natured Chet. Jeff waved from the opposite side of the boat as Tony climbed on board the vessel, then returned the wave.

Looking around after he had gotten aboard, Tony said, "Tell me about this boat. This is something else."

Chet said, "It's a V bottomed racing boat made of one-half inch thick fiberglass. It can go up to a hundred miles an hour. It carries two hundred and fifty gallons of high octane gas and gets about one mile to the gallon, depending on the speed."

Then he turned to Jeff and said, "Cast us off and let's show our guest some of the waters of offshore Louisiana."

Jeff pulled in the bow line and Chet started the powerful motor. Within minutes the three men were going first twenty-five, then sixty-five and then, according to Chet, ninety miles an hour over the calm waters of the Gulf of Mexico. It wasn't long and the boat was speeding past off-shore oil rigs as it made its way out into the beautiful, open waters of the Gulf.

After forty minutes of that high level of speed, a boat began to appear in the distance. Jeff took a screw driver from the utility storage compartment on the side of the cockpit and, after opening the door to the bunking area under the front part of the boat, Tony could see him undoing the screws holding a small portion of the front wall of that room to the large frame of the boat. The closer the racing vessel got to the boat, Tony was able to determine that they were approaching a dilapidated merchant vessel which was stopped dead still in the water. As they got closer to the boat, three men appeared on the deck of the small ship, each making himself available to grab the line that Jeff was now holding from his position on the bow of their racing boat.

Chet slowed their vessel to almost a stall and Jeff threw the line to the nearest man. Once the line was securely tethered to the mother ship, small packages wrapped in plastic and bound with tape began to be handed to him. Each package looked to be less than ten pounds in weight and less than a square foot in size. Jeff took each package and passed it to Chet who then threw the package on the floor of the cockpit of the boat. In all, Tony counted twenty-two packages as being transferred to the racing boat. After the last package had been delivered, the bow line was released from the mother ship and thrown to Jeff.

Jeff secured the line on board and climbed back into the cockpit. He then began transferring each package through the door to the interior of the racing boat. Looking through the doorway, Tony could see that there were bunks on each side of the room up under the front of the boat. After Chet pulled the boat away from the mother ship, he cruised at almost idle while Jeff took each package and stacked them inside the three feet tall, four feet wide storage area behind the front wall of the bunking room. He then used the screwdriver to secure the wall

269

back to the boat's frame. Tony checked his watch. The whole transfer had taken less than five minutes.

"You want me to drop you off at the Blue Barge?" Chet asked as he began to increase the speed of the boat. "I'll pick you up in a few hours if you want. We've got to get this shipment secured on shore and then we'll run the boat for about an hour or so."

"No. Thanks, but I'll go on with you. There are a few things I need to tend to on shore."

"Okay. Hold on. We're gonna get it on up there going back. Takes much less time that way."

Tony grabbed on to the boat, one hand on the side rail and the other hand on the forecastle as Chet opened up the throttle. The power generated by the twin motors of the vessel was something Tony had never experienced, but that didn't scare him. The thing that did bother him as they went back was that Chet had the boat going so fast that almost the entire vessel literally came completely out of the water and seemed to constantly be on the verge of flipping over backwards. For most of the way, almost the only part of the boat touching the water seemed to be the propellers. Chet was loving it. Tony was glad when they got back to the harbor.

Chapter Twenty-five

Juan Bartolli, known in his area of operations as "The Boss," decided he would go over to Bay St. Louis and see for himself what all the talk was about concerning the Baked Tomato. He also wanted to see who the fine looking animal was that the deputy was now having trouble keeping as his own girlfriend. Bartolli had always found it best to go check things out himself, especially if they were not going the way he wanted them to, which certainly seemed to be the case with this deputy. He talked with both the sheriff and with Tony before making that decision. After those discussions, he was sure he needed to go take a look at the man to get a first hand opinion of whether it was even going to be possible to get him to at least turn his head at times. He was also almost sure that the deputy had a source of information into his organization. He had to in order to now have been at the right place at the right time to make seizures that had cost him so much money in lost product.

Taking Larry and Johnny with him, the three made their appearance at the Baked Tomato at around 10:30 Friday night. Bartolli was wearing a white suit and vest with a black silk shirt. Matching white shoes made the 5 foot 6 inch, 165 pound man with his long, wavy, black hair look like a caricature out of some book. His wearing apparel did give him the appearance of looking much younger than his 46 years of age. Then of course there were those things that always seemed to get him attention, which he loved, in places where he was not known. They were the three strands of solid gold chains hanging around his neck along with the solid gold dollar coin hanging from the longest of the three.

When the three of them first walked in, Bartolli was leading the way flanked by the 6 foot 4 inch, 310 pound Larry on his right and the 6 foot 2 inch, 290 pound Johnny on his left. Needless to say, when the three of them walked into the Baked Tomato, there was a brief pause in many of the conversations so that the observers could take in exactly what they were looking at. As the three of them surveyed the room just inside the entrance, many of the observers began making whispered comments about the new attendees. The first comment made at Karen's table was from Carol, the redhead, who said, "Girls, it looks like we have a new play toy." With that being said, the other three girls slowly turned their heads at varying times to look at what she had referenced. Each one of them saw the spectacle, and the redhead knew who he was. Having seen Bartolli at a Mardi Gras party in New Orleans not too long ago in the same identical suit led her to say, "I do believe that is Juan Bartolli! Y'all know who he is! That's him!"

As Bartolli and his two friends began to make their way around to the left portion of the room, Mark noticed Bartolli immediately. He definitely knew who he was. Tony, who was standing next to Mark at the far right end of the bar, heard the words slowly come out of Mark's mouth, "What in the world is he doing here?" Looking at Mark and seeing him literally staring with his eyes, Tony slowly turned his head and saw the target of Mark's gaze. He couldn't believe what he saw. If only Bartolli could realize how ridiculous and out of place he and his two friends looked. It was almost like a scene out of some comedy show. Tony looked around and saw almost everybody in the place checking out the three new attendees. At least the band didn't stop playing because, if they had, the room most likely would probably have been silent as almost everybody looked in the direction of the three visitors.

Eventually the three settled at a table off to the left near the front of the dance floor. As soon as they sat in their chairs, all of the talking heads again began their chatter, most wondering who in the world the three clowns were, but the few who had some idea who he was were saying something similar to what Mark had first said when he saw them.

The redhead informed her table that the dandy of the group was worth about as much as the entire population of Hancock County. She also reminded them that he was somewhat of a shady person. It was at that point that one of the girls asked, "You didn't tell us the most important information. Is he married?"

Carol answered, "The last time I asked one of my friends over in New Orleans about him I was told that he was not married, but that he is into threesomes."

Molly said, "Threesomes? Don't we have enough here to reach that number?"

Carol laughed and then said, "Honey, you are the wrong color. He prefers Vietnamese girls. He has two that he sees most of the time. They are usually with him when he goes out. They take care of him, any way he wants, at any time he wants. Lots of drugs involved. I was told he is one of the biggest mobsters, if not the biggest one, in New Orleans. Which brings me back to my first thought, why in the world is he at the Baked Tomato?"

The group shifted their eyes back to where Bartolli was seated and saw the three men ordering their drinks from one of the waitresses. After a short period of time, the bar resumed its activities as the band began playing "Brick House." That song prompted Karen to stand up and say, "Well, girls, let's go put on a show for them." With that, she went out on the dance floor followed by two of her table mates, Molly and Sue. Soon other girls were putting themselves on display also, each one occasionally looking over at the table where the white suit and his two gorillas were sitting.

Mark looked around the room and saw Sheriff Burdette leaning against the back wall with his trusted Deputy Frank standing there with him. Mark wondered why Burdette was there tonight. He hardly ever came by so it was interesting that on a night that he was there, one of the area's biggest thugs was also there, in Bay St. Louis, Mississippi, of all places, and at the Baked Tomato at that. Tony's eyes followed Mark's gaze and he saw Burdette and Frank also.

Tony leaned in close to Mark and asked, "Why did you say what you did when that guy in the white suit and his two friends came in?"

Mark kept looking at the three visitors and said, "Because that is this area's richest and most well-known organized crime leader, Juan Bartolli, and he usually doesn't come over here. He has all he needs there in New Orleans. To be over here, with two of his men, means something is probably up. He doesn't make this trip just for the fun of it. He can have all of anything he wants over in New Orleans. This is very unusual."

Mark made eye contact with his boss, Sheriff Burdette, who slightly nodded his head in recognition. Mark then shifted his eyes, as did Tony, to the dance floor where Mark's former girlfriend, Karen, and her two friends were putting on their show. Mark wished she wasn't doing what she was doing out on the dance floor. As he watched her, he immediately made the comment, "She has no idea how dangerous it is for her to be dancing like that in front of him and his friends."

Tony had the same feeling, but was not going to express it. This was going to have to play itself out, if possible, with him only being an observer. It was at about that time that Bartolli and his man Johnny, after seeing a few other men begin to walk out on the dance floor and start dancing with other girls who were now out there, stood up and made their way onto the floor, specifically going over to where Karen and her friends were dancing. Bartolli lined up directly across from Karen, who greeted him with a faint smile. He quickly proved himself to at least be able to keep a beat, which Tony noted was more than Mark usually could do the few times he had witnessed Mark on the dance floor. Bartolli's body guard, Johnny, though was totally incapable of keeping a beat. Instead, he eventually just stood somewhat close to the two girls who were with Karen, trying to move occasionally to the music.

Tony could now see that Bartolli was trying to initiate a conversation with Karen as they danced by leaning forward and saying something and then her leaning forward and saying something. It was then that Tony thought to himself that it was

275

time for him to keep an eye on that situation. He looked at the deputy and noted that the deputy did not give any indication of being bothered by what was going on. Tony could only come to one conclusion and that was that nothing good was going to come out of what was happening right there in front of them. He felt that Karen had no idea how precarious her situation could be if she ended up just sitting with him or, even worse, leaving with him. He wouldn't put it past Bartolli to spike her drink if he could get her over to sit at their table with them. And there was one thing about it all. Karen was definitely the best looking woman in the place and Bartolli had noticed that immediately. Of course Karen had, probably knowingly, gotten him interested in talking with her by her provocative dancing, thinking maybe she would get Mark jealous to some extent. Tony felt himself getting uneasy and he wasn't even her boyfriend. What he knew she did not realize was how dangerous the man was that she was dancing with. He was the type of man that would do whatever it took to get her out of that bar with him. She was becoming more and more at risk every moment but still didn't know it.

The song being played by the band ended and the two continued to stand out on the dance floor talking. Bartolli's thug was nearby trying to convince Molly and Sue to come sit with them. It was then that Tony decided he had to go into action. Call it whatever it needed to be called, he got out of his chair and casually walked around next to the bar to a point where he was directly opposite Karen as she stood there on the dance floor facing the bar talking with Bartolli. Tony could hear an occasional word which led him to believe Bartolli was indeed trying to get her to go sit with him at his table. Tony made sure to catch Karen's eye and shook his head in a negative manner, indicating that Karen should not do what she was being asked to do. Bartolli, seeing Karen looking over his shoulder at someone, turned his head to see who it was she was looking at. At that point Tony quickly turned to face the bartender and pretend to order another drink. When he turned around again after ordering his drink, he could see that Bartolli was still pleading his cause. The problem seemed to be that Karen was at least listening to whatever he was saying. Tony again, this time more obviously, shook his head from side to side as if to say, "No, don't do that." Her two friends remained nearby in a continuing conversation of their own with Bartolli's body guard.

As the music began again, Karen broke off the conversation with Bartolli with a smile and walked up to the bar area to stand next to where Mark was seated in his usual position at the far right end of the bar. After a few moments, Tony casually walked over to where the two were and asked Karen to dance. As they walked out to the dance floor, Tony noticed that Larry, Bartolli's man who had remained at the table, said something to him that caused Bartolli's head to jerk around to look at Tony. The man must have seen what Tony had done and told Bartolli about it.

Tony quickly said, "Karen, listen to me. Do not, under any circumstances, do not go sit with that guy in that white suit, or even dance with him."

"Uhhhhh, a little jealousy, huh?" she cooed as she smiled at him.

"Please, it's very serious, do not dance with him. Definitely do not go sit with him, okay? Please, just trust me on this, okay?"

Karen leaned back and looked at him as they slow danced. After looking into his eyes and seeing how deadly serious he was, she said, "Okay. If you say so."

He immediately answered, "Good. Now walk back with me to where Mark is and, Karen, stay with Mark, okay?"

Karen was now listening closely to what he had to say.

"In a minute, go over to your two friends and get them away from that guy. Do not let them go with them. Those are really dangerous people, okay? Really bad."

She studied his face for a moment and then said, "Okay."

Tony said, "I am going to leave, but please, go stand over there with Mark."

With that he slowly walked away from the bar area and down next to the wall on that side of the room. Standing at the back of the room, when Bartolli finally looked his way, Tony motioned with his head for Bartolli to follow him. He then turned and went through the front door entrance and exited the building. As he stood out front, it wasn't too long and through the doors came Bartolli and his two enforcers.

"What did you tell her?" Bartolli immediately asked as he walked up.

"I told her that you are a very important man that deserves to be respected. I also told her she didn't need to be using you to make the deputy jealous. I mean, how in the world am I going to get his cooperation if his girlfriend is being hit on by the guy I am trying to make a deal for."

Bartolli stood there looking at Tony, processing what he had just been told. Tony could tell that even Bartolli understood what he had just said. Then he continued.

"Mr. Bartolli, you really don't need to be here. Your being here puts a lot of pressure on the deputy, it really does. You don't need to be seen in the same town with him while I am trying to get him to eventually help us. And he certainly doesn't need to see you hitting on his girlfriend. That's not going to help me get him on our side at all."

The one thing Tony was beginning to understand about Bartolli. He was not stupid. Arrogant? Yes. Strange? Yes. Dangerous? Absolutely yes. Offensive? Sometimes, yes. But above all, he was not stupid and he showed that again by the decision he now made.

He slapped Tony on his left shoulder and said, "You're right. I should have thought about that. You are right. But Tony, get this taken care of, now! I am tired of screwing with this guy. Get it to happen soon or else I am going to deal with it my way. If he doesn't come around in the next few days, I am going to blow the sonofabitch up in his fucking patrol car, next Thursday night, right out front here so everybody sees it. Next Thursday night, you hear me?"

With that, he turned and said to his two companions, "Let's leave this piece of shit place." The three of them then walked off down the street, the two men nodding their heads towards Tony as they walked past him. After he watched them walk into the night, he breathed a sigh of relief. A disaster had narrowly been averted.

Tony walked back into the place and up to where the deputy was still seated. Looking around the room, he did not see Burdette or Frank in the room. They must have also left, he thought. Not two minutes after he had returned, up walked Karen who said, "You owe me a dance."

He answered, "Who, me? I do?"

"Yes, you do. Come on, mister." She turned and walked out onto the dance floor, turning around to make sure he was following. Tony shrugged at Mark as he turned and followed her to where she now stood.

"Do you want to tell me what's going on?" she asked the minute they came together for a slow dance.

He looked at her. He didn't want to be dishonest but, at the same time, there was no way he could let her have any idea about what was going on. He shook his head and finally said, "I can't. But please remember what I told you. Stay away from that man, okay?"

She answered, "Okay. I haven't seen you that serious before. It's another side of you."

He remained serious, saying, "Just remember one thing. I think a lot of you. You have been very nice to me. You are so beautiful, and I mean that. You are a wonderful person. Just take care of yourself. Be careful, you hear me? There are things going on that I can't explain to you. The only thing you need to remember is just to be careful. Okay?"

She looked back at him as they moved to the slow, sensuous beat of the music. She really liked this handsome, smooth man. Oh, she had dated smooth men before. Mark was not necessarily one of them, but this handsome man was. There was something about him that just really stirred things inside of her. Oh, his looks counted. The fact that everybody seemed to now think he had lots of money also counted. But the thing that counted the most to her was that he had tried to protect her tonight. He genuinely seemed concerned about her safety and welfare. That showed her he cared, probably more than even he realized. She held him a little closer. She also felt safer with him now that she had been through that experience tonight.

The music stopped and they both walked up towards where Mark was seated. The redhead was there.

Mark said, "Carol here said that, since you want to date other

280

people, she is available for whenever I want and for anything I want."

Karen looked at Carol and said, "You just said that? To him while I was out there dancing?"

"Well, honey, you have said he could date anybody he wanted to. I mean, you were out there on the floor dancing real close to Tony."

With the speed of lightning, Karen's right hand came up and slapped Carol on the left side of her face. Then she said, "Get away from me, bitch!"

Carol eased a step back and then turned to walk away with her left hand up against her face where the blow had landed.

"And stay away from him. He doesn't like fat girls anyway!"

Tony felt a smile come across his face. As he turned to look at Mark, Mark broke into a grin, which was followed by outright laughter from both men.

Chapter Twenty-six

The next day, in Dallas, Texas, retired federal Judge Curt Allen made his way to the office of the Chief Justice of the Fifth Circuit Court of Appeals, George S. Brand. He had been summoned by Judge Brand to be in his office at the appointed time of 10 a.m. sharp. The chief judge's office was easily accessed being on the fifth floor of the federal building in downtown Dallas. Judge Allen had been to that office several times, mostly while he was still an active jurist. Having been retired for three years now, he had not been there recently. He wondered what this was all about, having not been told the purpose of his being there.

"Judge Allen here to see Judge Brand," he said to the secretary after entering the judge's outer office. The secretary, he noted, was not one that he knew so she had no idea who he was or how important he was. He made a note to make sure she remembered his name before he left.

The secretary said, "Please have a seat, judge, and I will tell him you are here." With that, she got up and went through a door in the back of the room, closing it behind her. Her absence from the room became more noticeable the longer it lasted, which seemed to the judge to be more than the amount of time necessary to announce his presence in the outer room.

The secretary finally reappeared, holding the door open as she said, "Please come on back. Judge Brand will see you now."

Allen stood up and, making sure his coat was being properly worn by adjusting the single button closing the coat, he strode towards and then through the door, immediately entering Judge Brand's chambers. He saw Judge Brand seated behind his desk, but he noticed that the judge was not standing to greet him nor was he offering his hand to shake. He also noticed a strange looking man standing behind the judge and off to his right side. What made the man's appearance catch Allen's eye was that he was wearing blue jeans, nice blue jeans but still blue jeans, and a western long sleeved shirt. The thing that most caught his attention was that the man was wearing a white ten gallon hat. Inside that office, the office of the chief judge of the Fifth Circuit Court of Appeals. As Allen neared the judge's desk, he also noticed that the man wearing the hat was also wearing cowboy boots. Must be some friend of the judge, Allen concluded.

Brand's booming voice said, "Have a seat, judge. Thanks for coming here on such short notice. This shouldn't take too long."

Seeing Allen glancing at the man in the cowboy hat, Brand said, "This is Brad Jackson. He's a Texas Ranger. He is here because I asked my good friend, the Governor of Texas, to loan him to me. I could have had a U. S. Marshal here, but I am going to try to do this with the least amount of disturbance possible. Brad served with me in Vietnam. He was with our Special Forces unit there in the Mekong Delta. I have known him a long time and the best thing about Brad is he can keep a secret."

Leaning back in his chair, the judge continued, "I don't want you to say a word in response to what I am going to say next. Just sit there and listen. I think you will understand why once I am finished."

Looking directly at Allen now, Brand said, "I have been informed by very reliable sources that you have been using your privileges as a retired federal appeals court judge to walk the hallways and go into the offices of the court in our buildings in New Orleans and here in Dallas for the purpose of influencing judges that have certain cases that are before the various panels."

Allen leaned forward and opened his mouth to speak, only to be interrupted by the chief justice who said, "I said, don't say a word. I am not asking you for comment. I am not asking you to say anything. This is a serious matter because the information provided to me has already been checked out and found to be true. Brad here has already gotten a couple of confessions, and I might add they were not hesitant at all about blaming you for everything."

Leaning forward in his chair now, Brand continued. "So here is what is going to happen. You are going to get up in a minute and leave, never ever to grace the halls of any offices of the Fifth Circuit Court of Appeals again. Your two friends are going to retire over the next couple of months, never ever to act as judges again. This system does not work with former political hacks like you doing things like you have been doing. We all knew about your past political campaigns, how you manipulated votes for your candidates, how you falsified voters' records for your candidates, and how you got your appointment through political favors owed to you. But those of us who care about this system we have thought that maybe you would grow up, at least act like a grownup, and conduct yourself like a federal judge should. Instead, you decided, after you retired of all things, to try to bastardize the system. Not only have you put at risk your future, and that of your two fellow judges, you have risked the reputation of those of us who take this job and our positions seriously."

Now pointing his finger and looking right at Allen, Brand said, "You are not from this point forward, to have anything, anything at all, to do with the Fifth Circuit Court of Appeals in any way whatsoever. If you do, rest assured that this matter will be referred to those who will properly deal with you to take care of the problem, once and for all. Now, get your sorry, good for nothing ass up out of that chair and get out of my office. Brad here is going to escort you to get your things and then he is going to go with you to the airport and put you on the next flight out of here." Motioning to Jackson he said, "Get this piece of shit out of here."

Within the next two hours, Allen was taken out to the airport and put on a plane back to Louisiana. Ranger Brad Jackson did not wave to Allen when Allen looked back at him from the top of the stairs next to the plane's doorway. Jackson stayed watching the plane until it took off, leaving Dallas and Texas and taking Allen with it.

*   *   *   *   *

After their last conversation about Kennedy, Tony could not get the subject out of his mind. He had, after all, read everything he could about Kennedy and the assassination, but it seemed to him that, for whatever the reason, Mark knew a lot more about the subject than he was letting on. That only raised Tony's interest even further. Even with everything that was happening, he still wanted to find out more about what this deputy in Hancock County, Mississippi, knew that maybe Tony had not been able to find out through his extensive readings on the subject. So on this particular Saturday night, Tony went to the Baked Tomato early enough so that he might be able to talk to Mark without, hopefully, many interruptions so that he could ask follow-up questions, depending of course on what Mark's answers were going to be.

Getting there a little after nine, as he walked into the big bar and dance area Tony could see that the patrons who had come by on their way home after work were beginning to make their way out of the bar. As they were leaving, another group of people was beginning to show up for the evening's activities. The band didn't start until nine-thirty so Tony knew he had some time during which he hoped to get into more discussion with Mark about Kennedy. Tony made his way over to where the deputy's normal perch was at the end of the bar. But instead of sitting next to him, he remained standing and leaned against the bar in the area between the two chairs. That way he could carry on a more personal conversation with him. He was beginning to feel as if the deputy was a close friend, which bothered him given what he was supposed to try to get the deputy to do, and that was at the very least look the other way at certain times, for which he would be well-rewarded.

"Hi there, deputy," Tony said with a grin on his face.

"Hello there, cowboy," Mark answered back.

"Oh, man, you are still calling me cowboy. You're not going

to let me forget that, are you?" Tony said as he motioned to the familiar bartender to bring him a Bud.

"Things like that help keep a man humble, don't you agree?" the deputy answered.

Looking back at the deputy, Tony said, "You know, you could sort of forget you ever heard about my experience with your girlfriend's horse."

Now with a big grin on his face, the deputy quickly and firmly responded, "Not a chance, cowboy."

Tony answered, "Not even if I sweetened the situation by offering you a small payment of some sort?" Tony was now watching Mark to see how he responded since it may give him some idea about how a more serious offer might be received.

Mark looked at him with a quizzical look on his face and then answered, "You know that it is bordering on something illegal for you to try to bribe an officer of the law."

"I was afraid you might look at it like that. I bet you are the one officer in this whole county that wouldn't take a nice contribution to look the other way about something at some point in time, now would you?"

Looking now more seriously at his questioner, Mark said, "You already know the answer to that question, especially for something serious, and that same answer holds even for something as insignificant as putting the word out that you know how to fly without wings from the back of a horse."

That answered his question about the deputy helping out and Tony admitted to himself that he was glad that Mark had handled it that way. He would have been disappointed if there had been any other answer. Tony did feel though that he had to change the subject quickly so that at the very least Tony could pretend he was just kidding around.

"I want to tell you thanks for making me think more about the Kennedy assassination. I've told you how much I have studied that. I have read everything I can get my hands on about him and his family and that assassination." Seeing that it appeared Mark was also happy that the subject had changed, Tony continued.

"I could look at that scene of Marilyn Monroe singing 'Happy Birthday' to him over and over. You've seen that, haven't you?"

The deputy nodded his head in the affirmative and then took a sip of his coca-cola.

"I mean, she might as well have been nude with that dress of hers being so tight and almost completely see through. Ohhhhh!" Tony moaned as they both now pictured the scene.

"I have even wondered about her death," Tony continued. Taking a sip of his beer, he then said, "That just didn't sound right, at least to me it didn't." Turning to face Mark, he said, "You know that she supposedly had been to bed with Bobby Kennedy, the President's brother, as well as the President."

Mark leaned back in his chair and said, "I had heard that or read that somewhere. Well, they both were attractive guys with lots of money and very famous. That is an attraction for lots of women. You know that Sam Giancana's girlfriend was at the White House seeing Kennedy, more than once. You do know who Giancana was, don't you?"

Tony quickly replied, "Even I know who Giancana was, and I'm from Sicily. He was the top mob guy in the whole country over here at that time."

Then Mark leaned over towards Tony and said, just above a whisper, "Well then, why is the mob boss of bosses letting his

289

girlfriend, the beautiful Judith Exner Campbell, go have sex with the President of the United States at the White House? Better yet, Mr. Detective, why is the President of the United States having sex with the girlfriend of the nation's chief mob boss, and at the White House of all places?"

"Well, now wait a minute. How do you know they were having sex? She was just taking messages from Giancana to the President and from Kennedy back to Giancana. The organization had been chased out of Cuba, just like the rest of the Americans, but they still had better contacts down there than the CIA. The CIA knew all of that was going on. They were the ones training the Cuban invaders, in Honduras and other places in Central America. But maybe you can tell me this, Mr. Deputy. How does someone like John F. Kennedy, who was raised along with his brothers and sisters in Boston, and sent to the best schools up there, end up even knowing Sam Giancana, of all people?"

The deputy smiled and, after a moment, answered, "It went way back. His father made his fortune during the roaring twenties shipping illegal booze. Some people say he was involved in shipping booze down here during that time. The Kennedy family even had some property down here. And it has always been thought that John Kennedy won only because the organization delivered the electoral votes of Illinois and West Virginia and that, without their help, he would not have won the election."

It was quiet for a moment, then Tony said, "You know more about all of that than I would ever have expected."

"I read the newspapers. There has been speculation about all of that for years."

After a few silent moments, the deputy said, in a very low voice, "Oswald spent some time in Russia. That doesn't mean much unless you consider it in light of what was going on at that time. It was called the 'Cold War.' You know what that term means? Why they called it that?"

Tony answered, "I have heard the term but what does that have to do with anything?"

"Well, do you remember hearing about the Cuban missile crisis? Now think about that, the Cuban missile crisis. Kennedy and Russian Prime Minister Nakita Khrushchev, the showdown. So close to nuclear war. And history says that Khrushchev backed down. This is the same guy who went to the United Nations up there in New York City and took off his shoe and banged it on the table there because he was upset that he wasn't getting his way."

"I remember reading about that."

"How do you think he felt after being backed down by Kennedy in front of the whole world over Russian missiles being put in Cuba? Do you think he might have been just a little upset about that?"

Taking a pause for a moment to take a sip of his Coke, he continued.

"Remember, the Cold War was just that, a war. It just wasn't being fought by the armies of the two countries. It was being fought by their intelligence agencies, the CIA and the KGB. They were killing each other's agents, and friends. It was a very serious competition."

Tony stood there looking at this deputy sheriff of Hancock County. He was amazed that Mark seemed to know so much about all of this. Yes, there had been a lot of information in the papers and magazines and on television over the years. Yet, this information he had just been told all seemed to be something more than that.

At that moment, up walked the bartender who leaned over and said to the deputy, "There may be a problem over at the other end of the bar." He then quickly moved away as the deputy got out of his chair in response to what had been said.

"Keep this chair for me, if you would. I'll be back in a little bit." As the deputy moved around the bar to its opposite end, Tony began to go back over all that had been said. With the number of people now coming into the dance area, Tony knew there would be no more discussion during this evening about the Kennedy subject.

Later that night, after he had returned to his little house, Tony sat in his chair with Buddy in his lap as he went over everything from Kennedy to Bartolli. What bothered him the most as he thought about it all was that he now knew for sure he was not going to be successful getting the deputy to look the other way concerning Bartolli's operation.

Chapter Twenty-seven

On the following Thursday Tony pulled up in his distinctive 1956 blue and white Ford and parked in one of the parking spaces next to the city park. He had to get a meal. He had spent most of the night thinking about the brief conversation he had with Burdette in late afternoon the day before. During that conversation Burdette confirmed that, since Tony had not been able to get Mark's cooperation, the planned bombing after closing that evening of Mark's police car was on.

Tony liked Mark, much more so than either Bartolli or Burdette, that was for sure. That had become clear to him when he had seen Bartolli trying to dance with Karen. He was glad, so glad, that she had not agreed to dance with him. Nothing good would have come out of that. Sure, he took a chance of Bartolli seeing him mouthing the words to her to not dance with him and knew Bartolli had been told about that. But he had felt that the entire situation was going to begin to get out of hand if he hadn't done what he did.

He had later spent the evening thinking about his life. He was having bad feelings knowing that his very nice friend, Mark, was going to be blown away the next evening because of a decision by Bartolli, who in his opinion, really was not worth the cost of the bullet it would take to kill him. As he got out of his car and shut the car door behind him, he wondered again for the umpteenth time since late the night before, what was he going to do. Just stay out of it all was the best thing, he kept thinking. He was a visitor to this country and he should not get involved doing anything that affected one of Bartolli's decisions.

As he turned to walk down to the cafe on the waterfront one block away, he looked over at the park and saw her. There was that nice older woman, Miss Helen as he had called her, sitting on one of the park benches. She noticed him immediately and motioned for him to come join her. She was good company and he had enjoyed their last conversation so he walked into the park and over to where she was seated. It was a beautiful day and it might be good for him to just sit and again enjoy the company of his new friend.

"Tony!" she said with a big smile. "Please come sit with me. I really enjoyed talking with you the other day. Make an older woman feel good by indulging her wish that you join her for just a little bit, okay?"

"That would be my pleasure, Miss Helen," he answered with an equally big smile. Tony eased himself onto the park bench next to her and, crossing his legs, asked, "What brings you out here today?"

"Actually, Tony, I have been coming here for several days, hoping I would see you."

"Really? Well, I am honored. Sorry I haven't been by here, but things have kept me away from downtown."

"Well, I am so glad that you are here now. Thanks for joining me. I have been thinking about our conversation and finally made a big decision."

"What would that be?"

"I am going to tell you a secret, a secret that you must not tell a soul."

Tony intently looked at this lady. He could tell she was as serious as she could be.

"Miss Helen, if you are going to tell me a secret, please know that if you want, I will never tell anyone. I was known back home in Sicily for being able to keep a secret."

Helen looked at Tony and could tell he was not just saying that to make her happy. He really seemed to mean it. She hoped so because what she was going to tell him would probably change his life. At least, she hoped so. Regardless, she had realized, while thinking about whether to tell him or not what she had on her mind, that she might not have many more opportunities to tell him. She felt that her time would soon be gone and there was this one thing that she just had to tell Tony, now that she had met him. It had never occurred to her that she might meet a child of Nick's because she had thought he was dead. What little information she had received as a result of her previous discreet inquiries to the United States Department of the Army indicated that Nick had died just a few days before the war in Europe was over. Things had been settled in her mind when she had found that out. Now, she knew differently, and this handsome young man, his son of all people, was sitting on the park bench with her.

Looking at him, she said, "Please don't think badly of me, but there is something that my heart tells me you need to know. And I think you need to know for other reasons I will tell you about in a few minutes."

Tony now could sense how serious this really was to her. He said, "Okay. Regardless of what you have to tell me, I can't imagine myself thinking badly of you. So, please, go ahead and tell me. I really would like to know what it is you have on your mind."

After a moment's hesitation, Helen turned a little to face him, looked him in his eyes, and said, "Your father, Nick, is the grandfather of my grandson, Mark."

She watched Tony's face while his mind tried to process what she had just said.

"Oh, that's not possible, Miss Helen. He was in Sicily for ----." He went silent as his thoughts caught up with his mouth. Then he tried again.

"Are you saying ------? Are you saying that Mark is somehow kin to my dad?" Tony asked with a quizzical look on his face.

Helen nodded her head slightly in the affirmative as she looked at him. Then she turned away, embarrassed and condemning herself for even bringing it up. She had thought it would be a good thing because she sensed her grandson was in trouble. She looked down, all of a sudden feeling terribly out of place.

"No. please, " Tony said, seeing her own reaction to what she had just told him. "Please tell me more. You know how much my dad meant to me. So please, tell me. I don't understand."

Feeling a little better because of what he had just said, she tried again.

Hesitantly, she said, "You are Nick's son. He went back to Sicily to help with the war effort there, married your mom after the war as you mentioned the other day, and you were born."

"Yes, that's what we talked about the other day. Now, what are you saying?"

Helen took her time, clenching a handkerchief in her clasped hands that were in her lap, knowing that what she was going to say in explanation was going to pain her. Finally, she got her courage together and started speaking again.

"Nick was here before he returned to Sicily. He and his sister, Madeline, who we talked about last time. Well, while he was here, I was married to Sheriff Bill Patterson. We had a son, Bart Patterson. What I am trying to tell you is ---". Helen gasped as she got to this part of what she was trying to say. She was on the verge of beginning to cry. She knew she had to say it quickly, now, or she might not ever be able to finish telling him.

"Tony, what I am trying to tell you is----------- that--------- your father, Nick, was Bart's father." She could not bear to look at him after she had said it.

Tony was in shock. His first thought was that this little old lady was off of her rocker. His second thought was that somehow she was mistaken. His third thought was, again, she was just crazy, telling him this on a park bench a mere few weeks after she had first met him. But the more he thought about what she had just told him and how emotional she was while telling him, the more he thought that maybe there actually was some truth to what she had said. The quietness was broken as she began to softly sob. It was then that he now felt what she had told him was indeed true. This very classy, older woman would not be sitting there on that park bench in the center of town telling him what she just had, and crying like she was after she had told

297

him, unless there was a lot of truth to what she had just said. That meant that he and Mark's dad, Bart, had the same father! And the hard part of it all was that Bart's dad must have had an affair with this sweet lady sitting next to him while she was married to the well-known and well-respected sheriff, Wild Bill Patterson.

He put his right arm around her, hugging her and trying to comfort her. She put her head on his shoulder, continuing to cry.

After wiping the tears from her eyes, she said, "I loved him. I loved him so much." She then began to sob almost uncontrollably.

Tony just continued to hug her. There was nothing he could say and the more she sobbed, the more he realized just how deeply she had loved his father. He didn't say anything as she cried. After a few moments she gradually began to get control of herself to the extent that he felt he could talk with her a little more about it all.

"Does Mark know this? Did your son, Bart, know anything about this before his death?

She quickly answered, "No, no. Mark has no idea and, please, I don't want him to know. It would serve no purpose for him to know, none at all."

After the passage of a few seconds, she continued, "And Bart had no idea. Ever. You are the only person, outside of your dad, that has ever known about it because I never told anyone and I am sure he would not have told anyone either."

Tony, with his arm still firmly around Helen, thought for a few moments and then asked, "Why didn't you two get married? You could have gotten divorced and you two could have gotten married."

Helen answered almost immediately. "Oh, I wanted to do

that. I wanted that so badly. But your father didn't want me to do that. He was so involved with Capone and all of that and he was afraid that Capone would have had us both killed if I left my husband. After all, he was the sheriff and I think they were involved together doing a lot of illegal things. I think my husband was very important to many of the things that Capone was doing."

Tony replied, "Well, I have to tell you, Miss Helen, I could understand his feeling that way if that was the case."

"You can?"

"Yes. He did that to protect you, and also him. I mean, if Capone's operation had been hurt in any way by your involvement with each other, from what I have heard about him, he would have not thought twice about killing both of you."

"Really?"

"Yes. For sure."

Tony wanted her to feel better about it all, but the bottom line was that what he was telling her was the truth. He felt sure Capone would have done that, especially if Sheriff Patterson had caused problems because of Nick's involvement with his wife. From what Tony knew and had heard, that absolutely would have been what happened. He felt his dad had evaluated it correctly. Tony had heard years ago that Capone had, himself, killed over 40 people for various reasons, many of them members of his own gang. He decided he needed to tell her that.

"Miss Helen, I have heard that Capone, himself, killed many of his own people for various reasons. I think that is something that absolutely could have happened." Watching the older woman's reaction to what he had said while sitting there next to him with his arm around her, he could feel her body relax a bit.

299

"But Miss Helen, I have to ask. Why did you tell me about this?"

After dabbing her eyes again with her handkerchief, she looked at Tony and said, "Because I think something bad is going to happen to my grandson, Mark." As she said that, what Tony had been told the night before jumped back into his mind.

"Why do you think that?"

"It's just a feeling I have. I am so worried about him. I don't feel good about his safety."

"But why tell me about your concern for him? Have you told him?"

"Oh, so many times. I really wish he would quit that job, quit working for that man, Burdette. I don't think he can trust him. I think it's just a matter of time before something bad happens to Mark because of him."

"But why tell me?"

"Because you are his father's brother. I felt that if you knew about it, maybe there's something you could do somehow to protect him."

Tony felt like he had just had most of the air taken out of his lungs. This woman, with her over sixty years of going to church and playing the piano and organ at church, was having some apprehensive feelings concerning her grandson. It was as if the Lord was sending her a message, and she was relaying it to him.

"I think you, of all people, can maybe help my grandson. I have heard a little bit about you since I first met you and I took a chance telling you what I did, hoping that you might do something. You know his father, my only child, was killed, supposedly in a botched arrest or something. I have never thought that's what really happened. Will you promise me you will try to see what you can do to keep an eye out for him? To help him if you can?"

How in the world was he going to not say "yes". She was in essence the mother of his half-brother, which as far as he was concerned, meant that Mark was his brother's son. Did this ever change things. After thinking about it all for a few moments, he felt he had to say something to her and he did.

"Miss Helen, thanks for telling me about this. Really, I know it took so much courage for you to do that, but from the bottom of my heart, thanks. And yes, I will see what I can find out; see what I can do, but again, thanks for confiding in me. I promise I will never say anything to anyone, and I also promise I will see what I can find out and do, if something is indeed necessary."

She turned to face him, leaned up and gave him a kiss on his cheek, and said, "God bless you. Please take care of yourself too, okay?"

"I will. Can we get together again sometime maybe?"

"I would love that. I really would. But I have to tell you, I have cancer. It has spread. They don't give me too much longer to live. I am in a great deal of pain. Really, I think the Lord was letting me stay around just so I could meet you. Now that I have met you, I think he wanted me to tell you what I did and wanted me to hear what you had to say. I am more at peace now than I have been in the last 50 years. May God bless and keep you safe, honey."

"Thanks, Miss Helen. And you too."

With that, he leaned over and kissed her on her forehead. Then he stood up, took one last look at her, gave a wave goodbye with his right hand and walked away. One thing was for sure. If he survived all of what was going on, he would never forget the smile on her face if that was to be the last time he looked at her. She was finally at peace. He hoped he would have the chance to see her again but something in the back of his mind told him he may not.

There was no way he could go eat now. No, instead he went back to his house, let Buddy into the living room and sat in his chair with Buddy in his lap, thinking for the rest of the day. He was torn about what to do. Having been told that Bartolli was going to have Mark's car bombed that night when he left the club, and then being told that Mark was literally his brother's son, he was at a crossroads. The one thing he was going to do was get downtown before dark. He wanted to park his car so he would have access to it should he need it. Because of all of the downtown activity around the restaurants and bars along the waterfront, he felt he needed to get there as early as possible.

At around 6:30, as it began to get dark, Buddy was put back in the bedroom and Tony left for town. Once there, he looked for parking spaces near the Baked Tomato but could not find any. With it being Thursday night, it seemed everybody wanted to park near the place so they would not have far to walk when they were ready to leave. Tony still didn't know what he was going to do. One voice in his mind said that he had to do something because it was his brother's son. Another voice was telling him at the same time to stay out of it, don't listen to some little old lady, and that Bartolli and the mob would be very angry if he took an action that adversely affected what they wanted to happen.

He ended up parking his car about six blocks away from the waterfront. As he began walking towards the bar, he noticed that there were several small churches in the block nearest to where he had parked. He decided to check the front door of one of them along the way and found it to be unlocked. He had been told that the churches in town usually left their doors that way so that anyone with a problem could come in and pray. He felt the need to do that. It was only 7:00. Burdette had told him that the bomb would go off around 2 a.m. that night. As Mark was leaving after the club closed. The bomb would be caused to explode when Mark got into his car.

Tony opened the door to the small church he had picked, waiting at its entrance so that his eyes could adjust to the darkness inside. He noticed as he felt his way down the center aisle that there was only one light on, that being a small spotlight in the ceiling that was pointed at the cross on the altar. With pews on both sides of the main aisle, he worked his way down to the third row from the front. He genuflected and then eased himself into the pew to his left and sat down. It was certainly peaceful and beautiful inside. Dark wood paneling was along both side walls and also behind the altar to the front. Two large stained glass windows were located along the side walls of the building. Benches were located on both sides of the altar area which, Tony guessed, were for the choir. To the right up in that area was the organ.

As Tony sat there, he went over everything in his mind. It all seemed to be confusing. So many things had happened, not the least of which was his meeting earlier that day with Helen at the bench in the park. He had no idea that he ever would have heard the information she had told him. Eventually, after about ten minutes, he got down on his knees on the prayer bench. He then folded his hands on the back of the pew in front of him. He soon became deeply involved in his prayers.

It was about the time he was asking the Lord for guidance that he heard a noise towards the right side of the back of the church.

He looked over his right shoulder and initially saw nothing but dark shadows. Just when he was about to look back forward, he heard a deep baritone voice say, "Your prayers will be answered."

Hearing that voice almost shocked him, because he had not seen anyone else in the church just a few moments before as he had walked down the center aisle. Looking more intently, he gradually began to make out the figure of a man, who also appeared to be leaning on the back of a pew as he kneeled, at the far end of the row on the right side of the center aisle, about six rows from the back of the church. Tony felt he had to say something, not being sure of what he had just heard, so he said, while looking in that direction, "What did you say?"

There was a brief moment of silence before the voice spoke again.

"Your prayers will be answered," the deep baritone replied. Tony could better see the man now. It was a black man, with what appeared to be short grey hair and a trimmed grey beard.

Tony said, "Thanks for saying that because I really need him to do that."

Turning to face the altar again, he thought about what had just been said. Tony then eased himself up off of his knees and sat back in the pew, eventually turning once again in the direction of the voice.

"I didn't see you when I came in," Tony said. Thinking he might confirm that the man was some sort of maintenance employee, he asked, "Why are you here at this time of night?"

The voice responded, "I work around here." After a few moments of silence, the voice asked, "Why are you here?"

Tony answered, "I have a major problem I have to work out. I came in hoping I would get some guidance."

After a moment of absolute silence, the man replied, "In quietness and trust is your strength."

Tony thought about that statement and realized how appropriate it was for his situation. The more he thought about what had been said, he knew what he had to go do. He immediately felt better about it. After thinking about it a few more moments, he got up, sidestepped his way out of his pew, and began walking up the center aisle to the front doors. As he reached the pew where the voice had come from, he looked at the black man and said, "Thanks for what you said. Good luck to you."

The black man, while looking at him, slowly nodded his head. Then Tony walked the remaining distance to the church doors. As he opened the door on the right to let himself out, he turned to take one last look at the grey headed, bearded black man with the deep voice. He was nowhere to be seen. Tony's eyes quickly searched for the man but could not find him. He was gone. Tony felt a chill on his neck as he turned and exited the church.

He walked farther down the street until he reached Beachfront Road, which ran between the bar and the restaurants overlooking the Bay of St. Louis. Mark's deputy sheriff car was not yet parked in its usual reserved parking place located about a half a block down the street from the south side of the Baked Tomato, so Tony took a seat on a stair step in the shadows of a nearby business building. He watched as the clientele of the bar he had now visited so many times began to show up, mostly in groups of from two to four and sometimes more. He wasn't going to be able to go inside the place this night. He wanted to watch everything that happened outside concerning his deputy friend's car while the deputy was at work.

At around 9:00, the deputy pulled up in his official car with

Hancock County Deputy Sheriff printed on the door of the driver's side and parked it in its reserved space. Once the motor was off, out came the tall, lanky deputy who locked his door and then walked over to the side entrance of the Baked Tomato. Tony had to chuckle to himself as he watched what actually looked like a cowboy walk to the door. The deputy's boots, white ten gallon hat and western-styled leather holster holding his .45 caliber pistol indeed gave him the appearance of someone who should be on a wild west television program. But the people he met on the street along the way seemed to like him, several giving him a warm and friendly greeting as he made his way to the doorway. He responded to each one, actually tipping his hat to a couple of the ladies whose paths he crossed.

After the deputy had entered the building, Tony stayed in his somewhat hidden location for quite some time before he had to get up and relieve himself in the nearby bushes, while still keeping an eye on the deputy's car. He then casually walked across Beachfront Road to look at the waters of the Bay of St. Louis as they reflected light from what appeared to be a full moon. As he stood there, he went over the whole situation in his mind. To cause a failure of a hit undertaken by his new mob "friends" was an action that certainly would cause repercussions. Continuing to look at the beauty of the moonlight reflections, he thought about what could possibly happen both if he did something to prevent the car bomb from killing Mark and what would happen if he didn't do something. He began to feel better and better about doing something to help him. He really liked Mark, and that was before he found out he was kin to him. Tony began making excuses for the event not happening, at least not tonight. The Boss could have waited longer before issuing that order. The Boss could work around Mark and still be highly successful.

It appeared to Tony, though, that Burdette wanted it to happen and the sooner, the better. Tony thought it was pure jealousy. He could understand why, for sure. Nothing about Sheriff Burdette made anyone, especially those with any judgment at all, feel like they could trust him. Burdette had every appearance of someone that could not be counted on, by anybody, for almost anything. Tony knew that if the sheriff had grown up in his hometown, he never would have made it past the first grade without being in several fistfights. In fact, as Tony thought more about it, he felt sure that Burdette had missed out on one of childhood's premier events for boys, getting into a fight in about the first grade that at some point was in doubt about who was going to win. Such an event had a way of shaping a young boy's personality, and almost always it was for the best.

Tony had been in several as he had come along, including some in his karate classes that had been touch and go for a while. But the one thing those fights had done was encourage Tony to make sure that, whatever a particular fight was going to be about, it was worth taking place because the ramifications of those fights, especially if a person lost them, were potentially life altering. Bloody noses, swollen eyes and lost teeth were bad enough in themselves. Mix those in with broken arms and legs or damage to other areas of the body and he had quickly been taught two things: number one, don't fight unless you absolutely have to; and number two, if you do have to fight, do whatever it takes to win, including cheating. Yes, Tony would bet that Burdette had never even been in a fistfight and certainly, if he had, he had not lost one. At least he didn't act like he had.

Returning to his somewhat concealed perch on the steps of the nearby building, Tony continued his observations. Several times two or more people, usually all boys but sometimes including a girl, would come outside from the bar, go over to some parked car and end up sitting in the car smoking what appeared to be marijuana joints or cigarettes. After a period of time, some of those participating in such activity would get out of their cars and go back inside the bar, a few having difficulty making their way as they walked.

As time went on, a boy and a girl who had come outside together managed to fog up the windshields of the parked car they were in. What that couple didn't know, and apparently didn't care, was that they were parked a mere seven parking spaces away from the deputy's car. What Tony began to admire as time went on was that the couple did not leave their car, even though their time in the vehicle now was coming close to totaling one and a half hours. However, he was worried that the two innocent young kids might get hurt by the explosion, depending on how big it would be. His concern for them only heightened his concern for Mark. The more he thought about it, the more the decision was clear to him. He had to try somehow to keep the deputy, his new friend and apparently close relative, from getting killed. He would deal with the ramifications of that decision after the event, if he was successful.

He was almost falling asleep when he noticed a man, carrying what appeared to be something in the shape of a small shoe box, walking towards the deputy's car. In one quick motion, the man bent over just as he walked on the sidewalk next to the car and slid the box up under the vehicle. Then just as quickly, the man walked away from the car and on down the street in a direction going away from the waterfront. When the man was almost two blocks down the street, Tony saw him open a car door and quickly get inside, quietly closing the door after him.

After remaining concealed in his position for about twenty

minutes, Tony decided that he would go take a look at what had been placed under the deputy's car. He eased away from his position and walked one block over away from the night club so that he could circle the area. Eventually he showed up on the street where the deputy's car was parked, appearing as if he had just come from the front entrance of the bar. He pretended to be drunk, staggering along the cars parked near the deputy's and falling down once before he got to the deputy's car. As he got next to the front of the deputy's car, he stumbled, again falling over but this time into the street so that he could look underneath the car. There was the box! And it had an antenna protruding out of one end. Tony gradually straightened himself up and continued staggering, turning on a street that would take him away from the observer's car. When out of sight, he quickly jogged back around to his concealed position, which again gave him a complete view of the location. And he waited.

While waiting, the more he thought about everything, the madder he got. Bartolli had been told, time and again, by the Godfather and other family heads, to not get involved in drug running. Yet, as Tony had been shown, not only were Bartolli and his allies involved in different aspects of bringing drugs into the country, Bartolli was getting even more and more heavily into it all. In addition, one of the cardinal rules had always been, Tony had always been told, to never kill police officers, regardless of what was involved. The reasons for that were that most of the officers were Italian and possibly relatives of those in organized crime, but also, it made sense to not make the police mad by killing one of their own men. Sometimes there were areas of cooperation the two sides were able to agree upon, but if there was a murder of a police officer, it would only incense the police and drive them into making sure all activities were stopped. That was certainly not to the benefit of the various families. His mind was made up. He was going to try to keep his friend, who was in essence his nephew, alive.

After almost all of the evening's attendees had left the building, Deputy Sheriff Mark Patterson walked out to his car, opened the door and was about to get in. Tony felt himself jumping up, running across the street, yelling at the deputy. He ran up to the car, grabbed the deputy by his left arm, and pulled him away from the car, literally dragging him across the street. It was at that time that a huge explosion took place.

WHAM!!!!!!!!!!!!!!!!!!!!

The car erupted in an orange, yellow and red ball of fire. The left side front door was blown completely off and all windows were blown out. The explosion knocked Tony and Mark to the ground, even though they were on the opposite side of the street by the time the bomb went off. Tony looked up from his new position on the ground in time to see the car up the street, where the bomb planter had been seated, pull out and disappear into one of the side streets.

Tony turned himself over on his side as he was lying on the ground and looked over at the deputy to make sure that Mark was alright. Mark slowly sat up on the ground, staring at the fire engulfing his car. He then looked over at Tony. They both then struggled to stand up, as they watched the fire continue to consume the car.

Mark looked over at Tony and said, "We need to talk."

Tony looked back at him and, after a pause, answered, "Yes, I guess we do."

"Let's walk over to the city park. We don't need to be around here," Mark said as he began walking in the direction of the park.

Tony looked over to see a few people starting to cautiously come out of the bar. He also noticed the young couple opening the door of their car with the fogged up windows.

"Let's go this way," said the deputy and they went two blocks over before walking back away from the Bay of St. Louis toward the park. When they got to the park, the deputy walked to the very same bench where Tony had sat with Helen earlier that day as she had made her disclosure to him about Mark's father. Now here he was again. "You got something you want to tell me?" Mark said as they now sat facing the road that ran by the park.

Tony looked at the deputy, his face visible from the reflections of the street lights. Thinking for a moment about how he was going to tell his side of things, Tony decided to start at the beginning.

"You know why I am here, don't you?"

"Why don't you tell me?"

After another moment of contemplation, Tony said, "I came here for the reading of Madeline Benedetti's will. My father was her brother. I am the only heir."

Shifting his position, he continued, "To resolve everything, I had to involve everybody. New York, Chicago, Detroit, all of them. Back when, Al Capone's money led to the success of rum running operations at many different locations all over this country. It was said that at one time, if his company had been listed on Wall Street, it would have been in the top ten companies in the country. Even though various other locations around the country were not really involved in the operations down here, in order for me to enjoy my life and not have to worry about them, I had to include them. My dad told me it might have to happen that way after he died, if Madeline died after him, and that is exactly what happened.'

Taking a moment to think about what should be said next, Tony continued.

"I was never involved in much in Sicily. My dad wanted me to stay away from the so-called "mob businesses" and I did that. He sent me off to school, in France, trying to keep me out of it all. When I got the call from my Uncle Marty in New York ----"

"Are you talking about Marty Gable?" Mark interrupted.

"Yes. My uncle is Marty Gable." Even in the limited light, Tony could tell Mark was impressed. "You know about him?"

"Yes, I know about him. Who doesn't?"

"Well, after the estate was divided up, Uncle Marty arranged for me to stay down here and for Juan Bartolli to sort of show me around. Turns out there was one thing that Bartolli wanted me to do."

Tony paused before dropping this piece of information on Mark.

"He wanted me to try to get you to back off from seizing his shipments. It seems you have been rather successful in some of the things you have done recently and he wanted me to see if I could stop that, to somehow get you to look the other way sometimes. I guess I failed at that."

"Why did you do what you just did?" Mark asked in a sincere tone of voice.

"Because I have come to like you, to consider you as a friend, almost like a brother I never had. I thought it was an irrational decision made by a mad man, and I didn't want to see a man get hurt, maybe killed, that I now consider a friend."

He took a deep breath and then continued.

"I will have to admit that Uncle Marty told me to be on the lookout for illegal drug activity down here. He said that the families have not authorized Bartolli to get involved in the illegal drug trade business. In fact, I got the impression they despise it. They think it breaks up traditional families. Well, Bartolli could care less. He made no attempt to hide it from me. In fact, he almost flaunted it. He is making too much money from it and you have hurt him in his chase for all the dollars he can get."

"What are you going to do now?" Mark asked.

"I really don't know," he slowly answered.

It was quiet for a few moments until there was the distant sound of an approaching fire truck's siren.

"I would like to know one thing," Tony said breaking the silence.

"What's that?"

"How did you know about when and where to hit Bartolli's shipments?"

Mark did not answer immediately, instead spending a moment to decide if he wanted to share that information with this man who had just saved his life. Fully realizing that indeed was what had just happened, that his life had in fact been saved by Tony, Mark felt he could tell him.

"He has two Vietnamese girlfriends. One of them was a source for us when I was in Vietnam. She was the girlfriend of a South Vietnamese officer we really respected. He helped us with the Phoenix program, an assassination program that worked well for us over there. They were assassinating our Vietnamese allies so the CIA started that program to counter that and it worked.

She and her Vietnamese Colonel boyfriend really helped us. The information they got helped save the lives of a lot of our boys over there. We basically pacified the whole Mekong Delta area. So when it all fell apart at the end, efforts were made to try to get our friends, like them, out of there because they would have been tortured and killed if they had gotten caught. The CIA was able to get her out, but the colonel didn't make it."

Taking a moment, Mark continued in a lower voice, "She got over here and ended up in New Orleans. I ran into her over there and got her to start helping me. She got with Bartolli and it was good for us for a while. Then he got her into heavy drugs. She ended up giving away an undercover informant that she knew about and Bartolli killed him."

Tony listened, feeling even better about his friend and relative. After a few moments of quiet contemplation, Mark said, "You know they are going to come after you. They are going to come after you regardless of your ties to Marty Gable. Bartolli thinks he is invincible, that nobody can touch him down here. He even has it arranged to where if anybody in any other crime family sends any of their people down here, they have to notify Bartolli before they come into the area. A few times he has refused to give his so-called "permission" for them to be here. For Gable to send anybody down here to help you would be like an act of war between the families. Though he might want to help you, it will be hard for him to do it. He has his own problems up in New York that he has handled so far but he has to be careful."

Tony thought about what Mark had just said. After a few moments of contemplation, he said, "I'm going to call him in a little bit. Ask him what I should do. Like you said, he probably can't do anything, but I am not going to run from Bartolli and his group for the rest of my life, having to constantly look over my shoulder and all. Am not doing that."

Mark said, "Knowing Bartolli, I hate to say it, but I do think that he would send somebody to find you, either here or over in your home area, if you are not over there to see him tomorrow. He would not think twice about sending some guys over to do a hit on you in your home country. In fact, he would probably think that would be a neat thing for him to have pulled off."

Sitting there without a word being said for a few moments, the two men gazed into the night air.

The deputy eventually said, "You alone are not a match for Bartolli and his group. The more I think about it, you are going to get a call or a visit early tomorrow morning from Bartolli's men who will want to take you out to the farm so you can tell him yourself what happened with your pulling me away from that car and saving my life."

"Well, you know that your boss, the sheriff, is one of his key men, don't you?" Tony asked.

"Have had that feeling for some time now, actually. Too many things have happened that messed up seizures and botched arrests."

"It wouldn't surprise me if the sheriff himself showed up tomorrow morning at my house, with one or two of his friends, to take me over there to see Bartolli."

The two men continued to sit there, not saying anything else as the reflections of the flashing lights now stopped. As Tony thought about the events of the day, he felt he had to ask Mark about something that had stayed in the back of his mind since it had happened.

"You know that church over there, on the south side of the

street that runs down by the bar? The one about three or four blocks away from there? All white wooden building?"

"Yes, a small church, steps in front of it."

"That's the one."

"Why," asked the deputy.

"I was in there earlier tonight. Thought I was by myself. Thinking about what to do about you. Then I heard this noise in the back and I looked back there and there was this black fellow a few rows from the rear kneeling in one of the pews. He made a comment that really just showed me the way as to what to do. He said something like 'In quietness and trust is your strength.'"

"That's from the Bible, Isaiah 30, verse 15, I think," Mark said.

"It is?"

"I think so. Who was the guy?"

"It was an older black man, grey hair, grey beard. Said he worked around there. When I was leaving, I was at the door and I turned around to thank him again for what he had said and he was gone. Just gone."

After a moment of silence, Mark said, "Sounds like Bernie."

"Bernie?"

"Yep. Bernie. A couple of other people have had that same type thing happen to them there. Black man is there, only says a Bible verse. Scared both of them to death almost, but what he told them helped them. Both of them. Yep, it sounds like you were with Bernie."

"So where does he live? I would like to go thank him at some point, if I get through all of this."

"The other two have never seen him again. Nobody knows

anything else about him. But I think if you said a prayer to the Lord for his telling you what he did, I think that would take care of it."

After a few moments of silence as Tony considered what the deputy had just said, Mark continued.

"Tomorrow is going to be an eventful day for you. You have to focus on tomorrow, or you and possibly others may not be around afterwards. Because of that and because I know you are interested in that Kennedy thing, I am going to go ahead and mention something to you now."

The deputy stopped for a moment and after taking a deep breath, continued, "Oswald went to Russia. He was over there for a while. Now think about that. It was impossible, absolutely impossible to get into Russia at that time. I have been told that the KGB looked at every person from the United States who applied to visit their country during that time and sometimes they drafted plans for compromising those who were considered possible targets. What do you think they prepared for Oswald? What all happened to him while he was in there?"

"All I know is he came back to the United States after spending over a year or more there," Tony answered.

"Do you know how he got back into this country?"

"He obviously was let back in somehow."

"I will tell you that it would have been almost impossible, impossible for him to get back into this country without the permission of somebody, some person in one organization in particular."

"What would that have been?"

"The CIA. And guess who came back with him? Do you know?" Mark asked.

"He got married while he was over there, to a Russian girl. She came back with him, Marina Oswald," Tony said.

After looking at Tony for a brief moment, Mark said, "We have to go now, but I am going to leave you with this. How did he meet her? He was a defector. How in that controlled society was he going to meet her? What do you know about her? What do you know about who her parents were? How did Lee Harvey Oswald manage to get back into this country, with Marina as his wife, at that time? How did both of them get into this country?"

After a pause, Mark then said, "Sorry to bring this to an end but you have a call to make, and I do also. We can't spend any more time here. We both have things to take care of. There's a pay phone about four blocks over. Let's walk over there and use it." With that, Tony got up and followed close behind Mark as he led the way to the pay phone.

Once there, Tony called Uncle Marty and asked Marty's permission to defend himself and do what he had to do to order to stay alive. He told Marty about the local group's heavy involvement in the shipment of illegal drugs, mainly marijuana but also other things. Marty told him to wait by that phone for twenty minutes and that he would call back there.

Precisely twenty minutes later, Marty called back and told him that the board had authorized him to do whatever he must to defend himself. He told him that the shipment of drugs was not something that they had authorized Bartolli to be involved with and that he had done it in defiance of them. Marty also said, however, that they were not in a position to make available any manpower on such short notice and that Tony would therefore be on his own.

Then, as Tony stood there beside him, the deputy made a call. When the call was answered, the deputy identified himself only by the name of "Crockett" and said, "The situation we talked about requiring the "Yellow Canaries" is imminent."

The reply was, "I'll call you back at this number in 15 minutes." Then the call was terminated. Mark said to Tony, "I am going to try and get you some help. All I can promise you is that I am going to try.

Tony stuck his hand out, saying, "Thanks, my man. I feel really close to you. Like I said, I almost feel like you're my brother. That old black man in church said to 'trust' and I am certainly doing that. I'm trusting you to come through."

Clasping the extended hand, the deputy shook his hand while saying, "Well, let's see if we can do something so that you can survive tomorrow. If they come to pick you up, try to delay going down there until at least 9 or afterwards. If they don't come pick you up, go out to the farm anyway but don't get there until 10:30."

As the two prepared to go separate ways, Tony said with a smile, "Okay, here I am, my life depending on somebody or something you mention 'yellow canaries' to? I think I am in deep trouble." He then let out a forced chuckle.

Mark smiled back, saying, "Remember, try to keep things going until at least 10:30 or so. I am going to wait here for my phone call, but its time for you to get back to your house. And again, thanks for what you did."

Tony said, "Just don't be late tomorrow, ok? I really will need your help out there tomorrow."

"I'll see what I can do to help you," Mark replied. "And Tony, if Burdette is there when things start happening, just remember that he uses his gun with his right hand, but if he pulls out a knife, he will use it with his left hand."

"Ok. Thanks for whatever you can do," Tony said.

Mark then waved goodbye as he turned and disappeared into the night.

Chapter Twenty-eight

Tony was sitting in his favorite chair in the small living room at his rental house.

He had been awake most of the night thinking about what all had happened and what else might happen in the new day. He had gone over everything so many times in his mind that he was at the point of being ready to just get things over with, regardless of how they might come out. Oh, he wanted to live, that was not the question at all. There were many more girls that he wanted to enjoy being with and many other experiences that he wanted to have in this thing called life. But he did not want Bartolli or Sheriff Burdette to be able to continue causing so much misery, and he especially did not want them around so that they could make another attempt on Mark's life, whose father he now knew, thanks to Miss Helen, was in essence his very own brother. He also didn't want to go through the rest of his life worried about being killed by Bartolli or Burdette and their friends.

Tony heard a car pull up in front of the house. Buddy started barking, as he usually had the few times previously when a car had stopped there on the street. He got up and, after putting his puppy in the bedroom and closing the door, walked over to the front door of his house, getting there just as knocking began to take place on the opposite side. Mark checked his watch and saw that it was a little before 9 a.m. Opening the wooden door, he saw Burdette standing there on the other side of the screen door, in slacks and a western silk shirt, wearing a gun belt and holster which was holding the .38 automatic pistol he liked to wear. He also noticed Larry, one of Bartolli's enforcers, standing in the street next to the car. He saw that the huge, casually dressed man was also wearing a .38 revolver on his belt. No greetings were said and there were no smiles.

"Come on. We need to get on over there. He's expecting us," Burdette said as he began to pull open the screen door.

"I'll follow you in my car," Tony said.

The sheriff responded, saying, "No. He said for me to bring you over there and I intend to do that, any way I have to," as he put his right hand on his holstered weapon.

The move had its clear intention of letting Tony know that, if need be, Burdette would shoot him right there, right now. Tony had thought about that prospect many times during the previous night and had decided it would not do him any good to take a firearm with him. Burdette would only take it from him to begin with and if Tony tried resisting, even if he won, Bartolli's small army of ruffians would forever be after him. No, he would go to the farm and find out for himself what Bartolli, and Burdette for that matter, had to say. The longer he could keep them occupied, the more time Mark would hopefully have to get some help out there. He surely was counting on him, but the one thing he was not going to do was run from Bartolli and Burdette for the rest of his life. If at all possible, one way or the other, it was going to be resolved today, if he had anything to do with it.

Tony stepped through the doorway, closing the wooden door behind him. There was no need to lock it. He had other things to think about, and worry about. Burdette then said, "I have to pat you down. We wouldn't want you to be carrying anything, now would we?"

So Tony stood there with each arm held out to the side as Burdette ran his hands over his clothing, eventually moving down to Tony's ankles. Convinced he wasn't carrying anything, he then motioned Tony towards the car. The enforcer warily eyed him as Tony approached the car, opened the door and sat in the front passenger seat. Burdette got in on the driver's side as the enforcer got in the back seat, sitting right behind Tony.

"Larry has his gun pulled and pointed at your back, Mr. Smart Guy, so don't try anything stupid. You've already made one mistake, pulling that sorry deputy away from that car before the bomb went off. We don't want you doing anything else dumb like that."

Burdette started the car up and, after pulling out onto the small street, he added, "At least you did one smart thing." Looking over at Tony with a sneer on his face, he continued, "We thought you might make it difficult for us to get you in this car, but you didn't. That was smart on your part, but that's about the only smart thing you've done since you got here."

Tony felt the urge to slug Burdette, not waiting for whatever Mark was going to hopefully do. But if he was going to deal with Bartolli and Burdette, it would be easier getting into the farm with Burdette driving than trying to run past the guards that he knew would be posted at the gate on the road leading from the highway to Bartolli's house. So he kept telling himself, patience is a virtue. Wait for the right time and this definitely was not the right time to make any sort of move, especially with a gun pointed at him from the back seat. As that voice had mentioned in the church, he was having to have a whole lot of trust at this point.

Most of the drive was made with nothing being said by any of them. After taking the turn off of Interstate 10 and heading south of New Orleans, Tony figured he might as well say something.

"How long have you been working for Bartolli?"

"I'm not answering any of your questions, asshole!" Burdette said as he quickly turned his head to glare at Tony.

Turning his head back so he could watch the road, he continued, saying, "The first time I saw you, I didn't like you. Told Bartolli that but he wouldn't listen to me. He wouldn't listen to me because of your New York 'friend,' Marty. But I told him to not show you too much, that we didn't know anything about you, regardless of the backing you had from Marty. I mean, you come over here from Sicily, of all places, and we are just supposed to treat you like a friend, right off the bat? Give me a break! And I was right. Was I ever right. Here you go off saving that deputy's life when you knew that Bartolli had ordered him killed. Who do you think you are to interfere with that? And don't forget, Larry still has his gun pointed at your back."

Tony just stared at Burdette, repeating over and over to himself that he had to keep his self control and not let this complete jerk upset him. More important things had to be dealt with, much more important than feeling good about himself for slugging

Burdette. Besides, there was that issue of that gun pointed at his back, about which he felt sure Burdette was not exaggerating.

They finally arrived at the entrance to the farm and pulled up to the guardhouse and gate. Tony glanced at his watch and noted that the time was 10:17. The man there, with an M-16 slung over his shoulder, recognized Burdette.

Burdette said, "Call Mr. Bartolli and tell him we are here and are on our way to the house." The guard nodded his head and picked up a phone as Burdette pulled away driving towards the mansion. During the few times he had been out there, he had never seen the guard there armed like that. Bartolli was probably being careful in case Tony did cause some sort of problem.

Once they had pulled up in front of the house, Tony opened the door and got out, to be met by Larry holding his .38 revolver pointed at him. Burdette got out of the car, motioned Tony towards the front door of the house and followed Tony to the door, with his right hand on his holstered gun as he walked next to Larry. As they approached the front door, it opened and there stood a man Tony recognized as another one of Bartolli's enforcers. This one had been the man that had carved up the undercover informant who had been turned in by the Vietnamese stripper.

Tony remembered how this one seemed to really enjoy what all he had done to that informant. He now had the same smile on his face that he had shown as he had worked over that informant before he had carved the man up to feed to the pigs. Tony had not been able to watch all of that but knew he would never forget this man's face. Now feeling a shove in the middle of his back from Burdette, Tony began walking in the direction the shove had been made, which Tony knew led to Bartolli's wood paneled office. Walking through the door of that office, Tony saw Bartolli sitting behind his massive desk at the far end of the room.

"Tony, Tony, Tony!" Bartolli said, staying seated, as Tony walked towards his desk. "You have created a problem for me. Instead of helping me solve one of my biggest problems, you have helped him survive!" Bartolli motioned Tony to one of the two chairs facing Bartolli's desk, in particular the one which the War of 1812 cannon on his desk pointed towards. Tony made special note of that, and also noticed that Larry was standing to his left right next to the chair that Tony was seated in, his gun still in his hand but at least not pointed at him.

"Why did you do that? What were you thinking? Ray and I have talked about it and cannot figure it out. So tell us, very precisely, why did you do that?"

Tony was ready for that question. He had thought about his answer to it over and over the night before. He had finally decided how he would try to deal with it, hoping to stall for a little time so that Mark might eventually show up and help him somehow.

"Mr. Bartolli, I am wondering why you let Ray Burdette here get you into so much trouble? You have lost shipments to his deputy, of all people. His deputy! Wouldn't that provide a hint to you that maybe, just maybe, your sheriff here might be letting some of those seizures, maybe all of them, happen?"

"I've wondered about that," Bartolli quickly answered. "I really wondered about that. Why would this deputy in his office be so successful in grabbing some of my largest shipments?"

"Well, good. What did you decide or find out about all of that?"

"I decided that was nothing to be worried about, him being

326

possibly involved with that somehow. Do you want to know why I decided there was nothing to all of that?"

"Yes, because I have wondered why those seizures were taking place."

"I am not worried about it because of what the sheriff here has done for me." Bartolli was smiling now. Looking at Burdette, he said, "Why don't you tell our little Sicilian friend here what you did for me?"

With Larry still standing on the left side of his chair while holding his gun in his hand, Burdette walked over to the corner of Bartolli's desk and stood just a couple of feet from where Tony was now seated. He then began talking.

"There used to be a sheriff in Hancock County, named Bart Patterson. He was some kind of world war two hero with General Patton in Europe, drove tanks over there and all. Came back after the war and went to work for his daddy, hired by his daddy, the sheriff at that time by the name of Wild Bill Patterson." Burdette sarcastically exaggerated the word "daddy" as he said it.

"When his daddy, the sheriff, finally passed away, they made Bart, his son, the sheriff. I had been working there for a couple of years and they just passed right over me and got the son to take over. Said I needed more, I think they called it, "people skills." Juan here recognized my abilities and convinced me I should join up with him because I was not appreciated. But there was old Bart, old war hero Sheriff Bart, and if he lived as long as his daddy did, hell, it would be another twenty years before I could be sheriff and I really wanted to be sheriff. I deserved it! Juan convinced me there might be a way to sort of short circuit that time frame and all. So he devised a plan and I agreed with it. It was put into action by me telling Sheriff Bart that I had an informant that he just had to meet. The informant, I told him, was responsible for giving us good information a few weeks earlier that had led to a little drug bust. He agreed and we set the meeting for out at the road that dead ends into Point Clear Island. There's this nice little cleared area there that's hidden from everything else so that it's private and all. Kids go parking out there sometimes on the weekends. We set the meeting up out there for Monday night at midnight. I knew nobody would probably be anywhere around there then and they weren't." Burdette then moved his left hand to the back left pocket of his pants.

"I told the sheriff we needed to take his car and that I would drive since I knew where we were going to meet the informant. We pulled up and parked on one side of that clearing. On the other side a car was already there, parked. I told the sheriff I would get out and go get the informant and bring him back to our car. So I went and got the guy and brought him back. We walked over to the sheriff as he was sitting there on the passenger side. I got back in the car on the driver's side and, while our 'informant' stood next to the passenger's side of the car, we started talking. I told the 'war hero' that it was time for the office of sheriff to be vacated. You should have seen the look on his face!" Burdette broke out laughing, with Larry laughing also, and Bartolli smiling.

"Well, of course he tried to play hero, reached down to pull his gun out of his holster. My 'informant' reached down inside through the open car window and grabbed his right arm so he couldn't pull his gun out. Then I said, 'Here is your resignation, sheriff!' "

As Burdette said that, he pulled a large switchblade knife from of his left back pocket with his left hand, pushed a button and out came the blade.

"I shoved this right into his stomach, just below his heart. Oh you should have heard the sound! I actually enjoyed doing it. The 'informant,' well that was Larry here, standing right next to you. The old war hero lived for about twenty minutes. We watched him die, slowly, and there was nothing he could do about it. "

Tony was in shock, and could barely manage to look to his left to see Larry standing there smiling, and nodding his head in agreement.

Bartolli then said, "That is why I know the sheriff here is not part of letting that deputy know about shipments and all. You have to remember that the deputy is the son of that former sheriff that he is talking about,"

Burdette began to hold the knife up, twisting it in the air as he then said, "I had to do this to him. Twist it some, shove it in him a little more. He was a tough old dude, but Larry here kept his right arm penned up against him and I used my right arm to keep his left arm from doing anything while I was twisting this very sharp knife here in his guts with my left hand. We just sat there and watched life ease away from him. I loved every minute of it. Guess I had more "people skills" than everybody knew. I had some skills with this thing that he definitely didn't know about." He pushed the button that let the large blade be folded back into the handle of the knife. He then put it back in his left rear pants pocket.

Tony was in total shock. He had just been told how his brother had been killed, and it was by these three who were in the room with him.

329

He quickly came back to the present as Bartolli said, "You haven't answered my question, Sicily man. Why didn't you let that hit go down so we would be rid of that deputy?"

Coming back to the present, Tony took a moment and then answered, "I wanted you to let me ------"

WHAMMMMMMM!

A large explosion went off on the left side of the front of the house.

WHAMMMMMMMMMM!

A second large explosion went off adjacent to the right side of the front of the house.

WHAMMMMMMMMMMMMMMMMM!

The second explosion was followed by the loudest of the three explosions. It was just outside the room they were sitting in and its shock wave completely shook the house. Burdette had tried to pull his gun out of his holster but dropped it when the third explosion took place.

Tony swung into action. He grabbed Larry by his right arm, turned the gun towards Larry and helped him pull the trigger so that he shot himself. He then quickly turned around to see the cannon on Bartolli's desk moving so that it was aimed at him. He ducked to the side as Bartolli caused the cannon to fire like a pistol. Then he heard a noise as Bartolli and his chair disappeared behind the desk. He quickly stood up to see Burdette looking for his gun but not finding it. Burdette faced him and then pulled his knife back out of his rear pocket with his left hand, pushing the button so that its big blade came out and locked in place. Burdette stood there now holding the knife in his right hand while just about six feet away from Tony. Tony grabbed the chair he had been sitting in and threw it aside so that there was a cleared area between him and Burdette. He could hear gunfire coming from outside the house.

As they stood facing each other for a brief moment, Tony said, "Come on, shithead. You want to gut me like you did that sheriff? Huh? Come on!"

Burdette made a little fake move, trying to judge how quick Tony's reaction might be. Tony remained cool, watching Burdette's eyes and remembering that Mark had told him that Burdette was left handed with the knife. Burdette began passing the knife back and forth between his hands, a sneer on his face. Burdette finally positioned the knife so as to use it like a tomahawk and it was in his left hand. Tony moved quickly, grabbing Burdette's left wrist with both hands, instantly pivoting in a karate move he had practiced hundreds of times, and in one motion brought the knife down and forced it into the center of Burdette's body just below his ribs. Tony then used his weight to shove against Burdette, forcing him to fall backwards down onto the floor. Tony landed on top of him as his hands still forced the knife further into Burdette. Now Tony's face was just inches from that of Burdette.

Tony said, "That sheriff you killed that you were just bragging about. That was my brother, asshole! Have a nice trip to Hell. I'm gonna watch you die like you watched him."

With that, Tony then jerked the knife up, gutting the sheriff. Within a matter of seconds, Sheriff Raymond Burdette had quit breathing.

The doors to the room burst open and in ran Mark. He quickly went over to Larry and made sure he was not a problem. He then came over to Tony as Tony got up off of Burdette. Mark had a rifle draped over his shoulder held there by a canvas strap and was also holding an M16 at the ready. Giving Tony a quick look, he asked, "You okay?"

"Yes, but Bartolli disappeared."

"How?"

"He just disappeared through the bottom of the floor right behind his desk."

They both went around behind the desk and looked down at the floor. They saw the trap door there which covered the area into which the chair, and Bartolli, had disappeared. Hearing more gunfire from outside the sides of the house, they both looked at each other. Then they heard the motor of a boat. They ran through double doors behind the desk and out onto the back patio which overlooked the bayou. There they saw a boat speeding away at full throttle on the canal that led straight back from behind the house out to a small island at the mouth of the canal. Open water could be seen in the distance on the other side of the island. There on the back of the boat was Bartolli in his white suit, standing there shooting them the bird with his right hand.

"He's getting away!" Tony yelled as he watched the boat racing down the canal. Mark stood there, searching back and forth on the ground below. Seeing that nobody was going to be shooting at them, he leaned his M16 up against the wall of the porch.

"Mark! Do something! He's going to get away!" Tony then reached over to grab Mark's M16. Tony used his hand to block the attempted grab, looked at Mark and calmly said, "I'll take care of it." Tony stepped back as Mark then reached around and pulled the strap attached to the rifle off of his shoulder.

Looking at the boat and then back at Mark, Tony said, "Hurry, damn it!"

Mark took his time, bent down on one knee and braced his rifle on the top portion of the small wall that bordered the patio area. Tony could see that Bartolli was still standing on the back of the boat and that he was still shooting them the bird, with the middle finger of both hands now raised towards them. The boat was getting ready to reach the small island at the end of the long canal where it would turn to its left to go out to open water.

Tony looked at Mark, then quickly back at Bartolli and his boat. He then started shaking his head negatively, saying, "You are never going to hit him at this distan----"

BAMMMM!!!!!!!

Tony shuddered at the sound of the rifle and then looked back at the boat. After a split second, he could not believe what he saw. The now small figure of Bartolli, standing on the right side of the back of the boat, was hit almost between the eyes. A large part of his head flew off with the impact of the bullet striking his skull. It also caused his whole body to be thrown back against the side of the cabin wall of the boat!

Tony looked back at Mark in pure amazement. He managed to finally, slowly say the words, "You hit him." He quickly looked down the canal to confirm what he thought he had seen and then, seeing the boat now stopped, he said slowly with still some feeling of disbelief, "You got him!"

Mark stood up as a yellow huey helicopter flew over going down the canal towards the boat. Mark looked up at the helicopter and said, "That's what we call a 'yellow canary'."

As the helicopter neared the boat, two shots rang out and the captain of the vessel crumpled, dropping the weapon that he had just pointed up at the copter. Mark and Tony watched as the copter hovered over the boat while first one man and then another one rappelled by rope down onto the back of the boat. Once on the boat, the two boarders turned the vessel around and began guiding it back towards the dock next to the house.

Then a bald headed, rather large man ran out onto the balcony carrying a .45 revolver in his right hand. Dressed in white pants and a white golf shirt, the man looked at Tony and then said to Mark, "Should I shoot him?" Tony's mouth opened as the man raised his weapon, pointing it at him.

Mark said, "No, Colonel. He's alright. He's a friend." The man showed a little doubt on his face but began to slowly lower his weapon, which made Tony feel better.

Tony then said, pointing towards the boat, "He just shot a guy off of the back of that boat when it was way down almost at the end of that canal there."

The Colonel looked down the canal and said, "Yes, but that's not a tough shot for him. It might be for a lot of people but not him. He used to make those all the time in Nam. Some say he had around 60 kills over there with that rifle of his." They both were now looking at Mark as he completed slinging his rifle back over his shoulder.

Looking back at Tony, the Colonel said, "I know for a fact it wasn't 60. It was almost twice that many. They put him up for a Silver Star, you know, the second highest military medal next to the Medal of Honor. It was awarded to him, but he never would accept it."

Looking back at Mark, the Colonel said, "I have to go tidy up a few things." Tilting his head to one side, he said, "You sure he's alright?"

Mark answered, "He is."

The Colonel then said, "Okay. But he's your responsibility. Agreed?"

Mark looked at Tony and then answered, "Agreed."

As the Colonel turned and went back into the house, the boat was leaving the dock area going down the canal once again. At that point, a second yellow helicopter flew over the house with a man standing in the doorway who gave a wave to Mark, which he returned.

"Who are these guys?" Tony asked.

Mark looked at him for a moment, deciding how much, if anything, to tell Tony. After a pause, he said, "They are members of a special unit. Some of them were in my old Vietnam outfit." After giving Tony a moment to think about that, he then continued.

"Sometimes there are unique security issues that need to be dealt with. It doesn't happen often, and has never happened before in this country, but in this case the Oil Cartel finally got tired of the misuse of their facilities by these guys."

Watching the boat now reach the end of the canal and make a left turn to get into open water, Tony asked, "What are they going to do with that boat?"

Mark answered, "Sink it. They'll take it out about a quarter mile or so and sink it. The chopper will bring them back."

By now, the gunfire had stopped. Mark could see men completing their search of the compound. Also, the bodies of Bartolli's men were being carried and then laid out next to the pig pen back away from the house. Seeing eight bodies now lying out next to each other, Mark asked, "How did your guys get to the security guards? I worried about that when I saw them as we came in."

Mark answered, "Silencers for the two in front. For the one in the back, a garrote."

Tony, being surprised by the answer, said, "You mean that your guy got close enough in the broad daylight to use a garrote on the guy in the back?"

"Look. There are none better. These guys, the members of my team, are the best at what they were trained to do. The very best. Once the decision was made, this was not that complicated a mission. Getting everybody down here and in place was the difficult part. We almost didn't make the starting point in the time schedule you and I had talked about."

"I wondered about that. You were a little late," Tony said with a smile.

"Yes, we were a minute thirty-eight seconds late, but we made it," Mark answered with a return hint of a smile.

Tony quickly said, "And I have never been so glad to hear explosions go off so close to me." He then let out a chuckle.

At that point a yellow helicopter flew back over the house coming from the direction of the boat.

"What is going to happen to Bartolli and Burdette's bodies?" Tony asked as his eyes followed the path of the helicopter.

"They have a couple of quaint little ways down here of dealing with people that nobody wants anyone to find out what happened to them. Bartolli had people cut up and fed to his pigs. A lot more people than anybody would ever guess. Back in the '20s, they used to take people out into the Gulf of Mexico and cut them up and feed them to the sharks. Bartolli is going to get the same solution he utilized on the victims brought here - the pigs. We don't have time for the shark option."

336

Now turning to face Tony, Mark said, "Burdette is another story. He is going to be taken back to Hancock County, to a remote country road out near Devil's Swamp. He will be shot a few times with a .45 in his chest area, from the front and the back. It will look like a drug deal that went bad."

Tony could now see in the distance three men picking up one of the bodies, which was now nude, and taking it behind the shed next to the pig lot. Hanging from their belts were machetes in scabbards. They had come prepared.

Tony and Mark turned and started walking first into Bartolli's office in the house and then down the hallway towards the front door entrance. The bodies of Burdette and Larry having been already moved, two of Mark's associates, both wearing gloves, were making sure that their cleanup efforts had been successful in the office.

As they approached the front door, Mark turned to face Tony and asked, "What are you going to do now?"

"What do you mean, what am I going to do?"

"Where are you going to go?"

Tony was puzzled by the question but said, "Well, now that you mention it, I think I will go back to my little house, if you can arrange a ride for me."

It was then that Mark looked at him, and after a short pause, said, "Tony, you can't do that."

"What do you mean, I can't do that?"

"It's just not that simple. You can't stay around here and continue on as if nothing happened. Remember, you were the one meeting with them. You were the one that made trips out here. You made the trip out here today in a car that was driven

337

by a man that is now going to be found dead. And oh by the way, he was the sheriff of that county over in Mississippi. Now you are the only one who met with them that is still alive. You can't stay here. There's going to be an investigation after it is discovered that none of them are alive. Somebody might want to talk with you. You don't need to be around."

After thinking about it a moment as they reached the front door, Tony said, "I would like to at least see Karen before I leave."

Mark stopped him as they were now at the front door. He said, "Look, you saved my life. Well, I just saved yours. The best thing for you to do right now is walk out that door and get out of here. Right now. If you stay here, I cannot guarantee that you will stay alive. You have to leave, now. Go away and don't come back. Ever."

"Ever?"

"Ever," Mark answered in a firm tone.

After thinking about what he had just been told for a brief moment, Tony asked, "What about my motorcycle? What about Buddy? What about my stuff at my house?"

"Karen will take care of Buddy. Your motorcycle is out front. We picked it up after you left this morning. Your stuff was gathered up also and will be disposed of in another state." With that, Mark opened the front door and there was his bike, loaded on the back of a pickup truck. Two men were untying the ropes holding it in its stand-up position.

Thinking for a moment as he watched the two men's effort with his motorcycle, Tony said, "Okay. If that's the way it's going to be, since I am going away, you have to tell me about what the real story is behind the Kennedy assassination."

Mark looked at him, noting the sincerity in his voice and the look in his eyes. Tony then continued.

"Look, you know how interested I am in that and I think you know what happened. I really think you do. I don't know why you know, but I do think you know. I promise I won't tell anybody, I really won't. Okay?" He continued to look at Mark, hoping that Mark would be understanding. "Really, I promise," Tony added, looking at Mark straight into his eyes. Finally, Mark responded.

"Okay," he said, and after a brief pause, continued.

"But if you ever do say anything, anything at all, to anyone, anyone at all, somebody, somebody will come after you and I won't be able to do anything about it. Nothing at all, you understand?"

Tony nodded his head in the affirmative, looking back at Mark. Mark repeated, "Do you understand?"

Tony answered, "Yes, I won't say anything, ever, to anybody."

After a moment's pause, Mark put his right arm around Tony's shoulder and they began walking towards the back of the pickup truck as the two men wrestled the machine down a wooden board towards the ground.

"Sometimes, there comes a time where it's in the best interest, of even very diverse groups, that something happen," Mark said leaning closely to Tony's left ear. After a couple of more steps, he continued.

"Remember I told you about the five thousand pages of documents that are still classified?" Mark asked as they slowly walked. Tony nodded his head as they now reached the rear of the truck.

"And that they were to remain classified for seventy-five years?"

Tony nodded his head again.

"Well, there are reasons for that. Those files have been sanitized, so to speak, but they still have information in them that shows that........."

(CLASSIFIED)

"VAROOOOOMMMMM! VAROOOOMMM!"

The motorcycle's loud engine came to life at the insistence of one of the two men who had unloaded it. He now revved up its engine so that it emitted a throaty noise so loud that it sounded like a cannon continuously firing. Standing there as the noise finally subsided, Tony's mouth dropped open in complete astonishment.

"Oh, my god," he slowly exclaimed. In almost total shock, he stared at Mark, visions running through his mind about what he had just been told. After a moment, a light slap on his shoulders by Mark brought him back to the present. He adjusted his vision on the deputy, now more in the present.

Mark asked, "So where are you going to go? I need to have some idea of where you are going to be."

Tony thought for a moment, then slowly turned toward his bike and began shuffling over to it. Arriving next to it, he put his left hand on the handlebar and slowly threw his right leg over the seat of the bike. After spending a moment settling on its seat, he turned and looked at the deputy. A slight smile came across his face.

"I think I'll go to Hollywood."

The deputy smiled and said, "I'll check in on you when you get settled."

"Now how in the world are you going to be able to find me out there?"

Mark answered, "I'm sure it won't be that hard for us to find you if we need to,"

A full smile came across Tony's face as he answered, "No, I don't guess it would be for you."

"You probably do need to keep a low profile for a while. If you've got any money from that estate in the banks down here, don't contact them for a while."

Tony looked at Mark and slowly nodded his head in agreement. He then revved the engine up and put the motorcycle into motion. As he made his way down the long driveway, he raised his left hand in a wave just before he disappeared into the distance.

Chapter Twenty-nine

The tall glass and metal building stood out in Riyadh, Saudi Arabia. The desert around it was completely bare and even though there were so many buildings that bespoke of the wealth of the country, this particular building still stood out. Its appearance easily brought to mind one word, elegance. It was a display, a foremost example, of what the ruling family that ran the country could do. The building simply dominated the skyline.

On the eleventh floor, access from the one elevator allowed to stop at that floor was strictly controlled to the hallway going to the special conference room. The hallway's path went past security checkpoints and ornate metal doors with remote control locks. Someone casually getting off of the elevator would never find their way to the conference room, at least not without guidance from one of the several male assistants and security guards waiting behind the bullet proof counter immediately facing the doors to the elevator.

Zack Purdy, the head of security for one of the largest petroleum companies in the world, had no problem getting into the room. He had been put in charge of establishing the entire security setup in the building when it was designed and built. With his company being the lead company of the five international corporations in the oil cartel, Zack was provided with great leeway by not only the boss of his company but also by the leaders of the rest of the "five sisters," as they were called. With Zack's extensive connections and background in the intelligence business worldwide, nobody with any knowledge of his past history ever wanted to do anything that might draw his ire. That included the leaders of the Saudi royal family.

Not even the top officials of the "five sisters" wanted to upset Zack. They all wanted him, and his groups of action personnel and contacts, to be available to provide any encouragement, or muscle, that might be needed to accomplish the goals of the cartel. It seemed that, more and more often, some country's despotic leader or some group of dissatisfied civilians seemed to think they could make monetary demands on the various oil companies, even seizing employees or facilities, until some large amount of blackmail money was delivered to them. None of them had ever figured on having to deal with somebody like Zack, and his numerous, well-placed and well-trained friends. Not many people outside the very upper level management of the cartel even knew Zack existed, much less what he did.

It was 8:55 in the morning as the representatives of the "five sisters" drifted into the conference room, each one making sure they were a little ahead of the 9 a.m. time for the meeting to begin. Zack was already there, as usual, seated in his customary position at the head of the elongated, solid glass conference table. He had his high-backed leather chair turned facing the beautiful view outside of the floor to ceiling glass wall that served as one side of the conference room. Zack's long time assistant and right hand man, Paul Ryan, was seated to his left. The other four members of the group took their places as they came in, two being seated on each side of the conference table. All were in casual clothes that made them appear as just tourists in the country on a vacation trip.

A Saudi uniformed aide appeared in the door way and asked in perfect English, "Anyone for coffee?"

One of the men, seated closest to the door, raised his hand a little and said, "Yes, the usual, please. Two crèmes."

"Yes, sir," the aide responded. "Anyone else?"

Seeing no positive response, he promptly exited through the doorway, quietly pulling the door shut behind him. Zack then began the meeting.

"Just so you all will know, some of our friends are working today, trying to read our conversation by using a new instrument that supposedly can pick up what is being said in this room by the vibrations off of the glass of these floor length windows here."

Each of the other men immediately gave Zack their full attention so that they would be sure to hear the rest of any information he might tell them.

"The guys are not sure it will work so we felt we should try it out for ourselves and see. There may come a time that we might need to have access to something like that, if it does work. We also may need to know how to stop it, if we don't want it to happen. We'll let you know how the tests go."

Turning his chair around to face the attendees, Zack then said, "I guess the first thing we need to catch up on is how that little operation over in Louisiana went. Paul here will bring everybody up to date."

Paul's mere presence gave an indication of power. His 6'2" frame carried 230 pounds with no effort, the result of numerous hours lifting weights. While Zack could control a room by his presence and intellect, Paul's influence was strictly muscle, combined with what Zack appreciated the most and that was Paul's dedication to making sure that everything possible was undertaken to ensure that whatever he was assigned to do was successfully accomplished. They had gotten to know each other while both were serving in Vietnam in the U. S. Army's military intelligence. That experience had frequently brought them both into contact with various operatives of the CIA involved with the Phoenix assassination program.

"As you all know from our last get together, we had to activate our 'yellow canary' group for that mission down in Louisiana. It was very similar to those that group had previously performed for us in Venezuela and Nicaragua. A situation was brought to our attention by some of our CIA friends concerning the use of some of our company's offshore drilling platforms as an entry point for the shipment of massive amounts of marijuana and other illegal drugs by a group down there associated with the organization. We monitored the activities for a while and, because of the increasing volume, we finally notified a friend of ours in New York who happens to be the leader of that group. It turned out that the Louisiana bunch had been specifically told to not conduct those activities but they didn't listen."

After pausing for a moment to look around the table, Paul continued.

"We got notice from one of our people, who is a law enforcement officer down there, that action needed to be taken because things were on the verge of happening which would have brought a lot of adverse publicity not only to our company but also to the industry we are all involved with. Our New York organization friends were told that the Louisiana group had gotten so confident and arrogant that they were probably going to take out one of their own local associates, who happened to be close kin to our friend in New York. Well the organization took immediate action to disown the Louisiana group and agreed to let us deal with the problem, since it would have taken them a few days to get manpower down there and we already had moved our 'yellow canary' group to the area. That group was able to go in the next day and close down the entire operation. That action also prevented the termination of our friend's relative. The event was completed with no casualties to our team and very limited repercussions."

After he finished his last sentence, Paul looked around the table to see faint smiles and a couple of heads gently nodding at the news.

Zack then said, "I think it would be appropriate for us to provide the same bonuses to those who took part in that, just like we did when they performed those other two operations. We can take it out of that Swiss account that we all contributed to back when to deal with things like this when they come up. We can use that little bank in the Cayman Islands again that we used before to run it all through."

A man with a full crop of silver hair said, "I think that would be a very appropriate thing to do. You have our concurrence."

The others around the table nodded their heads in agreement.

"Good. I didn't think there would be a problem, but I wanted to make sure we were all on the same page."

Turning to look at the man sitting immediately to his left, Zack said, "Paul, good job. Thanks for taking care of that situation for us. Before we leave the subject, if you would, tell the group about the CIA's interest in what happened."

Paul glanced around the room as he quickly gathered his thoughts about what he was going to say.

"All of you know that our friends in the Agency were the ones that asked us in the first place if we knew about the shipments taking place down there utilizing our platforms. When we told them we didn't and would appreciate them letting us deal with it, they agreed and went on to tend to other more pressing concerns. They seem to have their hands full anyway with things happening not too far from where we are sitting right now. We then started checking things out to see how big of a problem we had with some of our employees. Needless to say, based on what we found out, we are glad they let us deal with it."

After a moments pause, Zack said, "Anything else needed on this?"

Glancing around the room and hearing no further comment, he said, "Okay. Now let's talk about that situation over in Indonesia. We will probably need more information on that before we decide what to recommend to our bosses. I am sure they will go along with our recommendations, as long as we have things checked out there. We already have our 'purple parrott' units in place in that area. They have been provided with more men and more firepower than the 'yellow canaries' unit because of what all they may have to do there. So let's talk about that before we get into that Iranian problem that seems to be getting more and more out of hand. If the Shah there doesn't start coming around to our way of thinking about production and also quit asking for a larger share of our income, we might have to make some really hard decisions there. It is simply amazing that they think they can change a deal after the millions of dollars our companies have spent and there won't be any repercussions. The problem with both of those situations is that, when the esteemed former Navy submariner, our new President Jimmy 'Peanut' Carter, fired all of those hundreds of undercover CIA contacts like he did a few short months ago after going into office, the Agency and the country, and us, are now partially blinded. We don't know as much as we did before his foolish decision to do what he did. So Paul, bring us up to date as much as you can on both of those, if you would, that Indonesian situation first."

About forty minutes later the meeting broke up. Everyone left the conference room to return to their "tourist" roles, except for Zack and Paul. Zack leaned back in his chair and turned it so that he again faced the floor length windows. Paul turned his chair so it was now facing Zack. He then took the opportunity to lean back and take a deep breath.

After a moment of quietness, Zack said, "That boy down in Louisiana, the deputy sheriff, shot that guy at how far?"

Paul looked at Zack and said, "About 1600 yards." With the hint of a smile coming across his face, he then added, "Hit him right between the eyes. Colonel Parker said that he had heard of the boy doing something like that before in Vietnam."

Zack smiled and said, "I remember hearing about that boy when we were over there." After a brief pause, he then said, "That was a pretty good shot."

"Yes, sir," Paul answered. "It sure was. If you'll remember, the VC at one point had about a $25,000 bounty on him."

Zack nodded his head as he remembered that information. After a quiet moment, he looked over at Paul and said, with a slight smile on his face, "Let's give him a little extra bonus when you make those payments. I'm sure the group would approve." Then after a brief chuckle, he continued, "We do want to make sure he stays on our side, don't we."

Paul nodded his head in agreement.

"You just never know when we might need his expertise again," Zack said.

"I'll take care of it," Paul answered.

Both men now had wide grins on their faces.

Epilogue

The Vietnamese stripper was poisoned the same day as the attack.

The rig boss working for the oil company had an "accident" at the drilling rig, disappearing after falling off into the Gulf of Mexico.

Sheriff Burdette's body was found two days after the raid in a deserted area of Hancock County near Rotten Bayou. There were packets of cocaine in his pant's pocket and he had been stabbed and shot numerous times. No one was ever indicted for his murder.

Sarah Montgomery was released from the state penitentiary at Parchman, Mississippi after serving two years. Her extensive work with prison ministries led to a recommendation by the prison warden that she be released early. Upon her release, she went to work with Catholic Church charities along the gulf coast.

Sarah's lawyer, Bradley Hamilton, was eventually disbarred for stealing the money of three of his clients from his office escrow fund.

Kovac had a serious heart attack a year after Sarah's sentencing and was paralyzed from the neck down. Alone by himself in a nursing home, nobody came to visit him because of how badly he had treated everyone.

Judge Jonathan Banks developed a serious drinking problem and was eventually removed from office by the State Judicial Performance Commission.

Two judges on the Fifth Circuit Court of Appeals in New Orleans retired within six months of each other, much to the surprise of almost everyone.

After keeping a low profile for a while, Tony eventually took a job utilizing his Karate skills as an extra in several of the new action movies in LA. He was recognized by movie critics as potentially a new Hollywood star.

Deputy Sheriff Mark Patterson married Karen two weeks after the raid. Their honeymoon was to the Cayman Islands. While there, Mark went to visit the Cayman Islands Bank where he made a wire transfer of $175,000 to his previously established account at the Everglades National Bank in Jacksonville, Florida.

Upon his return from his trip to the Cayman Islands, Deputy Sheriff Mark Patterson was appointed Sheriff of Hancock County. He and Karen kept Buddy. Eight months after their wedding, the couple had a baby boy.

The second highest award given by the United States for military bravery, the Silver Star, was sent to Mark Patterson by a New York congressman, following a personal request by an important constituent of his, Martin Gable. Gable provided the details in support for sending the award following research conducted based on information provided by Tony.

Sheriff Patterson kept the Sliver Star medal and Karen had it mounted and displayed in a prominent location over the fire place in the living room of their home.

A traveling circus revealed that someone had released several of its animals from their cages, including a huge black bear, while the circus had been in the area. That bear is still seen in the woods from time to time in the area near the former pig farm. Its presence became so legendary that all local hunters agreed through the years to protect the animal and not let anyone harm that bear.

Author's Notes

This book is fiction. Any resemblance to actual events that may have taken place is coincidental. My interest in writing this book was simply to tell an interesting, captivating story. I hope I have accomplished that and that the readers enjoy the time they spend in the world created by my efforts.

Having said that, I will take this opportunity to mention a few observations. My first comment is that people in general are interested in events, especially events that involve famous or well-known individuals. Where those events, such as the Kennedy assassination, have a profound effect on their lives, or are at least perceived to have such an effect, people generally want to know more about it. An investigator would probably want to know exactly what happened, when it happened, where it happened, how it happened, and a competent investigator would definitely want to know why whatever happened did happen. There may be other parts to the equation, depending on the event, but generally the what, when, where, how and why questions tend to provide sufficient answers so that a conclusion can be reached that is satisfactory to those who care.

It is usually rather easy to figure out what happened, when it happened, where it happened and how it happened. Even inside those questions, if answers are provided that are not exactly correct, the resulting conclusion will be skewed so as to not be accurate. For an example, witnesses to events sometimes have different points of view, such as their locations from which to observe something that happened. One witness on one side of Dealy Plaza, for example, may have heard a sound that seemed to be like a shot coming from a location other than the Book Depository, while another witness at another location in the Plaza area may have an opposite opinion altogether. Yet because of acoustics of an area, both may be correct. Things, such as sound and light for example, can be misleading, to say the least. Throw in an individual's own limitations or impairments, such as hearing loss or eyesight limitations, and one can understand the statement, "Things are not always as they seem."

In addition to the above, now throw in the "why" question. To this writer, this question would appear to be the one that can usually be the most important. It has the opportunity to explain things that seem to make the answers to the other questions make sense when those questions, taken by themselves, lead to completely different conclusions. Most readers have probably experienced in their own lives events that just did not make any sense. No matter how a person looked at the event, it just didn't add up. A friend of mine once made a statement about an event I could not understand that has stuck with me through the years. His comment was, "Any time you see something that doesn't make any sense, follow the money and it will." I have found that piece of advice to be accurate many more times than not. As far as determining an answer to the "why" question though, there may be other factors involved, depending on the event, which could definitely affect how such event is viewed. For example, common human frailties such as pride, anger, greed, envy, jealousy and any host of other like qualities can have an enormous effect on a person's opinion or conclusion about an event.

All of the above is mentioned so that hopefully the reader will appreciate the general haze and sometimes complete fog that is present when events, both insignificant and significant, are examined. In our society, it was anticipated by the founding fathers of our country that the press should and would play a significant role in seeing to it that facts were presented to the public. Such presentation would allow the members of our democracy to be informed and therefore able to make good decisions, not only concerning those who represent us but also concerning events, especially those events that help shape the nation. However, the pursuit of facts is often times not easy. Such pursuit requires, among other things, a lot of effort, in some instances dogged persistence, and competent judgment at all times. It also requires a complete appreciation of the circumstances surrounding the event. Absent any of these, the bowl of facts becomes incomplete. As might be imagined one fact, just one particular fact, can and will completely change a conclusion concerning an event. A complacent, some might say lazy, or biased press may not put forth the effort that it might take to reveal a fact or facts that would dramatically change a conclusion or conclusions that the public might reach concerning an event.

The John F. Kennedy assassination has kept the interest of our country ever since it happened. That event has transcended time. It is one of those events in one's lifetime that a person remembers exactly where they were, what they were doing and who they may have been with when they found out about it. That event was the termination of the life of a handsome, dynamic man at the height of his existence, who was rich, powerful, charismatic, and had a beautiful wife and family. And oh, by the way, he just happened to be President of the United States after a hard fought election, the conclusion of which was in doubt until favorable, questionable results came in from the states of Illinois and West Virginia.

His father was, at the time of the election of his son, one of the wealthiest people in the entire country and had served his country as ambassador to England. Joe Kennedy had been a political ally of President Franklin Delano Roosevelt and had spent time in Hollywood as a financial backer of various projects there in the movie industry. He had wanted one of his several sons to be President and had accomplished that goal when John Kennedy occupied the White House.

So why would anyone want to kill President Kennedy? He was beloved by the nation when it happened. He was beloved by the world when it happened. Really? He was? But he was shot and killed, wasn't he?

There have been, over the years, numerous books that have dealt with this tragedy. Interest in "Camelot", as the Kennedy presidency was called by some, continues to this day. The discussions in this book are probably similar, for the most part, to discussions that occasionally take place even now about that era and, in particular, that event. Time has cooled the intensity of the inquiry but not the interest. One would expect that additional time will further cool such intensity. Some might say that is exactly what the drafters of the legislation limiting access to, what was at one time, several thousand pages of Kennedy Assassination file documents, intended. It continues to this day.

About the Author

Mack Cameron was born and raised in Laurel, Mississippi. He was on crutches as a child from the first grade to the middle of the fourth grade. Through the grace of God, he got off crutches and took up tennis. He went to the state high school singles finals four consecutive years, winning the championship two times.

He attended Mississippi State University (MSU), receiving a Bachelor's Degree and a Master's Degree in Political Science. At Mississippi State, he won four Southeastern Conference (SEC) individual tennis championships while a member of MSU teams that won two SEC team championships and finished as high as number three in the nation.

Upon graduation, he worked in Washington, D.C. as Staff Assistant to U.S. Senator John C. Stennis. He then served as an officer in U.S. Army Military Intelligence. After completion of his active duty military service, he attended law school at the University of Mississippi (Ole Miss) where he won the American Jurisprudence Award in International Law, served on the Law School Honor Council, and coached the tennis team.

After graduation from Ole Miss, Mr. Cameron served as Assistant Legal Counsel for the United States Secret Service under Presidents Nixon, Ford and Carter. He returned to Mississippi and has worked as a Special Assistant Attorney General in the Mississippi Attorney General's Office under four Attorneys General.

Mr. Cameron has served on the Mississippi State Bar Ethics Committee and is in the State of Mississippi Sports Hall of Fame and the Mississippi State University Sports Hall of Fame. He and his father, C. B. "Buck" Cameron, were the first father-son duo in the State of Mississippi Sports Hall of Fame. He is a member of the Mississippi State Bar Association and is a real estate broker. He is also the author of "The Bluffs of Devil's Swamp," the first book in this series.

www.ingramcontent.com/pod-product-compliance
Lightning Source LLC
Chambersburg PA
CBHW070308040726
47501CB00018B/448